HOT TICKET

HOT TICKET

Edited by Linnea Due

alyson
books

LOS ANGELES • NEW YORK

Manufactured in the United States of America.
Printed on acid-free paper.

This trade paperback original is published by Alyson Publications Inc.,
P.O. Box 4371, Los Angeles, California 90078-4371.
Distribution in the United Kingdom by Turnaround Publisher Services Ltd.,
Unit 3 Olympia Trading Estate, Coburg Road, Wood Green,
London N22 6TZ, England.

First edition: July 1997

01 00 99 98 97   10 9 8 7 6 5 4 3 2 1

ISBN 1-55583-379-9

Library of Congress Cataloging-in-Publication Data
Hot ticket / edited by Linnea Due. — 1st ed.
    ISBN 1-55583-379-9
    1. Lesbians — Fiction.   2. Lesbians' writings, American.   I. Due, Linnea A.
PS648.L47H68 1997
813'.01083538'086643 — dc21   97-4995 CIP

Cover design: Bruce Zinda

Contents

Introduction

Eros flits through the imagination, picking up a touch of pollen from this garish red flower, leaving it behind on that pale yellow bud. Given the right context and coloring, almost anything can be erotic.

Because I have a few kinks in my tail, what got me excited as a seven-year-old were accounts of dingy Paris basements with their walls oozing water, jackbooted Gestapo interrogators, and braver-than-brave U.S. pilots who'd rather die than give up the smallest secret. Name, rank, and serial number, fingernail by fingernail. Erotic merged with holding on to dignity in the direst straits, staring down one's tormentors with steely resoluteness, staying human in the face of horror.

This merger between heroism and eros has had interesting repercussions in my adult life. I've been lighting among associations drawn from this wartime scenario for decades, as if I were shifting a garden from one location to another, plant by plant. Subtle changes through the years have transformed the garden to something quite different, but if I meander along its paths, I can detect traces that lead back to that basement in Paris. If you can remember what you found erotic as a child — or what you eroticized in order to withstand — I highly recommend an exploratory ramble in your own garden. You'll be amazed at the vestiges that linger from seven to seventeen, from twenty-seven to forty-seven.

How do we expand our idiosyncratic erotic territories to include someone else's? To universalize the particularity of experience is the alchemy of art, and in matters of the erotic, we are all artists of our own lives.

The stories gathered in this collection of travel erotica exemplify that alchemy. When we travel we literally and symbolically break new ground, setting off from one point to end up someplace else surprising. Being static is death to the erotic; these stories are all about movement, about knocking down the barriers that prevent us from broadening our horizons and making the transformations that keep our erotic imagination fresh.

In Jane Futcher's "Caribbean Wave" and Elaine Apthorp's "Stealing Home," the marriage of childhood fantasy and the erotic is made explicit. Other stories, such as Shelly Rafferty's "State of Desire" and Kate Allen's "Everybody's Going to Seattle," bring past relationships into the present with mixed results. Other stories detail bottled-up erotic energy breaking past grief, satiation, or convention with the explosive force of a champagne cork heading toward the ceiling. Longing takes on an exquisite life of its own in Barbara Wilson's "Salt Water." And Lucy Jane Bledsoe's "Reconnaissance" pulls the threads together: An otherworldly sighting terrifies her character out of self-imposed dormancy, thrusting her into a new landscape of desire.

About the stories submitted: Of those that specifically deal with conveyances, trains by far lead the pack, with public bathrooms a frequent site of dalliance. The threat/thrill of discovery and voyeurism in a semipublic, semiprivate space sends many of these stories soaring. This tells us something about human nature, about how our sexuality is inseparable from who we are, seeping into our interactions with everything and everyone around us, no matter how hard we try to keep it confined to arenas we've deemed appropriate. But appropriate is as deadening to the eros as rigidity — we thrive on challenge and cross-pollination. So we seek each other out, all us artists and gardeners, to cultivate plots of land large as the universe, quixotic as the imagination.

Linnea Due

State of Desire
by Shelly Rafferty

In the nursery I found Nina studying the colorful map I had hung over the radiator. It was May, although the house didn't seem to have noticed, because the radiator gurgled and emitted a low, gentle thermal of heat.

We looked at Arkansas. I put my finger on the pink state and suggested Hot Springs for a vacation spot. I was pressed up against Nina in a casual way, the back of her gabardine trousers familiar against my thighs.

Behind us my newborn snored. His pacifier exhaled a rhythmic burble. Nina had come to see him, her curiosity piqued by the event of his birth. He cooperated by napping peacefully.

"Or the Carolina shore," I said next, leaning in over her right shoulder. The fragrance at her neck wasn't magnolia or dogwood but something softer. I pressed closer, suddenly recognizing the scent as one she used to wear when we were lovers years ago.

She didn't resist my kiss at the nape of her neck. As my tongue followed the cylindrical topography of her spinal column, she found Wyoming and wondered aloud about the Grand Tetons. There were so many places we could have gone, but we never did.

I let my hands settle at the handles of her hips and rested my chin on her left shoulder. Silently we swayed and remembered and stared at the map.

"What about New Mexico?" she asked, moving a finger to trace the almost square. I watched her travel the perimeter slowly, finding the eastern border at Texas, each mile summoning a long-gone way we used to be with each other. I reached up tentatively, my hand caressing the bowl of one breast. Her breathing didn't change, but she leaned forward ever so slightly, her long thighs tilted against the low, warm steam of the radiator.

"Too hot," I said, the inflection of my voice permitting her to infer a question if she needed to. My thumb skated across the roughness of a nipple. She spread one whole hand across the

Southwest. Her pinkie leaked into California, her middle finger crossed the Colorado River.

I dropped my hands to the equator of her leather belt and knowingly slipped the tongue through the buckle. Nina ignored me. Her hand traveled north through Oregon and on to Seattle; mine traveled south. Her zipper went down noiselessly; her panties were moist with sexual precipitation. I hesitated.

"The Pacific coast," Nina murmured. "Lots of rain."

"Yes," I said. I angled a finger, no two, inside the dark valley of her crotch and found slick quicksilver.

The radiator gurgled as she reached for the Great Lakes; I could feel its hard spires against the back of my hand as I pushed in deeper behind the isthmus of her pubic bone. And pulled back. And pushed in again.

Turbines and railroads and industrial pumps dragged us across Huron and Michigan and onward to the lazy steadiness of the Erie Canal; we navigated it slowly, pausing only to breathe deeply before dropping through each lock without waiting for the water to rise; as we approached the Hudson, small rapids foreshadowed the mountains to the north.

I kept to my course. Into the rough Adirondacks, where streams rushed with late-spring thaw, Nina reached wide to the East. We both knew where we were headed. In one hand I held the globe of her breast and in the other a hidden hot spring.

I knew all the wilderness of her.

In the Green Mountains we paused on the plateau. The radiator shuddered and hissed. Nina turned her head and found my mouth. And we came into Canada, together.

Stealing Home
by Elaine Apthorp

Ria Quesada, four years old, stood up beside her mama on the bus seat when she saw the letters of her favorite word: *Park.* "Mama," she announced, "we're almost there." A block down the road the playground came into view.

"Señorita Einstein, reading at four," boasted Mama's friend Meg, the wife of one of Papa's teammates, who had come along with them again. From her seat behind Ria and her mama, she reached forward to tousle Ria's hair playfully, but Ria ducked to shake off the touch. Meg was always saying nice things so Ria would like her and not act up when she was around. "And she has eyes like an eagle!"

"When she sees something she wants," said Mama, sounding tired. So when the bus stopped and Ria hopped down from the seat to lead the way eagerly through the narrow dusty aisle, she held her mama's hand and pulled her along as if Mama might not follow if she let go.

Soon Ria was taking running jumps into the sandbox, sliding on her hip the way she'd seen her father do. For a while she cried out "Safe!" triumphantly when she came to her sliding stop, but no one was watching her, and it seemed foolish, so she stopped. Now she was calling out to her mother in English, "Mama, see!" Mama, sitting on the grassy slope above the sandbox, looked over occasionally to make sure her daughter was not up to anything too alarming, but she was preoccupied, and Ria knew it. Meg lay beside Mama in the grass, up on one tanned elbow, twisting a piece of grass in her fingers and talking to Mama with a smile in her eyes.

Mama's attention was hard to get anyway. She was always looking away, out of windows, though there was never anything interesting there, and Ria had learned to take things apart and hide the pieces so that Mama, when she did look back, would come and talk to her. It was only because she needed the pieces, but she always spoke to Ria very gently and carefully at such times; so Ria had become ever more inventive in devising complicated mischief puzzles for her mama to solve. But when Meg was around it was hopeless. And Meg paid Ria more attention than Mama did, which made it worse somehow.

Now that they were talking, Ria knew Mama would not listen for her, but she called one more time for her mother to look anyway, this time in Spanish to annoy her, because Mama knew she ought to talk to Papa more but would not speak to him in his own language, even at home. Mama said he talked too fast and she would never learn that way, but Ria knew that wasn't so, because she could understand him fine, and she was just a little girl. But even her clever little dart of spite drew only a perfunctory glance from her mother. Meg was more entertaining: Now she was pretending to smoke her twisted piece of grass as she looked into Mama's face with her slow, soft little smile and made her mama laugh…Mama, who almost never laughed. There was something not right about it, like a secret. The air between them was different and strange.

On alert, Ria stood up to stare intently in their direction, letting the sand slip through her fingers and down her legs — a hot, dry, powdery feeling that went with the not-right feeling in her stomach — as she watched the two of them up on the slope so private. Then she saw her mama bend down, pulling her long yellow hair away from the side of her face, bending down till her face was so close to Meg's, and then she put her mouth on Meg's mouth and they were kissing. They kept kissing and didn't stop. Ria opened her own mouth, but the shout on her lips stayed there unreleased. She started to walk toward them slowly, not right in her chest, too fascinated to look where she put her feet lest she lose sight of them somehow.

It was very bad; she couldn't take her eyes off of it.

She kept walking toward them until she could see Mama when she stuck out her tongue and put it in Meg's mouth and they did it harder. Ria could see how their tongues made their cheeks bulge out; they were sucking and pumping in each other's mouths as if they were drinking very fast from a tall glass — so thirsty, they were going to drink it all.

Ria Quesada, thirteen years old, sat in the backseat of the bus with her knees up and clutched under her folded arms and said not a word all the long way out of town to the ballpark, ignoring her father's gentle questions and angry remonstrances — it being a point of honor with her that, since she could not pretend that she didn't understand her father's Spanish, at least she could refuse to speak it to him. When he looked at her now, she knew he saw her mom's face, not her own, even though Ria didn't look at all like her mother, being as brown and lean as he was and staring back at him with his own sweet dark eyes. But her rage to punish him gave her no peace. She struggled to go numb, truly numb, stared out the window, and tried to focus hard on nothing. It was her mother's trick, and it occurred to her to wonder uneasily if her mother had learned it the same way she had.

It was the same each time they brought her back from California, where she always went — went like the fish she'd seen on TV jumping stupidly up waterfalls, evidently because they didn't know any better. Ria did know better, but she went anyway. And paid for it, as she had this afternoon.

After he'd picked her up at the bus station and brought her home, he had slapped her around for running away again and putting herself in such danger and being a whore to shame them, until the tears came, not to her eyes but to his; then he hugged her hard and told her again and again, his litany as unvarying as the rosary, how her mama didn't care about Ria, she wanted to go to hell with that bitch, had tried for custody only to hurt him more, didn't really want her, didn't keep her, had called the cops to get rid of her. It was true enough to pummel her already wretched heart, and she ground her teeth in rage because she could say nothing to contradict him. The slapping was better than the hug and the litany, and all of it was better than what followed.

He went into the kitchen like he'd done half a dozen times before on similar occasions and got his bottle and sat there at the kitchen table just pouring it down. He was getting drunk on purpose so he could talk sneaky-sweet to her and make her lie down next to him on the bed because she was sorry for him and scared of him and loved him and was stupid like the fish. At first it would be just stroking her hair and her arms, and then he would say they were taking a nap together so he could rest before his game, but he would snuggle up against her like a long-trembling spoon and cry into her neck until his whiskers cut her skin. Then he would begin to rock into her thigh until his cock got hard against her buttocks and he put his hand there to jerk himself off.

Conveniently she had already scrubbed his come from her thigh and gone to her room and shut the door before Marta, the new wife, came home from her day-care job with groceries and the little boy in tow. But the sticky, translucent mucus of his semen, spent across the skin of her inner thigh, with its faintly acrid smell, lingered in her memory as she sat on the floor; and now that it was over, the nausea had come.

The bile rose in her throat when she heard her stepmother's voice as she came noisily through the front door of the crummy apartment, all keys and crackling paper sacks, calling for her irritably, "*¿María, estás aquí? ¿María?*" She had spied Ria's windbreaker there on the entry floor where her father had thrown it. "*¡María Elena! ¡Ayúdame! Estoy cargando demasiado,*" she complained and was silent a few beats, listening for Ria's voice, for Ria's feet coming to her call. Ria shut her eyes and counted too, grinding her teeth. *No, I will not carry your goddamned groceries. I am carrying enough.*

"*¡Por Dios! ¡María!*" Marta shouted, her voice a little hoarse between indignation and hurt, so mystified that her stepdaughter was too selfish to help and stayed in her room like she was too good for them all. Ria stayed where she was, trying to concentrate on the good feeling of the wall, which was only plaster and innocent of everything, while she toyed with the idea of telling Marta that her husband was more interested in his daughter's body than in her own. But she did not tell Marta anything at all.

She never told anyone. Ria was a liar and a thief and not as good at either as she had needed to be, and so she tried to convince herself that no one would believe her if she told about it anyway. But that was not the reason, and she knew it: She did not want her mother to know any more bad things about him than she already knew. Not because it would make her mother feel yet more guilt but because in Ria's fitful estimation her mom was happy and her dad was miserable and she felt closer to him for that, having been left too and being still able to pretend — when she didn't let herself think too hard — that he loved her. He did not touch her that way often, and he was always sorry afterward: bought her pitiful things he couldn't afford anymore, told her he was crazy, like that would explain everything and like she didn't know that already. He was pitiful. She was ashamed. She hated all of them.

And she began again to plot her next escape. Maybe not to Mom this time. She was sick of that closing door. Mom had no visitation rights, yeah, yeah, yeah. She could not keep Ria legally and would not keep her illegally. It was dopey to expect her to go underground for her daughter's sake, like mothers did in the movies. She had fought the good fight in the courtroom and lost, and she would fight no more, ta-da. She was happy there in Santa Monica with Meg, had work she liked, cherished her freedom. Ria could see it in her mother's eyes, weary, pleading: Let me go. When her daughter came to mind, Ria knew, she was only a great tragic stone of guilt that pulled her down and robbed her of the peace she had found "at such cost." So Meg had put it once, treating Ria to lunch, leaning into Ria's intellect, as she so often did, to trick her into sympathy. Ria had no idea how hard it had been, how long her mom had stayed for Ria's sake, how painful it was that she could not have her with them. Cost — to her mom. *Fuck it.*

Maybe, Ria thought as the bus made its final groaning turn into the weedy parking lot and she filed out behind her father and his teammates and headed grimly toward the ballpark, *maybe she would go to someplace none of them had ever been, where they could not find her if they looked so she would never know they had not tried.*

But it was worse on the street. You didn't have to be pretty to suffer there; it just made it more certain that you would, and she knew already, only too well, how beautiful she was. She was already menstruating and doomed to brassieres, shapely and graceful like her mother, with her father's lovely smooth complexion. Her hair ("a woman's crowning glory," Marta cooed when she was trying to make friends) was a striking blend of Mom and Dad: just straight enough to fall the way they liked it on TV, long against her slender shoulders, and kinky enough to catch light in every sleek dark ringlet tumbling down. She was quick and strong and could fight when she couldn't run, and she had learned to protect herself. But that didn't mean she wanted to live on the streets.

And so she descended one more time, stone-faced and silent, into the ballpark jail where, chain-link–fenced in her baseball prison, she wandered among the same old strangers whose faces always turned upon the diamond…a cruel place that had destroyed her parents, as it would many a young family now turning their faces with pitiful anxiety toward the lion pit between the white chalk lines, watching stupid as lambs while husbands and fathers marched out to die from decimal points and the hapless flailing of little sticks and fancy leather, a colossally stupid way to die.

There had been a time when Roberto Quesada's pitching arm was made of gold: This his daughter knew because everyone said so. But she knew it the way that she knew Columbus sailed the ocean blue: The important facts came afterward and were not about gold but the cost of it. Ria herself had been only a toddler when the gold gave out in her father's arm, and so the world of her childhood was to be an aftermath in which she tagged unwillingly behind her father while he kept throwing and throwing, worse and worse, less and less often, through the long downhill slide of baseball death. Trade upon trade, reassignment upon reassignment, crisscrossing a continent of smaller and smaller towns, he went on performing his slow, solemn ritual dance in propitiation of his absent gods, pursuing a distant glory that bewildered her, since she could only follow her father's gaze — always outward onto the baseball diamond — without ever seeing what he saw there or had once seen.

There had been a time, she remembered, when she was too small to know better, too small to have imagined how soon and how completely her world would break its axis and spin out into chaos; a time when she had sat up in her mother's lap in bright orange plastic field-level seats in a gigantic, brilliantly lit, magnificent bowl of a stadium, and she had waved a tiny Pittsburgh Pirates pennant and screamed "Pa-a-a!" joyously when her mother pointed down to the distant lanky figure on the mound. But that was a long time ago, before she had learned, as she figured all kids must, what frighteningly hapless creatures her parents really were.

Meg had told Ria that she was wise, pretending this was a gift, an advantage. But Ria knew that her perception was a grim anchor she was chained to that held her invisibly captive. Feelings were hard to bear, but understanding was worse. For still — after all of it — she cared for her parents, was even like them, both of them. It made her angry; she was alone with it, as with everything else.

As for the game, she could not look at it anymore. She was foraging under the bleachers for dropped change, rings, cigarettes, and other interesting salvage when she heard the crackle and boom of the microphone being turned on in the announcer's booth behind her. The announcer's voice, high with forced enthusiasm, promised a "special pregame exhibition." Ria happened to look up with casual interest (for the pregame stunts and giveaways tended to be at least sort of diverting, unlike the games themselves), but what she saw through the feet and candy wrappers between the tiers of bleacher boards made her stare.

"Oklahoma Tech's *woman wonder,* Karen Vender — *The Strike-out Vendor!*" the announcer promised over the crackling PA system and hustled through some names and numbers indicating the honors and achievements of this celebrated freak of nature — but Ria's eyes were taken up in a vision that made those tedious baseball words real to her for the first time. In the litany of statistics, the hard empty mathematics of her father's obsession that she had come to hate, she heard at last the music that had charmed and captured him. And singing tingling warm through every nerve she heard, she felt the wild, exquisite notes of another music playing upon her body...the music her mother had once heard long ago and followed as helplessly as her father had followed his.

For the woman wonder herself had jogged calmly out of the home dugout and into the lights, and there she was, astonishing, a figure so majestic that she seemed both utterly new and impossibly familiar, like the template of an unremembered dream — a lean, muscular female giant, broad of shoulder and narrow in the hips, with hair the color of bright summer straw, decked out in a uniform of shiny gold and gray, her colors matching from the cap on her golden head to the long gold-and-gray socks that followed the contour of her muscular calves. She paced out her own mysterious distance from home plate and, kicking the grass to mark an imaginary pitching rubber, turned back to face the backstop, where now the home team's bored backup catcher crouched behind the plate. Then she began, methodically whipping a baseball the size of a grapefruit into his mitt behind the plate while three of the home team's batters sauntered out to hit, grinning at the silliness of it all and a bit embarrassed. Nine pitches later they would all be sitting down again, a great deal more embarrassed, with "Strike three!" "Strike three!" "Strike three!" ringing in their ears.

Ria stood transfixed where she was, as if between herself and that great quiet presence lay nothing but air. Was it the air that bore this magic current, this almost tangible field of energy, or was it her own body, like a lonely tree on a hill of grass, calling the lightning to it, welcoming that transfiguring fire? Ria felt the burn of it behind her raptly gazing eyes, and gladly she felt her body its conductor, a circuit to receive and transmit and receive again the natural electricity of an exceptional athlete just coming into her prime — who was gathering herself to deliver another pitch from a windmill motion so sudden, so violent, and yet so perfectly smooth that it literally took the breath of the thirteen-year-old girl standing under the bleachers. And she knew that she had never seen, never imagined anything so achingly beautiful in her life.

Ria Quesada, twenty years old, was riding at the back of another bus; still dressed in her grass-stained Bruins blue and gold, she knelt with her face between Coach Gail Hartley's legs, sucking her anxious cunt in the dark. The coach held Ria's head as if to control the situation or make her stop or keep her quiet, but her hands kept slipping against the famous dreadlocks of her famous young pitcher's hair, and she knew as well as Ria did who was in control.

What she could not know was how little Ria was thinking about what she was doing. Ria's mechanics, in cunnilingus as in pitching, were astonishingly good for one so young; so good that, while her body carried on a fine performance with every appearance of passionate zeal, Ria could devote her mind to intense contemplation of something quite different. Right now she was working out the thesis for a paper on the metaphysics of Spinoza in which she was trying, for her own amusement, to get that philosopher into bed with Kierkegaard, the early Scandinavian existentialist. The real irony of the pairing, she was thinking now, would be lost even on her professor. At Kelley Complex in San Diego that weekend, after a three-hour bus ride and a taxi she couldn't afford, she had seen Karen Vender pitch again, and she had been floating in a liquid dream ever since, almost physically sick with longing for her magic Swede, who had no idea with what passion the gorgeous young Latina sitting behind the backstop had watched and worshiped every move of her body.

Gail Hartley's cunt, therefore, was a feeble substitute for what Ria longed to taste. But it was exciting to fuck her here and in precisely this way, splayed out on the plastic toilet with her shorts around her freckled ankles, too hot for Ria's touch to care who saw her being fucked at will by a sophomore half her age and ten times as intelligent. And with such a satisfactory audience too: Ria couldn't look behind her to see, but she liked to imagine all nine of the lesbian players and most of their six straight teammates were peering over their high-backed seats with prurient enthusiasm.

If one of the watchers was Paula Meisner, loud-mouthed freshman homophobe, then so much the better. Maybe old Gail had fucked one phenom too many and would at last get her skinny butt kicked out of the program she'd so recently inherited; it would serve her just about right. Gail was a fat-headed little Napoleon and a racist bitch of the worst kind: She would recruit you, and she would fuck you, but she wouldn't start you until she ran out of blonds — and in softball they never run out of those, it being (Ria smiled to herself) the only women's sport where slow, overweight wanna-be jocks could hold their own. You didn't believe everything you heard in this game, but Ria had witnessed enough with her own eyes to believe that a sickening percentage of the Gail tales she'd heard secondhand were only too accurate.

Nevertheless, Ria had been so extraordinary a performer in the few games she'd played last year that Gail had had no choice but to concede midway through this year's season that Quesada was her ace. Ria was so much stronger than anyone else that, in this afternoon's doubleheader against Long Beach, right after the last out had been recorded in Ria's first-game victory, Gail had run

Ria right back out to pitch the second game. Exploiting her athletes for the sake of her own win-loss record was even more compelling a practice for Gail than racial favoritism. Ria knew exactly what her momentarily fawning and cooing coach thought of her, and it gave her no consolation that her own sheer talent had finally planted her on the mound where she deserved to be. Still, Ria admitted, there was some pleasure to be had in topping the coach so deftly that Gail had no idea that she was babbling words her newly minted protégée had coaxed her to say and saying them loud enough for half the bus to hear.

Like the rest of her teammates — who had sprawled out as comfortably as they could in various positions of repose (the coach could pray they slept) against tall, narrow seats of the bus — Ria had had no opportunity to change out of her uniform at the end of the day's doubleheader. But she wished fleetingly that she'd kept her kneepads on as well: It was a bit uncomfortable kneeling on the metal flooring with her shoulders barely able to squeeze through the narrow doorway of the chemical toilet, all the while propping the door open with her foot to keep it from rattling from the motion of the bus.

This she did out of simple courtesy. She didn't really desire to waken any of her teammates who weren't already peering back into the darkness to watch the show, and for the sake of the coach's orgasm she wished to maintain at least the illusion of secrecy, to keep her conquest happily focused on the bliss of her surrender. As the coach ejaculated into Ria's face, lost, perhaps, in the fantasy that her latest nubile sophomore hunk had fallen for her charms and had to have her, Ria was suddenly sick of the whole thing, vaguely nauseous. She was half inclined to punch a hole in Gail's sopping cunt. *Goddamned chickenhawk,* she thought. *Why don't you get off with somebody your own age for once?*

It had been a trail of many buses that had led her to this one, and somehow the lameness of the situation seemed an appropriate comment on the journey she had taken to get there. At some point in her teens, Ria had given up hope that she was important to her parents, and yet she was proud. So she decided to be important to herself. She had cultivated skill in all things with a kind of cold flamboyance and was fitfully brilliant in school despite the incoherence of an education continually interrupted by the will of the baseball gods.

Like her father, she had kept moving from one lousy place to another, always losing ground. There was no point in all her miserable leavings and returns, and she knew it. But movement was the only thing like peace, a place between nowheres where she was at least going. Her childhood and her teens she had burned in silence, a prisoner in each of the ratty schools and between them all, riding — between two social workers, between two policemen, and at last between empty seats on the Greyhound she'd put herself on once more when, emancipated by the court, she was at last free to be nobody's.

The next bus she'd boarded had pointed to Westwood and the UCLA campus, close enough to Emancipated Mama to qualify Emancipated Daughter for in-state tuition. She had guilt money from both sets of her emancipated parents; the mixed testimony of spotty preparation, abysmal math, debating championships in two different states, and a soaring IQ earned her admission to the university, with majors in philosophy and legal studies. She was off to pick up the sort of English that her mother couldn't understand any better than her father.

But that was secondary, really, to another objective. UCLA had meant Gail Hartley, who had trained six all-American pitchers during her distinguished coaching career. For reasons she would never tell her father — or anyone else, for that matter — Ria had decided to be the seventh.

So one spring morning in February of her eighteenth year, she had walked on to the Bruins' softball diamond, smoking a cigarette, an old mitt of her father's under her armpit, surveying the field; she took a long, slow drag, pronounced her famous surname to the assistant coach, and then watched Gail Hartley's eyes as the words were repeated to her; watched as, in the hard blue calculating hunger of those eyes, she saw rolling out toward her the thin red carpet white people sometimes toss before swift dark feet — the one folks lay, the one folks walk when they are going to use each other.

She had ridden so many buses as Ria Quesada, runaway brat, that she felt no difference as Ria Quesada, useful commodity. She told herself she didn't give a damn about it either way. That arbitrary gift in her that Gail would value was her ticket onto the next bus, after all, and that was all she asked of them. She had learned not to ask for much. By her own strength she would reach out and seize what she could. But love could not be seized. So why was she doing this foolish thing, riding bus by bus toward the place where love might be, knowing she could not ask, could not take, must simply move to the place and wait, wait?

For though Ria's hands were gripping Gail Hartley by her thighs, lifting her pelvis to finish what she'd started there, Ria's mind was back at Kelley Park, sitting in the bleachers behind home plate, fucking Karen Vender only with her eyes. Karen was one blond who had deserved the stature Gail had given her when, as a rookie coach at Oklahoma Tech, she had ridden Karen — the first and greatest of her all-American arms — all the way to two national collegiate titles. Wondering whether Gail had ridden Karen any other way only depressed Ria; she preferred to believe her hero had had better things to do with her body…better than Ria had now.

That last Saturday had been only the second time in Ria's life that she had seen Karen Vender pitch, and yet Ria's eyes had followed the contours of that body with the acuity of an artist returned at last to the presence of her own lost masterpiece, recalling every brushstroke, every perfect choice, every precious detail of it despite years of separation.

For years she had lived on two posters and a slowly mounting crateful of National Tournament programs and subscription magazines — many months' worth of *Softball West* and *Women's Fastpitch,* two issues of *Women's Sports and Fitness,* and one bittersweet *Sports Illustrated.* Somehow Gail Hartley had come away squeaky-clean when the infamous Oklahoma Tech scandal had handed the university four years' NCAA probation as well as the four-page exposé in *Sports Illustrated* in which appeared the only picture of Karen Vender that Ria could hardly bear to look at, ashamed at her desire to stare. Splattered between action shots of two football players accused of taking cash bonuses for signing their letters of intent was a shot of Karen, out of uniform in a quiet gray crewneck sweater with the collar of a carefully ironed work shirt pitifully neat against her neck, sitting in a courtroom chair with her eyes turned miserably inward and looking as though she were listening to humiliating testimony — which she was. The caption beneath the photograph glibly summarized it: "Illiterate all-American Karen Vender (above, center) struck out in the classroom; her 000 SAT score was one Vender stat that never made the media guide."

It pained Ria to look into the face above that caption, with her lost eyes hunted and blank with numbness and disappearance, as if the spirit, desperate to escape from her body, had only burrowed too deeply inside it to be found. But Ria found herself drawn to the photograph anyway; it exposed Karen in a way that was strangely thrilling, so much so that just to touch the cover of that magazine, let alone to open it to the sacred page, made her blood race and her cunt throb as if she were touching Karen's body.

She was shy enough about her obsession that she marked Karen's pictures with Post-it notes laid discreetly upon the pages; she could find her idol easily by a quick flip-through, but no one else would notice what made the journals so indispensable to her that she packed a couple in her suitcase even for the shortest journeys. Ever since her fourteenth summer, when she had first figured out how to massage into climax the warm ache that throbbed between her legs when she thought of Karen, she had been masturbating to those pictures, and she could no longer come without one of them in view.

Her sentimental favorite was the cover shot on the earliest of her annual National Tournament programs, which she'd sent for through the mail. The camera had caught Karen's supple, powerful body arrested in its motion at the very end of her delivery, a split second after releasing the pitch. Her right arm was cocked tightly at the elbow, the tanned forearm thrust almost straight upward parallel to her body, the long, sensitive fingers of her pitching hand bent loosely in a kind of gently closing fist, the palm curved slightly outward. When she had first seen that picture, she had not known what that hand position meant. Now she had learned to imitate the pitch with her own version of the notorious Vender Drop. But for several years, when she traced the dramatic line which that upthrusting forearm made against the background of grass and sky, she knew only that Karen's arm was the most powerful lever ever to hang off a female shoulder and her hand the most unbearably beautiful instrument in creation.

She had fantasized for months about simply kissing that hand and holding it warm against her own cheek; but that was at fourteen, before she had found an opportunity to experiment with another girl's body. Her fantasies had progressed with experience: These days her imagination would not settle for less with Karen Vender than everything she had ever taken from the girls she'd seduced in high school and the women she'd seduced in college. She wanted Karen bent over a weight bench taking Ria's fist deep inside her and moaning, "Fuck me, I belong to you." She grinned at the hilarious egotism of her scenario, and yet one of her objectives for her weekend expedition to San Diego had been to listen hard in hopes of hearing what Karen's voice sounded like so she could hear her say those words in her fantasy exactly as they would have sounded.

After she'd sat down at the perfect spot, right behind home plate and almost at field level, after the scarlet-and-gold–clad Delta Rockettes had made their traditional sprint from the dark dugout to their positions afield, Ria, her eyes riveted on the dugout, caught her first sight of Karen Vender, returned to her own magnificent three dimensions once again. When Ria's eyes adjusted to the darkness of the dugout, she saw that Karen was down on one knee, helping the catcher fasten her last piece of equipment — one of her shin guards — before she herself took the field. The catcher was a husky butch with a good deal of weight on her frame, but Ria could tell that Karen would tower over her when both were standing. She was so tall that even down on one knee, she had to hunch her shoulders to get low enough to reach the catcher's calf, but she did it without hesitation. Oblivious to the clapping and chanting that had started to build from the spectators — softball aficionados all, most of them had set their alarms this morning and staggered to this 9 A.M. game expressly to see the legendary Vender pitch — Karen focused entirely on her teammate's need.

There was something in the gesture, such unstudied kindness, that it touched Ria in a place too painful to go to. To rescue herself from that place, Ria speculated that Karen did seem like exactly the sort of person who would let herself be butt-fucked over a weight bench; but then Ria heard herself thinking — with absurd seriousness — that it would not be right to do it to her. Ria's heart was so full at the sight that she thought, with confused alarm, that she was going to cry — something she never permitted herself to do and quite untenable in one who'd learned very early that her strong suit, in bed and out of it, was detachment.

Ria Quesada, twenty-five years old, stood in the center of the glass-walled hotel elevator, arms folded, trying not to think too much about where she was headed and what she was about to do. She focused instead on the disastrous meeting downstairs from which she and the other distinguished and aggressively recruited members of her new team were fleeing, like so many rats deserting a much-advertised *Titanic* before they could be identified as investors, let alone passengers. Ria realized, for the first time in the two months since she had signed on to this dubious voyage, that she had been fantasizing that at last she had found herself in a community of people she could admire, people with whom she could wish as well as need to belong. And where she had cooked that up she couldn't imagine now. They were only a thrown-together fourteen-car pileup of jock dykes with grass between their ears and, when it came down to it, nothing much else in common.

Shop Shop Markets Inc. was all that had brought them together: a regional retail chain selling international cuisine that was now shooting for nationwide expansion. Its president, Li Chuen, blending fatherly pride with advertising acumen, had thrown $100,000 at Dusty Winston (ex-coach of the U.S. National Team) to piece together around his youngest daughter, Su, a kind of Technicolor dream team of standout fast-pitch players, picked as much for appearance as for skill, to float his national campaign both on field and off. They had gathered in Houston that weekend for the strange purpose not of playing softball but of shooting commercials: commercials in which their most photogenic and racially diverse nine had posed, in full uniform, behind a phalanx of shopping carts, the two tallest — Su Chuen and Karen Vender — holding up softball mitts absurdly full of soup noodles and frozen enchiladas.

Su was a passionate soul — during her collegiate career at Stanford, Su's penchant for throwing bats in disgust on those rare occasions when she failed to hit the ball out of the park was legendary — and though she bore her humiliation in grim silence all through the afternoon's interminable shoot, she was clearly boiling mad from the word go, controlling herself with enormous effort. Ria suspected Su was more miserable for her teammates' sake than her own; she must be feeling, as she had since the team was first assembled, that every indignity any one of them endured was her fault. Su was loyal by nature, having a sincere reverence for her elders that Ria wistfully admired. And Ria knew — because she shared it — what was making Su writhe. It was bad enough that oneself was made ridiculous, but the idea of Karen waving noodles at America in the twilight of her career was too much to bear.

Karen had endured it all without a murmur of complaint, not even in her eyes, until one wan little smile crossed her face on the eighteenth take, when the director asked "the big horse in the back" to switch her mitt from her left hand to her right so that the image would match that of left-handed Su. Characteristically, Karen had made no protest, silently cramming the glove down onto her pitching hand as best she could. It was the rest of the team that cried out indignantly that Karen was right-handed and the mitt would look backward to anyone who knew the game.

Only Casey Steele, the catcher, was more amused than offended. She pointed out sardonically that pitching out of a mitt would significantly alter Karen's technique in the future, but she guessed the American Softball Association would sanction the change in honor of the corporate interests of Shop Shop.

"If you really need a left-hander," Ria had spoken out at this point in her dry-ice tone, "put Steele back there. Her mitt's already on the wrong hand." This broke up half the line with laughter, but it only jacked up the tension another notch, because even the youngest players knew this was a sensitive point: As a left-hander Casey had no business playing catcher, where she had to slide-step to the right for every throw to second, most batters being in the way, and where to make a tag as quickly as a right-hander, she had to straddle the plate like a goalie so every slide to home became a collision. And she'd been allowed to do so all her long career entirely because (so the story went) she was the only catcher in the game who could handle the Vender Drop consistently and communicate effectively with a pitcher so dyslexic that not only letters and numbers but also the basic finger signals — one for riser, two for drop, three for change of pace — confused her. Casey was an inveterate clown, as happy to make fun of herself as of anything else; but just beneath her manic good-humored persona was a fiercely sensitive butch painfully conscious of her mediocrity as an athlete. Her pink-cheeked, gregariously cheerful face had a smile like a crocodile: She refused to be laughed at when she had not herself devised the joke.

"Hoo, girl, you go!" Jill Rockney, center fielder, had laughed into Ria's ear. "I see you got the death wish in you."

Ria shrugged. She didn't give a shit. She had achieved what she wanted: No one was laughing at Karen anymore.

But some sort of stupid reckoning was inevitable, and that evening, when they'd all reassembled in Su and Wendy's suite — ostensibly for supper but really to bitch about the afternoon — Ria had come "spikes up," as Jill liked to say, ready to do battle. The form of combat when it came, however, had taken her by surprise; Casey spent most of the evening with her saber-toothed grin pointed not at Ria but at Karen. She ripped her famous battery mate all evening, jovially but ruthlessly, from the moment they'd all sat down to the moment they made their hasty departure, pausing only a few minutes to shoot down a secondary target or two. Ria had merely been one of those.

They had sat in the living room in various configurations — lovers in one another's laps, enemies exactly polarized across the coffee table — in assorted postures of disgust, ignoring the chips and dip Su had ordered from room service and the meat loaf Karen had cooked that morning for the occasion, though they drank the beer and soda like a row of water trucks lined up at the loading dock to be filled. They were in no mood to socialize; instead they were intent on hashing out the indignities of the day and everyone's doubts and complaints about the way their spring tournaments had gone so far, which was not very damn well.

"And how *can* we be losing?" Casey had asked — in her tone of mock bewilderment — "with the Old Gray Mare herself in our stable, laying her best horse apples on the mound for the honor of grocery shoppers everywhere?"

"That's a shitty attitude, Case," Su snapped.

Casey grunted and let out a hard laugh. "The Manchurian Candidate speaks!"

"Oh, come on, Casey, give it a rest," pleaded Sandra.

This precipitated a bizarre fight between Casey and Sandra, in which the shortstop, despite her righteous cause, seemed to be sliding miserably down a hill, her eyes beseeching Casey not to punish her. After five minutes of shouting back and forth, Casey looked her meaningfully in the eyes and said, in a weary tone, "Just sit down, Sandy, you're making an ass of yourself."

"There's an ass here all right," Ria purred coolly. She took a drag off her cigarette before she added, "But it isn't Sandy."

"Why María Elena, how subtle!" Casey replied, exaggerating the rolled *r* and leaning long into the soft *e* until it sounded like a bleating lamb, as if there were something inherently ridiculous about Spanish pronunciation and, by implication, Ria herself.

Wendy Perez, the other Latina member on the team, had a long fuse — for which everyone was regularly grateful, as she alone had the ability to calm her lover, Su, when Su was in one of her bat-throwing moods — but Su did not. "Fuck you, Steele," she growled, "you racist bitch." And the room erupted in shouting and broken glass.

But Ria was present only in body.

Casey knew nothing of her history, surely. But as Ria had observed from their very first team workout, the veteran catcher had an unerring intuition when it came to sensing weaknesses of others, and she'd realized early on how little Ria wanted to hear her given name. And she had scored with it all right. For a few moments — it could have been one second or twenty years — Ria Quesada, who could outfence any opponent in two languages, could not respond; she was too far away. While the chairs scraped and the voices rose and the glass broke and the scuffle erupted, all was silence in Ria's mind, all but a single voice... She was sitting on the floor in a grimy rented room in Oklahoma, hugging the wall and hearing *"¡María Elena! ¡Ayudame!"* with her lower back still aching from her father's thrusting pelvis.

Why was it, she thought, trapped in the glass-walled elevator, looking bitterly at all the little houses on the street below with their deceptively peaceful lights in the windows and suspecting that behind each glowing window there was discord — why was it that she felt so responsible, a secret party to the whole lame fiasco that the meeting had become? She was ashamed that she had not returned Casey's cruelty with the withering retort it deserved. *Flashback,* Ria told herself. *I couldn't help that.* She'd had them before, and she'd have them the rest of her life, she figured. But there was something else to her shame: She had not defended Karen either.

Casey had defused her enemies with her usual aplomb — turning astonishingly sweet and self-deprecating, gradually making their rage look overblown and a little funny, her bullshit and their reaction both follies she was glad to concede and laugh about. Ria felt slimy witnessing the whole performance: the cruel gibes at Karen's expense, the ugly shouting match, the sullen silence with which they'd clambered in twos and threes to their feet, reached for their gear, and hurried away from one another. In the midst of this exodus, Casey had had the gall to offer in parting one more jest at Karen's expense: "Don't forget, everybody, take a little of Horse's Mystery Meat with you — it's a great insect repellent." Ria's heart went out to Karen, but she felt deflated, as she often had that spring, to watch how little respect the hero of her childhood commanded among her peers; it was sweet to have been defended by these semistrangers, but it was bitter to see how little they cared, after all, for Karen. As for the fight, she didn't give a rat's ass except that she felt bad for Su, who had never gotten a hit off of Ria in the three years they'd been opponents on different teams but who had vigorously supported Ria's recruitment and made an effort to include her in get-togethers.

Such support had mattered a great deal to Ria, much more than Su could have known. For Su's friends, the older players, were Karen's too. And Ria had deserted her Eureka team — on the heels of a national championship season — for the untried experiment of Shop Shop entirely so that she might finally have her chance to jump Karen Vender's bones.

Ria felt almost homicidally angry that evening. She calmed herself now by reflecting that if she hadn't taken herself out of the danger zone, she would have done such violence that she'd have brought her long journey to a halt so painfully close to her destination. A sense of urgency mobilized her: This team would not stick together much longer. If she lost her chance before she could summon the courage to take it, she would regret it forever.

For the two months Ria had traveled in Karen's company, their only real contact had been on the practice diamond, where for half an hour at the end of each workout, while Dusty Winston kept the video camera rolling, Karen had helped Ria fine-tune her delivery. She was a gentle teacher, full of praise, and Ria felt nervous and shy in her eagerness to be worthy of every compliment. Karen crossed no boundaries, radiated no quest for intimacy; her touch seemed only serious and kind. But when Ria masturbated now, it was to the memory, tingling in her fingers, of Karen's touch, gently and patiently retraining Ria's fingers around the ball to clean up her drop-ball grip, and the sweet warmth of Karen's shoulder brushing hers as she guided Ria in slow motion through her delivery.

In such moments Ria felt so close to Karen that it almost scared her. So she fell back on her usual detachment, disciplining herself to appear as casual and indifferent as the rest of the younger players while she watched and listened, learning, learning all she could, before she made her move — and tonight, she had decided, was the night. For in all her outrage on her hero's behalf, Ria knew her real motive for riding this elevator was not to console Karen or to defend her honor but to take her now, tonight, when the long day's humiliations had left her, Ria hoped, vulnerable enough to drink in kindness and in kindness be seduced.

She was so absorbed in her reverie that she was a little stunned to find herself at the door to Karen's suite. *Well, this is it,* she thought, rapping her knuckles on the door, feeling her heartbeat jacking up. As she stood perspiring in the hallway, suddenly it occurred to her that others might have found their way to that door ahead of her; perhaps Sandra or Su had come home with

Karen or followed her home on some mission of consolation or self-justification. Worse yet — Ria kicked herself inwardly that she'd forgotten this — Casey Steele shared the suite with Karen, as she often did on the road, and it made an angry heat rise up into Ria's nostrils to think of having to put up with another minute of Casey's self-centered braggadocio. But she'd hardly had time to be mortified at this possibility when Karen opened the door and asked Ria inside with a wave of a dish towel.

Ria studied Karen's features for pain or anger or unrest, but as she led Ria into the kitchen — Karen appeared quite alone in the suite — she looked calm, almost impassive. She moved a little slowly down the hall, with a slight stoop to her shoulders, so perhaps she was more tired than usual, but then Karen always looked tired.

"Beer?" Karen asked.

"Sure, thanks."

Karen fetched a beer from the refrigerator and with the reach of one long arm passed it to Ria's hand. Ria took a long, grateful drink, then pressed the wet can against her burning temple.

"Mind if I do some of this…?" Karen gestured apologetically at the dishes that littered the table and sink.

"Oh, yes, go right on," Ria said, suddenly embarrassed at her own unsolicited visit. "That was a mess tonight," she offered by way of explanation.

Karen nodded and turned toward the table. "Yeah, guess I'm a messy cook, all right." She indicated the dishes. "You know, I don't cook a lot, and then when I do it, I try too hard. Doesn't matter. What is it Casey says? *Esmoknix.* Something like that. She says that's German for 'It makes nothing.'" She looked at Ria in the doorway and smiled kindly, her wan smile a good-natured imitation of cheer. Then she grinned. "That's me cooking," she said. "'Makes nothing!'"

Ria blushed at Karen's mistake and said, "I meant the meeting," before she could stop herself.

Karen turned quickly back to the dishes and looked down at them solemnly. "Yeah. Well." She seemed frozen, as she had been at the meeting, by a sudden awareness that the joke, yet again, was on her. Ria felt senselessly unkind. Now she wanted to say to Karen, "You're not stupid, just preoccupied, and I didn't explain

myself," but she could not find safe words. Karen laughed sheep-
ishly and went to work.

The glaring yellow light over the kitchen table set Karen's
large, familiar figure in relief; her long, lithe back bent and swayed
easily, swiftly, and purposefully over the debris as she cleared it
away in silence. Pausing over the work with that slight stoop in her
shoulders — Ria remembered then that Karen must have been up
at 5 this morning — she blew out a soft breath of air as she considered the pile, her long hands tentatively fingering the dish towel
as if she were marshaling all the formidable resources of her body
for this simple task.

Ria leaned back slowly against the kitchen doorway, watching
her intently. She thought Karen Vender looked ready to run the
last six miles of some marathon from hell, six miles she would have
to run over again anyway because this marathon would never really end. And it struck her, for the first time, that Karen nearly always
looked that way, that even at her freshest and happiest she seemed
to be trudging through something: a female Sisyphus staggering
patiently behind her rock.

That was how Karen was: weary and peaceful. She'd look into
the sea of faces looking back at her and never expect to be seen.
It was hard to tell whether she even wanted to be. Off the mound
she always seemed to be embarrassed by attention. But sometimes
Ria caught Karen's mild gray eyes searching a room as if she were
looking for something or someone who would not be there, who
would never be there. What was she looking for? And those faces
that searched Karen's, even as they dismissed her, took her for
granted, teased her — they expected her to bring something sweet
and generous into the room with her, something that rescued
them all.

Karen had just dropped the dishwashing liquid and was foraging for it patiently amid the suds. Water drops coursed up her
strong, tanned forearms to pool at the inside of her elbows, and
the muscles slid and pulled in her long, powerful back. *Our grand
old warhorse,* Ria repeated to herself. *Jesus, the bitch has got me saying it.* Karen was a lovely name, yet nobody on this team called
her that. Casey's "Horse" had stuck to her, like "Spider" to Sandy
and "Look Out" to poor Jill (who didn't need to be reminded of

her wild throwing arm). Then there were the ornate racial slurs
with which Casey so deliberately peppered her speech. *The Manchurian Candidate,* Ria brooded, *what crap* — carefully passing over
María Elena.

Casey, the author of all these irritating aliases, had given herself something jaunty and butch so she could slip free of her own
given name, Mary Catherine. Karen had submitted to Casey's
stampede — and though "Horse" alone of all the herd had stuck
to her, Casey continued to advance new names, each one more
condescending than the last. She did this, Ria guessed, just to see
the color rise in Karen's face and that wan smile unsettle the soft,
solemn line of her mouth. Why did Karen put up with that? Why
had she ever put up with her at all, let alone for fifteen years as
battery mate on 500 diamonds?

"What do you see in Casey?"

"Hmm?" Karen looked up, attentive and preoccupied at once.

"Casey Steele. She treats you like you're some kind of mascot.
Why do you take that from her?"

"Oh, well," Karen said, thinking of the statement and the
tumbler in her hand at the same time and looking about the teem-
ing counter for some place to put either. "Casey's just...playing
around."

"Doesn't seem like playing to me. More like putting you
down. Which is incomprehensible to me. She's a mediocre ball-
player — it's no secret she's only played majors all these years
because she was your catcher — and she struts around like you're
some kind of dumb appendage. It makes me want to slap her."

At this Karen laughed, a weird little "Hah!" that she tried to
cut off before it slipped out.

"You think it's funny?"

Karen looked miserable. "It's complicated to explain and not
very important," she said at last, making a little clatter with the
dishes.

"Try me."

"Well, if you knew Casey, you'd know she's really kinda inse-
cure. She don't mean no harm. You just don't want to do the alpha
dog thing with her. When she's hurting, she don't care what she
says, she's just got to bite back harder."

"You mean I'm supposed to be scared of her?" Now it was Ria's turn to laugh. "Come on. She's about as scary as the Pillsbury Dough Boy." Now she had Karen laughing, and the sweetness of that made her want to keep it going. "If all six-foot-four of you weren't around, she'd get her ass kicked all the time."

"Maybe so," Karen laughed. "She always tells me I'm her bodyguard and to keep my eyes peeled for incoming missiles from ex-lovers. When we were kids I sort of was. Her bodyguard, I mean."

"Lovers" dropped so easily from Karen's lips because it was a joke and all about Casey, who provided the one subject besides pitching that Karen seemed able to talk about comfortably — Casey, whose words she seemed so relieved to recite. But Ria had never heard that word come out of Karen's mouth before, and it caught her breath. The room seemed full of it — lovers, not in the past with an *x* but with a question mark. Maybe it was only her own body full of it, her heart a little fast because they were alone together and that had never happened before.

Ria had done her research: She had asked around, carefully casual, asking without seeming to care about the answer. Supposedly Karen and Casey had never been lovers, but that was hard to imagine. Two lesbians don't play ball together for fifteen years on a half-dozen teams in three different states without something happening, especially when one of them was as gleefully predatory about sex as Casey seemed to be. The thought of Karen and Casey sharing an intimate past was depressing. It seemed like yet another bond between the two, which, even in the breaking, would have nothing to do with Ria. The pain in that thought made her cruel.

"Do you like that?"

"Like what?"

"Being sidekick to an asshole," Ria said.

Direct hit. Karen gripped the dish in her hand as if suddenly she had no idea what to do with it. The expression in her eyes was painful and eerily familiar. Karen Vender could neither fight nor flee. She would not hit back.

So easily and coldly I kill, Ria thought, but it was her stepmother's voice: Marta, invincible conscience, accusing, *"Escucha*

tus, pensamientos. ¿Qué estás haciendo?" as if she could hear and
expose the evil turning of Ria's thoughts. Helpless, Ria hurtled
down that bottomless well of memory again. *"¡Por Dios, María!"*
Marta had known what Ria was: a hunter, a spy in her own family, too good for everyone — and that was what people told themselves when they knew down deep in God's eye they were no
good to anyone. Direct hit. *"¡Recuerda tu padre!"* How the fuck
could she forget? She honored her father against all deserving. It
was he who could not honor her. *How you lie,* said the Marta-ness
in her heart. *How you steal from your own self.*

In childhood she had learned to control such situations, all situations, with a shrug and a cool, impassive face, a cigarette, and a
silence that said, *Father is not worthy of my respect, and neither are you.*
If she did not speak, she would not confess. Then swift and silent
she would make her move and set off running: silent hunter, silent
thief. Winning was so easy, like squashing a bug. But empty. You
ate and were hungrier than ever, traveled so far to find nowhere.

A sense of this poisoned power she seemed to have, always too
much, never enough, bathed Ria with shame. She was crawling
painfully, hand over hand, up the wall of her well, up toward the
kitchen of the present, alarmed that she could see the room without being there. "I'm sorry," she heard herself say, "that didn't come
out the way I wanted it to," because she knew that it had. "I know
you guys are close. I just can't figure out why. You're such a sweet
person, and she's such a jerk."

Karen could not turn away quickly enough: Ria saw the blush
in her cheek, red fire beneath the sun-gold tan, and in that instant
Ria returned to her body, feeling her own blood rising and diving
within her, her heart pumping a little faster in its current from
brain to groin and back again. *I desire, therefore I am.* She said a
prayer of thanks for the gift that Karen had given her unawares.
She heard "sweet," and she likes it.

"Casey's all right," Karen said. "It isn't right, I know, she teas-
es people so hard. But she's just playful mostly and doesn't mean
nothing by it. She's not a bad person. Got her trouble like anybody else."

"I.e., she's a jerk," Ria said shortly. She was tired of hearing
about this woman, though Karen didn't sound like a lover when

she talked of her. Karen sounded more like a roadie on someone else's world tour, pathetically proud of her inside information. That was depressing too. Ria had worshiped the idea of Karen Vender, Strikeout Vendor, for so many years, it was deflating to find her hero not the center even of her own adventure.

Ria said, "A person can be clever without being cruel," and then almost laughed, because it seemed to her that she had always been both and could not separate the two any better than Casey did. Casey was just less skillful — a bull in the china shop where Ria was a sliding, sinuous cat. Now Ria was plotting how to fuck Karen even as she spoke, which did not feel innocent. She was thinking that if Karen was impressed with such a swaggering phony as Casey, a truly dominant woman could knock her off her feet with a whisper.

"Maybe I'm nice because I'm not clever," Karen said, her voice light, the pain in it very old. The lightness sounded like the little plop a pebble makes when dropped down a deep well. Someone with a well that close to dry would be wary of visitors who stopped to drink. Maybe Karen was single on purpose.

When Ria had first joined this team and set about her quiet campaign, it had been hard for her to believe that Karen Vender, so handsome and gentle, was single. But in time she understood. Karen hummed at so low a frequency that, despite her size, she disappeared into her surroundings as if camouflaged to resemble anything she touched or stood beside. Maybe that was why Karen chose to stand in the shadow of her wisecracking catcher. Casey drew attention away from Karen. And now it occurred to Ria that maybe Karen wanted it that way, that she did not want to be seen.

Ria wanted Karen's body so much, she could hardly bear it, but she could see how others might have felt the same way, only to be rebuffed by this curious vanishing act. It was as if Karen were continually excusing herself and hurrying away from the table before one could form the words for even the shiest introduction, a request to pass the salt. And there was Karen's emblematic signature of victory, her disappearance from the field before even her infielders could offer her so much as a pat on the back or a passing high five. So long ago on that minor league baseball diamond in Oklahoma, Ria had watched while Karen Vender turned for the

dugout at a jog the instant the umpire began the ritual punch-out
signaling the last strike three, almost before the last unhittable rise
ball went whistling from her hand to become only a hard sudden
breeze in the batter's face, invisible and gone. Karen was in a quiet
hurry to be elsewhere, a moving target harder to hit than anything
she threw.

Maybe it was less painful to her to be ignored entirely than
to be seen only as a beautiful animal to be captured and used —
as so many must have seen her, as Ria herself had seen her, as she
was seeing her now. But if Ria came on to her and Karen resist-
ed, Ria knew she would crumble into a sorry little heap of
shame, blow away like cigarette ashes swept from a table by one
firm breeze. Some killer cat she was! Ria tried to shake herself
free of the thought, which led inexorably to *"¡Por Dios, María!"*
Only movement could distract her; she had to be faster than the
voices in her head.

They would not take the fire in her body — this at least was
something all her own. She was so close to the feast that she could
taste it, desired it with all the lust and yearning in her heart: She
knew how Karen would feel, how deeply she could be kissed, how
deeply entered, how deeply taken. The pull of Karen's body was
irresistible.

"Stop it," Ria said harshly, slipping down off the counter and
up behind her.

"Stop…?" Karen looked confused, her pitching hand gripping another tumbler like a buoy not to be submerged, a landmark
to steer by in this sudden squall.

Ria reached across Karen's body, yanked the glass from her
hand, and threw it behind her so hard, it shattered against the wall.
Once she had touched her hand, she felt the sudden electricity of
the contact so intensely that she nearly lost her balance. She
slipped her left hand around Karen's neck and with her right slid
across her waist down the natural hollow of her hip to seize her
hard by the groin. The feel of Karen — her long, hard body, her
moist skin, the sweat hot against Ria's fingertips and palms where
she covered Karen with her taking hands, all of it — sent such a
shudder through Ria's own body that she was alarmed, for once
in her life frightened by her own act.

In a single second it all dropped through her consciousness, all at once: Maybe this was the wrong thing, was terrible, was trouble. Karen would think she was too young, too aggressive, invasive, ignoring boundaries she had every right to expect Ria would honor. Karen would be angry, and Ria had never seen her angry before. And Ria would be all tumultuous apologies, miserably exposed: She would have to withdraw.

She would have done so — had she not felt the hard muscles in Karen's stomach relaxing instantly at her touch, her whole body giving itself up to Ria's hands, shivering hot with an answering desire every bit as potent as Ria's own.

Ria kissed Karen's neck and caressed her hips, her buttocks, her thighs. A bead of perspiration slipped down the soft part of Karen's jaw below her ear, and Ria kissed it, licking the wetness with her tongue, feeling the sweet invisible down of hair that lay close upon her cheek. Her pitching hand, its grip relaxing to Karen's openness, nestled between Karen's thighs to brush and then settle over her groin, warm and moist through the thin summer pants. At this touch Karen's head fell back, and her broad, firm shoulders collapsed into Ria's. And Ria, feeling Karen surrender completely to her touch, felt a rush of power thrilling through her own body like threads of flame flashing outward from her chest and pelvis. "Karen," she breathed, pressing the yielding length of Karen's back closely against her breasts and caressing Karen's groin until the soft cotton there was soaked. She unzipped Karen's pants, feeling her buttocks tighten and release to the command of Ria's fingers freeing her of her clothing, Karen's strong arms lifting above her head as Ria pulled the tank top over her head. When Karen was naked, Ria slipped her first and middle fingers, already moist, deep into the hot, sweet softness in the cleft of her cunt.

Karen moaned, a high sigh of sweet release, lifted out somehow free from all trace of her flat Southwestern drawl: a voice before speech and beyond it, that could say what it was to be a woman in passion, that could say *ecstasy* in Karen's first and truest voice. Ria listened, rapt, to that voice, willing it to go on and on singing the whole song of Karen that maybe no one had ever heard from beginning to end. Karen tried to turn around, to give her breasts and belly and cunt fully to Ria's touch. But Ria wanted to hold her back-to-breast, still drinking, drinking her fill of this sweet power. So she held her fast with a fierce tenderness, pressing Karen's buttocks into her own pelvis. Her fingers in Karen's cunt played with Karen's genitals now lightly, now wildly, now deeply, now quickly, now deliberately. She teased Karen's clitoris with this systematically discontinuous touch until, half mad with the stimulation, Karen relaxed, surrendered there too, her clit now trained into submission to any touch Ria chose.

Her left arm pinioning Karen's, Ria slid her left hand across Karen's chest to squeeze and fondle Karen's breast until the taut nipple pressed helpless into her palm and she must kiss her there. Ria turned Karen in her hands and began to rock her slowly as if they were dancing, for between her thighs Karen had become a hot sea of cream, rocking softly pliant beneath Ria's hand, Ria's fingers plotting a course through swiftly parting waters. Karen was so tall that Ria need not bend at all when she placed her lips on Karen's nipple, took it into her mouth, and gently sucked; then firmly, carefully, with both her strong young arms, she took Karen down onto the tile floor. Now so weak in her submission, no longer in control of her body, Karen could not hold herself steady in any posture but had to be assisted to the floor, entranced and limp-limbed, like a deeply sleeping child undressed and carried to bed without a murmur of awareness. Karen yielded so eagerly and completely that it was as if she too had been waiting all the years just for this, as if the well in her were so full after all that Ria's touch had made it overflow.

Karen lay under her hand, unable to do anything but respond and resound. Ria's palm was cupped over the pubic mound still pulsing with blood, still shivering hot in the aftermath of orgasm, the little aftershocks of that great rending of her earth slowly decreasing in magnitude, Ria's slender fingers lying at rest against the hood of Karen's clitoris. Deep between lips Karen could not close until Ria chose to withdraw, Ria's hand touched Karen at the center of the conquest, at the hot tip of this continent, an iceberg turned volcano that Karen could not submerge. In her palm she felt the pulsing of the mons as it weakened, the heartbeat beneath the breast as it slowed…and she found herself absurdly hanging on, lying silent across Karen's hot body as it cooled, listening to it intently and wistfully as if for distant music as it moved farther and farther away.

It was time to move, to turn from this, to reach for her cigarettes, to prop herself up lazily on one elbow and take a long cool drag to calm herself, time to think of something calm and amusing and powerful to say to Karen Vender, Strikeout Vendor, this girl with Meg's face and her father's arm who, she had believed for so long, knew a secret about herself that made her proud, even though no one watched or hoped or waited for her. But there was no secret here. There was only Karen, an easy target after all: dull sidekick, shy butt of jokes, losing her fastball, pushing forty alone, with all her money in a duffel bag, too simple to be ashamed that there was so little left or to be angry that no one cared.

Or maybe too wise, Ria thought wryly. It seemed to her now that there had been yet another gap in her own education, more costly than any algebra she had missed: She had never been to the place where serenity was taught. And for an instant she felt, she knew, what the world must have looked like to Karen all of her life: a sea of directions written in a code that her severely dyslexic perception, ill-diagnosed and unaided, could never wrestle into meaning. But Karen had taught herself everything she needed to survive. She memorized landmarks that would be bulldozed and replaced the next time she looked for them and dared to live in the perpetual unfamiliarity of the world, always losing something, never lost. Karen had taken both her gifts and the loss of them, her privilege and her handicap, the way Ria had taken plates of food at runaway shelters and detention centers on all the circular journeys of her childhood: What you got was simply what you got — you ate it or you died. Karen was just doing the next best thing still possible for her, eating as served; and when she could no longer have that, she would take less.

If low expectations could've made Ria happy, though, she'd have had no bitterness to smoke, she would not have taken the long journey to this bed. It was only a road trip to the past she had taken, just to make sure she had left nothing behind. Now it was over and done: One of them should make for the dugout, look for the bus, and get on.

But Ria had stopped this bus, caught the invisible, held the ball, still, in her grasp. Karen was going nowhere. Precious and particular, a solitary woman who for Ria's pleasure and her own had let herself be so vulnerable so easily, she lay here and now, with her strong sweet body still against Ria's hand as if it were not over.

And Ria did not want to move.

Night Train to Florence
by Gabriella West

Liz and I were both studying Italian at an Irish university, which is why we found ourselves together one late summer afternoon on the streets of Milan, hurrying toward the train station (which our guidebook told us was a monument of Fascist architecture) to catch the train back to Florence. Then something unexpected caught our attention. On a sunny, deserted street, two girls in dresses were throwing a Frisbee back and forth almost dreamily. They were pretty girls with long hair who smiled at each other; they were our age — eighteen, nineteen — and seemed curiously absorbed in their game. Liz and I stood and watched them, astonished. Liz was not good at pausing — it was not natural for her to watch others with interest and without expectation — but I liked to shape stories in my head, and by the time we had reached the end of the street, I'd convinced myself that what I had just seen was so strangely unreal that if I looked back, the girls would have vanished.

Liz too seemed slightly shaken by the experience, which surprised me. I wondered if she felt the same twinges of jealousy that I did. The girls had seemed such good friends! Traveling around northern Italy with Liz had been a mixed experience so far; there hadn't been the deepening of the friendship that I had hoped for. We had fought several times, over nothing really: just our different rhythms. Liz was excitable and had great stamina; I was slower, more thoughtful, and tended to expect her to be the leader. Her grasp of the language, after all, was so much better. We were here because our university required us to go to Italy for two months during our three-year course. We had become wearily familiar with trains and ferries, hostels and quick snacks from railway bars. Liz required regular infusions of coffee to keep her going. I didn't but accompanied her to cafés. Neither of us had enough money to eat properly.

"You've lost so much weight!" Liz had said approvingly after our first month as I sat up on a bed in a Florence hotel. She was skinny, with a short mop of fuzzy, thick blond hair and glasses. I was her complete opposite: plump, long dark hair, with full breasts and wide hips. Uncomfortable with my femininity, I hid myself as best I could, though it was difficult in the Italian summer. We carried large bottles of water with us, and I sweated a lot, although Liz, annoyingly, didn't.

We had covered a lot of ground. It shocks me now to think of how many towns we visited and for what short periods. Liz had it all mapped out in her head. We had passed through Perugia, Bologna, Parma, Ravenna, Assisi, Florence, Siena, Pisa, Lucca, Bergamo, Brescia, and now Milan. I was looking forward to getting back to Florence, where I would take the train home and Liz would stay on. She planned to go down south to Rome and Sicily. I didn't envy her that journey. She had so little money now. We both had the kind of families in which asking for more money was difficult — not even an option really — and anyway, we were too proud. We were very much on our own.

As we sat in the train for the long trip back to Florence, I remembered one shining moment of togetherness at the beginning of our travels. We'd taken a bus to San Miniato, on the outskirts of Florence, and had climbed the hill to the little yellow church. I had loved it the year before when I'd come on my own and wanted to show Liz the view of the city from that spot. We sat on a bench and sipped cheap white wine from a carton we'd bought in a shop. We had only one plastic glass, so we passed it back and forth. Quite rapidly we got drunk, since our stomachs were empty. We laughed easily. Everything suddenly seemed alive, vivid, and there was something charged in the air between us. Liz had lively blue eyes behind her glasses; both of us liked to laugh, but life had not been kind to us.

One thing the two of us had in common was our romantic inexperience. Nobody had ever asked us out. I had fallen in love with my best friend in school, but Liz did not know this. I felt like telling her then. We were up there, outside the city, shaded by a cypress. The heat was gentle and steady, and it supported us as we gulped down our drinks. We would have a good time in Italy, I thought, and I was grateful to Liz for letting me come along. So I told her so.

"Oh, I'm glad to have your company too," she had said, smiling. "It's going to be difficult when you leave. I'm dreading it."

I'd believed her. But then on the train, as we sat across from each other in a daze, as she began to gush about what she would do after I left, how great it would be to see Sicily and Rome, I felt suddenly useless. I had in my hands a novel called *The Woman of Rome,* and as I tried to tune Liz out, I found myself reading something about the different levels of desire that people have for one another, how no two people, even if they love each other, ever feel the same thing at the same time. A feeling of sadness grew and grew. It was so true. Liz seemed not to notice my mood. Her face had become all pink; she was like a child, I thought scornfully.

I tried hard never to get excited about things; it was safer. I closed my eyes, feeling tears prick at my eyelashes. She didn't care. I had wondered if she was attracted to me, if possibly something would happen during this long journey together, but obviously she was interested in only herself.

The thump of the train dulled me into a stupor. I was aware of the Italian families chattering to each other; at least they seemed warm and expressive. I had never sat in a train carriage with my family, and if we had, we wouldn't be speaking to each other except to utter sarcasms or reprimands.

Liz had a harshness too, I thought; she was utterly pragmatic. And yet a year ago on her eighteenth birthday, she had seemed so vulnerable when she confessed to me that she thought she might be a lesbian. "Oh, I'm sure you're not," I had responded numbly. I wanted to add, "I think I am," but I had been afraid to. We had sat together in the cold hallway of her flat while people danced and chattered and drank in the other room. She had wanted to be with me, not them; I recognized this but felt threatened somehow. I wasn't ready. Earlier she had left the party to cry in her bedroom, and I had wanted to go in and comfort her, but something had stopped me.

Would it always be like this with us? Would we never be able to comfort each other, connect in any deep way? It looked like it, I thought grimly, and I didn't see much hope of someone else coming along either.

"What did you think of those girls?" Liz said suddenly. She had a rather sharp way of looking across at me sometimes.

"What do you mean?" I muttered. I didn't maintain eye contact for very long. I felt like a sulky child.

"Oh, you know…the ones on the street. Do you think they were tourists?"

"They must have been. They had backpacks."

"There was something hippyish about them," Liz said thoughtfully.

It was 1986, and nobody wanted to look like hippies. The '60s had not yet come back into vogue. But Liz and I shared a fondness for that time.

"It was like an old film," I said. That was the way I had experienced it, and I was surprised when she agreed.

"I know," she said. "Like a silent movie."

We smiled at each other. Film was another great love that we shared. Liz kept a list of all the films that she saw and graded each one on a scale of one to ten. That was one of our first conversations, I remembered, at the university accommodations where we met. I'd been fascinated by this attention to detail. It was so English (which she was).

"I'm dead tired," I said helplessly. I was afraid I sounded pathetic, like a baby, but Liz nodded and rubbed her eyes.

"I wish they'd shut up," she said in a low voice. The other inhabitants of the carriage were blithely unresponsive to our presence. It was like this always. If you were visiting a country, you were somehow unreal to its inhabitants. Liz and I moved through Italy in some kind of limbo. We had very little contact with outsiders. This satisfied me, though I sensed that it made Liz anxious. The men we encountered seemed to regard us as a couple. That was ironic, I thought. We were far from that.

But I didn't know what it was like to be in a couple anyway and certainly not with a woman, though I was even more clueless about men, never having felt any desire for them. It reassured me a little that Liz's attraction to men seemed so shallow and of such recent origin.

The train rolled on and on. It was funny in a way to be returning to the beginning of our trip, like the source of a river.

At each stop the train emptied. We would reach Florence in the early morning.

I was still feeling a little clutch of sadness. Liz moved over to sit next to me. I was surprised but felt so numb that it didn't matter. She had moved because an elderly man sitting close to her was smoking a particularly foul pipe. He pulled his hat down over his eyes and appeared to be falling asleep.

"He's got the right idea," I whispered to her. We began to giggle over what we could throw into the bowl of his pipe to snuff it out and to try to figure out how to say in Italian, "Put that in your pipe and smoke it." Then we laughed about the German man in the train to Pisa who had slapped his wife proprietorially on the thigh and asked inanely "Pisa?" even though we had just set out from Florence. All our good memories seemed to be in Florence, I thought dreamily. We were resting against each other now, and the warmth somehow helped. Yes, we'd both agreed, he was a sexist pig. Liz got very offended if men behaved like chauvinists. Her father was an insensitive boor, she'd told me, who liked to pick the hairs out of his nose while he sat in his armchair at night. She'd always sided with her mother against him.

Liz pulled a little bottle of wine out of her rucksack, which was always stuffed to bursting and which she had affectionately named *il vècchio gòbbo,* the old hunchback. Sometimes she referred to it as *il vècchio gobshite,* a coarse Dublin term that cracked me up. I was thrilled by the wine, and we began to drink it greedily.

It was almost completely dark in the carriage. I could sense Liz's nice, clean English smell and wondered if my sweatiness bothered her. She rested her head on my shoulder, and I marveled once again at how coarse her hair was. *It's like a boy's,* I thought affectionately. I was the one who always wore men's clothes though — jeans and shirts. Liz preferred a more crisp and feminine look — white blouses, skirts. I envied her hairless legs.

"I'm getting maudlin," Liz confessed. "I'm so scared of your going... What am I going to do?"

"You don't need me," I replied. There was no bitterness in my voice. I just knew it was true. "You'll do fine without me. You'll be able to chat up men."

There was a pause. "I don't really want to," Liz said. She sounded quite subdued. "I mean, even if I do, I'm not sure that's what I really want."

I didn't know what to say and cursed myself for not having the right words. But somehow it didn't matter. I was tipsy, and so was she, and we were in a night train careening through the Italian countryside, and the old man's pipe had gone out, and nobody could see us. So as she looked at me plaintively and rather shyly, I reached out and touched her face. Just quickly. It was almost involuntary.

"I've never kissed a woman," Liz said. "Have you?" She looked at me with great intensity, but her curiosity seemed more cerebral than sensual.

"Yes…" I said hesitantly. My memories of kissing my school friend were so precious to me, yet they seemed very far away. I had resigned myself to never being with anyone else again, since it seemed that I had lost the part of me that would take the risk of reaching out to a friend.

Her eyes gleamed. "I *thought* you had," she murmured. She appeared to admire this. I almost smiled.

She reached into her rucksack and pulled out another bottle. "Let's go the whole hog," she suggested. Then we laughed because the English phrase sounded so funny.

"Where are we?" I asked wildly. "Isn't it strange — we could be anywhere." The train did indeed lurch to a halt on occasion, but no one ever came in. We had already had our rail passes stamped, so we were pretty much going to have privacy for the rest of the trip.

"You could stretch out," I suggested. "Except there's only really room for one of us to do that." The old man was still huddled in the corner. Now he was snoring faintly.

"But…not if we stretch out together!" Liz was giddy now. She got up, pushed me down, and then climbed on top of me. We entwined our legs around each other.

"How does this feel?" she asked.

I didn't know. Maybe it was the wine, but my skin was burning. We looked at each other for a long time. Then she took off her glasses. She put them down on the floor. I lay there waiting.

She seemed to know exactly what she wanted to do. I was grateful for that.

She kissed me on the lips, first tentatively and then using her tongue. I had never had anyone's tongue in my mouth. I pressed back against the seat, pulling her down hard on top of me. Her skin felt so silky and soft; she was very pale despite weeks in the Italian sun.

We kissed for a while. I found myself undoing her bra and running my hands over her breasts. It was weird. I sort of knew what to do even though I had always assumed that I would freeze up in this situation. Liz seemed quite determined to make the most of our opportunity. Before I knew it she had unbuttoned my shirt, pulled my breast out of my bra, and began sucking on my nipple. She used her teeth.

I gasped. She was so enthusiastic in her movements. I felt myself drowning in a sea of wetness. I pulled her other hand down into my jeans. Again she seemed to know what to do.

Her fingers brought out waves of pleasure. I began moaning gently. The old gentleman's snores were louder if anything, more explosive. Her fingers worked hard against my groin, flickering against my clit, penetrating me. My breasts were so sweaty now, my nipples huge and erect.

"I want to go down on you," she whispered in my ear. Her voice was low and throaty. She seemed possessed.

"No, no…he'll see," I muttered.

"Nobody will see," she said impatiently. "Don't you want to?"

My face was burning red, partly from embarrassment, partly from arousal. She propped the rucksack up by my head at the side of the seat so that my view of the old man was blocked. Then I felt cool air on my legs. She had pushed them apart.

It was strange to have something happen that was so outside my usual fantasies. Oral sex had been something I'd always dreaded. I'd felt the shame about my body that most young women feel. I didn't want that level of intimacy. It seemed terrifying. But I couldn't say no.

At first I felt nothing, and the roughness of her tongue just seemed pleasant. I worried about having to fake it. Then she seemed to find a rhythm, for I noticed that my body was responding, my thighs were tightening. Then there was a point where I realized I didn't want it to stop. My breathing was rough and ragged. I began to beg. Suddenly I felt her fingers going inside me, and I almost screamed.

She pushed up on top of me, still fucking me with her hand. Sweat was dripping off her face and onto my breasts. I felt myself rising off the seat, desperate to get more of her inside me. Suddenly she was on the seat, I was on top of her, and I stopped moving. A shudder rose up from the depths of me; I held my breath, trying to keep the sensation, and then, pushing down against her, I came. My face was wet with sweat, my ears burning, and as I relaxed against her, I felt her idly stroking my cheek.

"What about you?" I managed to say. I felt too tired to do anything more. I hoped she wouldn't be disappointed.

"I'm okay," she said. I realized that she was still fully clothed more or less. I wrapped my arms about her. "I think I like doing it more than it being done to me," she continued.

I didn't understand this but let it go. I still couldn't really move. I had no clue how to process what had happened.

"Well, you'll remember that, won't you?" she said gently. She reached down to fumble around for her glasses. I looked at her face. She was so relaxed and calm that it made me realize how overwrought and tense she usually was.

"I'll try," I said with a smile. There didn't seem much more to say. I pulled on my clothes, and we rested together. Soon we fell asleep.

We awoke as the train was pulling into Florence. The old man had left the compartment, but on the seat across from us — a perfect, surrealistic vision — lay his pipe.

The Ladies' Room
by Judith Stelboum

I don't know about you, but I feel uncomfortable and out of place in the ladies' room, bathroom, rest room, WOMEN, CHICKS, HERS, SETTERS. I used to collect all the cute names, like some people collect matchbooks.

I don't know if I'm supposed to dress for the ladies' room. Maybe they should have some regulation ladies' outfit to slip over what you're wearing before you go in, just so you look like a "lady."

I always check the door twice to make sure I'm in the right room. I walk in, and these two women (ladies) are combing their hair in front of the mirror. They're both wearing these tight little miniskirts, heels, and stockings. I can't help looking at their legs first. Nice! Then my eyes move up their bodies, noticing the thin see-through blouse of one and the tight sweater of the other. Their outfits reveal high, full tits on the one with the sweater and hardened nipples on the one with the blouse. One of them has thick, long wavy hair. Voguey. Hair you can really grab and hold, wrap around your hand.

They're putting on lipstick and checking out their eye make-up. I don't have to check the door again…no doubt about it. It's hard to believe…but…this is my room too.

And I think, *Well, we do this the same way, anyway. Don't we?* So they're talking, and I listen as I pee, because I'm beginning to doubt that I really am in the right room. Something about Timmy and Danny and restaurants and Chrissie's wedding, and I hear them giggling. Maybe I should check the door again?

Anyway, I come out of the stall, and they're looking at their nails…so I look too. Wow, it's enough to give you the chills. Those nails…like something out of a horror movie; long and red like some animal all bloodied from a recent kill. Except these ladies can't retract their claws. But they're admiring the nails. In fact, they're now talking about Patti or Sue or someone who does nails. I'm fascinated and hang around washing my face and hands just to

44

hear the rest of it. I feel like I'm in some foreign country observing the local customs. So interesting!

One of them has permed red hair, which I think has to be dyed because her eyebrows don't match her hair and her skin is sort of olive color. Redheads are always fair-skinned; at least, from my personal experience this has been true. Trust me on this one! I know what I'm talking about.

Anyway, the redhead begins to get nervous because she senses that I'm eavesdropping, and she pokes the other one. Okay, so now they look at me. Believe me, you know I look nothing like those two. I'm wearing my uniform: black jeans, white shirt, black leather jacket, dark aviator glasses.

I can see the contemptuous look on their faces as we stare at each other in the mirrors over the sinks. So I want to whip it out and dangle it in front of them. You know…I wanted them to see something familiar. Something they both would recognize as part of their world. But the truth is, no matter how long I've been playing with it, how hard it's been sucked and pushed and pulled, it just ain't gonna get that long. And I'm not packing that day anyhow, because…who would have thought I needed to?

I walk over to the door, lock it, lean against it, and say, "Excuse me, this is the ladies' rest room, and would one of you ladies — *women* — like to rest here with me for a while? I see there's a chair over there. Would one of you like to sit on my thighs? Would anyone like to sit on my face? Would you like some fingers for an appetizer or more for a main course?

"Or if either of you ladies would like, I can just lay out my leather jacket on the floor, and we can do it there. Don't be bashful or shy, baby, speak up. Tell me what you want! Personally, I like to talk while we're doing it. Don't you? I think it adds to the excitement."

Their contempt has turned to fear. They're clutching each other, mouths open, shaking. I think they're about to scream. Well, one is, anyway. The one with the longest nails. Yup, it's the redhead.

So I continue, staring at the redhead. "Well, I can 'do you,' but you could never 'do me.' No, sir — oops, *madam* — not with those nails anyway. Next time you see Patti or Sue or whomever, tell her that those nails are just too long for real lovemaking."

I walk over to the redhead and stroke her cheek — palm first, then with the back of my hand. She recoils from my touch, her eyes wide, face turned away from mine. I have all I can do to keep from smacking her hard, leaving my hand and signet ring imprinted across her face. Well, Timmy or Danny would have done it better, I'm sure.

"Don't scream now!" (Isn't that what all the rapists say?) I place my finger against my lips. "Shh." I'm laughing as I move toward the door, turn the lock, and walk out.

Picking Up Daddy
by Robin Sweeney

"You will know me, boy, by the way I cut through the crowd, like an animal tracking its prey, until I find you and make you mine."

That's what Griffin's latest E-mail said before she got on the plane in Philadelphia and came to claim me, a continent away, in San Francisco.

I stood waiting outside the gates of United Airlines. The collar she had sent me was in my right rear pocket, my boots polished, my jockstrap holding my packing dick in place just like Daddy told me. My on-line daddy was coming to make me her boy, and I was going to pass out from anticipation.

Griffin had found me my first night on-line, and she spoiled me for all other cybersex and on-line cruising. Hell, she spoiled me for most in-person sex and cruising too.

It was a complete accident that she was able to find me. My first night wandering around the possibilities of America Online, barely computer-literate, I found the gay message area. There I found the leatherwomen board, and I posted an ad:

> Jaded boy looking for other boys to play with, although her heart would still belong to Daddy if she'd show up already. Not into fakes or pretending. Looking for a real connection. I'm a sick fuck into most kinks who likes to pitch as well as catch and who is looking...

Turns out that "sick fuck" was a little too much for the family standards of America Online. (The pitching and catching part was apparently okay, though.) The on-line monitors who pull "objectionable" ads deleted my post, and I was certain no one would see it.

Griffin had seen it, though. In that window of opportunity between posting and pulling, Griffin read my ad and decided to respond.

"Fairly presumptuous, aren't you, boy?" her first subject line to me read.

Holy shit, I thought. *It worked.*

"You sound like the sort of lost boy who starts acting loud and tough to try and scare away the noises in the dark. You've probably started topping the girls in town, maybe even being someone's daddy, in an attempt to get your needs met. After all, if you can't get what you want, you might as well make someone else's fantasy come true, right? That's not working, or you wouldn't be putting personals on-line.

"I am willing to allow you to write me if you lose the poor attitude and present yourself properly. If you are not capable of this or are not interested, you need not respond. Otherwise, you have twenty-four hours, boy. Yours truly — Griffin."

I was a newbie on-line, but I had been around the block as far as women go. I wanted a daddy badly, but I hadn't found one. I dated a lot and had flings that I really enjoyed, but I always ended up topping my girlfriends. Griffin had pegged me right. I had been doing S/M for a while and had gotten a fair bit of experience. The type I like — women who look like sixteen-year-old boys — tend to be novices. I liked playing with them just fine, but having to explain to somebody how to tie my wrists to the bed just didn't inspire me to bottom.

Also, like most people I met, I was afraid of getting what I wanted. I didn't like to give it up to just anybody who asked. Daddies were supposed to know how to take a boy down. Most of the ones I had met weren't up to the follow-through I craved. I didn't want to be just submissive, I wanted to be told how to behave.

That's exactly what Griffin did. I checked her profile:

Griffin. Also known as Sir.
Female, single.
Macintosh PowerBook 145.
Occupation: student, cook, and daddy top.
Likes leather, dykes who are boys, taming the untamable.
Quote: "Come closer. I won't bite…until you ask me nicely."

I wrote back. I had no idea how she wanted me to present myself, much less how to do it in writing. If we were at a party or a bar, I'd bring her a drink, be respectful, and call her Sir. How was I supposed to do that on-line?

"Good evening, Sir. I appreciate your letter to me and hope that you find my response timely. I am interested in learning more of what interests you in a boy. True, I haven't found many people I want to submit to, but I try to remain open to the possibilities.

"Sir, I apologize if my ad was too brazen. I never expected an answer, much less from someone who was going to give me an opportunity to present myself properly. Please, Sir, would you tell me exactly how you would have me present myself? Respectfully yours — Jay."

Twelve hours later my computer "said" to me, in a way that was grammatically incorrect but delightfully enthusiastic, "You've got mail."

"On your knees, boy," it started, "is how I would expect you to present yourself to me. On your knees, head up, and eyes forward until I told you different. Arms behind your back, left hand holding right wrist. Legs spread — and don't let your ass touch the heels of your boots. Look me in the eye, boy. You're not a dog, and you're not a slave.

"You're a boy, and I expect you to do us both proud.

"Now, tell me more about yourself, boy. What should I know? How would I tell who you are in a crowd if we were to meet at a bar?"

That was the start of almost endless letters back and forth. We didn't do what I later found out was typical in cyberspace. I didn't lie to Griffin, and she didn't tell me anything less than the truth. I explained my life in San Francisco, working at a retail store on Castro Street, living with a bunch of roommates, and playing with lots of women.

And looking for Daddy.

"My friends call me Jay, and my mother still calls me Janice. I prefer Jay, although I'm sure that's not a surprise. I'm not as tall as I act, Sir, which means I end up looking up at people more than I'm comfortable with. Five-two should be taller than it actually is, Sir. I'm a big boy, not fat, really, just solid. (I like to think that makes me more fun to hurt, but I'm not sure if that's out of line.) I'm pale, with light brown hair that I keep in a flattop. I wear jeans and T-shirts to work and dress shirts and ties to play parties. (It's that F. Scott Fitzgerald fetish, Sir.) I just turned twenty-six and have lived in San Francisco for three years.

"My eyes are blue when I'm calm and go green when I'm horny or sick and turn gray after I've been beaten. And please, Sir, will you tell me about yourself?"

"A younger daddy," her next note said, "is what you're going to get with me. Are you a sick enough fuck to still treat me with the respect due Daddy? I turn twenty-one next month.

"I'm a student here in Philadelphia, although my family lives in New Hampshire. I miss that part of the country, but I don't miss my father and his homophobic bullshit. I came out my senior year of high school — which reminds me, boy: Tell me your coming-out story.

"I go to college at the University of Pennsylvania, which is exactly as uptight as it sounds. Full of frats and the boys who fill them, who aren't half as interesting as the boys I meet on-line. I'm out of place here and wouldn't have survived if it weren't for the people I meet on-line and the women in Dangerous Women, the S/M support group here.

"I work, study, read, write, terrify my dorm mates, and cruise perverts, both live and on-line. I'm five-ten, dark-haired, dark-eyed, part Irish, part German, part Cherokee. I lift weights, cook professionally, and can't wait to be done with school.

"Now tell me what hankies you'd be wearing when you'd cruise me at the bar and how you would get my attention."

I did just that, spinning a fantasy about picking her up at the Eagle during a beer bust in front of all the fags who don't understand why two women would be there and going out into the alley and fucking like wild things, me on my hands and knees, getting plowed by her from behind. She wrote back, adding flourishes like handcuffing me over a motorcycle and inviting other people to join her in fucking me.

I loved it.

With words she painted a picture that I longed for. I tried to offer her as much from my writing as possible. We exchanged fantasies and conversations about our real lives. We gossiped about people we knew on-line and even managed to have arguments.

We wrote back and forth and sent pictures. At one point we exchanged phone numbers and started talking on the phone as well. We kept fairly different schedules, though, and I've never been that comfortable with phone sex. The phone didn't match the intimacy of our writing somehow. Early on I knew that I wanted to meet her and be her boy FTF — face-to-face, in computerese. Griffin cinched my interest and made me want to really be her boy about two months after she first answered my ad.

One day there was a package on the kitchen table for me when I got home. I didn't recognize the address at first glance. Who did I know in Philadelphia? Then I realized. The package was from Griffin.

I was so excited, I could barely open the box. There was a note on top of the tissue paper that filled the small box.

"Boy," it said on the outside, and I unfolded it.

"I found this collar on one of my travels along I-95. In one of those little towns in New York in a mom-and-pop store. I bought it that day and have kept it oiled and ready for the person I wanted to wear it. I didn't know who that would be or when I would find them, but I knew I would someday have a boy who would deserve this.

"You must oil it once a week and wear it whenever you write to me or whenever you read your mail from me. You are also to wear my collar to the next leather event you attend where you are not otherwise engaged, and when you are asked whose collar you are wearing, tell them it's your daddy. Much love — Daddy."

The collar was a plain black band of leather with a shiny chrome buckle. I held the collar up to my nose, and I smelled the oil she had rubbed into it and swore I could smell her too, even though she was thousands of miles away. I had never met her, but she had reached out, found me, and claimed me as her boy. I had never worn a collar before, though I had wanted to, and had told Griffin that when I was someone's boy, I wanted to wear a collar to mark me as belonging to Daddy.

I wore it that night when I wrote to her on my knees in front of my computer.

"Daddy," I wrote, "thank you for the collar. i am wearing it now as i write to you. i can't begin to tell you how thrilled i am by having a collar from you, how much it makes me feel cared for and like i am your boy. i can't wait until i can actually see you, feel your touch, and be in your service. i treasure the token of your esteem that you have sent me. thank you, Sir — your boy, jay."

We continued writing for several weeks, the collar never far from me. Griffin made me tell her all my fears and fantasies and would leave messages in E-mail telling me to put clothespins on my chest or ordering me to beat off while I read. I crafted long and complicated stories for her involving more and more of my desires to please her and serve her as my daddy. I practiced polishing boots so that I would be competent to take care of hers. I started wearing my keys on the right and telling people, "No, thank you, I'm taken."

Except snuggling up with a computer isn't easy, and even the most delightful messages don't fill emotional needs after a while. Griffin realized this, of course. She was my daddy, and she was perceptive.

"Boy, I know that it's hard being so far away, and I would understand if you need to find a flesh-and-blood top to serve. However, you should not make plans with anyone for the week of March 2nd through 10th. Be at the airport to pick me up. Attached is my itinerary."

So here I stood, at the airport as instructed. Daddy's flight was announced, and passengers started filling up the gate area. I didn't see her in the first crush of people and worried fleetingly that she wasn't on the flight.

Then, just like that, there she was. The grin on her face I recognized from photos, but now she was real and in front of me. Her black leather jacket hugged her broad shoulders over a black turtleneck tucked into blue jeans. Her crotch bulged in a way that let me know she was wearing a dick, and her boots glittered with their shine.

"Hello, boy," she said as she dropped her carry-on bag and wrapped her arms around me.

Finally I was touching Daddy. Even better, Daddy was holding me. I put my head on her chest and tried to breathe calmly.

She smelled like sweat and leather and some sort of spicy scent, and it was intoxicating.

I felt her pull the collar out of my back pocket, and she put it around my neck. I watched her face as she buckled the collar on me. She looked at me and growled.

"Mine."

"Yes, Sir. Please."

She kissed me then, first soft and friendly and exploring. Then she grabbed me hard and pulled me against her, one hand reaching for the collar around my neck. Her mouth took over mine, the kiss becoming ferocious, and I melted into her arms. All my fantasies, all my desires, and all that E-mail were fulfilled with that one kiss.

She pushed me away and turned on her heel. She didn't look back to make sure I followed; she just assumed that I would. That was a safe assumption too as I grabbed her bag and scurried to keep up with her long strides.

She headed into the women's room and moved to the far stall, one of the larger handicapped-accessible ones. She held the stall door open for me, and I blushed as I hurried past the lone woman at the sinks.

Daddy sat on the toilet, legs spread, playing with her bulge.

"Down, boy," she said, and I dropped to my knees. I couldn't believe she was doing this in the San Francisco airport, but I didn't want to stop.

"Take care of my boots, boy."

For a second I thought she wanted me to polish them, and I panicked. My boot-polish kit was at home. Then I remembered one of her earlier E-mails to me about a boy needing to love Daddy's boots with every part, including a boy's mouth. I leaned over and put my lips on Daddy's boots.

She groaned and shifted her weight and put her other foot on my back, pressing me onto the tile of the floor. I spread out full-length and tried to put my entire being into licking the boots of the woman I had just met and knew so well. I licked and kissed and moaned under her boot and thrust against the floor, rocking my hips. My packing dick pressed up against my cunt and drove me crazy, and I heard Daddy unbutton her jeans above me.

"Up, boy, and suck me off."

I scrambled to follow her instructions. Her dick hung out of her pants, and I dived for it. For so long I had beaten off at night fantasizing about a daddy to service and, please, a big daddy dick to fill my mouth. After Griffin started writing me, I created endless dreams about her, how she would take me and make me her boy, make me suck her big cock.

And there I was, forcing as much of Daddy's dick down my throat as I could. Daddy grabbed my head and groaned. I closed my eyes, rocking back and forth over her crotch. I opened up my throat and swallowed her as well as I could. Daddy was real, and her dick was too, at least as far as we cared.

Griffin pulled me off her dick, grabbed me by the collar, and pulled me closer. She started kissing me hard, harder than she had at the gate where I had waited for her. She undid my belt buckle and unbuttoned my jeans. I held on to her shoulders as she groped my packing dick, the pressure against my cunt almost overwhelming, my psychic attachment to my dick making me throb.

Daddy pushed her hand past my dick, past my dripping cunt, and, kicking my legs apart, started playing with my butt. It felt so good, I moaned in her mouth. She fingered me gently, and I could tell she had smoothed her manicure down to almost nothing for this. She pumped her fingers into my cunt once, twice, then pressed the moisture into my ass. My butt opened around her finger, and I let her inside me.

"Oh, please, Daddy," I whispered. "Please fuck me, Daddy. Please?"

Griffin nodded and kissed me again.

"Yeah, boy. Daddy's going to fuck you. Take my dick in your ass and make me happy, boy. Yeah, I'm going to fuck you." While Daddy said this, she pushed my jeans all the way down past my knees and turned me around. She pushed me over so that my nose almost touched the floor and I could see the pumps of the woman two stalls over. "Beat off, boy, and come for Daddy while I fuck you."

I felt lube trickle over my ass, and Griffin's fingers started spreading me open. I had practiced with butt plugs so that I could take Daddy's dick, like she had ordered me to in E-mail, but I was nervous. Griffin's dick wasn't the biggest strap-on I'd ever seen, but it was pretty hefty. I felt her press her dick against my ass. I started touching my clit under my packing dick, breathing deep and trying to take her cock in my ass. Daddy pulled my hips closer to her, rocking me back toward her, and her dick started going inside me.

Then, so slowly that I could barely tell she moved, her dick slid into my ass. Daddy pulled me back, and I moved against her, and her cock filled my ass completely. Just as slowly she pulled back out until her dick almost left my ass, and I heard myself whimper.

"Yeah, boy," she murmured above me. "Daddy's here. Fucking you. Making you mine. My boy."

She plunged back into me and started to move in a rhythm so sweet, I had to bite my wrist to not cry out. She grunted and moved inside me, and I rocked back in response. I beat off as Daddy hit her stride, pushing me on and off her dick. Soon, almost too soon, I came, with Daddy fucking my ass.

I lay there panting as Daddy pulled out. I felt her clean me off. I couldn't move; everything felt too good. Daddy buttoned her jeans and slapped my ass once to get my attention. I got up onto my knees and turned around.

"That's my good boy," she said. She wrapped her arms around me and hugged me close, like Daddy should.

"Let's get out of here," Griffin said. "Take me home with you, boy. I need to have you fuck me now, and if we wait much longer, it'll be here in the airport bathroom. And I don't come as quietly as you do."

I left the stall in front of Griffin. I walked proudly in front of my daddy and smiled at the woman doing her makeup at the sink as she looked quizzically at the two rumpled and grinning leather dykes leaving a single airport bathroom stall.

In Security
by Michelle Latiga

I'd stopped in Amsterdam for a few days' R&R after a particularly long business trip to Berlin. Just three days. But enough to decompress. A nice little hotel overlooking one of the canals, Nutella on my breakfast toast, Campari at a sidewalk café, watching puppeteers in the square, and a few visits to the wonderful women's bars — just what I needed to shake off the tension of Germany before going back to the insanity of New York.

Amsterdam is known for its tight airport security. Long waits while luggage is being checked and searched are not uncommon. So there I was, lugging the suitcase that contained my business drag and hefting my backpack over my shoulder, ready to return home from another successful though predictably uneventful business trip. I looked at my watch. My flight wasn't for another two hours. I'd have plenty of time to grab a drink and watch the other travelers. That is, if I ever got past the tight security.

I love airports, which is probably good since I travel for a living. What I love most is just watching the people as they move around the world. The looks on faces: excitement, boredom, elation at seeing someone again, that wistful last look back as they walk down the ramp to the plane. It's such a strange world, all tied up in just a few acres of space. I usually try to get to the airport early, just to watch the people. And fantasize: That magnificent woman could be waiting for me to come home after a long trip; that handsome butch might just walk up and offer to light my cigarette. Ya gotta dream.

I pushed my luggage down the floor, following the line of tourists waiting to go through security. Although there were four or five inspectors, the line moved slowly. Some poor soul, obviously a diabetic, had all her insulin and needles in her bag but no prescription. The security guards were having a field day, going through the clothes in her luggage, piece by piece, layer by layer, opening every bottle and tube of cosmetics, looking through every page of her books. It was embarrassing, so I made a mental note never to forget to bring the prescription slips for any meds I had with me. It was a good rule to remember, sort of like the one I learned when I tried to go through a metal detector wearing ben-wa balls. Okay, so I was hoping for a bumpy flight, but you gotta do something when you're stuffed into a narrow seat for seven hours.

I looked at my watch. Hopefully, the line would clear soon. I'd already scoped out the passengers around me: a couple of groups of business travelers, a family with teenage kids on their way home from vacation, several college students — no one really interesting. No one that set my fantasy gauge in motion. Patience would have to prevail.

As my turn finally came, I hoisted my bag up onto the inspection table and set my backpack beside it. I knew I didn't have any contraband. I never do. One of my biggest fears is ending up in some foreign prison, unable to contact anyone, maybe even not understanding the language. I'm really careful that everything is totally legal.

The security guard smiled at me as she asked me to unlock my suitcase. I smiled back. In her starched and pressed light blue uniform shirt and navy trousers, she was very attractive: dark blond, as most of the Dutch are, average height, nice build. And she looked vaguely familiar to me. Maybe I'd seen her at one of the clubs, maybe she just reminded me of someone I used to know. After a while everyone looks familiar.

I waited patiently as she inspected my suitcase and started to feel through the clothes for any hard or boxed items hidden there. I studied her hands, long, thin fingers on wide, strong palms. Nails short but well-manicured with a light polish. She obviously took good care of her hands.

My fantasy mode kicked in. A blond in a uniform — ah, love. She looked me straight in the eye. Maybe I was smiling too broadly. Be cool.

As I watched her go through my underwear, my mind began to wander: *What if I were still in those panties, that bra. What if…*

Oh, stop it, I chided myself, trying to wipe the silly grin off my face. *It's going to be a long flight. Don't get started now.* I took a step back just to relieve the pressure building up between my legs.

I glanced down at my watch again. Forty-five minutes had passed already. Damn. Another fifteen minutes here, and I'd have only a half hour before my plane started to board.

I looked up to see the luggage inspector studying me rather intently.

She'd opened my backpack and was going through the pile of magazines and books I'd stashed away for the flight: two back issues of *On Our Backs* and a copy of *NightHawk.* She flipped through the magazines, her face completely impassive as she scanned the pictures of naked women loving, touching, teasing each other. Then she went through the rest of the bag, taking too much time to look at every page of my passport. Casting a last glance at the back cover of April's *On Our Backs,* she carefully placed everything back in the backpack and leaned it against the closed suitcase.

Looking at me intently, she leaned forward. "Would you empty your pockets onto the table, please," she said.

I reached down into my jeans pockets with both hands. There was my cigarette lighter, a few guldens, a quarter, a box of wooden matches from one of the bars, my keys, and two sticks of gum. She looked at them without comment.

"Would you step around the table, please," she said, not really a request as she reached for the metal detector wand on the bench behind her. I stood stock-still as she ran the wand up both my sides, just touching me lightly in such a slow, provocative manner that I felt the sensations clear through my body. I shivered as it passed just a little too close to my breasts. The wand remained silent. No metal on (in) me this time! It was only my mind that was buzzing uncontrollably.

Then she turned and motioned to another security guard who'd been pacing back and forth along the line of tourists. The second guard walked over. I assessed her: taller, slightly larger in build but with the look of someone who was athletic, well-toned. She looked kind of familiar too. Did I suddenly know everyone in the airport? Or had I just been traveling too long? Sometimes crossing several time zones and being away from home do strange things to your mind: You start looking for something familiar rather than exotic just to keep from being alone.

The two talked quietly for a moment, the second guard nodding and glancing at me as the first one spoke. I couldn't hear what they were saying, but I was beginning to get a little worried. Was something wrong with my passport? What was the problem?

Finally the first one turned back to me. "Please come with us," she said, picking up my backpack, turning and leading the way toward a door at the end of the room. The second guard stepped back to let me pass, then fell in line behind me.

"What about my stuff?" I asked, looking back at my suitcase.

"It'll be safe. No one will touch it." The guard's voice behind me was stronger yet more soprano than I'd have thought. It was a nice voice, but I was starting to get concerned. I'd never been detained going into or out of a foreign country before.

When we were in a small windowless room, the second woman turned and locked the door.

"What's this about?" I asked, trying not to let my nervousness show in my voice.

"Do you have anything to declare?" the first guard asked, ignoring my question.

"Declare? No! I've got nothing illegal!" I protested, perhaps too loudly. "You can search my bags again."

"We need to search you," the second woman said. She turned me around toward a metal table against the far wall. "Lean against the table and spread your legs. We have to frisk you."

What to do? This was getting weird. I knew I hadn't done anything, but there I was, in a locked room in a foreign country staring at two uniformed guards, one who stood at least four inches taller than me. I hesitated, trying to pick the right response.

"Turn around and spread them!"

I obeyed that time without hesitation.

I could feel her right behind me, too close. Her hands started at my shoulders and worked their way down my arms, then back to my torso. Slowly, ever so slowly, feeling each of my ribs, her hands descended to my hips, then down over my ass. Was it my imagination, or had her hands lingered just a bit too long on my rear? I'd never been frisked before, but this was nothing like I'd ever imagined. The touch was almost that of a lover, gentle but insistent, demanding. I could feel the pressure begin to rise again.

Then she bent low behind me. I could feel her hands around my ankles, moving up my calves, over my thighs, and stopping between my legs. I gasped. I could feel her probing the crotch of my jeans. I was starting to sweat.

"Wait," I stammered. "What is this about?" My breathing was ragged. Fear? Excitement? It was hard to tell.

"Are you hiding something?" the first guard asked, stepping up to me.

"N-n-no. I have nothing to hide."

Someone's hand was in the rear pocket of my jeans.

"Nothing to hide, huh?" Two long white tubes of thin paper twisted at the ends fell to the table in front of me. I stared at them in disbelief.

"Those aren't mine! I didn't have them when I came in here. I never saw them before!"

"Are you saying I didn't just take them from your pocket?"

"You couldn't have!" I protested. *Damn!* I thought back, pressing my knuckles into the table, hoping the pain would wake me from this nightmare. I knew I shouldn't have tried that one joint last night at the brown bar, but this was Amsterdam. Marijuana cigarettes were sold openly in those bars. It'd been a kick, something to laugh about later. But where had these come from? I didn't remember having more than the one I'd smoked. I'd never have bought more. My mind raced. Had someone planted them on me last night?

"You can get in deep trouble carrying things like that around."

"Those aren't mine, I tell you, they're not mine!" I was definitely sweating. Was this the beginning of my worst fear? Why me? My emotions were flying in all directions. I really didn't know whether to laugh or cry.

"Maybe we should check more…thoroughly," the first guard said, looking up at the second with an evil grin.

"Do you think a full body-cavity search is in order? You never know what else she's trying to smuggle" was the reply.

"A full — you gotta be kidding." My mind was racing. What was happening here? Was I being set up? These were government security guards…weren't they? Weren't they?

The taller guard pulled me back from the table. Her hands were on my sides, slowly working across my stomach and over my breasts. She held me closely as the first guard started to unbutton my shirt. She pushed it apart and stepped back to look at me.

"It would probably be in your best interests to cooperate fully," the taller one whispered in my ear. Too close to my ear, actually, as I felt her breath against my neck. Little shivers of sensation ran down my body.

"These look good. Very nice," the first guard said, releasing my bra to let my breasts hang freely. "No place to hide anything here."

Maybe it was the fear or the worry about missing my flight or even the excitement of looking into the dark blue eyes of the uniformed officer in front of me, but my nipples sprang to attention.

I looked from the first guard back over my shoulder to the taller one. Both wore very serious expressions. I couldn't measure what was really happening.

"Maybe I should taste them to make sure there's nothing on them. You know how creative smugglers can get."

I gasped and almost burst out laughing at the absurdity of the statement, but as her mouth surrounded my breast, I could only draw a sharp breath and lean back into the woman who still held her arms around me.

All of a sudden it didn't seem to matter what was happening. My mind was objecting, but my body was reacting to the intense licking of my breasts. I felt the bolts of sensation run through me, stopping in my cunt.

As the guard nibbled first one breast, then the other, her hands kneaded them roughly. Then I felt the taller one reach down and unbutton my jeans. My head was spinning. There I was, sandwiched between the two women, two *uniformed* women, feeling like my body had turned to jelly! And my jeans and panties were now somewhere around my ankles!

I felt fingers weaving their way through my pubic hair and into the hot wetness there. As the first worked my nipples forcefully, fingers found my clit: stroking, rubbing, flicking decisively. I heard myself moan as the tension in my crotch heightened. Then a hand curved deeply into me, in and out, slowly at first, then more insistently. I started to writhe as the intensity increased. I felt my body pushing against the hand, and I could feel the heat rising through me.

These women were good together — very good together — first one taking the lead, then the other. I was completely off-balance, rising almost to climax, then floating back into the sensations. It seemed like I was forever floating between them. I wasn't sure where or who I was. I'd completely lost track of time and space — except that hot, wet area between my legs. Suddenly it all swept over me. Shudder after shudder, every fiber in my body exploded.

I began to realize I was leaning forward, wrapped in the blond's arms, trying to calm my breathing. Her face against my neck was warm and comforting. Her caressing of my body was gentle and strong.

"I told you she'd be good. We should have done this last night."

I looked up to see the taller woman hoist herself up onto the table, take one of the joints, and light it.

"Just a cigarette," she smiled, waving it in the air, "hand-rolled."

Nice scare tactic. It sure had had its effect. I shook my head as I pulled back from the blond's arms.

"But…" What was I going to ask? My head was still spinning. I was in a daze.

"We saw you at the bar last night. We were going to ask you to come home with us, but you left before we could talk to you. You're not angry, are you?"

I shook my head. Angry? That was hardly the word I would have chosen!

She held the cigarette out to me, and I took a drag. I still wasn't sure if I was dreaming.

"Are you all right?" The shorter one reached out and brushed my hair back, caressing my face as she did.

I looked down at my jeans. "Yeah, sure, fine." I wasn't really sure. I reached down and pulled my pants back up. I looked from one to the other. "Do you do this often?" I asked.

The shorter one grinned at me. "I guess you'll have to come back to find out."

We laughed, the tension gone.

"The minute I saw your reading material, I knew that you were...sort of an adventurer."

"But never quite this much," I said, smiling. Again I just shook my head.

"Well, we've inspected everything now," the taller one said, hopping down off the table. "I guess there's no legal reason to detain you. You'd better get dressed. You still have a plane to catch." She ground her cigarette out on the floor and looked at her watch. "And you'd better hurry."

I nodded as I quickly fastened my bra and buttoned my shirt. How would I tell anyone about this? Who would believe me? Even *I* wouldn't believe me!

I brushed my hair out of my face and followed them out into the terminal.

"Come back again sometime," the shorter one said, handing me my stamped passport. "And have a good flight. I'll call the gate and make sure they don't leave without you." She picked up the phone on the security desk, not moving her eyes from mine.

I picked up my suitcase and threw my backpack over my shoulder. "I...uh..." What could I say? "Thank you" was all I could think of.

We smiled at each other, and I started toward the gate area. God, I love airports.

The Festival Virgin
by Bonnie J. Morris

On the fourth day of Ceci Blum's first camp-out at a women's music festival, someone on her work shift called her a sheltered Jewish princess. This, on top of discovering live mold growing inside her sleeping bag, sent Ceci stomping out into the rainy night.

Fierce downpours had canceled the nighttime stage concerts, so the rain crew moved a few comedians into the dining hall instead for an abbreviated, cozy show. Ceci heard laughter and cowgirl whoops as she trudged toward the cedar-scented light and warmth emanating from the camp lodge. *Saturday night, and I ain't got nobody,* she thought bitterly, blowing her nose. Her fingers itching from mosquito bites, she finally managed to open the heavy doors and poke her head inside.

The crowded dining hall bulged with womankind. At one end countless pairs of wet socks dangled over the blazing stone fireplace. Food tables had been shoved back to accommodate rows of wooden folding chairs. It might have been any Camp Fire Girls leadership council or folk festival milieu in America except that naked breasts predominated in glorious variety. There were white-haired women with creased faces and strong hands, toddling girl children beaming through face paint, women of fine bulk and women of thin sinew, deaf women and interpreters signing their conversations with urgent grace. Ceci saw black, brown, tan, golden, red, pink, and creamy white skin glistening in folds and ripples, the sheen of skin spiraling outward from the central configuration of breasts and bellies. Enormous breasts like full and intricate baggage; smaller breasts erect and goose-bumped by the outside chill; breasts scarred or missing from cancer surgeries; breasts stretched from lactation and some, presently, swollen with milk for the nourishment of a dangling babe in arms. Muscles and veins ran beneath the rolling flesh. Here and there were sunburned white women ruefully atoning for yesterday's nudity, women rubbing lotion onto one another's chests with glad palms.

The smell of 200 body oils, anointments, and perfumes as well as healthy body sweat filled Ceci's nostrils, congesting her head further yet conveying a subtler message of adult female sensuality that was pleasing to heart and mind. Well-trained in chemical analysis from her graduate school studies at MIT, Ceci quickly identified musk oil, patchouli, eucalyptus, Eternity, Jontue, Cachet, orange blossom, White Shoulders, rose water, Millionaire, Love's Baby Soft, Chanel, Youth Dew, and Arpege as well as a secondary wave of Hawaiian Tropic, Coppertone, Nivea, baby powder, lanolin, Noxzema, and swirls of marijuana smoke. Struggling to breathe, Ceci peered through the sea of multicolor breasts and interesting haircuts, hoping in vain to find a seat.

Two lesbian comedians, perched on stools at the front of the hall, teased and sassed their captive rain-damp audience. "What's the real reason lesbians have short fingernails?" asked performer number one.

"Whee!" shouted the crowd.

"Because no one has any fingernails left after pulling open those discreetly stapled issues of *Lesbian Connection*," answered performer number two.

Ceci tried not to look too longingly at women kissing, women touching one another's bare limbs, women wringing out wet shirts and applauding the entertainment with bare-assed, unself-conscious approval. Steam rose in a cloud from the toasting socks, the drying hair of 200 heads, the bodies pressed close together in patchouli harmony. *Am I the only one here without a date?* Ceci thought miserably, sitting cross-legged atop a fruit crate. She fished through her knapsack for an aspirin and caught sight of the physics textbook she'd inadvertently brought with her to the festival. Hypnotized by reading matter under any circumstances, Ceci opened the book and began studying for the class she'd have when she returned to MIT the following Tuesday.

"Don't tell me you're reading a *book* here," laughed the woman nearest to Ceci. All she wore, Ceci couldn't help noticing, were high-tops and a tool belt. "Live a little, girlfriend!"

"But I love reading," Ceci replied, feeling defensive.

"*I* love women," Tool Belt tossed back, returning her gaze to the two comic performers. "Only live once, kid!"

Ceci scrambled to her feet, splintering the fruit crate into fifteen pieces. *That's it — I'm out of here,* she thought grimly, her wet feet slapping flipperlike toward the exit. *I don't fit in. Nobody thinks I'm a* real *lesbian.*

Half running and half walking, she plunged out of the dining hall and down the hill toward the circle of workers' cabins.

I'll just sit here for a moment and bawl, Ceci told herself, ducking into the shelter of a wooden porch. She sat down with a defeated shiver, letting the familiar player piano of self-pity roll out its song inside her head.

The 25-year-old daughter of Holocaust survivors, Ceci had grown up well aware of her family's experience in wartime Europe, listening to adult discussions about oppression and persecution from the time she could first comprehend words. Ceci, raised in America, with her good grades and her accentless English — she was the one who could succeed, her parents believed, and they had encouraged her every academic triumph in school, urging her on from high school to college to the Ph.D. program she soon hoped to complete. When schoolmates and other children called her "egghead," "teacher's pet," or "geek," Ceci's parents reminded her that it was no shame to be a bookworm, that they of all people understood the name-calling that came with being "different." But when Ceci showed no interest in dating or marrying a nice Jewish boy, expressing instead a timid interest in the nice Jewish girl next door, her parents were thunderstruck. *"Schanda fur leiten!"* they cried — a scandal for the neighbors!

Ceci had discreetly withdrawn from their cries of shame, moving to an apartment in Boston and burying herself in her studies. Occasionally she made the trip by subway to Am Tikva, Boston's gay and lesbian synagogue, trying to weave together the parted strands of her own life. Then, one afternoon last spring while browsing in a women's bookstore for histories of women in science, Ceci had noticed a flier for the women's music festival and thought such a getaway might allow her to meet other young lesbians in a setting far removed from her parents or the university halls.

But she hadn't counted on meeting so many lesbians who laughed at her for being, as they put it, a "festie virgin," unfamiliar with camping, with festival weather, with S/M workshops and tofu surprise.

She sat on the cabin porch, mulling over all the new ways she failed to fit in.

One: I'm skinny and pale, burn easily in the sun, carry around an inhaler, have no athletic muscles to speak of, no softball history. I don't shoot pool, don't lift weights, can't seem to learn the two-step.

Two: I would rather study my schoolbooks than go to a female ejaculation workshop.

Three: I have no sexual experience beyond my fantasies, have never kissed another woman, never even made the first move. I lack the romantic and physical frame of reference these veterans take for granted. I'm a nerd in Jewish culture because I'm an unmarried woman; but I see that I'm also a nerd in lesbian culture because I'm a grad student. Where is the woman who will love me for myself? Why is it a crime to like reading?

Ceci's frustrated sniffles had alerted someone inside the cabin. The screen door opened, and a woman's voice called out, "Hey. Who's there? What are you doing sitting wet and alone in the cold night air?"

It was a worker named Trudy. Ceci had met her at the gathering for Jewish lesbians Friday night, had wanted to hold her hand during the joyful Sabbath dancing. Trudy's wild hair blended with the porch's shadows and dripping plank walls, making her seem larger than life as she stood in the doorway.

"It's you," Ceci managed to say.

"Yeah, you were expecting maybe Barbra Streisand? Oh: the MIT scientist! I remember you from last night. So why weren't you at the Jewish lesbian workshop this evening? I know: You assumed we got rained out. We had it in the kitchen at the last minute." She paused, the door still swinging in her big palm. "You don't look so good. That's not to be rude, you understand."

"*Oy,*" Ceci chuckled, rising to her feet. "I'm sort of on your porch unintentionally. I was feeling sorry for myself. I wanted a quiet place to think. I didn't mean to wake you."

Trudy had arms like strong young palm trees; they swung out akimbo as she edged onto the porch. Ceci looked up into a face that was ten serene years older than her own, a Jewish face more Russian than German, and beautiful teeth that flashed as Trudy demanded, "What's the matter? Someone hurt your feelings?"

"Well. This woman on my work shift called me a Jewish princess because I didn't know how to hammer a signpost. I'm better at indoor things..." Ceci trailed off, blushing. Did "indoor things" suggest she was an ardent lover? That wasn't what she had meant to say.

Trudy snorted her contempt for Ceci's workmate. "Listen, one minute. One minute. I took back some cookies from the kitchen tonight. They're hidden under my cot. Hang on." She disappeared into the cabin once more.

I must look hideola, Ceci thought frantically. She stabbed both hands through her thick brown hair, trying to rally her rain-plastered haircut and succeeding only in cutting herself on the left ear with her women's-symbol ring.

Trudy returned to the porch steps with a blanket and two enormous cookies. "They're kosher," she assured Ceci, who looked carefully into the dough. "I baked 'em myself."

"It's peanuts I'm allergic to," Ceci explained. "But these don't have any. Mmm, so *good!*"

"*L'chaim. La briut!*"

"To your health too," Ceci said shyly. They munched in silence, and then Ceci burst out, "I feel so *isolated* at this festival. I wanted to meet lesbians, but everything is so *outdoors* and *wet* and *stressful.* I've learned everything I know about lesbian culture through books, and I guess I'm just not ready for the *embodiment.*" She smiled at both herself and at the joke, feeling better.

Trudy was nodding. "Everyone suffers from festival syndrome, though. You don't have to be a festie virgin or a sheltered nice Jewish girl to feel overwhelmed, pal. Did you go to Alix Dobkin's workshop? She's the most visible Jewish dyke here. Anyway, she says that part of being at a lesbian festival is being frustrated and miserable because our *ideals* are being tested. We create the matriarchy here bit by bit every summer, with no real blueprint to work by. We know what we *don't* want and so are critical of each other's mistakes or weaknesses." She paused to lick chocolate crumbs from her fingers. "This year I'm here at the festival as a worker, and so I get an actual bed in a worker cabin. A real mattress instead of a leaking tent makes a difference in *my* attitude. The first time you go, you have no idea how to meet and maintain your own comfort level — or what the hierarchy of status in the worker scene is all about. Everybody's first festival is an overwhelming experience. Mine sure was."

"Tell me about it," Ceci suggested, luxuriating in the sensuality of chocolate.

Trudy shifted the blanket across their legs and gave a preliminary chortle. "Well, sister, I must say, the sight of you eating chocolate takes me back to my first festival. It was — hmm, I'm dating myself here — 1980, and I was twenty-one. Let me tell you that *back then,* when *I* was a festie virgin, women's music festivals were still in their infancy and offered even fewer comforts to the campers who came. I was just finishing college, but I was as *out* as the backyard and just aching for an armful of women. When I saw my friends' brochures for this festival, I packed my sleeping bag and canteen in like ten minutes — although the actual festival was still four months away.

"Our women's group chartered a Greyhound bus and driver to take us here, and the trip was at least twenty hours long. And every last dyke on the bus was in a couple except me, so I had to take that really attractive single seat in the rear by the bathroom. All through the night, women stumbled past me to pee, and two lovebirds tried to smoke a joint in there and got a stern lecture about 'foreign tobaccos' from our driver.

"We pulled into a truck stop for breakfast. So like sixty dykes poured into the restaurant for coffee and hash browns. We took over the bathroom, washing our faces, brushing our teeth, changing clothes, loading up on tampons from the dime dispenser. One woman, who had actually been my therapist for a year, washed out her menstrual sponge in the sink! The straight patrons were absolutely aghast. This trucker asked if we were on our way to a Girl Scout reunion. Other folks just stared. We had a dyke waitress, though; she ended up driving to the festival herself after work that night.

"I was so excited when we arrived that I didn't even bother to set up my pup tent. I slept in a community tent with women from all over the country and sang all night. But I wasn't prepared for the dreariness of the *food!* Fifteen years ago we didn't get nice, thick veggie burritos with sauce or lasagna with cheese or any of the amazing soups-for-1,000 you now enjoy. No, we had boiled gray potatoes with yogurt dip three times a day, livened up with the occasional old carrot. There sure weren't any concession stands selling ice cream and Oreos on the side either. The only type of munchie for sale was popcorn, which you had to call 'momcorn.' Had I known beforehand, I would have packed a muffin at least or some tea bags! So to make a long story short, I cruised a woman for no other reason than her giant bag of M&M's. I was desperate."

"What happened?" Ceci was fascinated.

"Oh, I laughed and talked and ate *her* chocolate for hours. We even wrote to each other for a while. Heh. Plenty of funny things happened at my first festival — like I was lying down in front of the day stage, wearing sunglasses and nothing else, and this woman swooped down on me and delivered a long, wet kiss. When I sat up and removed my shades, the poor lady gasped, 'You're not Claire!' and raced off in mortification."

They laughed together.

"And now you're laughing rather than feeling sorry for yourself," Trudy observed with satisfaction.

"Yes." Ceci had begun to yawn in spite of herself. She wanted to hear more stories from this fearless Amazon, who spoke with the same Yiddish lilt as Ceci's own parents. At the same time, she longed to lie down and sleep in a warm, dry place. The prospect of returning to her damp, mold-coated sleeping bag in the woods was wildly unappealing.

"Tired? You can sleep in our cabin, Doc. We have an empty cot going to waste. It's pouring out there." Trudy stood up and stretched. "I have a spare sleeping bag you can use — I'm about to turn in anyway."

"Oh...no, n-no," Ceci stammered, feeling the back of her neck heat up like a cheap hot plate. "I know this is supposed to be the sleeping space for festival workers." She gazed longingly at the silent interior of Trudy's cabin.

"They're all *asleep;* they won't mind. You want to catch a cold, wandering around wet and miserable in those soaked jeans? Come on. Indulge yourself, sister; spend tonight on a mattress under a watertight roof."

This offer was simply too tempting for Ceci to decline. Trudy scooped up Ceci's knapsack, and together they tiptoed into the silent cabin.

From the beds around them came the soft breathing and assorted snorts of twenty slumbering lesbians. An occasional syllable of dream babble floated down from an upper bunk. Ceci heard her own rubber-toed sneakers squelch a wet trail into the rear of the cabin, where Trudy carefully moved an empty iron bed frame out from the far wall. "Here! Put this on." She handed Ceci a dry flannel nightshirt.

Ceci stretched out gratefully on the soft mattress. It was heavenly to be in something resembling a real bed after sleeping on hard, rooty ground for four nights. She felt her body relax for the first time in days and let out an involuntary moan.

"Is this your first camping experience?" Trudy whispered, sitting down on the next cot and removing her boots.

Ceci sighed into the dark, trying to speak as quietly as possible. "Yes. I've never had much outdoor experience. My parents certainly didn't take me camping; they were so overprotective! They were active Scouts themselves as kids, but later the woods held all sorts of terrors for them when they were hiding from the Nazis." She shuddered at this image.

"Your parents are survivors?"

"Yeah."

"Mine too."

"You're *kidding*!" Ceci leaned up on an elbow, astonished.

"Sure. It's not so unusual to find daughters of survivors at lesbian festivals. There are other women like us here."

Like us, Ceci thought, her heart pounding. *She's so big and strong, and she thinks I'm like her! How did I end up on her porch? I wished myself right into Jewish lesbian space!* She moved her face closer to Trudy's, straining to catch the whispered words.

"My mother grew up in Poland and during the war was hidden by a group of Catholic nurses at a regional hospital. It made such an impression on her that she spent years urging me to become a nurse. Apparently that hospital was a center of resistance activities, with nuns using drugs to bribe the Nazis to leave the kids alone. You haven't lived until you've heard my mother tell her story about picking the pocket of a totally stoned Nazi morphine addict."

"So did you do as she said? Become a nurse?"

"No. I'm a paramedic and drive an ambulance. Same thrill of saving lives, but I get to wear dykier clothes and map out traffic routes. I know what you mean about having overprotective parents, though. My mother's chief complaint about my lesbianism, for instance, is that I've somehow *willfully chosen* an endangered cultural identity, whereas she couldn't 'help' being Jewish. She doesn't *get it* that lesbian identity, like our Jewish roots, comes with a will to survive against odds, an ability to live as outsiders *and* insiders. I know she just wants to spare me from the hatred *she* put up with in her life."

"How was it…coming out to her?" Ceci wanted to know, thinking of her own parents' stupefied expressions the night she was caught making a valentine for Miriam Dinnerstein next door.

"Well, she's known for years and years. I wrote her a sort of manifesto in eleventh grade. Her first reaction was to say she'd love me even if I were a murderer, which wasn't exactly the analogy I'd have liked. But we've grown closer since my father died, and she's met my partners over the years with open arms and steaming trays of kugel. She's really tried to love the women I've been with. But I'm, like…uh, not with anybody right now."

This last remark seemed to hang in the air.

Good God, thought Ceci.

She lay on her mattress watching her own heartbeat actually pushing the bedcovers up and down. What should she say next? Could they keep talking? Other women were trying to sleep. Ceci felt her teeth grinding together with frustration. *I don't know what to say. I really like her. I don't know what to say. She's the one woman I've met here who knows what I'm all about. She likes me just as I am. And I am hopeless! Hopeless! I can't move. I am utterly incapable of turning this situation to my advantage. A real lesbian would lean over and kiss her. Why must my mind be so much quicker than my body? Look at her: She is so handsome and strong. If I don't touch her, I'm going to implode with desire. And there is* no privacy. *Women are sleeping all around us!*

Ceci flinched as Trudy's elbow brushed against her. "You're really tense, girlchik. Would you like a back rub?"

Even Ceci knew this was the oldest line in the book. Or so everyone said. Aloud she breathed, "Sure."

"Don't worry," Trudy whispered, pushing their two beds together to form one large square and then rolling up the sleeves of her faded festival sweatshirt. "I'm real good at this — CPR training, you know." She deftly turned Ceci onto her stomach and began kneading the muscles of her back and neck with warm, skilled hands.

"O-o-oh," said Ceci.

"Shh," laughed Trudy. "This doesn't hurt? This feels all right?"

"Yes," Ceci responded, desire slowly gathering in the pit of her stomach and pleasantly pinwheeling outward from there. She breathed dizzily into the pillow.

"You have beautiful bones, nice bones." Trudy worked seriously, moving her palms with competent pressure around Ceci's ribs and shoulder blades. In the darkness the only sounds were women breathing and skin on skin.

Outside, the rain dripped sensuously from tree branch to tree branch.

Abruptly Ceci rolled over and pulled Trudy on top of her.

For a moment neither of them spoke. Then Trudy whispered, "Are you sure this is what you want?"

"I want," said Ceci, wrapping her leg over Trudy's, astonished by her own bravado.

"How quiet can you be?" whispered Trudy.

"I don't know," Ceci answered truthfully, her fingernails pulsing. "I've never done this before. I really am a festival virgin."

Trudy paused.

"But I want you," Ceci said again, her voice barely audible.

Trudy slowly lowered her mouth onto Ceci's in the dark. The bedsprings squeaked approvingly.

"*Gevalt!*" gasped Ceci. She glanced wildly around at the beds filled with sleeping women. "I'm sorry. *Oy,* don't stop. I'll really try to be quiet!"

73

Trudy smiled, her white teeth shining. "No problem, Doc. Just keep your tongue in my mouth."

Outside, the rain gradually slowed to drizzle, then to a fine mist. Animals emerged from their burrows, sniffing the air, eager for a few hours of night foraging after the prolonged storm. Two raccoons lumbered onto the porch where Trudy and Ceci's cookie crumbs remained.

Inside the cabin the temperature had risen several degrees.

Trudy had magically zipped their two sleeping bags together so that she and Ceci could lie in a private cocoon of warmth. Ceci found herself naked against Trudy's bare hipbone. They both sighed at the mutual contact of warm flesh.

"Oh, my God," groaned Ceci.

"*Shah, shah,*" soothed Trudy into Ceci's breasts. "Listen. All around us, hear the sleep of sister passengers who travel with us on this journey. Deep in the belly of this ship, we all sail toward America. There will be women's land there; safety and warm dances."

"Yes," Ceci heard herself repeating over and over.

Trudy's hand cupped the back of Ceci's head and kneaded the tense little muscles there, then brought Ceci's face toward her own again.

As quiet as a pond, they exchanged tongues, feeling the tiny soft hairs at the corners of their mouths.

"A *shayne maidel,*" Trudy said, exultant, and entwined her toes with Ceci's.

"Oh, please, yes. Speak to me in Yiddish. I can't believe you know my language!"

Trudy whispered the lilting, caressing words Ceci longed to hear and then said in a low voice, "Shall I make love to your Jewishness, my sister bride?"

The Song of Songs, Ceci thought. *She's going to recite the Song of Songs. I am so turned-on.* Aloud she whispered, "Say it to me, as much as you know."

"Oh, that you would kiss me with the kisses of your mouth, for your love is better than wine," Trudy chanted, in Hebrew now.

"Yes," gasped Ceci.

"*Ani l'dodi v'dodi li* — I am my beloved, and my beloved is mine; my beloved is unto me as a bag of myrrh that lieth between my breasts; my beloved is unto me as a cluster of henna in the vineyards of Ein Gedi. Behold, thou art fair, my love; behold, thou art fair; thine eyes are as doves."

"More," Ceci said, running her fingers across Trudy's lips.

"Behold, my love, our couch is leafy, the beams of our houses are cedars. I adjure you, O daughters of Jerusalem, by the gazelles and by the hinds of the fields, that ye awaken not nor stir up love until it please."

"It pleases me," Ceci affirmed, breathing unevenly. Steam began to form on the cabin window just above their beds. Trudy slid down, her tongue writing the passages of poetry across Ceci's erect nipples.

"Rise up, my love, my fair one, and come away; for, lo, the winter is past, the rain is over and gone, the flowers appear on the earth; the time of singing has come, and the voice of the turtle is heard in our land."

"Slower," Ceci gasped, watching Trudy's hand gradually disappear between her legs.

"Thy two breasts are like two fawns that are twins of a gazelle, which feed among the lilies. Come with me from Lebanon, my bride; thou hast ravished my heart, my sister, my bride; thy lips, O my bride, drip honey — honey and milk are under thy tongue."

"Slower."

Then, for a long time, no words, only motions and reactions.

Desire, longing, too much, shy, shy, start over. Now keep going.

Trudy curled against Ceci's body, stretching her warm tongue down to where her fingers had played.

"I sleep, but my heart waketh," Ceci panted.

"Open to me, my sister, my love, my undefiled; for my head is filled with dew, my locks with the drops of the night."

"Yes," moaned Ceci, her thighs trembling. "And I rose up to open to my beloved, and my hands dropped with myrrh, and my fingers with flowing myrrh. I opened to my beloved."

"This is my beloved, and this is my friend, O daughters of Jerusalem," wrote Trudy's tongue.

"Don't stop."

"The roundings of thy thighs are like the links of a chain; thy navel is like a round goblet, wherein no mingled wine is wanting; thy belly is like a heap of wheat set about with lilies; thy neck is as a tower of ivory; thy nose is like the tower of Lebanon…"

"I broke it in tenth grade," Ceci moaned.

"I will climb up into the palm tree, I will take hold of the branches thereof; and let thy breasts be as clusters of the vine; and the smell of thy countenance like apples; and the roof of thy mouth like the best wine, that glideth down smoothly for my beloved, moving gently the lips of those that are asleep."

"Amen," from Ceci.

"For love is as strong as death; many waters cannot quench love, neither can floods drown it."

"Keep going, keep going, don't stop; tell me more. It doesn't have to be from Song of Songs; I feel so close — "

"My heart overfloweth with a goodly matter; my tongue is the pen of a ready writer," Trudy recited.

"It sure is," Ceci breathed.

"And Ruth said: 'Entreat me not to leave thee and to return from following after thee…' "

" 'For whither thou goest, I will go.' "

" 'And whither thou lodgest, I will lodge. Thy people shall be my people.' "

"Slower. Slo-o-ower. Just a little bit more — "

"And Miriam took a timbrel in her hand, and all the women went out after her with timbrels and with dances, and Miriam sang unto them." Trudy raised her head and looked up at Ceci's flushed jawline. "Come into the Red Sea with me, girlfriend. We're crossing it, you and I, *now*. Hear it roaring on either side of us? No waters will ever close over our heads. We can run through it, come out alive, *now*."

Ceci heard the crush of parted water, the beckoning desert beyond both hard and hopeful. She saw on that far side Trudy dressed as Miriam, dancing with music, her brown feet bare. She felt her entire skin begin to tingle, a sensation so intense that it had a color all its own.

"Keep going. Keep go — *oh!*"

Water/hold me/the stone tablets of commandments smashing at our feet.

Thy people are my people, the lost tribe of lesbians.

Eventually Ceci became aware that she had not, after all, managed to keep quiet. Two festival workers were leaning over their bunks and staring down at her. Mortified, she ducked her head under Trudy's armpit. But secretly she thought, *I'm not a festival virgin anymore.*

"Say," said one of the awakened women. "Was all that from the Bible?"

"Hebrew Scripture, word for word," Trudy affirmed without a flicker of embarrassment at being overheard.

The awakened women looked at one another. "How come *we* never learned that stuff in Sunday school?"

Reconnaissance
by Lucy Jane Bledsoe

The air in the desert is like hot breath, menacing and demanding in the way it is all over you, all around you. You have no
choice but to give in, let it have your skin. We lay naked, belly up,
on top of the cotton blanket, a good couple of feet between us,
our legs and arms spread to allow the air, which hadn't cooled a
bit since the sun dropped below the horizon, to bathe our bodies.
So much dried sweat from the long hot day covered my skin, I was
a regular salt lick — an uncomfortable thought. Who knew what
night creatures would emerge to feast on any juicy snacks they
could find? The immensity of the desert and the company of an
entire ecosystem of creatures and life-forms that have adapted brilliantly made me feel like a sacrifice. As a pale water-loving crea-
ture with nothing protecting my life from this hot sand, this dry
wind, this unrelenting sun but a thin furless skin, I was fodder.
Especially at night when the desert comes alive.

As if mental exercises could ward off the nighttime army of
scavengers and bloodsuckers, as if marking myself geographically
would offer proof of my existence, maybe hedge against my disappearance, I placed myself. The immediate boundaries of this
desert were comforting enough. To the north, water. A fat, wet
aqueduct twisted like a snake moving west and away from its
source, the Colorado River. To my east, the Chocolate Mountains,
hardly intimidating with their edible name. The coast ranges to the
west conjured everything the desert was not: soggy, dense foliage,
dark green. Finally to my south, the Mexican border, music, tequi-
la, bright colors. This was the Colorado Desert, a region 2,000
square miles huge, located in southeastern California. Was it comforting to think of this desert as small compared to its neighbor to
the north, the formidable Mojave? No. Any desert too big to
escape on foot is boundless.

I struggled to my feet, walked on sand as fine as pastry flour,
soothing to my scorched soles, and opened the cooler. I found the
big plastic jug of lotion. The lotion smelled like gardenias, lush and

green, as I squeezed an enormous mound of it into my palm. I began with my ankles and moved up, palming the cool creaminess into my skin. Finished, I stood and let the whisper of a breeze dry me. I applied another layer.

What next? I looked at the woman lying tangled on the blanket, the woman with whom I'd lived happily for years. I lay back down beside her. Though it was a moonless night, I could see the black immensity of the mountains behind our camp. In the other direction, at a greater distance, were more mountains, but from here on my back I saw only the immediate ones and the stars emerging in the violet sky above. How foolish to go against nature like this. Why was I trying to sleep at the time all desert natives knew to come awake, scavenge, commune, eat, and love? My brain cells, which had slowed to a state of involuntary meditation during the heat of the day, were bursting to life, one by one, like the stars overhead. Like the creatures emerging from their sand tunnels and plant cabanas. Adapting, as if evolving into a desert animal in a matter of minutes, I too began to revive as the night came on.

A trace of coolness in the air. At last. The desert at night is even fresh.

I rolled to my side, the movement of my body making a tiny breeze, and whispered, "You still awake?" I reached out and touched a thigh. Ran my hand up to her waist. Her skin was dry, papery. No answer. How does it happen that the more years you spend with a person, the lonelier you feel? It has something to do with the impossibility of being known, really seen and heard, in the way you long to be known, seen, and heard. So that the more years you put in with a person, even as a deep kind of comfort develops and passion endures, the more you feel devastatingly alone, alienated.

Three stars shot across the sky, beacons or messengers, beckoning or delivering. Hard to say. My friend stirred, groaned, asked for a Coke.

I rose again and got two Cokes from the cooler, relieved that she'd awakened. I brought the bottle of lotion too.

"I was never asleep," she said. "Just trying. It's noisy out here."

"Yes." Skittering, scratching, even sighing.

I handed her the drink, then got our short chairs. We draped towels over the plastic, then sat, still naked, drinking, my friend on one side of me, an agave on the other. Its knifelike leaves folded over except for one, whose sharp point tapped my shoulder. It almost hurt, but I didn't move because it reminded me I was there. An eight-foot stem shot from the center of the plant, looking exactly like a giant asparagus stalk pointing at the stars. The native Cahuilla used the agave for food but also for tattoo dye.

We had arrived in the desert early that morning, planning to stay a few days, as long as we could hold out, hoping to see the desert blooms. It was March, much hotter than most Marches, yet heavy rains had fallen the previous week, causing flash floods in the canyons. The flowers were phenomenal.

"Is this a safe place to camp?" my friend asked now for the first time. During the day it had been too hot to ask questions. We'd driven the four-wheeler off the paved highway and up a dirt road until the dirt road withered to a path. We parked and carried our things a bit farther toward the mountains, then camped in the spreading fingers of an arroyo, far from the base of the mountains where it became a canyon but close enough to discern rivulet paths from the storms last week. She had asked a reasonable question. Why would we assume that no rains would fall this week? Would a flash flood be just inches or several feet deep by the time it reached us?

"No," I answered. "Not really." But we didn't move, and I knew that she wouldn't bring it up again. After all, though we were sincere about wanting to see the desert blooms, that was only the metaphor for our being here. The flowers were like the top of a mountain, a destination so that you can take the journey. Camping in this wash, planting ourselves in the heart of change, that was our real reason for coming. In spite of its flat, uneventful appearance, no ecosystem is as quickly changeable as the desert. A simple spring downpour can dazzle the grays and reds and browns with the florescence of desert bloom in a matter of hours. Even the shape of the land transforms daily, the winds constantly reshaping the dunes and the floods tearing soil from the arroyos and replacing it in the washes. I came here to feel the immediacy of change, as if I could quicken my capacity to handle it.

I picked up my foot and placed it on hers. My toes caressed the fine bones straining against the skin of her foot, the sand on my sole scratching her. She moved her foot away from mine. We drank more Coke.

Tonight we were mostly silent, but in the daytime we had talked of desert spirituality. Stumbling away from our shade, a bright umbrella plunged deep into the sand, we had hovered over a desert blossom we found fifty yards from camp. Hot-pink petals on the flat beaver-tail cactus. Beside it a barrel cactus shimmered with crowns of yellow flowers. And all around, like ghosts, the ocotillos growing from the sand like heat waves. Soon, overwhelmed by the sun, even though we were dressed like sheiks in our layers of white cotton, we staggered back to the shade, such as it was, and pulled more cold drinks from the cooler, opened our clothing, and rolled the bottles over our thighs, our foreheads, our necks. Replaced them, found colder ones, peeled off the tops, and threw back our heads. Drank. Talked some more about spirituality. If you could call it talking. Out here conversations minimize.

"That flower."

"I never knew fuchsia before."

"You could drink it."

"Yes."

"Breathe it."

"Yes. Taste it."

I got up again and walked to a beaver-tail cactus. Like a mule deer I stretched my neck, leaned down, and pulled off part of a bloom with my lips. It tasted like flower petal — satin fuchsia.

And somehow felt like I'd seen God. It's the heat. It's the slight anxiety about creatures you don't understand. A slivering in the sand nearby. A scuttling across your foot. Sometimes, when the anxiety brightened for a moment into fear, I considered locking myself in the truck, locking myself against the reptiles and crustaceans and rodents that thrive here. But if I did that, I would die of heat. Better to chance contact with the desert fauna. And to endure the current of risk, slight and subtle but present enough to remind me of my vulnerability and of someone else's authority.

Tonight we finished our Cokes, and I offered to put lotion on my friend. She agreed. I started with her neck, moved to her shoulders and breasts. I spent a long time going down her arms and massaging her fingers with the lotion that smelled like gardenias. I couldn't do her feet because the sand grit scraped painfully.

We laughed, and she suggested a walk.

I felt a bolt of dismay at the idea of leaving camp. I glanced at the square of blanket snarled in the sand, then at the truck in the near distance. This had become home but truly was no safer than any other part of the desert around us, familiar only because we had designated this agave and these ocotillos surrounding our camp in their particular pattern as home.

We put on flip-flops to protect our feet against thorns and headed into the desert. The silver chollas looked luminescent, their spines glistening like starlight, like mist. Earlier, in the daylight, I had put my nose in one of the silver cholla's blossoms, the color of unripe apples, sour green with a reddish tint along the outer edges of the petals. Above us the stars looked both hot like dry ice and cold like the blue roots of flame. Nowhere else am I more aware that I am staring into not just the sky but the universe.

"It's a trip out here," I said inanely, wanting only to break the spell of silence.

I looked at my friend. Naked like me except for flip-flops, she didn't even turn her head, as if my words had been swallowed by the bigness before they could travel the few inches to her ear. I looked behind us. I could no longer see our blanket, but the truck stood out like a dark tank, out of place and useless. And getting smaller as we walked on. I began to wonder why we were walking.

"Because we can't walk in the day," she explained in answer to my question. "It's lovely. Look."

I did look, and it was lovely, but the space was beginning to feel too big; it pressed in on me like it had the intensified gravity of a black hole. I loved the wilderness for reminding me of my place in the wider realm, for reducing my fears to biological reasonability, but out here the ratio was too exaggerated; I felt on the brink of being squeezed to absolute nothingness. I wanted to touch my friend, to know my flesh by traveling hers.

She walked a distance away from me, though, maintaining the gap when I tried to close it, moving as if I were the repellent end of a magnet. Maybe she was reveling in the loneliness.

I sifted a handful of sand through my fingers, kept walking.

"Look." My friend finally moved toward me, touched my shoulder.

I looked to the mountains, not the ones buttressing our camp but the ones in the other direction, in the distance. "What?"

"Do you see that light?"

I scanned the night sky, now looking away from the mountains and toward the expanse of desert, and saw an odd white light with yellowish tinges. It bobbed gently as it moved slowly in a path perpendicular to ours.

"A single headlight," I said. "We're probably getting closer to the highway. Some car with one headlight out."

"No. Too high in the sky."

Soon I realized there was a second light behind it, then a third. A string of seven lights, all bobbing gently in the night sky, at least a mile or two away, moving slowly in single file like a family of ducks.

I was pleased to have a mystery to solve, a topic of conversation between my friend and me, something to engage my attention other than the vastness. Not only do I write science textbooks for a living, but I'd also just completed a long chapter on astronomy for which I'd read much more extensively than necessary for the writing. I also spent many nights in the outdoors. I'd seen a lot of strange stuff in the sky, and none of it had ever frightened me. Most of it I assumed to be satellites.

These were no satellites. They were far too low in the sky. Nor were they airplanes or any other craft with an engine, for they were absolutely silent.

I racked my brain for explanations.

Of course, I knew what my friends would say, what would be "obvious" to anyone to whom I described this experience: the military. The desert is known to be a playground for bomb testing and other military maneuvers. A couple of years earlier, I'd spent an entire backpack trip diving for cover as the sky exploded time and again. Later I learned that they were researching the sound barrier, and the multiple explosions were sonic booms.

So I tried to look at my bobbing lights as a military experiment. In this age of supersonic jets and space shuttles, softly bobbing lights are hard to explain. They were perfectly silent. They moved slowly, deliberately. Weather or surveillance balloons were possible, but why at night? Why over the state park? We were a long way away from the Nevada border and the larger deserts where military experiments are common.

My mind, charged with adrenaline, ran through and rejected all the possibilities, which made these lights, by definition, bona fide UFOs — as in flying objects I could not identify. Instantly I saw my face in blurry lurid color splashed across the tabloids: EXPERIENCED SCIENCE WRITER SIGHTS UFO. If I had not yet disgraced myself in other ventures and claims in my short life, this certainly would do it. Just last year I had hired an astrologer to give me career advice, and she had nailed my issues so accurately, I had no choice but to declare myself a believer. *I'm becoming a quack,* I thought now, *a kook.* To bolster my flagging self-respect, I reminded myself that the tabloids weren't the only ones reporting on UFOs. Since the beginning of time, very respectable publications and people had described inexplicable phenomena in the sky. Even biblical stories have been interpreted as UFO sightings, including that of the prophet Ezekiel, who reported seeing a fire-spitting, gleaming bronze craft from which four living creatures emerged. And what about Alexander the Great, who claimed that he and his army had been harassed by a pair of flying objects?

So I was in the company of prophets and world conquerors. Somehow that was more disturbing than comforting.

As the bobbing lights drew closer, I reined in my imagination, surely fueled by too much reading, and forced myself to think harder about possible natural explanations.

None fit. All the literature on UFOs that explained away sightings as atmospheric abnormalities used examples that were obvious: shooting stars, Venus on particularly bright nights, strange reflections of the sun, even the reflection of a camera lens on window glass. The lights approaching me were not reflections of anything, nor were they misinterpreted heavenly bodies. They were too low in the sky; I could see the dark backdrop of the mountains behind them. Most of all, it was the way they moved that began to truly unnerve me.

The string of seven lights, bobbing ever so slightly in the night sky, changed their course. They had been moving in a line perpendicular to us, toward the mountain range in the distance. As we stood and watched, utterly naked save for the flip-flops, the lead light turned slowly, imperceptibly at first but by now decidedly, and headed directly for us. There was something else: I had the sense, the strong sense, as did my friend when we talked about it later, that these bobbing lights were guided by some kind of intelligence. They headed for us as if to sniff us as an animal would do, moving neither randomly nor by a prearranged pattern or blueprint — without precision and *with* decided will. They seemed curious.

As they approached us, my fear intensified. In fact, I have never been more frightened in my life. Not when I developed early signs of hypothermia while skiing in a whiteout. Not the time I clung to the edge of a crumbling cliff, looking down hundreds of feet below me. Not when I stood alone for the first time in my new room, a room that was vomit green and maybe eight feet square, after leaving home at eighteen. While experiencing these earlier fears, I somehow had remained engaged. I had known I couldn't indulge the fear because I had to act.

This time there was no action to be taken. The seven bobbing lights were approaching, dipping lower in the sky as if to get a better look at the two naked women in flip-flops. Yes, I admit that I did go so far as to imagine some form of spacecraft landing, of a hatch opening, of little beings waddling toward me. Pointing. Laughing. Forcing me into their spacecraft. Explaining in perfect English or in garbled alienese that they wanted me for science experiments or — worse — were taking me home to their planet.

I did imagine abduction. In detail. And for those moments this science writer truly believed it was possible.

Begging my friend to come with me, I began to run. Where do you run to in the desert? It was irrational, of course. There was nowhere to go but back to camp. At least that was a home of sorts, and I needed to get there. As I ran, panting, I looked over my shoulder. The lights kept coming, bobbing, taking their time, while I, a naked bundle of human cells, ran through the desert night. I quit looking over my shoulder and just ran.

In hindsight I'm glad she tackled me, though if I'd been a few years older, I'm sure she would have induced a heart attack. My scream seared the cooling desert air. The impact of her body knocked me face first in the sand, silencing the scream and restructuring my fear. Like the way an injection of energy can transform the molecular structure of a substance, the skeleton of my fear, though still fear, took on a powerful erotic charge. I was grateful for the length of my body against the earth. And for the length of her body against mine.

She apologized for the attack from the rear.

"Don't move," I said. The pressure of her body relieved my loneliness, wholly.

It was not, she explained, that she was any less scared than I but that her fear had taken another form. My running terrified her, made her feel we'd provoke a chase, like running from a bear.

We lay in the sand together, our bodies wet and gritty with perspiration plus sand, our gasping the only sound for miles. The lights, still in a line, oscillated in the not-far distance but seemed to have stopped their approach. As if they'd seen enough of these pitiful earth creatures, they turned, again imperceptibly at first, and headed for the mountain range. We watched them retreat as we made love, voyeurs to the aliens, their menace feeding our passion. Eventually the first light rose slightly and skimmed the peaks, then dropped behind the mountains out of sight. The rest of the lights followed, one by one, each rising to miss the peaks, and disappeared behind the range. Then, feeling equally foolish and anointed, somehow favored, we talked hungrily, the human voice an oasis. We tried to imagine the bobbing lights being piloted by American soldiers in green camouflage suits running surveillance or tests or simply joyriding in some new or not-so-new toys. With the military, we agreed, anything was possible.

But that was just the point: Anything *was* possible. And as we talked, the military explanation seemed just a wee bit more absurd than other possibilities. The idea that only this one planet, only this one speck in the universe, sponsors intelligence is illogical. Think of the ant making a journey across my friend's hip as we lay in the desert sand. I am sure that it, along with all its comrade ants, perceived itself to be the top rung in the order of things, entirely oblivious to the existence of humans and most other species, even though by some remote chance this one was traversing a human body as we spoke. Isn't it possible, even likely, that we are the ants to other forms of life or intelligence in the universe? Couldn't we be just as oblivious?

My friend brushed away the ant and rose to her knees. She walked on them to a nearby succulent I couldn't identify. She weaved her fingers among the thorns in order to grasp a fat leaf and tore it from the plant, then crawled back to me. She broke off one of the thorns and used it to trace the tattoo on my breast. Then she dug her fingernails into the flesh of the leaf, accidentally piercing her palm with a thorn, and cursed. Still she continued until she managed to break the rubbery flesh. A clear gel oozed out. She scooped a fingerful and applied it to my skin, cool and slippery.

And as I relinquished myself once again to her hands, I realized that all of us — the bobbing lights, whether military or alien; the ant traveling the landscape of my friend's body; and even I — were on reconnaissance missions. Hadn't I come to the desert to watch, to see, to measure myself against what I found here? We are nothing but this watchfulness, this constant reconnaissance in the hopes of finding fertile geography on which to feast, whether that geography be a piece of fruit, a person, a desert, a planet. What matters is the simultaneous feast; being laid bare; the sand in your crevices; the sting of the agave leaf, tattoo needle, or starlight; the place where your flesh intersects another geography. I closed my eyes to better concentrate on the sand scraping against my back, the something sharp — a piece of rock or a thorn — digging into my hip. In my left ear I heard the tiny clatter of a hard-shelled animal, and on my skin, the balm of her mouth and saliva, fingers, and cactus pulp.

Hourglass City
by Myrna Elana

Aara flipped her wrist and checked her chron. Time to meet Carmen for the vials of antidote that would keep her going for another month. She stretched her fingers as she walked, easing her joints, anticipating Carmen's heat and tightness on her hand.

She loved this part of the spoke; there were no battery lights, no fans, no sounds but the rhythmic slash of knife sharpening.

The Renderers used their dulled blades to cut messages into the corridors. Lit by black-violet glow strips, they came off the walls like dreams: MEAT! EAT YOUR MOTHER. Next to MY KNIFE UP YOUR ASS was a drawing of a large-breasted, thick-armed Renderer impaling the General with a boning blade. Aara flashed on an Egyptian workman's graffito of the female pharaoh Hatshepsut being sodomized by her overseer, her body masculinized, her crown in place.

This spoke of the city was dirty and poor and had no public services, but at least here there were some people with spirit.

The Renderers were the bottom-of-the-tier workforce: They took the turned-in and collected bodies of oldsters and other dead, butchered them, and rendered them down to food bars. The perfect place to hide — it had become her home in this underground city. The govt's security officers found the poor populace, death-inured and masters of knives, insufficiently deferential for their tastes.

She checked over her shoulder and took a last glance at the drawing. Wispy gray hair brushed her brow.

Up ahead flashes crossed the fork Carmen had named as this month's assignation spot.

Suddenly a scream cut down the corridor, echoing as Aara ran toward it.

Carmen, it had to be. She pulled her stunner out. Six Hell Hounds hulked out of the dark, swinging their flashes, the one in the lead carrying Carmen over his shoulder, blood running from her mouth. Aara flattened herself against the wall and held her breath. Her stunner was nothing against the Herdex annihilators holstered on each meaty hip.

Carmen would never forgive her if she got herself caught. An astringent tang bit her nostrils as glass crunched under the Hell Hounds' heavy boots: the vials of her hourglass antidote.

She held still. If only she could shoot syringes full of acid under each of the big men's skin. Make them howl the way they made their victims howl. The sounds of their boots and their nightsticks slapping their thighs faded.

Aara ran. She reached the last corridor, her body keen. Would someone be in her quarters, standing beside the door with a Renderer's blade?

As soon as they got Carmen under the Needle, they might find their way to her room. And they might already know who the antidote was for. Aara Naeracine Bokh: the official news nets branded her incendiary rebel, heretic, enemy publisher, revolutionary leader.

The antidote Carmen had been bringing her neutralized the hourglass drug the govt pumped into the city's water supply. Aara shook, trying to block Carmen's open face and rounded body from her mind, Carmen who could race from an undermarketer's front-shop in the city's hub to the Renderers' spoke with the hourglass antidote faster than anyone she'd known. Carmen might be forced to betray her and could be killed going under the Needle for the second time.

Slipping her switchblade down her sleeve, she keyed her door lock and sprang back. Silence.

Her sensors activated her battery-adapted lights. The abandoned supply room she'd appropriated lay open to her eye, its blank gray surfaces undisturbed.

With no wasted motion, she dialed open the wall chest for her disks and left one scrawled line detailing Carmen's capture for the women of her circle. Maybe the Welders would be able to help Carmen.

From the back of the closet she grabbed her uniform. The crisp fabric bunched in her hand. The Officer she'd stolen it from had gone drop-jawed with shock when she'd rammed her elbow up his nose as he tried to cuff her.

She zipped the trim black uniform, snugged the weapons belt around her hips, and fingered the kiss-my-knife creases down the legs. Moving fast, she laced the gleaming heavy-soled boots up to the knee. Metal spikes jutted from the heels and toes. Maybe she'd make it out of here yet.

She slipped her papers over her breasts, put her stunner in her hip pocket, and slid her switchblade up her sleeve. Aara combed her hair back and thumbed the comb into her pocket. Old and strong — that's one thing the big boys hadn't bet on.

In her pack she stuck a jacket, civilian coverall, water bottles, her makeshift water filter, food paks, medikit, flash, and bedroll. Camping time.

The floor panel closed over the battery-adapted printing press. Aara hefted her pack and locked the door behind her.

She couldn't stay in the corridors long, so she'd make the best time she could. Her chest began to ache from the rush of dry air in her lungs. The pain had to be from running — it was too soon to be feeling the effects of hourglass. She wouldn't drink any more water than she had to.

The last time her delivery had been missed — a runner had been killed by a Renderer who mistook her for a terrorist — Aara had been in convulsions in a matter of days. If Carmen hadn't made the run to a lab contact who shunted abortion supplies to Industrial Spoke women, she'd have died then, at the "old age" of fifty-one. Carmen had granted her more than seven years of life. Aara extended what little was quiet within her, that peace that kept her sane, toward Carmen.

Aara ran, pushing through the jabbing hurt in her chest. Up ahead she'd get out of the corridors. With the Hell Hounds after her, the dark no longer felt safe. The ache in her legs and chest began to warm her, relieve her. She sped up, leaning into the corridor's curve, following the glow strip, the pain washing through as good as sex, to the place she went with Carmen when her lover came so hard, she cried — finding the good pain in her own body.

She'd always known this could happen: The hourglass would claim her, take her life, probably her mind first. But having grown to a graying age, she'd come to think she would die in her own time. Damn. So much she still wanted to do.

If this had to be happening, she wanted Carmen with her. She slammed her fist into a corner, held the throbbing to her chest. They'd have spent the afternoon in the tunnels, skin getting slippery and drying in the chill, Carmen's ass against her belly, black curls fragrant and light on her face, her own arm and butt sore from pumping her younger lover. Her chest ached. Her lover's deep scent covered her; her hand convulsed inside Carmen's tight, sentient sheath, came out cramped and juice-wrinkled after wringing out every sound and need Carmen had in her.

The Welders could get bombs into the city's elite hub; maybe they could get Carmen out.

She bit the inside of her cheek; the deep tang of her blood helped take her down.

The ways became less familiar. Aara eased to a run-walk. The glow strips changed to yellow: the Sewing Spoke, the sweatshop. Machine hum filled the air — and women's curses. Bits of fiber blowing through the air ducts made her sneeze. But it smelled better here, the warm scent of textiles. She'd smelled human fat and gristle and decaying blood for too long.

In the amber-lit Goods Spoke, she keyed open a maintenance shaft. The clean, burning smell of working metal greeted her.

She slipped in, and the wall panel sealed behind her. The dark tunnel formed a high-tech cave with bare insulation and colored wires covered by a transparent guard sheath. There was room to lie down, turn around, and proceed at a crawl or crouch.

This spoke, which distributed coveralls and rations, was one of the few outside the hub that had climate control. The warmth felt good in her joints.

Aara sat against the wall and let down her guard a notch. Her feet hurt, and pains spiked through her chest; she needed to rest. A hollow, tram-hit ache filled her belly. There was only one place she could go: past the perimeter — outside into the Waste.

A deep breath, and she unzipped the black uniform and pulled out the news disks about the war and her manuscripts. She opened an insulation panel and secreted them in a hollow under the yellow fibers — a place her circle used to distribute news sheets.

She dug in her leg pocket for a pen and tapped it on the gray pulp of her manuscript's cover page. She wrote:

I'm going outside.
Life to you and freedom.
I'll be heading toward the sun.

The sun — the one landmark that would still be out there.

Earlier generations had left maps, but what good would they be in negotiating the surface of a blasted planet? With care she fitted the panel back into place. The metal jittered against the slot; the hell with finesse, she jammed it till it clicked.

Even in the dim tunnel, she saw and felt them trembling against her will: her hands. Her hands that had triumphed over stiffness to master the tedious art of hand-set type, her hands that had brought young women crawling to be taken and had taken them past the edge of pain to their truest, most radiant selves. She wrung her hands, gouging her fingers with her nails.

She'd pace herself and get through this, get out. Day or night made little difference in the dark tunnels. She was due for a rest.

Aara laid out her bedroll and stuck her pack under her head. Flicking her knife into her hand and leaving her boots on, she willed herself to sleep.

Hours later her dreams still crowded her. She packed up, ate one of her algae rations, took a sip of water. Thirst made her tongue swell, her skin tighten, her head buoy — but even with her homemade filter, the hourglass drug was getting to her.

Losing her hands' finesse was one kind of bad; worse had been the convulsions that racked her at twelve when hourglass entered the water and again at fifty-one, leaving her sweated and wetted and shit-fouled. Loss of control was only a matter of degree.

She swung down from the tunnel into the spoke. It was a dead time, and she could go faster through the corridor. Her night images kept after her as she followed the glowing orange line.

Wet lips and smooth flesh, a shaved slit, slick and opening to her fist — the scent of it was in her, pungent and clear.

At the quietest time of night, footsteps sounded behind her. She sprang into a side artery, her bones creaking.

A figure paused, moved toward her, and stopped again.

The dark gray uniform and black weapons belt denoted an Officer cadet. The short-haired head swiveled, amber light slid on blade-shaped cheekbones, lips so full, they'd be outrageous after being pumped by sex.

The coverall's top creases grazed erect nipples — a woman. The cadet turned again, the uniform hugging her ass, that seam sliding right between her cheeks. Well-muscled. Handsome.

Aara waited. The woman picked up her stride, walked past, without drawing a weapon. Aara grabbed her, pinned her arms.

The cadet squirmed in her grasp — a strong woman. Aara shifted to a headlock, evading her captive's donkey kicks, and tripped her down.

"Looking for me?" Aara flipped her over, knelt over her thighs, and flicked her blade against her throat. "Don't fight. I can kill you so fast…" She made her voice a caress. "I have nothing to lose."

The woman began to rock her hips beneath her. Aara searched the young one's face. The cadet's mound pressed up at her. The ploy smelled of a trap.

"Let's go somewhere more private," Aara said. The cadet's eyes widened; her body stiffened, but she didn't struggle.

She pulled the cadet to her feet, yanked her arms behind her, and slapped the self-tightening monocuff on her wrists. Her small breasts stuck out, nipples fingertip-sized and hard.

Shoving the cadet ahead of her, Aara marched her out. Officer reinforcements would be nearby. She couldn't leave the woman; she couldn't afford to give away her position. So, crazy as it was, she was taking the damned cadet hostage — the damned black-haired, brown-eyed, soft-lipped sinuous cadet.

She pushed the woman by the monocuff, which acted on the nerves of the wrists, numbing the arms. The scent filled her — this one, this woman. Aara shoved her forward.

"Hey!"

"Shut up." Aara pushed her to a near run in case the woman's voice had alerted sensors to their location.

Location! Shit! She slammed the cadet against the wall.

"Where is it? The tracer!"

"What are you talking about?" The cadet's too-loud voice filled the corridor. Aara cracked her across the face. The skin blotched red. The cadet's hot eyes narrowed.

"One simple, quiet answer." She bared her teeth. "Where's the tracer, and where's your wire?"

The cadet looked at the floor, teeth clenched.

Aara yanked down the coverall's zip. She gripped the cadet by the neck, choking her scream. Her thumb eased into the nexus of nerves below the jaw.

"Are you ready to tell, or shall we do this the hard way?"

"The tracer is at the nape of my neck."

Aara slid her fingers through the thick black hair, pushing her face into the cadet's. She ripped the tracer off and ground it under her heel.

"And the wire?"

"You mean it about killing me, don't you?"

"Being attractive is no proof against death. You're wasting my time, and I don't have much." She shoved her hand into the woman's coverall, feeling her armpit, her breast — an easy mouthful — and delved down her belly, inhaling her scent, toward her cunt.

"It's behind my left ear," the woman snapped.

Aara snatched it off, pleased to take a bit of skin with it. The cadet stared first at her and then at the ripped sutures hanging from the implant wire.

"Listen up, guys," Aara said into the wire. "I've got a bomb and your handsome gift, and I'm heading to your headquarters — the secret one." Maybe the bluff would distract them.

She dropped the listener implant and stomped.

Blood ran down the cadet's neck, and her eyes went glassy. Aara fingered a packet from her belt, bit it open, and slapped gel-skin on the wound.

"Come on, march." Aara prodded her ass.

Zagging out the smallest arteries, Aara made for the city's perimeter, the Row, making the best time she could with her cuffed captive. In an outlying corridor in the Welders' Spoke, she keyed open a maintenance panel to get back into the tunnels. The cadet stared open-mouthed, panting. Aara gestured at the crawl-way. The cadet turned in all directions, breathing hard. Aara gripped the collar and seat of the cadet's coverall and heaved her inside.

Aara took a deep breath of the hot metal emanating through the Welders' world. She wouldn't be coming back this way, and the women in this sector had always given her a glow — their big arms, strong stances, sweated jumpsuits straining over wide backs, the feel and smell of metal and oil all over them, those big metal hoods and the torches they used, the flare that left an after-image on your eyes, and the booming songs they belted out over the clang and crash of huge metal slabs and beams. Her first woman, a Welder who found her nosing around wet-palmed, took her down under an ancient truck and discovered she was wet everywhere, and right there, to the music and hot stink of rending metal, taught her the ecstatic nuances of pain; Aara's then-small body pinned in the grease, with those big calloused hands taking everything they wanted — nipples, cleft, and ass — the strained-to-shaking muscles of her legs, and her cries right into a mouth that tasted of metal as the woman drilled her untried cunt and pinched her nipples so hard that the Welder made herself come before Aara'd figured out what it was all about (but she caught on then with those big fingers prying at her cunt and ass).

Now Aara exhaled the heat from her lungs and climbed up into the shaft.

The panel sealed itself with a soft suck sound. The cadet raised herself up on her knees and rubbed against her as though they'd met for a tryst. Aara thrust her to arm's length against the wall.

"We've got things to talk about." Aara pointed to the floor. "Sit." Her captive sat.

Aara tucked down into a tailor's seat.

They sat knee to knee in the tight space. The cadet adjusted herself, leaning forward to take pressure off the cuff. Sweat glistened on her face in the blue light of the crawlway's luminescent strips.

"So what are you called?"

"Darce," the cadet whispered. Some act, or this was one scared rookie.

"Very well, Darce. Who are you working for?" She saw the guard go up in the woman's eyes.

Aara patted the Herdex on her hip. She hoped it was the Officers and not the govt's not-so-secret death squad, the Hell Hounds. The Officers tortured you, but the Hell Hounds kept you alive — one survivor she'd met had cut off her own hand to escape the holding cuff and the Needle, the biggest mind fuck ever known. It took everything you were and distorted it, replaying emotions at concentrated force, over and over, each humiliation, each murderous thought, each rejection, each grief, each instant of self-hatred — infinitely.

"So, Darce, I'm supposed to believe we two happened on one another by chance? You just happened to get tracer and listener implants? And you happened to be out looking for action with some nice old woman?" She ran her hand up Darce's thigh. Darce blushed and glanced away.

Aara slipped her switchblade down her sleeve and flicked it at Darce's breast. Smiling at her captive's refusal to move, she pressed the point just under the thickest vein on her throat.

Darce sat fixed against the wall, breathing fast.

"Good. You understand. Now — who are you working for, and what are your orders?"

"I'm with the Officers' municipal force — a beater, you'd say. The bulletin was just your description and orders that you be taken alive." Darce raised her brows.

"Taken where? For what?"

"Just to headquarters is all I know." Darce shrugged, winced as the monocuff tightened. Strands of hair stuck to her sweat.

"I don't believe you. You might be a private, you might be what you say, you might be a Hell Hound." She tapped her blade against Darce's mouth. "You know more than you're telling. The act's too cute." She spat toward the door. Darce turned away.

Aara grasped her arm and hauled her up to a crouch.

"Come on." They'd have to crab-walk a few feet, then they could make better time. Darce's fear-sweat overpowered that softer, tantalizing scent.

Her hostage dug her heels in. Aara pulled her arm, and Darce brought up her knee to kick; Aara flicked her knife open against her throat.

"Tch, tch. Don't be stupid. I'd rather not leave you for the Renderers." When she was a child, the sight of those women and men in blood-smeared aprons with their long curved knives had given her goose bumps — the threat seemed to have the same effect on Darce. She smoothed the sweaty hair off Darce's brow. "This way, my dear."

She led Darce far into the shaft, making a couple of turnings along the larger branches, taking her far enough in so that noise wouldn't bring other beaters.

Chill bumps came up on Darce's neck when Aara removed the monocuff. Darce rubbed her wrists, eyeing her.

"Strip." Aara smiled. It was cold in the unheated shaft.

"Look — " was as far as Darce got in protest. Aara pulled out a stunner and snapped the switchblade back up her sleeve.

Darce unbuckled the weapons belt and let it drop. Glancing up at Aara through the lick of hair that fell in her face, Darce unzipped her uniform.

Her hips shifted as the coverall slid open over her hard chest, her deep navel, her spiked pubes. Darce swung her head to one side, arching her back as her fingers slid over her crotch to her ass, opening the uniform all the way up the back of her crack. The silver teeth of the zipper framed and plumped up the plum-colored sex lips and the softest part of her butt.

She slid her fingers along the zipper's edge, pulling it away from her mound to improve the view. The coverall slipped down her shoulders, bound her defined arms as they pressed the sides of her breasts, thrust them together and out, the strike edges of her hands grinding into her sex.

Her whole body was a weapon. Aara enjoyed the dip of her waist as the coverall slid down her arms to her hips — a small waist that made Darce look almost fragile just right there, at that one important juncture of her body. If Darce chose to live, Aara would show her how to build up the muscles over her kidneys, give her body the kind of armor she hoped neither of them would ever need again.

Darce slid the uniform down her legs, her glance half-lidded, submissive, as though trained to turn her captor's aggressions to something she could more easily handle. What big eyes she had!

A muscle in Darce's cheek pulled her smile crooked.

"Cut the show, handsome. Just take it off."

Darce finished undressing in quick peeling motions. A blush stained her face.

"Shoes and socks too. Good. Now put your hands on your head and your back to the wall. Walk your feet toward me, and keep your shoulders on the wall. That's it."

Aara grabbed the coveralls and searched them, squeezing all the seams. She kept her eyes on her well-muscled captive, whose brown nipples stood in the chill.

The flat beater shoes made her smile. Cadets had to earn their Officer boots.

With the stunner trained on Darce, Aara fished out ID pak, short rations, and a Herdex. She weighed the weapon, the fastest auto multiphase available. The woman could have pulled the Herdex when she'd first sighted Aara, but she hadn't. Maybe they did want her alive.

She slipped the cock-handled gun into her pocket, thumbing the safety so as not to dematerialize a leg. The belt had a monocuff, flashlight, stunner, gelskin pak, and medikit; she examined each. The belt and other items she stuck in her pack with a glance at the ID: Darce Halbertson — for what it was worth, IDs being cheap on the undermarket.

Now she could pay attention to her companion's body. Young, so young, with that smooth, glossy skin. Breasts small and high, nipples pointing, nicely furred crotch. And that blush!

"Turn around." No reason not to indulge a little. No. Plenty of reason not to indulge. But, oh! The winged spread of shoulders, the pebbled backbone leading to the deep cleft in a round, outthrust, sculpted ass.

Prodding Darce, she led her to a pullout waste facility.

"Vomit."

Darce balked, refusing to approach the pullout.

"Look, I can kick you hard enough in the belly to make you puke. You choose."

Darce knelt and stuck her finger down her throat, choked up some water.

"Keep at it." Aara kept the stunner trained on Darce until she'd emptied her guts — it was the best way to dislodge an internal tracer.

"Now empty yourself."

Darce blushed. "Are you going to watch?"

"I'm going to watch every move you make for the rest of my life. Get used to it."

Huffing, Darce mounted the pullout and released her wastes after long piss- and shit-shy pauses.

"Good girl." Aara flushed the pullout; let them try to get a read on that. She handed Darce a water bottle to rinse her mouth.

Aara put the monocuff back on her. She wedged her switch-blade between Darce's back teeth to keep her from biting and probed under Darce's tongue, behind her molars, and behind her uvula, forcing her to gag. No tracer.

She wiped her fingers across Darce's breasts. Darce shook under her touch, breath coming fast, skin going scarlet down to her nipples.

"You sure know what you're about, don't you?" Darce said, averting her eyes. Aara smiled, pushing her away from the pullout.

She patted the firm round ass. "Sit."

Darce sat, pulling her legs against her chest. Her gaze flicked from Aara's face to the knife to the pocket bulging with the Herdex. Her blush deepened.

"I've heard you like to hurt people..." Darce pressed her breasts forward.

"Is that why you're here?" Aara's throat went tight, spit thick in her mouth.

"Do it," Darce whispered, wetting her lips.

Aara prodded her in the chest with the spikes on her boot.

Darce's face drew together, giving Aara a preview of what she'd look like in a few years. Her eyes went wide, and she started to glow, mouth open, head back.

"There are worse things than being uncomfortable." Aara pushed against Darce's resistance, watching her boot's steel points pierce the skin between Darce's breasts.

Blood welled up the spikes. Darce lost her balance. Aara fought temptation, breathing hard.

The cadet howled as her flesh pulled off the spikes, leaving cuts in her chest that looked like tiger claw marks. Blood ran down the creases below her breasts as she arched back, belly and pubes presented above her captured hands.

Turn-on jolts ran through Aara's body.

"My God, I wanted you to do that." Tears ran down Darce's face. She rubbed her leg against Aara's uniform, against her thigh. "I thought maybe they were wrong about you, all those Officers' reports calling you dangerous. I had to see for myself." Darce swallowed and tried to raise her ass off the cuff. "I used to read your writings and look at your picture — I couldn't believe you were so bad."

"Thank you." Aara squatted down and looked into Darce's eyes, then she gripped the short soft tufts at the base of her neck and kissed her. No way she could trust this woman, but her body wanted to believe this, just this, this response, this need — the one honest thing Darce could give her. Darce reached for her with her face, her tongue, her whole body, and Aara took in her breath, covered Darce's nose with her hand, forced her to breathe and then not breathe with her own breath until Darce lay panting and limp, surrendered.

"Spread your legs and stay still." Aara used her left hand, the one she usually fucked with, nails filed to the quick, to check Darce's cunt.

"So, Darce, when you were looking at my picture, did you think of me doing this?" She watched Darce's face tighten and then open as she fingered her slick pink folds and pushed a finger inside her, swirling just behind the opening and probing in a spiral all the way in, circling the cervix, sliding deep behind it, nudging the dip at its center. She pulled back out.

Winking, she held up two fingers, pressed her fingertips past the tightness, and then turned her hand. Darce's juices oozed into her palm.

She levered her hand into Darce's loosening slit up to the knuckles. She slid back and drove in deep — twice — and again hit her hard right on the tender place inside, already swollen with fluid. Her fingers knew she could fuck her hard enough to make her squirt.

Darce moaned and rocked toward her and whimpered when she pulled out.

"This hole passes the test." Aara held up her empty hand. Darce's face flamed.

Darce squeaked when Aara used her wetness to make her tightened asshole juicy.

"I have to be thorough, baby. No one's coming on this trip with me but you."

"You're a...dirty old woman!"

"You got that right." She slid her thumb into Darce's ass, and her captive gasped and squirmed. After three breaths she used the slowest possible motion to rim the inside of Darce's asshole.

Darce rocked her ass up as Aara's thumb began to retreat.

"Gotcha!" Aara crowed.

For thoroughness, though her own chest had gone bright red, she slid her middle finger into that now welcoming ass.

It was so hot and dark and soft, she wanted to live there.

She pressed her finger in and out, exploring that silky, vulnerable hole, feeling Darce right there up inside her most secret opening. Darce opened herself on a breath and beckoned her in with her whole ass.

Making her face blank, Aara withdrew and rested her hands on Darce's up-cocked knees. It was too much — to feel her own need, to miss Carmen, to want this stranger this much.

"That wasn't so bad, was it?" Aara eased her hamstrings, rounded her back, and creaked up to standing.

Darce averted her face, but Aara caught the shine in her eyes.

Gently, even tenderly, Aara inserted the spikes from the boot that hadn't been blooded yet into the curve of Darce's ass.

"Get up. The torture's over."

She stared at Aara over her shoulder, the humiliation plain on her face: Had this meant nothing more to Aara than a strip search? "The reports were right," she spat. "You are dangerous."

And so are you, Aara thought, shaken by the intensity of her own response. The temptation to rip Darce's cheek open with the spikes flared inside her, but she contented herself with a tiger swipe up Darce's flank. Blood flared in curved stripes, beaded and dripped down the pale flesh. The captive rolled over and presented her ass.

"We're done for now. Listen, you're going to be disoriented for a while. You're drinking filtered water, not getting as much of the hourglass drug as you're used to. Your thinking is going to get sharper, your emotions more intense. And as a hostage you'll…feel unexpected things for me." Aara bit her lip against the tenderness she felt for Darce. The blood and sex flush moved her in ways she hadn't expected now that Carmen was gone.

Aara washed her hands at the sink. The crusty pink soap seemed like an artifact from another age.

She avoided looking into her captive's face and hustled Darce out a branching tunnel. The cadet lost her wind before she did.

At a worker's rest area, she pulled Darce down to sit on a cot.

"Don't worry, I'm not going to commit further indignities on your person." She took a sip of water and handed the canteen to Darce, who emptied it.

She refilled it at the sink, running the water through her homemade charcoal filter. Her hands held steady. It was a gamble, trying to get by on so little water, but without the antidote she couldn't afford to have much hourglass in her system. A headache started building behind her eyes. She clipped the canteen on her belt and sat down.

Now that she could get her breath, she flashed on how Darce had felt inside, that hot darkness, her inner ass softer the deeper she went into it. Aara stroked the gun through her crisp uniform. The handle had a good shape — it might be just about the cadet's size, get her wet enough. The sharp sighting flange on the barrel had other possibilities.

Grinning, she pulled out the ID pak and worked it. Classification A-16. Darce wasn't an Officer cadet but a private, a member of the govt's security force.

She released the monocuff and shook Darce's hand. Darce stared at her.

"Nice to meet you, private. How long have you been following me?"

Darce yanked her hand away.

"It would help if you'd loosen up a bit — but have it your way." What did she expect from a private, friendliness? Aara's throat constricted. The two of them were stuck with each other. If they were going to survive — and more than survive — she needed to get through to Darce. And maybe she wanted more from Darce than good hostage behavior. The silk of the young woman's skin, the shine of her eyes had imprinted themselves inside her. She picked up the coveralls and pocketed the stunner, slipping her switch into her hand, flicking out the blade.

She kept her eyes on Darce as she began cutting into the legs.

"Hey! What are you doing there? Those are the only clothes I have!"

Aara grinned and handed her a strip of the strong fabric.

"Here. Tie your ankles together."

Darce glared at her but complied. Aara watched her make the knot too loose, probably expecting Aara to check, opening herself up to get conked. Aara humphed.

She stepped to Darce's side and gripped her arms, slapping the monocuff onto her wrists. Pinning Darce's legs with her own, she tightened the ankle knot. For good measure she tied her captive's legs together at two points: below the knee and around her firm, silky thighs.

"There you go. I'll be back in a while. Just moan if you need anything." Darce's scent tantalized her; she tried to ignore it.

"By the way, Darce, do you know how the city got its name? Do you know why your Officer's uniform has an hourglass on the lapel? I'll tell you. It's named for Operation Hourglass, which 'won' the war."

Darce's eyes widened.

"I don't suppose you have much to say about the war that reduced us to this, that destroyed our planet; what can you say about the regime that caused it, your precious govt that you still serve?"

"You want me to feel like I'm part of the problem because I support this govt. I want you to know I think that's crap." Darce's spit hit Aara's face.

Glaring, Aara wiped her cheek. She wadded a strip, pushed it into Darce's mouth, and tied another around her head to secure it. Even this far in, she didn't want to risk a scream.

Darce writhed appealingly, but Aara smiled and shouldered her pack. She rounded the turn and settled down a few feet away. Now she would get some sleep.

Aara emerged from surface dreams in two hours. Her heart pounded, her palms sweated.

No! Aara focused and pushed the tension, the clenching, the stoppage through and out of her system. She slowed her breath. The hourglass drug had begun acting on her muscles.

Maybe, just maybe she could survive without the antidote — if she could find drug-free water.

Breathing deep, she stood up and steadied herself, glad her captive hadn't seen. Maybe she should leave the private tied in the crawlway. No. She'd damaged, and she'd killed — but only when there had been no other choice.

Life mattered more now that there was so little left. How much? Hours? Days? Weeks? And of what quality? Would she go into convulsions, cardiac arrest, or — dementia? No good going down that road.

After a few deep breaths, she tightened her uniform. Smiling to herself, she combed back her hair and slicked it with spit.

She went round the bend where Darce slept. Gently she released the ties, but Darce only stretched in her sleep. Aara's muscles and joints spoke to her as she worked her body. The cold had settled in her bones. At least the uniform helped conserve heat.

What had made Darce take the path of a private? And were the two of them so different? Strong women who liked weapons and physical force, liked to control, believed they were changing things for the good. She deepened her groin stretch and groaned. Goose bumps stood out on the young woman's bare skin; she lay curled on her side, holding herself.

When Darce's eyes fluttered open, Aara smiled. She squatted down and removed the gag. Darce grimaced and spat. The fabric had left deep red marks on her face; her lips looked swollen — Aara's clit jolted.

"Have a good sleep?" Aara rose and palmed her stunner.

"Yeah, sure." The woman sounded puzzled, rolled to sit. "Why are you being nice to me?" She rubbed her eyes.

"Look, we have to travel together. And I'm not out to make you miserable." Aara looked away, too attracted to the way Darce's hair splayed over her eyes, the sleep wrinkles on the fine skin, the down on her arms, the crinkling of her big nipples in the chill.

"Right." Darce wrapped her arms over her chest.

"Here." Aara tossed her the thigh-length coveralls. Darce grimaced and stepped into them. She rolled up the shredded edges, giving Aara a good view of her muscled legs down to the beater shoes. She stretched.

"Well?" Darce stared at Aara.

"This way."

At a pullout she stopped to piss, standing as she preferred but facing out, with the stunner trained on Darce.

"What's that smell?" Darce wrinkled her nose.

"This is the Synthahol Spoke — the people's brew is made from urine and drugs." She laughed at Darce's expression. "Drinks for the hub are made from breast milk, harvested from women who 'choose' to live in heated, lit, vid-provided cells with full cannibal's rations — rather than working in factories, sweatshops, or rendering shops for subsistence and like as not homemaking for male batterers, their 'protectors.' The women, with the few men who produce viable sperm, carry to term, enforced — "

"You don't know what you're talking about!" Darce yelled, her face reddening.

"How do you feel about supporting the privileged few at the hub in living off everyone else, little private, little enforcer?" She clamped her mouth shut. She missed the women of her circle; she missed the precious few people in this city who used their minds to think.

"I wanted to make a difference." Darce's voice broke. "As a private I thought I could. But it only... Tracking down kids who write on the wall, oldsters who don't want to die, workers who leave their assigned spoke, interrogating undermarket smugglers. I once caught a young black woman who'd escaped; I didn't know what those round scars around her nipples were from." She turned her face away.

"I know you didn't know," Aara said, holding back the surge in her heart. This woman had thought some of this out; it was more than she'd hoped for. She touched Darce's shoulder, and sparks flashed through her.

Darce's eyes met hers.

"Let's go."

Aara kept to the tunnels, zagging farther from the hub. Darce had gone shaky from hourglass withdrawal, breaking out in sweats and dry heaves. They had to crawl, sneezing in the dust, taking care not to touch exposed wires.

At a low crawlway, Aara tied a tether to Darce's ankle and removed the monocuff. She pointed to the floor, and Darce glared back at her.

"Get on your knees and crawl," Aara snapped. Darce balked until Aara prodded her to her knees. After slapping Darce's ass to get her crawling, Aara followed, out of kick range. She prodded Darce often to keep a fast pace; the oily smell of motors invigorated her.

Halfway through Industrial Spoke, Darce pulled up short at a widening in the tunnel and turned around in the tight space.

"Enough already. If you're trying to tire me out, you've done a good job. I'm not going any farther."

Aara blinked. "Bullshit." She brought out the Herdex. "Move."

"No!" Darce knocked the gun aside. Aara grabbed Darce's arm and slammed the Herdex against the side of the private's neck. Choking, Darce dropped to her knees. Aara jerked her arm behind her neck so hard that she gagged, and then she jammed the Herdex into her ribs.

The big-handled weapon felt good; the private's shudders came through it into her hand. She stared down at her. A touch less control, and Darce would be dead.

"Get up and move." This time Darce didn't even look at her. She got up. An ugly flush spread on her neck where a knotted bruise formed.

Too tired to move. What crap! Darce was trying to get Aara captured. She pushed the pace, jabbing Darce in the butt with the stunner. Shaking, she locked the Herdex in her holster to alleviate temptation. How dare this damned woman risk both their lives!

"Don't push me, Darce. Just don't."

"I'm sorry." She turned her face to Aara. "I feel like I'm breaking inside. Maybe you're right about the hourglass drug. I feel too much now." Tears ran down Darce's face.

"Give yourself time. New things don't always make sense. And you're in withdrawal."

"I want the pain to stop, the confusion." Darce tripped, pulled against Aara's arm.

"Listen, when I first realized I couldn't go along anymore, I was scared. I was my mother's daughter, a dedicated govt scientist's good girl. Giving up the life I knew to go underground and be something I didn't have words for shook me. I was hurting myself in bad ways for a while." The cut scars on her thighs and the memory lapses from home-tube uppers and downers were her reminder. "All I could hang on to was a growing sense of who I was and what type of people I needed to be with — strong women who knew their own mind and were off the drug and wanted a better life than anything any of us had known." She patted Darce's shoulder. "I know about fear."

"I hate it that you make what I've dreamed of — my life, my career — look so ugly." Darce pressed her chin against her own shoulder, close to Aara's hand.

She could feel the heat from Darce's smooth cheek. "But you already knew it, or you wouldn't have come after me. Or at least," Aara showed her teeth, "you wouldn't have come after me to talk." She thumbed her own uniform's softened crease.

"Sometimes I've felt so strange, as if there was no one at all to talk to." Darce's eyes darkened, and Aara made herself keep looking, against the urge to shut back down.

"I know the feeling," she said softly.

A day later they reached the end of the last Industrial Spoke and the taller tunnels that led to the Row at the city's perimeter.

"Where are you going?" Darce asked, wheeling on her. "Where are you really going? Do you know where you are?"

"Do you know where you are?" Aara flung back at her. She took a swig of water and eyed Darce. Her hand shook, and she slammed the water bottle back onto her belt.

"I've been this far only once before." Darce swallowed and

glanced at the water bottle. "During training. We were taken out into the Row. We suited up in noncontam gear, and the commander opened a door, and I saw…the outside." Darce shook her head. Aara could hear the pounding of her heart. Outside. The Waste.

"Close your eyes."

Aara didn't want Darce to see her hands shake. Darce complied, little crinkles showing on her eyelids the way they did on a child's, showing the effort to behave.

Aara held the water bottle and let Darce suck from it. She wanted to hold the younger woman against her breasts and comfort her, nurse her.

She put away the bottle and used the back of her hand to wipe Darce's lips.

The cadet blinked at her. "No one has been tender with me in a long time — "

Aara couldn't look at her; her body kept surging, wanting her. She prodded Darce to move ahead.

"Please, would you just slow down and talk to me?" Darce begged.

"Look — we don't represent the same interests." Aara pushed Darce to walk faster.

"What *are* your interests?" Darce asked, squirming to look into her face.

"What do you care?" Aara's voice shook.

"Maybe I do care." Darce looked at her sideways. "If you'll just let me."

Aara tightened the monocuff until the private squeaked. It was one thing to control Darce, another to feel herself veering out of control, wanting Darce.

Darce dragged her feet, and Aara poked the Herdex at her tit, aiming for her heart.

"You said you wanted to find me," Aara said. "Why?" She hustled Darce along.

"Your name has been coming up on the news net for as long as I've been able to read. I wanted to see you for myself. Aara Naeracine Bokh. It didn't seem like you could be real — one old woman against," she swung her chin, "all of this."

"I'm not alone."

"Yeah, but you're known. Most of your people stay hidden, safe. They don't take the risks you do. I guess that always attracted me, that you're a fighter."

"Funny you joined the other side then."

"The city isn't perfect, the govt isn't perfect, but it's what we've got, and I'm grateful for what I have. I couldn't disgrace people who care about me by flaunting myself, even if I could agree with you. You revolutionaries make a spectacle of yourselves — "

"Is this about me, or is this about you?" Aara asked, so low that Darce had to offer her shell-curved ear to her lips. Darce shuddered against her.

"Oh, damn you," Darce whispered.

They passed a few oldsters, a sure sign they were near the Row.

"Most of the oldsters are women. Men turn themselves in or jockey for govt positions that allow them to age." Aara tightened her mouth. Her mother hadn't made it to fifty, riddled with the cancers epidemic among women.

Spikes shot between her ribs. This was her time to end, her time to go white-faced, to reach and cry and look for someone to make the pain stop. Weapons — God, no wonder she loved weapons so damned much. The word *redemption* rang in her head, and she stifled it, squeezing the Herdex's grip — she'd always have a way out. She bit her tongue, held it between her teeth, breathing.

Darce pressed against her. "Aara, come back with me. You can do more for your cause by coming forward. Think of the media attention. You can make a statement, and there will be a trial, and you'll have a safe cell, food, everything you need. My employers aren't into torture. It's a humane ending you're being offered."

" 'Everything I need,' you say. I need freedom, Darce, that's what I need. That includes freedom to share my ideas in forums other than the censored circus of our courts, whether you think what I have to say is crap or not. Don't feel bad," she said and squeezed Darce. "You've done your best. I'm incorrigible, everyone says so." For the first time in a long time, Aara laughed. From the corner of her eye, she caught Darce's smile.

She turned to be sure, and Darce kissed her.

"Don't start that again!" Her mouth felt too alive.

Darce looked right into her, pressed her breast into the gun, releasing her breath slowly.

Aara gripped her arm harder, against her own shaking.

At the end of the spoke, the tunnel ended, forcing them to descend the corridor — the way to the Row. It was barely lit and snaked with live power cords, making it necessary for them to go slower.

"Stop, please! Will you stop?!"

Aara yanked the monocuff, activating the nerve-deadening effect. This would be a bad place for a skirmish. She rammed the Herdex under Darce's shoulder blade, grinding the sharp sighting flange into the muscle until blood welled through the uniform. The blood relieved her, and she could go on.

"Just keep moving."

Aara slowed the pace even more at the end of the Row's corridor. She could hear and smell the people on the Row. There would be patrols here.

She keyed open a shaft and boosted Darce into it, followed, and let out her breath when the panel snicked into place.

With her boot spikes she prodded Darce. "Crawl."

"We're going back! We're going back now?" Darce's voice cracked; Aara didn't answer her.

They reached a room, one of the workers' rest areas.

"Take your clothes off."

"Could I just rest a minute?"

Aara nodded. She needed a break too. Everything in her was so tight, she wanted to run. They sat on a bench.

"Would you take this off? Please?" Darce pleaded. "I promise I won't do anything."

Aara measured her and released the cuff. "There. Now you'd better think about your options."

"Options?" Darce bit her lip as she rubbed her welted wrists. Bringing feeling back to the wrists and arms was one of the most painful aspects of the cuffs, one of the features Aara liked best about them.

"How do you feel about going back to being a private, serving the govt?"

"You mean you'd let me go?" Darce turned toward her. Her scent, while soured, was still strong.

"Leave that aside; just think about it. How do you feel about your job after some of what you've seen, after what we've been through together?" Aara could hear a drip in the pipes, smell the odd graphite tang of the outer city. Darce turned away, addressed the tunnel's wall.

"I thought being a private would be great, but I'm just taking orders. I thought I'd get to meet you — you're like a legend — and I'd capture you. It would make my career..."

"It doesn't sound as though this career makes you happy."

"Happy? Who's happy? I don't think even the govt members with their fine clothes and luxury quarters are happy. They are among the most unfit, unfocused people — " Darce stopped herself. "But you're talking about me, aren't you? No, I'm not happy."

"And what's going to happen to your career now that you've been captured by the old woman you've been stalking?"

"No one thinks of you as just an old woman!"

"You see what I've been saying? About the value of old lives? What if we saw no one as just an old woman? Think of how that would change us as a people, how honoring all our lives would lift us — "

"Stop that! I get so tired of all your ennobling ideals, your heresies!"

"Then why were you looking for me so hard? Why have you pored over my heresies?" Aara smiled. "And in case you haven't noticed, you've begun to speak a few of your own."

"It's not how you're making it sound!" Darce's blush came up purple in the blue glow.

"It wasn't that you needed me. You're more than this role you've taken on, and you know it." Aara touched Darce's hand. The soft skin, the energy meeting her, shocked her.

"Just stop. Please just stop." Darce held herself, her fine black hair falling in her eyes.

"If I let you go, your colleagues will want to find out everything about me you might know and might not even know you know. You'll be stripped of private status for failing, and you'll be used as an informer. Your precious govt will turn you over to the Hell Hounds."

"You're wrong! You're lying! They'd never — " Darce folded her arms against her belly.

"It's happened before. A woman I love, Carmen, was once an Officer. Something showed up in her attitude exam. They sent her to the Hell Hounds. She broke there. Do you have any idea what it means to have another human being, via the Needle, break your mind? This is a whole other dimension beyond the Officers' clamps and spiked boot kicks. Yes, they're for kicking. I hope you admire my restraint." She swung one boot, spikes licked by blue light.

"You can't know all this. The only reason there are any extreme measures is because the terrorists — "

"Is that what they tell you? They don't tell you that if something a bit off comes to light on the attitude exam, you can be examined more thoroughly — by the Needle?" She pinched Darce's chin.

"I don't believe it."

"Haven't you wondered about cadets, Officers, other privates who have disappeared?"

"It's a hard job. Sometimes people break down from the strain. A couple guys in my class — "

"Has anyone heard from those guys since?" She fingered back her hair. "Carmen broke, but women from my circle found her on the Row, took her in, made her safe to get through the nightmares, the aftershocks, the years of not trusting her own mind. This isn't just about living out one's age or reclaiming the outside." Aara dropped her hands.

"I can't think about all of this now. Please."

"Fine. Get undressed, and you can take the first shower."

"You really love her, don't you?" Darce looked at her too closely.

"Yes." Aara touched the hollow that used to be full of Carmen. "Yes, I really love her." She met Darce's eyes.

"Wash your coverall too, Darce. I'd like to get you back to your original scent."

Darce stared at her. "Living like this, with no control over anything, no future, makes me want to die." She spun away and turned on the shower full force.

Aara watched her abrupt, hard motions as she soaped herself and scrubbed the coverall, lifting her face to the spray, rubbing her welted wrists in the heat of it.

When Darce emerged from the shower, she threw her wet coverall at Aara and lunged for the Herdex. Aara kicked her in the thigh, a hard kick that rammed the spikes in and slammed her against the wall. Darce went down.

"I'm sick of this." Aara locked the Herdex in her holster. She sat on Darce's pelvis and slapped her face hard. Her handprint bloomed across the pale cheek.

She gave herself to the fury and pleasure of it, slapping the handsome face back and forth, her hand tingling, Darce's head rocking, face reddening, both of them breathing in gasps as Darce tried to buck her off.

"I want you, damn it," Darce yelled. "You know I want you. Damn you, I've wanted you all along!" Her lips swelled, split, blood ran down her cheek, and Aara grabbed her by her neck and licked the blood, kissed her deeply with it, their mouths filled with metallic tang, teeth and tongues still clashing with the heat of the fight.

"You're asking for it, aren't you?"

"Yeah, I'm asking for it." Darce stared at her with all her pride and need right there on her face.

Aara tortured the young breasts with her nails, squeezing them hard, pinching the nipples till they flushed with blood.

Darce moaned, her shoulders straining as she tried to get her hands free. Her breath came fast, and her hips rocked, and not all of the color in her face came from the slaps.

"You bitch." Darce drew the words out on a hot breath and cut her eyes at Aara. Her chest blazed.

"Shut up and kiss me." Aara bit her mouth, making her lips swell, tongue-fucking her face.

She dug her hands into her breasts, pulled her nipples, and twisted them, pinching deep. She rode Darce's energy, smiling into her wide-open face, slapping her breasts, then pinching them, pressing her into the good pain that made her gasp and jerk on her own pleasure. Biting each nipple, she sucked the taste of abraded flesh into her mouth. She drove her thumb slowly into Darce's ass, squeezing her tits in one hand and grinding both nipples between her teeth. Darce's whole body shook in climax.

Darce lay gasping, her body completely soaked with sweat. Aara stared at her.

"I didn't expect you to come so soon," Aara said. "We haven't gotten to foreplay yet, and you're ready for dessert." She wiped the sweat off her face, breathing deeply. Slowly she let her thumb slip from Darce's ass.

"I've been wanting you so much. Let me please you." Darce's eyes gleamed.

Aara unzipped her own coverall all the way to her ass and smiled. When Darce smiled back, she lowered her wet, aching cunt on Darce's face.

Darce's tongue met her with a rush, jolting her, lips and teeth gripping her, a soft flick of only tongue, her own sounds rising. Aara began rocking, riding Darce, leaning over to get her tits.

Aara increased the pressure on Darce's nipples until she screamed against Aara's swollen clit. Twisting the nipples, Aara jabbed in her nails.

Charged on Darce's cries, she hurt her just enough and came on her mouth.

Aara caught her breath, waited for the throbs and oversensitized feeling to subside. She reached for and stroked Darce's hands.

"Suck my clit. Tighten your lips on it for me." She rode Darce's face, jackknifing her clit into that perfect hole.

The pressure built, Darce's tongue flicking her head, her shaft held firm, caressed with each stroke, her lips and clit head swelling, going tight. She pushed, riding it, holding Darce's wrists.

Aara shouted, rammed out of her body on something near love. She lifted off Darce's face, slid down her body, and kissed her cunt-juiced mouth. She thumb-fucked her tongue, high on Darce's responses, her gasps, and her sweet, tight sucking. Smiling, she unholstered the Herdex, locked its safety, and stroked its big-knobbed black handle.

"Do you want this?" The thick, soft-yet-hard rubber grip was warm from her body, the perfect fit in her hand.

"Oh, yes. Oh, yes, please."

Aara slicked the weapon up and down Darce's drenched, swollen folds and ground its grip into her oozing slit.

She forced the whole length into the tight cunt.

"I want to hurt you. It's better for me the more I hurt you." Her voice gone fierce, she leaned in and bit Darce's neck.

"Then do it, I want you to." Darce's words came thick-tongued. "Hurt me. Please."

Grinning, Aara slid the weapon out and angled it. She'd pressed her hand over Darce's mouth, watching her wide eyes. Jerking the sharp sighting flange, she cut Darce's clit. Just enough to make her bleed.

She slammed her own cunt against the bleeding spike-puncture wounds on Darce's thigh, pressuring that deep bruising, the bleeding under the skin, using Darce's blood for lube to rock her clit on.

"So good, so fucking good — go ahead, take what you want." Darce's eyes deepened in surrender.

Skewering the knobbed handle into Darce's cunt, Aara pressed into her motion as her cunt took it in deep.

"Beautiful, baby, let me have it," Aara whispered. "Come on the pain for me; that's what I want, let me have it." Radiant, Aara fucked her with the gun as hard as she'd ever fucked in her life. Darce lifted her ass for it; tears ran down her face as she came on it again and again harder, shaking.

Aara stared at the blood running from Darce's clit over the big weapon's black handle.

She sucked the blood from the clit, taking Darce's heartbeat in her mouth, widening the cut with her tongue, pulling at it with her lips, sucking her blood until her own coming rose and nearly blacked her out as she drove the gun into Darce at an upward slamming angle that made her scream.

A long time later Darce stirred. "I liked that," she whispered.

"Yeah, I could tell." She'd never taken anyone like Darce, never touched a woman with such a fast response — who needed to be hurt as much as she needed to hurt.

"I want you to fuck me again. With your hand."

Aara tensed. What did this woman *really* want? "It's time we move on," she said finally.

"No, please. I want you — please?" Darce's red face and swollen lips were painfully appealing.

"There'll be plenty of time for that later." Aara stood and zipped up her uniform.

"Now, *please!*" Darce came up on her knees.

"If you're good, I'll fuck you at our next rest stop. I'd like to see what I can fit inside you." She closed her hand into a fist. Darce blushed and looked down at Aara's boots.

"I'm going crazy, Aara, I can't live like this; I never have any choice about anything. You make me want you, and then you won't... If you keep treating me like this, I'll kill myself."

"Shut up." She grabbed Darce's coverall, yanked the seam tight up the cleft of her cunt and ass, and made her stand. That cunt, puffy and oozing, so tender, to be pinched and then stretched... And that ass...

Darce pressed her face into her palm, and Aara's clit jumped. She made Darce look into her eyes.

"I'll fuck you hard enough to make you want to live."

Darce surrendered herself into Aara's arms.

"I'll make you keep that promise," she said and bit Aara's neck.

"Sweet bitch."

Aara opened the air lock that made the Row a defense and seismic buffer for the rest of the city. Nudging Darce through, she inhaled deeply and focused on slowing her heart. The air lock suctioned shut.

She took her jacket from her pack and draped it over Darce's shoulders to hide the monocuff and the bloodstain on her damp uniform.

"Come here, handsome." Pulling Darce close, she hip-nudged her to walk near the wall so she could take out anyone who attacked.

"The Herdex is set on max." Aara poked it at Darce's tit. "It's a bad way to die." This was the worst part. If Darce screamed, if a patrol came by...

Her senses sharpened. The Row was quiet, too quiet. A few old ones leaned against the walls. One old woman wore a yellow flowered dress, a costume amid the standard civilian coveralls. The oldster's eyes flickered in dreams; a urine puddle spread beneath her. Aara winced. She could be there — could have been there eight years ago. Breathing shallowly against the Row's stench, she walked slowly, calming her urge to bolt.

She'd never been outside. But she knew how to get there. Thinking about it made her sweat, made her stomach roil.

Ahead, a group of three gray-haired women huddled with their arms around each other; one of them winked. No, couldn't have been.

Time to leave this damned city and the death it held for her. She'd make her own death.

She shook it off — her circle would salvage her papers and her publishing system. The work would go on, that's what mattered.

Darce's nervous cough made her look into her pale face. Maybe she'd have some company when she died.

"Aara, look out." Darce nudged her, and she glanced around.

Hell Hounds, pushing through a knot of oldsters up ahead. Shit! But the Hounds hadn't seen them.

If Darce hadn't... She turned with Darce and retreated.

One of the three old women sitting against the wall signed to her. The old women spread their overcoats, creating a tunnel of shelter. With Darce, Aara dived behind them. The oldsters resumed their pose.

The Hell Hounds' boots shook the floor. Silver belt buckles, skewer handles, and whip hooks flashed across their tight black uniforms.

From between folds of fabric, Aara watched the men shine their lights into the oldsters' faces as they passed. By all the grace left in the world, they passed.

Heartbeats later the women leaned forward and brought the folds of their clothing back to themselves, wings contracting.

Aara and Darce scrambled out and bowed to them.

The oldest woman met Aara's eyes, rose, and embraced her. Aara kept the Herdex trained on Darce and hugged back with one arm. The woman's white hair hung down like a veil over full, pendulous breasts. Aara wished she could rest there as she'd sheltered in the warmth of the oldsters' bodies.

"Old lives are as sacred as young ones, Aara Naeracine Bokh." The woman smiled.

"My thanks to all of you." Aara kissed the woman's hand. Others watched with enlivened eyes. Aara gave her Darce's stunner. "This setting alleviates pain, the middle setting immobilizes, the highest setting kills." She demonstrated one-handed. Darce stayed still. The woman pocketed the stunner, nodding. She kissed Aara full on the lips.

"There are people outside. Those of us who can sense such things know it. Go in peace. You've made your mark here; you're on the right course."

Aara's gratitude for the words, whether they were true or not, made her chest open. "Thanks, thanks everyone. To freedom," Aara whispered.

"To freedom," the oldsters whispered back, a sound deep as the earth itself.

"Tell Carmen — Carmen Triana — I love her. And please, please help her."

Blinking hard, Aara led Darce away.

For once Darce moved as fast as Aara without being prodded.

"Thanks." Aara squeezed Darce's shoulder.

"No problem. I couldn't have given you to the Hell Hounds." She looked into Aara's eyes, then looked away. "Aara, I…I want to tell you…" She swallowed. "Listen, would you take off the monocuff?"

"Soon, baby, real soon." She put more control in her voice than she felt. They were so close now.

They came in sight of the door. Her breath sank in her body as she approached it. Until she made it outside, she could still be apprehended — or turn back.

Please let Carmen be all right. She dug her nails into her palm, brought herself back.

Her arm ached from keeping the Herdex trained on Darce. So the private hadn't betrayed her. She might still mean to escape — anyone would panic at going outside.

Swallowing the lump in her throat, she forced herself to keep walking. She could do it; she had to.

She steered Darce to the door. It looked like the air locks leading into the Row except for the word EXIT printed on it in green. Darce strained against her, and Aara held her close, nosing the Herdex into her breast. She keyed the door open, using the code her mother taught her against this day.

"Don't, please don't. I'll do anything," Darce said.

"You'll do it anyway." Aara's vulnerability to hourglass and her need for the antidote had made her aware, as not even history could, of the absence of freedom.

Aara took a breath and put her hand to the door's latch. Her muscles locked. It wasn't hourglass but terror that held her.

"Damn it." She pressed on the latch, and it stuck. Darce pushed at her gun arm.

"Don't do this, Aara. I don't want to hurt you."

Aara laughed. This was about her life, and the little private was threatening to hurt her!

No one had noticed them — she craned her neck to be sure. No one could reach her where she was going.

"Darce." With all her energy she found the peace inside and holstered the Herdex. She put her arms around her.

Darce trembled against her. Aara released the cuff.

"Will you come with me?"

Darce looked down, and Aara wished she hadn't asked.

"Yes." The dark brown eyes shone.

"Thank you." She brushed her lips across Darce's still-swollen mouth, so open inside herself that the feel of Darce's breath on her skin rushed through her, a good ache, the best pain. She swallowed, ran her hand down Darce's cheek.

With her weight Aara moved the latch. She opened the door. She hadn't realized she'd closed her eyes until she opened them. Darce struggled in her arms and screamed; Aara propelled them both through, slamming the door behind her.

And outside — it was pink.

Pink. Aara blinked and thrust Darce to her knees.

She swallowed and tasted the air. It didn't hurt to breathe. Maybe she'd find good water, a deep spring. Her mouth ached for it. A thrumming in her muscles warned of more pain to come.

Under her feet lay a soft, grainy substance the same tone as Darce's skin — sand. It moved with each step she took, rocking her. And in every direction above the horizon was pink.

Aara took deep breaths.

Darce remained on her knees, her face in her hands.

The outside, the Waste. It had been generations since anyone in the city had seen it, aside from a suited-up glimpse at a door-way. But there was still a deep memory and longing for the lush-ness, the land.

She turned a slow circle, blinking. Aara had expected any-thing — but not to find it beautiful still, not to be moved by the color that deepened even as she watched, by the soft earth under her feet. Tears ran down her face.

"It's amazing," she whispered. She pressed her hands together. She wished her mother had lived to see her make it.

Darce sobbed louder. "It's the end. The loss of everything. Nothingness. Worse than death."

Their eyes met.

"Kill me!" Darce shouted. "Kill me now."

Aara shook her head and helped Darce to rise. This wasn't going to be easy for either of them. Darce stared at the ridges left on her wrists, red and purple.

"Go to the door." Aara raised her hands, palms out.

Darce hesitated, then ran back to the wall of the city. Only a tight rectangle showed the door they'd come through. Darce threw herself against it, pounded on it, kicked it, screamed. She dug at the thin weal with her fingernails and screamed again, a keening that lit into Aara's bones.

Darce moaned and slid down the door, leaving streaks of blood from her torn fingertips.

Aara went to her. "There isn't any way back in."

"You crazy old bitch!" Darce screamed, lunging at Aara and toppling her.

Aara rolled and pinned Darce on her back, kneeling on her arms. Rearing back, she slapped Darce's face, gripped her jaw hard. She stared into the wide brown eyes.

"Bitch, bitch, bitch," Darce spat. "Kill me, or I'll kill my-self."

Aara pulled Darce's head back so that her neck strained and her mouth opened.

"Just stop, I'm warning you," Aara said.

The pink sky brightened. There was no other sound but their panting.

"Get up!" Aara licked her lips and stood. Her thirst had hit the burning point. If there was anyone alive anywhere she could get to, there'd be good water.

Darce sprang to attention at the order, and Aara enfolded her in her arms.

"You're a natural. No wonder you were a private." Darce's blush warmed her chest.

"I don't know, Aara. I don't know if I can live like this, with nothing."

Aara touched Darce's face, fitting her hand to the cheek.

"Just be with me now. Just now and then the next now. That's all you have to do. And I'll be with you through it all." Aara kissed her and searched her face until Darce nodded.

Aara took Darce's hand and led her toward the horizon. Straight ahead a banner of smoke surged across the pink. And a bright crescent — something left from the war? She squinted into the glare. It was the sun, rising.

A Light-minute
by M. Christian

How are you today? was all the message said. It was their ritual, a tight tradition between them. Sasha was a nighttimer, a sunset-to-dawn kind of girl. Before she crawled into her warm flannel cave and drew sleep up over her eyes (she'd written), she always left that message for Alyx to find in her own preferred morning.

Happy, Alyx sent back with a flutter of keystrokes, *love you.* Another ritual, much more recent. Alyx felt it, though, with a tug of hesitation, a grip in her chest of uncertainty. It might well have been totally true that Sasha was the love of her life — but they'd never met.

So much was known — despite all that was unknown (the sound of her voice, the way she smiled) — that Alyx was very certain about the feelings she had for the tiny dark-haired girl with the sweet little bulb of a nose, deeply tanned cheeks, and vibrant brown eyes (*I'm a Mediterranean princess who likes the night*): a color print of her framed neatly over the monitor. Even without hearing her voice or really seeing her face (beyond the picture she'd transmitted), she knew that Sasha somehow fitted perfectly into her life. Their conversations, though time-delayed, hummed and clicked with a familiarity that belied their three-month relationship.

At first Alyx was hesitant about venturing into the electronic unknown. The world was still much too loud, hard, and brilliant for her back then to learn the unfathomable language of baud, server, gateway, and the like. Jo had left her — taken her pictures, blankets, clothes, books, *herself* and left Alyx nothing but the little Santa Cruz bungalow. That and a series of pains when Alyx did anything — anything at all. Till, that is, her brother smashed open her front door, emitting a torrent of painful light and crashing street noise and slammed down a small box next to her antique computer. In a sympathetic whisper that sounded like a torrent of dishware pouring down a tin-shod mountainside, he had said, "If you won't go out, maybe at least you'll meet someone else."

The box sat for a long time, until one day after a slug of vodka it had seemed too much like the phantom boxes that Jo must have used to spirit herself out of Alyx's life. Anything at that point was better than boxes.

Boxes meant travel. Travel meant desertion. What she wanted was a house that she had to leave only when she absolutely had to.

There were two other messages waiting for her from Sasha. By the lengths of their setup, she judged one to be quite long and one surprisingly short.

I want a car. Never had one before. But when I think of us, I always see us driving somewhere. You with your copper hair and burst of a smile. Me, all clouds, rain, and small, warm fires. I always see us traveling, you and I. Not necessarily going anywhere specific — just going. A sense of movement. I know you like your house — you've told me enough times — but this is how I see us. Going. Not staying. Going.

I used to make out in cars — at first with boys and then with girls. Always liked that, being in such a tight spot but still with all those windows. Maybe I like to show off when I fuck — I don't know. I see us driving, maybe, somewhere hot and desert. Flat, hard lands with green cactus flashing by. I don't know how to drive, so why don't you? I'd sit on the seat next to you, letting the wind slap at my hair, buff my face. God, do I have an imagination or what? I close my eyes, and I can almost see it all. I'm wearing white pants — maybe jeans — and a simple tan shirt, probably a guy's. I have a bra on just because I don't like the ache my back gets without one. After we drive for a while, listening to stations pass each other on the radio, I start to get real excited...horny, you know. So I put a hand down between my legs, cup myself, and squeeze. I love to do that — especially when I have jeans on. I like the way it feels, to be trapped by that hot, tight material. Dipped in denim. I squeeze, and my thumb is right above my button. Squeeze and press, squeeze and press.

I hope by now you've noticed. I know you like to watch, and you know I love to show. Squeeze and press. I take your hand off the shift and put it on one of my breasts. I know it's awkward, but this is a fantasy, right? Squeeze my titty, Al, squeeze down hard. Yeah, I like it kneaded hard. I'd hope you'd be able to feel me get all stiff and hard under your fingers. I'd love for you to unbutton my shirt, get a tit out of my bra, and suck on it, but shame, shame, you've got to drive, watch the road.

Or try and watch the road. I'd take my shirt and bra off anyway (give the truckers a treat) and stretch out on the seat. Nice and warm...and hot and wet, right? I don't take off my pants because I like the way they feel around my butt and legs, but I do unbutton the fly. God, girl, I'm melting...there and here, right now sitting here, trying to think and type at the same time. It's getting kinda hard to do ;-)

Alyx sat down at her machine. She didn't know what to do. Sure, Sasha had reached out her tiny invisible hands before and coaxed many a heaving come from her, but this time it was different. It was hard to exactly define how different, but it was — Alyx felt the usual tug of her own hands down to her clit but also the hot stream of tears. She wanted to jerk off and cry.

Next to her machine was a window. Barely out of sight, a tarnished brass wind chime turned, suspended under the simple eaves: a mermaid. She was surrounded by thin steel bells, trapped behind polished bars. Caught by the boredom of the wind, she turned back and forth, chiming her frustration at being captured with a series of pleasant but nonsensical notes.

Jo had given Alyx the mermaid. She'd thought Jo had made all of herself vanish from the house (boxes), leaving nothing but the hurt somewhere before Alyx's breastbone. Jo had missed the mermaid.

Ah, but we must persevere — if just for the sake of love. Okay, for lust, girl. God knows I do lust after you, you know — got your picture up here right next to my machine, and I take your face (in my memory, natch — the picture would get wrinkly) to bed with me each night. Have I told you I like to lie in bed and fiddle myself and think of you? I do. The car trip is one of my favorites, because I remember you saying that you'd love to just "get out and go." Well, get out and go with me, sexy! Have I got to pulling over yet? Lemme scan back and — oh, my, how could I have forgotten that?

I mean, the whole idea of the thing is that. You'll see, you'll see. So there we are, tooling down the highway, me with my pants kinda shoved down and my hand...well, kinda shoved down, working myself up nice and slippery. You're still behind the wheel, eyes tearing themselves out of your head as you try to watch the road (somewhere boring) and me playing with myself (never boring). See, we're playing this game — or, rather, I am — it's called Make Her Pull Over. So the whole idea is to turn you on so much that you can't keep driving. And, boy, would I try and do that. I'd lick my fingers, tasting my own stuff. I'd circle and rub my special button till I wheeze and moan like a boy. I'd tickle my asshole too (I told you I like that) and see how many fingers I can hide inside myself. Have I told you this before? I can't remember, we've been doing this for so long. Well, if I have, then this is no surprise (ah, but you haven't seen me in action yet), and if you haven't, then it is — all of them! All of my sweet little fingers into my very hot and wet self. It's quite a party trick, definitely one that folks pay attention to. Quite hot too. Real hot, as a matter of fact. Right up there, fisting yourself is. Right up there.

Are you ready to pull over yet? Are you? Boy, you are made of some stern stuff, girl.

Alyx felt a familiar tightness and warmth spread through her. It was a good feeling, one of the things that at first she'd thought Jo had boxed up with the rest of her life and rushed into the U-Haul. Unlike the mermaid, she was grateful that it had been left behind.

Yet another ritual: She'd get up to *How are you today?* perk herself some coffee, feast on yet another breakfast treat (if she was feeling mighty slutty, it would be something from the tiny Korean grocer and not from the local health food store), and read Sasha's longer messages. If she'd spiced their correspondence, then Alyx would have something as she walked through her day — the images that Sasha wove so well spinning and cavorting in her back brain as she worked in her garden, went to the store, tried to paint again, or did any number of things that just seemed to fill up the space left behind by Jo. If it was a good one, if Sasha had been able to successfully work her way through the wires to Alyx's warm interior, then she might lie in bed that night with her trusty Hitachi. The next morning Sasha would get a *Very happy, thank you* to her usual *How are you today?*

Maybe it was the mermaid, crying in her pure tones of confinement — trapped too by Jo's departure. Maybe it was the dreams she'd been having — of the feeling of high-speed wind tearing through her hair and burning her eyes. A Route 66 kind of dream, a *Vanishing Point* kind of dream. The smell of baking asphalt, gasoline, hot vinyl, dust, and sun. The snapshot of the road ahead, unchanging despite the blurring speed, of a pyramid of stretched road — a perfect vertical of flashing meridian. In the dreams she always drove, always tore miles away between her tiny house, her rituals of waking, working, then sleeping (with maybe a masturbatory image of Sasha to make her smile for a moment, maybe two) — passing, with a flash of uncaring recognition, the figure of someone who might be Jo, hitchhiking.

Today the mermaid spun, maybe even angrily — turning her jail of bells into a flickering twirl of silver. Alyx listened beyond Sasha's electronic seduction as the chime spun and spun in a suddenly gusting wind.

She was hot. Mimicking Sasha in her story, she dropped a hand down to her own jean-covered crotch and squeezed, feeling the heat of herself through her thin hands and the wetness inside herself. Her nipples ached suddenly like two hot bites on her breasts, and she felt like crying out.

Don't you want to see me? Don't you want to drive on that road somewhere and watch me take my hand inside, hear the wetness of me, see the shininess of me? I want to show you.

Jo, hitchhiking on the side of the road.

Before she was even aware of it, Alyx lifted her sweatshirt and tugged at her right nipple, grunting ("Piglet," Jo had called her in the bedroom), and bent down in reaction so far, she had to open her eyes against the sensation (a rushing feeling, a shivering feeling) to make sure she wasn't going to brain herself on her monitor.

Alyx felt…different. Her safe routine flashed past like a billboard at 120 miles per hour — zap, gone. Nothing but the retreating metal or wood framework. *How shoddy!* she thought. Day in and day out, held together with nothing but its own momentum.

But passing it was scary too.

Part of her, the little Alyx, wanted to jump right back, turn around with a scream and squeal of tires, and go back along the same road. The garden still needed some serious work, she didn't have anything for breakfast tomorrow (Korean or healthy), and she was actually looking forward to finishing her current painting…but sitting there on her ergonomic chair (another gift from her brother), it all didn't seem to matter.

It's quite a sight, I can assure you. You know, when I first started to do this hand-vanishing act, I thought that everyone could do it, that every-

one out there had small hands and a hungry pussy like mine. Surprise! I did it for Socks (I told you about her), and she just about fell off the bed.

I want to show it to you. That's the only way, really — can't just sit here and describe it to you. It's one of those things that you just have to see for yourself. Let's take a drive, a little trip to God knows where, with a small lunch, some dams, and some gloves. Don't you want that?

Feet now up on the padding of her chair, legs as far apart as they could be, balancing on her heels, Alyx read and screamed *Yes!* in her mind. Rhythmically she squeezed and stroked her still jean-covered crotch: squeeze with her hand, stroke with her thumb, dance with her fingertips.

She knew where Sasha was leading; it was a ritual just as much as *How are you today?* was. They'd met on some computer board or other, when the wound from Jo was deep and bleeding heavily. It had started simply and grown, wandering from that small board to one of the huge on-line services. It had also grown between the two of them. Even though she'd never met or even ever talked to Sasha, she was bigger in Alyx's life than Jo ever was. But still Jo was a deep hurt, a fundamental unsteadiness. Sasha and Alyx were better than friends — but the hitchhiker on the side of the road kept them apart.

Sasha had been growing more and more bold about what she wanted. It was more than fair, Alyx knew. But reaching meant the chance of not being touched. That was still too hard to do.

Where are we? Oh, that's right — nowhere. We're two mean-ass bitches from hell, high on quim and pussy juice, screaming menstrual pain to the Goddess in the moon, tearing down a road to fucking nowhere. Sorry about that, A. Got a good whiff of my own steaming self and got me going there. Right — we're driving. You, you're driving, and I have my pants down around my ankles, my shirt off, my tits out, and my hand up my crotch.

Sometimes — and this is sure as hell one of those times — I love to stroke myself while I get my hand up there. Lucky for me I used to trade off hands (no cramp that way), so it isn't all that difficult to get myself off. Keep your eyes on the road now, girl. Don't go wrapping us around a phone pole or anything.

But I am quite a sight, I have to tell you — and I'm not bragging now. I love it, especially when I have both hands working on myself, the way my tits get all scrunched and pushed together. I got cleavage! Wish to hell I was just a bit bigger, though. Then I could catch a nipple in my mouth. Sad fact is, sexy, that I'm just a little too flat, and the best I can do is to breathe heavy or blow a little cool air on my nipples.

Won't you suck them for me while I get myself off? Don't worry about the road none — it's all a straight line from here.

Whatever spell Sasha had managed to weave, it definitely had caught Alyx. The rituals of her hiding fell away quickly, neatly, and she found herself — after a few quick fumblings of jeans, shirt, panties — naked and on her chair. The smell of herself was almost shocking. She'd always thought of herself as a neat girl, not one to really rut, but *damn,* she could smell herself strong and powerful. It normally would have distressed her to have such a strong reaction, but it was an unexpected day, a radical day, and the smell of her own cunt made her all the more feverish.

And wet — her lips were slick and puffy beneath her fingers. Radical, yes: Normally it took a quite a few strokes to get herself all wet and ready for a hard jill — but again Sasha had driven down her long and lonely road and revved her engine loud and hard. She was very wet, and, nestling like a marble in her folds, her clit was raging.

Please.

Reaching down, Alyx scooped a bit of her own juice and bathed her clit. A fire started down there and raced up to her chest, nipples (ache, ache), and mouth (she wanted desperately to kiss someone, anyone). Working herself a gentle froth from her own wetness, she stroked and rubbed her button, grunting (but not a pig, not today) and hissing as the come raced up her spine.

Watch me. Come with me, Alyx.

Sasha was dark and grinning in her mind. The wind buffets their faces, making crazy streamers out of their hair (Sasha black, Alyx dirty blond). She imagines and then sees, perfectly, Sasha with her legs up on the seat (just as hers were), one hand snaked into her cunt, the other butterfly-dancing on her clit. Sasha huffs and puffs and hisses and then screams (just as Alyx does, thinking of her).

Go with me, Alyx.

Panting, heaving, Alyx got up and cleaned herself off with a quick shower. Under the hot spray, her tiny house came smashing down around her again: the weight of the emptiness again confining her, trapping her (go to the market, try to paint, go to bed early). She came out of the shower shaking and shivering as if she were cold.

Two messages.

Call me, said the other and a phone number. San Francisco. An hour away.

She'd seen it before, of course, many times — as many times as Sasha had asked her to call, to pick up the phone, to reach out and start to move, to travel again. Go forward.

The speed of light was the next thought in Alyx's head. How long did it take the message to get to her from Sasha. How long would it take the call to go through. A second, a minute? How far away was the girl she knew, the woman she loved? A light-minute away? A world away? A call away?

Such a marvelous trip to start by just walking across her living room to the phone and dialing.

Might as well get started now.

Seduction.com
by Martha Equinox

Date: Wed, 15 May 1996 18:17:23
From: CecchiJ@pervert.com
To: ThompsCo@pervert.com
Subject: Networking for law offices conference

Hi, Corinne — Just wanted to touch base with you and tell you how much I enjoyed meeting you last weekend at the conference. It's possible I might be coming down to San Francisco in a few weeks, this time for pleasure instead of work, and I was wondering if you'd like to get together. My schedule isn't set yet, but the office owes me some time, and I might have a friend's place to stay in. I liked the little bit I saw of the city and of you. I'm interested in seeing more. Let me know.
Jean

Date: Wed, 15 May 1996 22:05:35
From: ThompsCo@pervert.com
To: CecchiJ@pervert.com
Subject: Your possible visit

Great idea, Jean — I liked what I saw of you too. I'm always interested in hot new play partners. I assume that's what you had in mind? Let's talk about this, see if we can make a good match. Usually I switch, but I haven't been bottoming lately. I know you're a top, but do you ever switch?

I am very interested in playing with you. I like smart, funny women, and you made legal billing problems a stand-up comedy act yet still sold me your company's products. Your hands are marvelous. I couldn't help wanting to feel them on my body or wanting to run my fingers through the dark waves of your hair. I like your body: tall, solid, and butch, that feeling of strength and

power coming from its pores. Did you notice that I kept touching you on your arm or shoulder to emphasize a point, brushing
against you as I walked around your display? You have very sexy
pheromones.

If we played together, what would you like to see me in?
Neck-to-ankle black latex? A rose-colored silk teddy with garter
belt and ankle-strap high heels? I think I'd like to see you in a
white button-down shirt and button-fly jeans. I'd like to unbutton
your shirt slowly, kneeling in front of you while you sit in a chair.
I'd pull your shirt out of your waistband, trying not to be too
clumsy. Do you wear undershirts? A bra? Well, since it's my fantasy, you'd have nothing on under your shirt, and I'd run my hands
from your shoulders to your waist, looking at your breasts and
skin. Your skin is such a beautiful rich olive, and I imagine it warm
and smooth under my hands, your nipples and areolas a rich
brown. I'd like to linger there, but I know too many butches who
don't give their breasts to a lover until long after they've given
everything else, so I'd just put my hands on either side of your
waist, sit back on my heels, and look in your eyes. Then if you
asked me what I liked, I'd tell you that I like dominance and submission play, points and sharps of all kinds, traditional beatings
with canes and whips, and creative sensory play. I like to fuck my
partners, and I like them to like fucking me.

What do you think ought to happen next?
Corinne

Date: Sat, 18 May 1996 09:35:07
From: CecchiJ@pervert.com
To: ThompsCo@pervert.com
Subject: My visit

I'm in my home office looking out the picture window toward
the water and the mountains. I live on Capitol Hill facing the
Olympic Peninsula and Puget Sound, and today is one of those
perfect days when the snow on top of the Olympics is so bright,
it hurts to look at it.

Sorry it took so long to get back to you. You took me a little by surprise, but I thought about our meeting and realized I shouldn't be. I'm always attracted to aggressive femmes. You girls are just so much fun to flip. Submission tastes sweeter coming from a woman who's used to being in control, and submission is what I want from you. I have a strong desire to see you on your knees naked, trying to find the words to beg me to touch you.

To answer your question, no, I don't switch, and don't think you're going to get my shirt off me so quickly. I'm a top, a sadist, not a masochist or a bottom. I don't like scenes where the bottom has a hidden agenda about flipping me. I've tried both sides, and I'm just not into pain or being told what to do. It always ends up feeling disrespectful and just pisses me off.

What did you mean "I haven't been bottoming lately"? All I want from you is masochism and submission. Think you can give me that? I'd guess your head is the hardest part of your body to give up, but maybe I can help you with that little problem.

When I think of you I see you restrained on a cross, facing me. I think I'll take the knife from my belt and cut your clothes off, then torture your tits for a while. Maybe I'll start with clothes-pins in rows across your pecs and upper tits and extend them up your inner arms. If you seem to be having a hard time, I'll slip my brass finger claws on, and with one hand holding your throat, I'll scratch the tender lower part of your breasts just deep enough to make bright red lines with a tiny bit of blood, then continue scratching down your belly, down your hips, into your inner thighs. If you object, I'll just tighten my hand on your throat until I'm sure I have your attention. Eventually, if you ask me sweetly enough, I'll take the clothespins off slowly, one at a time, enjoying the pattern of red bruises they leave behind. When they're all off I'll put the tit clamps on your nipples and slowly add weights, tightening the clamps a little more with each weight until your nipples are holding as much as they can carry.

By this time my hands will be sweating inside my gloves, so I'll put new ones on, lube up my hands, and begin to play with your lips. I'd like to take a long time exploring outside your cunt before I go inside you. I think I'll move to stand beside you so I can play with your ass with one hand and your cunt with another while I tongue your nipples where they stick out of the clamps. Soon I'll slide one finger into your ass, and depending on how you respond, I might slip one finger into your cunt. Just one. I'll hold your eyes with mine while I slowly unscrew the clamps with my other hand. I want to watch your eyes when I pull your swollen nipple into my mouth as I slowly fuck you.

I think by now you ought to be begging for more, begging to be fucked deeper and harder. I like to think about fucking you, taking a long time to fill you up so that when I do, you're so hot that you burn my hand.

Maybe I'd take you down and put you over my knee so I could spank and beat your ass and back. I think that might be so pretty, I'd have to put my fist in your cunt again. I like the thought of holding you across my lap while I fuck you blind.

Let me know just what you're prepared to give up for me. I'm burned out on being some woman's marvelous fuck machine, so I want to make sure that you're very clear about how much I'll want from you, and I want you to give it up to me with grace and style. I'm very attracted to you, but if I'm going to go all the way down there to do you, I want to know that I can have whatever I want. Jean

Date: Sun, 19 May 1996 21:13:47
From: ThompsCo@pervert.com
To: CecchiJ@pervert.com
Subject: ??scene??

I keep reading your E-mail, and each time it stops my breath and heats my cunt. I really like tit play. How did you know? I haven't gone under, gone into my deep masochism, in a long time, but the scene you described reminds me why I'm a masochist. It's been a long time since I've met a woman who makes me feel transparent and reminds me how hungry I am. I want this more than ever, but I don't know if I can get there. I'm having a lot of trouble with some aspects of bottoming right now. I don't think I can be submissive — just the thought of begging irritates me.

I've thought about this all weekend. I'm not being any good at giving up control lately, even though I really want to be able to give it up for you. My submissive side is on some sort of a sabbatical. Your fantasy about doing me made me weak in the knees, but you're right: The hardest part for me to release is my head. There've been some losses in my life recently, and death always pisses me off, you know? Maybe that's why my dominant side is so strong now. It's also probably why my masochistic side is so hungry.

We could have fun here if we can figure out a way to make this work. I have the perfect play space with my own (small) dungeon where we can make noise and be pretty out there. Do you know what an earthquake cottage is? After the '06 earthquake, a few hundred were built at the back of residential lots for families to live in while their homes were being rebuilt, and I've got one. It's completely private, at the back of a huge yard, and partially screened by bushes and trees. Everything around me is grass, flowers, trees, bushes, or the fences of the neighbors behind and beside. The smaller bedroom is my dungeon, and I just happen to have a cross that might fit your fantasy.

So here's what I'm thinking. I know you're a sadist, and that's what I want from you. I know I'm a masochist, and that's what I want to give you. It's just the dominance and submission part that I'm all fucked up about now, so I want to switch those roles. I am not talking about topping from the bottom but about dominant masochism and submissive sadism. I've done some of this kind of play, and I like it a lot; it lets both players go deeper into sadist/masochist play than they might otherwise get to go. The masochist has control over what kind of pain she gets, and the sadist is free to be extremely cruel without having to worry about pleasing the masochist or how close she is to the masochist's limits.

Please think about this. I am not talking about flipping you. There is no hidden agenda here, no expectation that you'll suddenly become a masochist, and no disrespect of you as a sadist. Just because I can't be submissive doesn't mean I stop being a masochist, and starting off in control lets me go there. Once I get really high, the tension of balancing dominance and masochism becomes unbearable, and I fall deeper into one side or the other. With a sadist who is also a true submissive, the scene can end with

my beating her or fucking her. With a sadist who is really dominant, the scene ends with my giving up everything to the sadist,
including my dominance.

I don't think I can get to my masochism without starting off
in control. I guess the question is, Can you let go of dominance?
Can I get you wet with the thought of torturing me, hurting me,
doing everything you want to me with no responsibility for
whether I like it? Can I make you hot by telling you I will give you
my body and I will lay out the toys I want you to use on my body
and I will move under your hands like no one ever has because
your sadism and my masochism will be perfectly matched? The
way it would work might look something like this:

We spend the first night fucking, rough trade, nasty and hard,
getting to know each other's rhythms in that sweaty, intimate way.
Waking up, we shower together, teasing and laughing but nothing
serious. We eat, get dressed, and go for a walk, shopping for chocolate and fresh fruit. We talk about roles and what turns us on and
anything else we want to talk about.

When we get back home, we start to move into the scene. In
the bedroom I take my clothes off for you, but you can't touch. I
tell you to dress me and hand you one piece of clothing after
another. I stroke your head and run my hands casually over your
body but pull your head back by the hair when you try to take my
nipples in your mouth. When my stockings are straight and my
spike heels are on, we walk down the hall to the dungeon. While
I pull a tall stool over to the cross and sit down, you cross the room
to the sound system and set up the music. My toys are hanging on
hooks on the walls, and we've added yours to the mix. I tell you
to gather specific toys and put them close to the cross — a few
whips, a nightstick and some canes, some scratchers and scrapers,
and the case of blood-sports toys.

I tell you which whips are okay to start with and that I want
you to begin on my back but to stay away from my ass for now.
As I move to the cross, I turn my head away while you weigh the
different choices, letting the falls drape over your forearm. I want
to be surprised. I feel your palm flat on my back, pushing me gently against the cross, and I reach up to grab the chains over my
head. For a moment, when your hand leaves my back, everything

stops, waiting, then I hear the air rushing toward me. The soft, heavy weight of deerskin smacks against me, and heat suddenly blooms in my cunt and across my shoulder blades. As I fall into my masochism, you watch me begin to move and breathe with each stroke, and you change to a sharper, heavier toy. I look at you over my shoulder and see your eyes hot on me as we both start to sweat. I tell you to use the bull-hide slapper and arch up, crying with each stroke. Do you feel it, how much I like what you're doing? I want you to feel it in every part of your body.

When I'm ready for you to work on my ass, I stop you, grab your hair or throat, and kiss you, maybe slap your face or take your shirt off and pinch you, then show you the next toys to use on me. By now I'm panting, and my voice is a little hoarse. I lift up the back of my skirt and tuck it into the waistband so my ass is naked for you. If you make a mistake, I correct you. When I'm so hot that I can't speak, you'll still know what I want because I'll show you exactly what to do.

When the pressure of balancing masochism and dominance is too much for me to bear, maybe your dominant side will pull out my submission, and you'll take me further down than I've ever gone. Maybe you'll be so hot in your submission that I'll throw you down and fuck you till you scream. Maybe I'll let you fuck me, maybe I'll cry and beg for you to fuck me. You never know how it'll turn out.

Think about it and dream about me.

Corinne

Date: Thurs, 23 May 1996 19:03:27
From: ThompsCo@pervert.com
To: CecchiJ@pervert.com
Subject: ??scene??

I'm nervous that I haven't heard from you. If you're absolutely not interested, let me know, and maybe we can try something else. I'd hate to lose touch completely.

Corinne

Date: Fri, 24 May 1996 12:22:55
From: CecchiJ@Lawware.com
To: ThompsCo@pervert.com
Subject: Possible scene

Sorry I didn't get back to you, but you gave me a lot to think about. I've had a lot of strong reactions to the scene you described, so many that I don't know what I think. Give me a couple of days, and I promise I'll get back to you.
Jean

Date: Sun, 2 June 1996 08:43:48
From: CecchiJ@pervert.com
To: ThompsCo@pervert.com
Subject: Possible scene

All right, I think I know what I want to say — or at least some of what I want to say. I've never done anything like the scene you described. I've never even heard of anything like that, and at first it really pissed me off. I mean, I told you I don't switch. Are you guessing I can be flipped, or has someone been dissing me?

Switching has usually been a disaster. I've never been able to be submissive, but last week I realized that might be because I'm not masochistic at all, and submission has always meant masochism in the scenes I've done or watched. The possibility of being sadistic and submissive at the same time, without having to pretend to be a masochist, is wild.

I haven't been able to get you and your fantasy out of my mind. I keep wanting to see you panting with pain and lust and know I did that to you — no, know that you used me to do that to yourself. I don't know how to do this. I want to be deeply sadistic to you, I want to see your eyes dilate with desire and endorphins. I want you to need me, my cruelty and my passion, to get to your hottest place, and at the same time I want to be controlled by you. I don't think I know how to be submissive, but the thought of being told exactly how to hurt you, knowing I'm doing it exactly right, turns me on. I've never liked being slapped in the face, but I keep waking up in the middle of the night because in my dreams you walk up to me and slap my face and I come. Sadism is usually more head than cunt for me, but this stuff is hitting me in a really sexual place, and that makes me very nervous.

Okay, okay, back up. Here's the practical stuff. What if I can't be submissive? What kind of dominant are you? I don't do humiliation, no contempt or bullying. That shit just pisses me off, and if I get pissed off, I will definitely *not* be submissive. And if I'm doing something, maybe whipping or caning, and you tell me I'm doing it wrong, I'm sure I'll get pissed off.

I don't know what to say anymore. Write me.

Jean

Date: Mon, 3 June 1996 20:33:07
From: ThompsCo@pervert.com
To: CecchiJ@pervert.com
Subject: Come here soon

I couldn't get to my E-mail last night until it was too late to write back, which meant I had to wait all day till I got home from work. It drove me crazy.

I like your dreams. I'd love to find out if slapping you at the right time can make you come. In fact, I can feel my cunt rise up just thinking about it.

I can tell that what I'm suggesting is working your nerves, but I like it that part of you is very excited by this. If it helps, no, I'm not into humiliation. I'm not into making you do something that offends you. What I want very much is to be masochistic for you in the only way I can right now. I want your sadism, and I want you, the flavor of you, the lust of you. I want to cry out in your hands. If you can give me your skillful cruelty, I can give you my pain and desire. If you can let go this amount of control, I can open to you physically and sexually in a way that no one else ever has. I need a sadist who's confident enough to let go. I'm dependent on you for this. My lust and need have your name on them.

I don't want to own you or control anything about you out-side of scene. I don't want a girlfriend or a best friend. I don't care what you call me. I'll call you Jean, unless you want me to call you something else that makes it easier for you. Do you want refer-ences? How can I entice you, convince you? I don't know what else to say except that I want you, and, yes, this is very sexual for me too.

I think you should come here soon. I was attracted to you when we first met and have only begun to want you more over the last few weeks. And of course I've checked you out, but no one has dissed you. Everything I've heard about you in scene and everything you've said to me in these letters makes me want to do this with you.

I can clear any weekend this month and take a Monday off work if I have some notice. You should have your own housing so we can have space if we need it, even though you might end up here the whole time. Gay pride is the 30th, if you're into showing off bruises. I know I'm just babbling, but as much as you can't get me out of your mind, I can't get you out of mine.

I keep thinking about you torturing my tits. I think about watching your face as you draw a razor blade across the top of my left breast toward the nipple, glance up at me, then keep cutting slowly and deliberately in a star-burst pattern around my whole breast. Your eyes are dilated and predatory, and the blood smell flares your nostrils. If one of the cuts stops bleeding, you gently spread the cut until it beads up, dark black-red in the light. I pant, and you press your other hand against my sternum to even out my breath, then cup the weight of my breast in your hand as you make another cut. The sounds coming out of my throat echo in yours. You bend to lick my breast, but I grab your hair and hold your head back, then reach to kiss you deeply and push my body into yours. My breast stings and bleeds more, and when I pull back, one side of your white shirt has lines and blotches of my blood in a circle. I hold you away from me with one hand and reach for the alcohol and matches with the other, then hand them to you. Slowly leaning back on the cross, arms up, I take a deep breath before I nod to you. You place a clean white towel across one of your shoulders, then dribble alcohol across the top of my breast.

Staring into my eyes, you light the match, wait for me to drop my head back, then drop it onto me. As the alcohol burns blue and my skin turns red, you press the clean towel against me, then pull me to you and lick the tears off my face.

I really think you should come here soon.

Corinne

Date: Mon, 3 June 1996 21:51:19
From: CecchiJ@pervert.com
To: ThompsCo@pervert.com
Subject: Lust and lubricity

I'm arriving SFO this Friday 6/7 at 9:12 P.M. on American and return to SeaTac Tuesday 6/11 at 7:45 A.M. I've got a car reserved, so don't come to the airport, I'll come to you. I decided I wanted to drive if we go anyplace. I'll call you Thursday night to discuss what toys to bring and for the thrill of hearing your voice. I'll pack lots of white shirts.

Jean

Pony Tale
by Shelly Rafferty

Dundee, DeMarco, and Hyde were clustered near the back of the eight-rider contingent. Ahead of them Murphy, in her red baseball cap, whipped up her pony to a lively trot and glanced back over her shoulder. "Pick it up, ladies," she encouraged. "We've got to make Acadia River before dark."

Jacziniak, just behind Murphy, rolled her eyes. "My ass is killing me," she muttered. "Why don't we stop now? I think my horse needs a break."

Murphy ignored her.

Dundee urged her companions to keep pace, busting DeMarco's bay in the hindquarters with her switch. She herself hung back a little.

The going had been hard.

In six days they had covered nearly 150 miles. The distance hadn't really been that difficult, but the discipline, the vigilance, and the endless conversation that had been required of her and Murphy had left them both exhausted.

But you couldn't let on. God forbid any of the women should think that you weren't as tough as they were.

And the trek had tested some mettle: On the second night temperatures had swung down to freezing. The next morning the women grumbled about their early start. Ojulu, from Central Africa, was terrorized by the cold and fought with Murphy about even crawling out of her sleeping bag.

Westover suggested to the others that they simply leave Ojulu behind. Gloves and saddles and boots and bags came to life as everyone prepared to break camp. Finally recognizing that she might remain the only worshiper in the cathedral of forest, Ojulu complainingly and slowly did her part. Putting on her boots, she'd started to cry and shiver with the cold; Jacziniak told her to shut up. Misha Ramsey told Jacziniak to shut up. Misha gave Ojulu her sweater.

Dundee and Murphy knew better than to interfere.

Now just one more day. Tomorrow the paddy wagon would meet them in North Bailey for transport back to Baedeker Bay Provincial Prison; horse trailers would be sent to collect their steady mounts. Most of the women — convicted of big-city crimes in places like Toronto, Vancouver, and Montreal — would never ride a horse again.

And that was regrettable, thought Dundee. You put women like these into the wilderness, and suddenly you knew who was going to make it on the outside. It was clear which ones understood that the goal wasn't in the *getting there* but in the *going*.

And to be fair, the trip had other, more visceral perks. Bathing in the river. Women in jeans. Rhythmic, shifting asses in leather saddles. In all, beautiful scenery.

Speaking of which, Dundee dug in a bit and caught up to DeMarco.

"You're on dinner detail tonight, aren't you?"

DeMarco shifted in her creaky saddle. Her muscular legs bent tightly down to the stirrups. "Right. A little beans and rice, I think." She dropped her reins into her left hand, fingered the rear pocket of her dusty dungarees, and pulled out the dinner schedule. "With Ojulu. I hope she's a better cook than me."

"You're in luck. She was in refugee camp in Kenya for six years, so the rice won't be much of a challenge. On a good day she might have had beans." The trail was angling up now through a sparse field. Far across the slow descent of meadow and hardwood forest, an elbow of the Acadia River was barely visible. Dundee trailed a hand along the front of her uniform jacket and buttoned up another notch. "You didn't cook for your son?"

DeMarco gave Dundee a sidelong glance, her dark eyes full of restrained anger. "Mickey D did most of the cooking. I was good at Froot Loops. Oreos. Sometimes I would remember to buy bananas or oranges."

Dundee blew her off. DeMarco's anger wasn't aimed at her but at a fate that had not been kind or fair or forgiving. *Don't take it personally,* she said to herself. Besides, DeMarco was doing well. Even if the only reason she spoke was a nod to Dundee's authority. "Well, cooking's not everybody's thing."

"Is it yours?"

DeMarco wasn't always trying to be a smartmouth, reasoned Dundee. She shouldered her attitude like a restless toddler too tired to control. Cocksure delivery, a stare that never shuddered, always a hint of spittle behind the perfectly straight teeth.

"I can't even flap a jack," smiled Dundee.

"I'm sure you've got some hidden talent," challenged DeMarco.

Dundee let her hand settle on the pistol in her hip holster. "It's hardly hidden."

"So you've got a gun. Possession doesn't qualify as a talent, CO." The use of her title — uttered in DeMarco's gravelly, ingratiating tone, *see-oh* — reminded Dundee of the line between them.

"Let's hope I never have to impress you then." DeMarco didn't need to know about her silver medal from the Correctional Officers' Games. Only Kenny Conway, a sergeant from Banff, had been able to outshoot her. Dundee slowly extracted her Ray-Bans from her jacket pocket and snapped them open. "Catch up to the others, Maria."

No doubt about it, Maria DeMarco was bad news.

On the other hand, the fact that Maria DeMarco — in addition to being bad news — was also a dyke was not lost on Dundee. Ever since DeMarco had signed up for shock incarceration camp, Dundee had made it a point to avoid her, to assign her to Murphy's teams, to forestall even the smallest gesture that might hint how incredibly attractive she found the former drug dealer. In a way Dundee even admired her: DeMarco's single-minded determination to get out of jail, regain custody of her son, and put her life on the right road had been apparent from the day she first arrived from detox.

Expressing any interest, however, was out of the question. It was unethical. It could get her fired.

Still, it hadn't been beyond Dundee's imaginative powers to see herself — in some other life — shuddering in some wildly sexual relationship with a woman like DeMarco. It had been a long time. Her last lover, Allie, had been a good woman but entirely too safe, too domestic. Friends had nonetheless envied Dundee's apparent settledness, blithely unaware of Dundee's growing boredom with the traps of monogamy, vacations in August, and Saturday-morning sex.

Dundee's eventual promiscuity had been purposeful: Allie left her, and Dundee was glad it was over.

Her friends called it self-sabotage, but Dundee knew better. She was free.

Around sunset, they set up camp.

Dundee watched Maria give the beans a stir. In the firelight DeMarco cut a handsome profile. Her short near-black hair lifted brightly off her serious brow; a square chin and long neck lent a certain elegance to the expression of unforced pleasure that often showed in her face. And although she laughed easily, Dundee knew, DeMarco could also be deeply contemplative and remote, separate from her peers, aware of her otherness. In those times the whole of Maria DeMarco softened, and her eyes became depthless black pools, and her mouth — moist and open with an unspoken thought dancing on her tongue — seemed a resentful invitation.

"You're off on some other planet, partner."

"Jesus, Murphy. You scared me."

"The local wildlife is dangerous, you know." Murphy raised an eyebrow and nodded in the direction of the cooks. She had a small clipboard in her right hand and knelt in the dirt next to Dundee. "But I must agree, she is a sweet piece of the street." DeMarco was standing now, stripping off her prison-issue jacket. The sleeves of her work shirt were turned up with a precise, even cuff.

"But she's strictly off-limits," said Dundee. Mechanically she took the small clipboard from Murphy and began to turn the pages. Progress notes for each prisoner.

"Off-limits for you or for me?"

"Well, your wife might have something to say about it..."

"Oh, yeah, right," said Murphy as if she had suddenly remembered her partner of the past ten years. She shrugged and smiled. "I guess it's your call then."

The teasing between them was old and comfortable. For years they had harmlessly joked about the good fortune that had befallen them: What could be better for lesbians than to work in a women's prison? Certainly the life wasn't exactly full of the B-movie clichés, but the opportunistic lesbianism in which most inmates engaged was strangely gratifying to both of their voyeuristic inclinations.

But as for relationships, fraternizing with prisoners was absolutely taboo. That hadn't ever been much of a problem. For one thing Murphy had been with Christy since the dawn of man and was more faithful than a good compass to true north. And for her part Dundee had simply made it a practice to never mix business with pleasure.

For a moment they both stared after DeMarco, who now had lowered her head and was commiserating with Ojulu over the bean pot. As if she knew she was being watched, she glanced briefly in the direction of her guards. Her expression was mildly unsettling. Dundee felt herself inhale deeply. Damn, DeMarco was sexy.

"What time do you figure for our ride out tomorrow?"

Murphy's question snapped Dundee back to the moment. She scanned the horizon quickly. A dusky gray-yellow mixed with the faintest red. Dundee frowned. "If it's raining, it'll be a slow trot." She quickly initialed the reports and handed the clipboard back to her subordinate. "Let's shoot for 5. You want the first watch?"

"Sure," said Murphy tiredly. "What the hell."

At 1:45 in the morning, thunder booms rustled Dundee from a drowsy repose. Why hadn't Murphy come to get her? She checked her watch and reluctantly slid out of her sleeping bag.

The steady drizzle wasn't heavy, but Dundee found her boots anyway and slunk her feet into them, ignoring the laces. She staggered from her tent and stretched, then plodded out to the fire. Slumped unnaturally under cover of a thin tarp stretched between two saplings, Murphy had dozed off.

Dundee couldn't help smiling.

They were all exhausted, that was the thing. And to where would the prisoners escape, anyway? Hell, these women couldn't tell a grizzly bear from a groundhog. Nobody was going to make a run for it in this wilderness.

Dundee stepped closer and debated about waking Murphy.

"Leave her there, CO."

DeMarco slowly emerged from the shadow. In the crook of her arm was Murphy's rifle. Instinctively Dundee reached for her pistol. Shit, she had left it in the tent.

"Surprise."

"Maria." Dundee's tone was measured. Quickly she scanned her memory for the proper procedure. Stay calm. Get her talking. Agree with what she says. Don't provoke her. "What are you doing?"

"Relax, Dundee. I'm not going to shoot you." Still, she shifted the stock of the rifle to a more or less level position.

"Give me the gun then."

"Can't do that, CO."

"Why not?"

"Because then you won't tell me what I want to know."

"Yes, I will."

"No, you won't." DeMarco gestured with the rifle. "Leave Murphy here. Come on."

"Where are we going?"

"Just down the shore a little. I don't want to wake the others."

"I could just start yelling right now."

"But you won't."

"What makes you say that?"

"Because you want to know about me too."

At the edge of the river, they plodded along in silence for a quarter mile or more. Large boulders, flattened by a thousand years of current, protruded into the swiftly moving water.

"Stop here," said DeMarco. She pointed abruptly with the gun. "Take off your shoes and throw them over there."

Dundee shook off her boots easily. "What do you want?" Strangely, she didn't feel frightened. The boots thudded in the sharp gravel several feet away.

"I want the same thing you do."

Dundee indulged her.

"You've been looking at me."

"Put the gun down, Maria."

"I will. But answer my question first."

Dundee frowned. "Was there a question?"

"Don't be coy." Maria stepped closer. "Now turn around." The muzzle of the shotgun slipped fluidly over Dundee's shoulder. It nuzzled the space under her ear. "You've been looking at me," DeMarco repeated. "Haven't you?"

"Yeah." Dundee swallowed. The shotgun barrel was so cool against her neck. "You are a dyke, aren't you?"

"You know I am."

"But you've stayed away from the other women."

"So?"

"We generally look the other way. I've just been surprised that you haven't pursued — "

"That would assume I was interested." The rifle muzzle slid down the outside of Dundee's arm. "The women here want something for now. As soon as they get out, they run back to their straight little lives and try to forget whatever they did in prison to feel human." She snapped the rifle upright suddenly. "I was human when I got here."

"What do you want from me?"

"You started this thing."

Dundee knew what she meant. "Well, you can forget it. I'm not coming after you."

"Of course you're not. You'd like to, but you can't allow it. Things would be different if you knew where this was going."

DeMarco came around to face Dundee and stared. Gently she stepped backward and lay the rifle in the slippery gravel.

"Where is it going?"

"You really want to know, don't you?"

"You've only eight more weeks, Maria. Why throw it all — "

Suddenly DeMarco was at Dundee's throat, her mouth a hungry fox, exhaling little bites even as she fiercely clenched at Dundee's jaw and neck with her hands. "Coercion, that's the excuse you need," her voice rasped.

Dundee wriggled a hand between the two of them and grasped the front of DeMarco's shirt. She pushed her away hard but didn't let go of her.

Coercion. DeMarco was right. She couldn't just have Maria because of her own authority. Her moral thermometer, no matter how occasionally shaky, clearly had a bursting point in matters of force. But she hadn't forced this situation. Maria had the gun, even if she did put it down.

This was it: Her opportunity to object.

But she couldn't. Right here, right now: a beautiful woman gasping, challenging, waiting in the grip of her fist.

"No witnesses," whispered DeMarco. "Come on. Kiss me."

Their mouths were not tentative but deliberate and quick. Dundee did not say anything as Maria tore open her shirt and took her nipple in her teeth. She hadn't expected such aggressiveness. She surrendered any thought of taking control.

And there was great relief in that.

DeMarco pushed her to the gravel and straddled her, chewed her lips and searched her mouth with a tongue that could not speak. Her hands were rough on her breasts, her mouth voracious and keen to be full.

They'd never be caught, that was for sure.

It wasn't something they would talk about. For a fleeting instant, as Dundee felt DeMarco's hand push inside her jeans, she wondered if Maria harbored illusions about what their encounter might mean. In the morning there would be no going back. There was only what lay ahead.

DeMarco found her saturated with wet. Her pulsing attack was unforgiving, her hand a steady drummer, her knee behind it keeping time.

Was this going somewhere? After all, wasn't this what Dundee wanted: an unfettered, dissembled opportunity to not be obligated? DeMarco's hand pushed deeper, faster. This was fucking, pure and simple. Nothing symbolic about it.

Oh, God. If only for a moment, it felt good to be imprisoned again. Maybe for once, it wasn't about *the going*. It was about *getting there*.

Dundee lifted up, let go, and overhead oriented with the stars.

Her Lady's Handkerchief
by Veronica Holtz

It was but a moment ago in time, in the space of a slash of the sword, when the European earth and its peoples lived under their quarreling monarchies. In the small realm of Talais, situated between the northeastern French territories and the Swiss cantons, a young queen was spared the fate of her husband by the swift sword of a woman during an attempted assassination. In reward for the woman's trustworthiness and bravery, Queen Sophia pronounced a royal edict — the formation of a legion of female warriors to dedicate their lives to the protection and bidding of their sovereign. In the ensuing years gallant warriors, unparalleled in their valor and loyalty to their queen, came from every corner of Europe and beyond to find acceptance in the guards — the Valiers.

The crowded Rue des Fourier parted in respect for one of the queen's elite guards. In full uniform a lean woman of seven and twenty stepped her steed lively down the street, her rapier hanging chivalrously at her side.

The young and gangly Simone ran to greet her. "Elan! Elan! You had audience with the queen?"

"Yes." Elan laughed at the stripling of a guard, who had not yet had the privilege of being in the presence of her sovereign.

"And did you kiss her majesty's hand?"

"Her hand was as soft and sweet as the finest cambric," the handsome Valier replied, knowing that Simone was in search of any tidbit describing the exquisite sensations that accompanied such an encounter. Elan glanced around the street. "Where is Jiuffe? Her majesty sends us to duty."

Down the passageway they saw the half-clothed Valier sprinting through the crowd with one boot hardly attached to her foot. Her unbuttoned ruffled shirt waved behind in her wake, leaving her breast guard in full view. Like a drunken juggler, she held her scabbard in one hand while stuffing her shirt furiously into her pants with the other. The hearty Valier ducked behind Elan and let out a muttered curse.

The red-faced Count de Aubergine had spotted her. Running as fast as his portly figure would allow, the nobleman pointed his sword wildly toward the culprit. "You there! You shall pay for your insolence!"

Elan cut off the count's attack. "Sir, what is your concern?" she asked courteously.

He puffed his cheeks out in comical fury. "I found this scoundrel ducking out of the bedchambers of my wife, and I demand justice for her actions."

"Sir, I commend your loyalty to your wife, but surely you are mistaken," Elan appealed to his civility.

"There is no mistake. This wretch was naked."

Jiuffe belted her scabbard and stepped forward with a concerned look. "Dear count, your wife was suffering from melancholia. And I, well-versed in the Eastern art of the medicines, undertook to cure her ailment. Upon examination I found her overcome with a high and volatile temperature. And as she was unfamiliar with my technique, I was compelled to remove my own attire to quell her fears. I assure you, she was well-attended, and you will find her quite recovered."

The old count stood in confusion, his thoughts tottering between revenge and indebtedness. The tale might have been well-taken by him but for two officers of the influential Minister de Limberger's army standing nearby. Valiers caused enormous jealousy among the regent's men, who sought every opportunity to challenge the female warriors.

"I curse the wretches who call themselves Valiers. They plague the morals of every man's wife," challenged one soldier, looking squarely at Elan.

"So, Jaros, has your wound mended since our last meeting?" Elan glanced amusingly at his twirl of a mustache.

"Quite."

"Good. Then prepare yourself for a fresh cut."

Elan and Jaros drew their rapiers and stepped *en garde*. Simone crossed swords with Jaros's companion. And the count challenged Jiuffe.

For all of his fervor, the count was intimately more acquainted with feasts and debauchery than with swordplay. Having passed up several opportunities to pink the man, Jiuffe nicked him nicely on the buttocks, though his swinelike squeal convinced her to regret her generosity.

"You are lucky I did not charge your wife for my services," she yelled, chasing him half a block down the street.

Elan clashed her sword with a defiant Jaros, testing his mettle with several dogged passes. Finally, having lured the weasel into a position of defense, she struck his sword downward. With a flourish of her wrist, she cleanly swiped the arch of his mustache, leaving a thin line of blood where one side of his carefully combed lip hair had been. Aghast, he thrashed his fingers against the burn, vainly in search of half his facial ornament.

In keeping with the finest etiquette, Elan saluted her defeated foe with a sympathetic smile. "My apologies, Jaros. Had my sword been properly canted, I would have carved your mustache in a more shapely fashion."

Simone was dancing frantically with the regent's older guard. As he stepped a few paces backward, Elan casually put a foot into his path, tripping him to the ground. In an instant three sword points hovered over him, and he conceded.

"Until next time, gentlemen." The three Valiers sheathed their swords and bid a triumphant good-bye, retiring to Elan's nearby lodgings.

"I pray it was worth your while?" Elan commented to Jiuffe.

Jiuffe lifted the Countess de Aubergine's handkerchief out of her pocket and sniffed it, satisfied that it held the most valiant reason to lose one's life.

Simone looked in awe upon Jiuffe's good fortune. The ladies of the court had been known to bestow lavish gifts of gold and jewels upon Valiers in their favor. But when a lady handed a Valier her personal handkerchief, it was proof of her loyal and lasting devotion.

"Ah," Simone groaned. "Someday I shall please a lady so that I may carry her handkerchief with me."

"And so you soon shall," declared Elan, whose name had often been whispered in connection with the most amorous intrigues of the court.

"Soon," Simone repeated impatiently. "I am a Valier and — "

Jiuffe laughed heartily. "Dear Simone, certain particulars cannot be taught. One is either born with the disposition to please a lady or not."

"And how am I to do that when I so seldom meet one?" Simone countered.

"You shall meet the finest of ladies in Valgras tomorrow," answered Elan as she changed into her traveling clothes. "The queen has commanded us to give the Lady Aure safe escort to the lands of the Marquis Lubene, her future husband."

Jiuffe repocketed the countess's handkerchief, the thought of her latest conquest discarded with the mention of the lady. "They say she is beautiful and of a restless nature."

"And of the highest virtue," said Simone, already defending the lady against Jiuffe's insinuations.

"No matter," imposed Elan. "She is the queen's cousin, and as Valiers we are charged to behave in a manner befitting her majesty's trust in us."

"On my oath to the queen," pledged Simone as if she were already sacrificing a great love.

"I have never behaved otherwise," commented Jiuffe nonchalantly.

"Then, come, Valiers," commanded Elan, brushing back her collar-length hair. "We will reach the inn this afternoon and have a night's rest before meeting her ladyship."

As the three Valiers arrived at the respectable inn of the Golden Fawn, Elan was preoccupied with her rapier's lack of balance. Such occurrences were commonplace when one was drawn into so many unnecessary duels. A simple reckoning of the weight would bring her sword back into excellence. The landlord informed her that the nearby blacksmith could repair her sword. And to Elan's good fortune, the weldsman understood her explicit wishes, as he himself had been in service to the queen many years before.

The sun had started to set when Elan returned to the inn. Exhausted, she walked up the back stairs to her quarters, the promise of good food and a warm bath in her head. She opened the door to the abrupt gasp of a young woman ducking under the quilts of the bed.

Elan threw her cloak and scabbard on the table. "If you are sent here by Jiuffe, I do not require company tonight. You may take your leave."

The woman, clothed only in a nightshirt, pulled her head indignantly above the covers. "Valier, do you mock me?"

"Most certainly not." Elan observed her thick-flowing brown hair and eyes that were expressive even in the dim light of the room. Not wishing the woman to take offense, she said, "Your beauty speaks like angels, and your eyes show the mischief you are capable of." She grabbed a handful of louis d'or from her pocket and offered them with outstretched hand. "Here. For your trouble."

To Elan's dismay the woman did not move to take them. She had possession of the most comfortable bed in the inn. And she looked as though she had every intention of laying claim to the running bath in the adjoining chambers as well.

Agitated by her impudence, Elan prompted, "What more do you require?"

The woman crooked an eyebrow and retorted, "My price is much higher than you could hope to imagine, Valier."

The blood rushed to Elan's face in hostile perplexity. She added a few coins to her palm, allowing each to clang against the other as she measured her temper.

Simone entered from the bath chambers looking both like an agreeable lackey and an anxious lover smitten with her first brush with nobility. "Your bath is prepared, Lady Aure."

Elan turned a deep crimson as she sunk to one knee. "Your ladyship." She sought to recover herself by displaying a humble stance. But the proof of her indiscretion lay in her palm. One hundred louis d'or jingled embarrassingly.

Lady Aure made a most amused face. "We were favored by the weather and arrived earlier than expected. I, being quite spent by my travels, was not aware that any further services would be required of me this evening."

Elan immediately replaced the coins in her pocket. "I beg your forgiveness, my lady."

Lady Aure eyed the Valier for a moment, then said, "I am indebted to the Valier who so graciously gave up her room and bath for me."

"It is my honor, your ladyship," Elan quickly replied. " We will take our leave." Seeing that Simone had no intention of moving, Elan slapped her into a bowed position, and the two Valiers retreated out the door.

"Deuce!" Elan cursed harshly on the landing. "Why did you not tell me her ladyship had arrived?"

"Jiuffe was waiting for you in the tavern," Simone explained. "And since Lady Aure is staying without servants, I volunteered to prepare her bath." Simone reddened with pride at her accomplishment.

"She travels without her own servants?" a puzzled Elan asked.

"She arrived with at least a dozen but sent them ahead."

"Ridiculous!" Elan grabbed a bottle of wine from the kitchen and retired to the stables, mumbling comparisons of her innocent mistake of identity with the audacity of a noblewoman to travel without servants. She finally formed a decent bed of hay and plopped herself down, when she saw Jiuffe stride across the barn, barely containing a haughty laugh.

"Such an impression you have made on her ladyship!"

"I see you wasted no time in coming to taunt me about it," Elan sneered back at her.

Jiuffe stretched out against the stable wall and gave a condescending snort. "My dear Elan, if we are not disgraced and turned from our commissions, we will surely be the new jest of the court. In any case you will be the cause of our misfortune." She motioned for the bottle of wine.

"If you are quite finished…" Elan began intolerantly.

"Unfortunately, dear friend, you have the enjoyment of my person tonight. As fortune would have it, I was dislodged from my room also. Her ladyship is accompanied by Madame de Lourette: a generous woman in her own right. She gifted me with this cushion so I would not want for comfort." Jiuffe leaned back against an elegant satin pillow, joyfully anticipating a situation rife with amorous possibilities. Elan had put herself on irretrievably wrong footing with her ladyship. And Jiuffe considered any advances by Simone toward either of the noblewomen unworthy to be designated competition. Thus, she dreamed that night of an open field filled with flowers, wine, and two noblewomen.

Elan nestled close to an old ragged blanket. She rolled from side to side in a blunder-weighted nightmare in which her path to higher rank disappeared.

And Simone slumbered in a bed, warmed by her encounter with the feminine side of nobility.

The next morning Aure awoke with great excitement. She opened the window and looked out over the beautiful provincial lands. A friendly breeze met her with good tidings and swept her thoughts to a place where she had longed to be. She confided her secrets to this magnanimous wind and remained in the prelude of her adventure until a knock on her door announced Madame de Lourette. The noblewoman entered, followed by Simone carrying a tray of fresh breads and tea.

"Put it there on the table, my cavalier," Madame ordered flirtatiously.

Simone placed down the breakfast. On her way out she bowed to Lady Aure and Madame de Lourette so low that it appeared as if she were kissing the floor. They broke into laughter at her departure.

"Elise, it so pleases me that you accompany me on my journey," said Aure as she poured them a cup of tea.

"Are we not the closest of friends?" Madame replied.

"Of course. But since your marriage I have seldom had the pleasure of seeing you. The count is very generous to allow you to join me."

"Allow me? I gladly rid myself of his air." Madame laughed at the perplexed younger woman. "My dearest Aure, I cherish the station I have achieved in life. But two years of such boredom has exasperated me in the extremity."

"You speak as the ladies in court who carry on with secret lovers," Aure admonished her.

"You will not judge them so harshly once you have worn the bodice of a wife." Madame lay across the bed. Propping herself on her elbow, she announced, "Aure, since we have taken on this expedition without telltale servants, I intend to enjoy the pleasures it offers."

"And so we shall, Elise." Aure sat down next to her.

"I have it on good authority that the queen's Valiers place little restraint on their desires."

"Elise! That is not what I meant."

"Of course, their oath to Queen Sophia would prevent them from pressing a lady. But it is well-known that they have received the favor of many a noblewoman."

"You are a married lady of rank," Aure reminded her.

"Yes, yes," Elise answered as if swatting an annoying fly. "I would never think to jeopardize my marriage. But I shall not deny myself such attentions when they should be so forthcoming."

Her remark, sounding so positive as to its result, prompted Aure to ask, "Has one of them signaled you in any ardent fashion?"

"No. Not yet. But Jiuffe seems to be a Valier of action. And the younger one...eh...eh..."

"Simone?"

"Yes. Somewhat uninitiated but zealous."

"And Elan?"

"Ah." Elise leaned forward and assumed a knowing air. "Simone tells me that Elan is quite tortured by her indiscretion last night."

"Then I shall speak to her and set her mind at ease." Aure did not wish to travel in animosity with the Valiers.

"But other than her faux pas," Elise grinned, "I daresay a woman such as that would throw a bodice into contortions."

After breakfast Elan went to see that the horses were prepared for travel. She stopped for a moment to admire a black steed the lackey had pulled from the stables.

An old groom stepped the horse about. "A fine animal, eh?"

"Yes. Worthy of the general of the calvary," Elan answered appreciatively.

"Or a lady?" Aure came forward and lovingly patted her steed. "She is high-strung, but we cover the ground as one."

Elan courteously gave her salutation, a bit disappointed that the talents of such a choice horse would be neglected by a noble existence. She used their meeting to broach the subject of their travels. "My lady, I understand from Jiuffe that we are to travel away from the main road."

"Yes. I wish to visit the fete at Darau. And we shall travel much faster without servants."

"Surely you know that the niceties to which your ladyship is accustomed are not to be found on the trail. We can reach your party on the main road in less than one day's ride."

"And are there not rumors of bandits on that very road, my good Valier? I do not believe my cousin, Queen Sophia, would deny me such a journey."

Elan took a step back in misery at the mention of her majesty's name. "Your ladyship, it appears you have the advantage over me. I am well-aware that you may destroy my whole future with one word to the queen. But — "

"Which word?" Lady Aure asked, fully expecting this discord. "That you mistook me for a chambermaid?" She lifted an innocent eyebrow in such a manner that Elan understood she had been reprieved. "Valier, I release you from this burden you carry. I disperse any power I may have over you to the winds."

Confused by this quick conciliation, Elan could only bow in the fashion proper for a Valier. "I am indebted to you, Lady Aure."

"My good Elan," Aure continued charmingly, "I promise that my impetuosity will not inconvenience you. I have been on the hunt and handle a horse quite well."

"That may be — "

"And as for any dangers, I put my explicit trust in the brave Valiers of the queen."

Elan could not argue against such an unassailable spirit. To refuse her ladyship, who had spoken with such reason, would deny Elan's own value as a Valier. The gentlewoman's vigor and intelligence were refreshing. Yet such qualities hardly represented those sought after by nobility. As they started their journey, Elan contemplated these contradictions, when Jiuffe joined her in the lead.

"Ah, what sweetness!" Jiuffe exhaled. "So clever is Lady Aure that she asks her questions through her attending lady."

"What questions?" wondered Elan.

Jiuffe smiled lustfully. "Madame has sent me with inquiries about the ways of the Valiers. Elan, keep the lead, and I shall stay behind. Such an inquisitive nature deserves my complete and undivided attention."

Elan glanced back at the noblewomen, when suddenly Lady Aure's horse bolted forward as if at the sound of a starting gun. Alarmed, Elan dashed after her. Elan sprinted past a grassy hill and through a mass of oak trees, just in time to see her ladyship disappear over the top of a precipitous incline. The Valier urged her horse up the steep ridge, fearing that the noblewoman could be thrown at any moment. She reached the other side, only to find Aure sitting with perfect composure in her saddle, her horse calmly munching the greenery underfoot.

"You look pale, Valier. Shall I gift you some smelling salts?" Aure asked wryly.

"Lady Aure, have you forgotten yourself?"

"Ah. You speak as though the horse were riding me instead of the other way around." Aure threw the challenge forward. "Perhaps you believe me best locked in my chambers, away from such pleasures?"

This unexpected defiance caused Elan to shift evasively in her saddle, her silence only intensifying the importance of her awaited answer. After a disconcerted moment she met the unwavering gaze of the noblewoman and courteously yielded. "Your ladyship, I am impressed by your ability. I humbly admit that I was surprised by your actions and sought only to keep you from harm."

The answer more than satisfied Aure. She stepped her horse down the hill, and they rejoined the others.

The lodgings for the group were not to compare with the inn along the main road. Still, everyone was in good humor because the fete at Darau was to commence in only a few days, and the conversation centered upon the baked goods, the games, and the famous race. Lady Aure took part with great interest. Madame even danced with Jiuffe. In return Jiuffe promised to bring a rare carafe of wine to her room. Whether truly rare or not, no one saw either Madame or Jiuffe until the next morning: Madame with her porcelain cheeks radiating color and Jiuffe fluttering her eyes toward her with private messages.

Left to pay the group's tab, Simone questioned the landlord about an extra charge for the broken bedsprings in Madame's room. She almost unsheathed her sword when he spoke of a loud and prolonged moan that had disturbed his other patrons. However, Jiuffe quickly intervened and paid the extra coin.

As they prepared to depart, Elan noticed Lady Aure in conversation with the stable hand. Though the boy seemed reluctant, the lady haggled like a trader and paid him a plump sum for his old lackey's cap and clothes. She joyfully stuffed them in her satchel and joined the others.

As they passed the farms and villages of the region, Elan's thoughts stayed, a trifle amused, with Lady Aure's purchase of the lackey's attire. Such clothes could never hold any worth to a noblewoman. Yet when Aure set off again galloping through the hillsides, Elan was reminded that her ladyship's actions had little to do with her title. She was about to go in chase, when Jiuffe jumped to the fore and rode after her.

Simone, who had been trying desperately to entertain the noblewomen during their journey, found herself as jealous of Jiuffe's action as she was suspicious of what had occurred between Jiuffe and Madame at the inn. She set herself under a flowing elm tree and retrieved her papers to pen her frustrations.

"You write, my young Valier?" Madame asked, appearing next to the elm.

Embarrassed, Simone hid the papers behind her. "I only gad a bit, Madame."

"Then you are a poet."

The compliment warmed Simone toward the noblewoman. She was at once convinced that such an observant mind could never be involved with Jiuffe. "Madame, would you care to hear a verse?" Simone asked tentatively. "I would value your opinion greatly."

Madame's fine lightness of hair and cultured face formed a perfect design of nature. She sat down and spread out the folds of her dress. "I would be delighted."

Simone sifted through several pages to find the verse most perfect for this occasion, guiltily bypassing those she had written in honor of Lady Aure. Finally she brought forth that which she thought to be her sweetest composition.

The Valier compensated for her verse's lack of imagination with such dramatic zeal that a willing listener could choose to ignore any disproportion. When she finished she found Madame charitable in her opinion, so much so that Simone's emotions hurried far ahead of what Madame had intended. The inexperienced Valier blurted out such fervent declarations that Madame stretched out her hand, as much to block Simone's enthusiasm as to gift her with the honor of kissing it. This gesture in itself sent Simone into ecstasy, and she vowed to celebrate her newfound love with another rapturous poem as soon as possible. Before Madame could protest, Simone grabbed her notebook and ran off full of romantic inspiration.

Elan laid out their lunch, concealing her concern as Jiuffe and Aure returned gaily from the pastures.

Jiuffe grabbed some cheese and a branch of grapes and headed in Madame's direction to attend her needs. With an amorous wink to Elan, she commented, "Lady Aure rides like a Valier!"

Jiuffe often spoke such revelations without the slightest notion of their significance. But Elan saw the fragments of the lady's interest in Darau and her purchase of the lackey's clothes from a purposeful weave.

Aure sat down comfortably on the grass, aware of Elan's grimacing face. "My good Elan, am I the cause of your displeasure today? Do you still doubt my — "

"You intend to ride in the race at Darau, don't you?"

Aure paused for a moment, then deflected the attack as well as any master of the sword. "You flatter me, Valier. Your imagination does you credit. But surely you know women are not permitted to enter the race."

Elan put forth her proof. "A noble traveling without servants. Bolting off at every opportunity to test her Thoroughbred's legs. Lackey's clothes? And don't deny the purpose for which you intend to use them."

Aure lost her pleasure in the situation. She intentionally directed her attention to the food laid before her.

"Perhaps Jiuffe enjoys the recklessness of your confidence, but — "

"Jiuffe does not know," Aure said, looking up at Elan. "No one knows. Only you." She softly tilted her head, adding, "And how could I expect you to understand?"

Deep brown eyes searched for an ally in the Valier, impelling Elan to contemplate her actions. What the noblewoman contrived to accomplish was well within her reach. Her steed was prime; her talent, unquestionable. Yet even if she managed to pass as a lackey or young lad, the scheme would surely be discovered. Then what penalty would fall upon the Valiers, indeed upon Elan, for allowing such amusement against all decorum that encompassed nobility?

"It is impossible," Elan concluded.

Aure threw a handful of grapes aside in a fury. "Impossible? That I have been scolded during my upbringing for my curiosity and skill I have learned to expect. But I will not accept such reproaches from you — you, who have the power to define your own destiny; you, who have entered into realms many of us only dream of. How can you abandon me when I have given you my confidence?"

"You have given me no confidence. I have guessed it from you," Elan retorted. "You are a lady!"

"And as such I am denied a pleasure even a young boy may enjoy. Valier, do you not take pleasure in the risks you take? This is mine. And if you do not share the purpose of my venture, I beg you keep your silence on the matter."

The candor of Aure's appeal penetrated Elan's sense of duty. The Valier was pulled into the woman's dream. To deny her this challenge would be to slay her very spirit. Elan's final resistance dissolved under Aure's imploring gaze. "I will keep my silence, your ladyship."

On the day of the fete, Madame complained of a headache and declined to accompany the group to Darau. Elated, Simone insisted on staying behind to tend her, explaining to Madame that she was well-versed in the Eastern art of the medicines.

Aure stepped out into the fresh provincial air, her lackey's clothes hanging agreeably on her frame. The oversized cap covered her bountiful hair, giving her a countrified appearance that complimented her aristocratic face. Though Jiuffe declared her more eccentric than her cousin at the sight, Elan found the noblewoman's spirit infectious. And the conspiracy of their secret grew even more comfortable when the lady insisted they call her by her familiar name to promote her disguise.

Great tents and booths covered the grounds at Darau. Several spits were laden with fat capons, pheasant, and fricassee of hare with flavors of wine, garlic, and herbs. The three women stopped at each booth to converse with the patrons and sample the delightful dishes or ointments or lotions for sale. When any fare was agreed to be worth the price, a sample was bought. Elan quickly found her saddlebags filled with delights.

Lounging for a prolonged time at one booth, Elan and Aure debated the tenderness of a piece of fowl by sharing it with each other. Their preoccupation with each other soon became tiresome to Jiuffe, so she grabbed a tankard of brew and departed to watch the show of magic.

At the call to the event of the day, Elan escorted her ladyship to register for the race. In good humor Aure ventured a comfortable tease. "Perhaps you will place a small wager in my favor?"

"I go only to oblige your whims," Elan countered with a half-hidden grin that betrayed her enthusiasm for Aure's initiative. A doubt on the noblewoman's face caused the Valier to add, "I shall take the greatest pleasure in your endeavor."

The starting pistol cracked the air. And Elan found herself excitedly cheering on the slim lad on the stark black Thoroughbred. As the horses rounded the flags set at the wide oak tree, Aure held neatly to third place. On the flat, even grounds of the meadow, she kept pace. Aure overtook the second rider by flying over a brook and cutting closely to the shrubs on the other side. A group of five ran so close that all were still clearly in the running.

On the third leg of the race, they pierced through a mass of trees, disappearing for a moment from view. Suddenly a great brown mare jumped to the forefront, followed by a chestnut, then a gray. Elan strained her eyes in their direction. Yet as the whole of twenty horses sped out of the brush, Aure was nowhere to be seen. Panicked, Elan rushed to her horse and charged to the far woods. In a small secluded clearing she spotted Aure.

"My lady!"

"Elan. I knew you would come."

"Are you harmed?" Elan exclaimed, jumping from her horse.

Aure twirled herself fully around, throwing the cap carelessly from her head. "Not a hair. Did you see me around the turn?"

"Yes."

"How I jumped the brook?"

"I cheered you on."

Aure claimed a smile of satisfaction. "Then you did enjoy it?"

"Immensely."

"I believe I could have won. Do you not agree?"

"I do. But why did you step from the race?"

Aure stopped for a moment, checking her enthusiasm. She touched her lips in thought and breathed deeply. "All at once it became most important that I see you."

The gentleness in her tone led the sentiment beyond the limits of ordinary politeness. Elan felt she had just heard words more intimate than those spoken by any bedfellow.

Sure of her position, Aure stretched her hand out toward Elan and closed her eyes in anticipation. Unexpectedly the gentlewoman became a force stronger than Elan herself. The Valier took hold of her hand and imagined how soft it would feel against her face, how wild in her grasp, with fingers so long that they could reach inside of her with a stroke more dangerous than any sword. If Aure's hand held such powers, how could Elan dare to look upon its master?

She started to lose all faculty, as if she were being devoured by a powerful sorceress. Her innermost thoughts became infused with unbearable want. She thought to throw herself against Aure and tear through her clothes, to knead herself into her flesh and envelop her in a merciless heat. Elan dropped the hand abruptly and stepped back. Aure's eyes sprang open, and they saw in each other the true stakes of their game.

"You deny me this?" Aure asked in a choked voice. "You, who have been gifted the handkerchiefs of the most brilliant women in the realm? Is mine so unworthy to be among them?"

The token of the sport of love became a horrible jest to Elan. She desired nothing of the handkerchief. It would only pierce her like the fiercest dagger if she were destined to look upon it rather than its owner. "You are of the cruelest heart," she rasped.

Aure shrunk backward, scalded by the words. "I pray a sword cuts you to the ground, you wretch!" She jumped to her horse and galloped back to the fete.

Elan did not follow her. She crouched down and gently picked up the lackey's cap that Aure had left behind. Holding it closely against her cheek, she breathed in its aura, unable to deceive herself about what command it had over her.

Aure joined Jiuffe at the show of magic. Center stage a magician floated a golden cloth over his hand, and a white dove appeared to the amazement of the crowd. Yet Aure did not see his marvelous feat. Confused with emotion, she drifted in an unfamiliar daze until the sight of a large bearded man jolted her. Impulsively she shouted, "The pendant!"

Before Jiuffe had a chance to stop her, Aure, clearly in a rage, strode defiantly toward the man. Without taking heed of his size or his foul manner, she demanded, "Where did you come by this pendant?"

"Perhaps I bought it," he mocked to his companions.

"It was a gift. My servant would never have given it up," she persisted fearlessly.

"Your servant?" He laughed so hard, the coarse stubble on his face shook. Pointing to her clothes, he asked in exaggerated wonder, "A wench like you has servants?"

Elan and Jiuffe quickly appeared at Aure's side. "Do you question the friend of a Valier?" Elan glared at the beast.

He pulled aside his outercoat to display his shiny épée and answered, "Only the friend of a dead Valier."

They drew their swords, three against two. Elan evened the score by smashing a full tankard against one man's face. Then she clashed swords with the beast. His blade was thick, but its master was full of wine, and Elan quickly grounded him.

"Aure, our horses," she commanded as she saw two more thugs running up to challenge them.

Jiuffe dealt her foe a wound in the shoulder and jumped atop a wooden table, ready for the next. He lunged at her, and she deflected his sword, weaving back and forth at each pass.

The other ruffian engaged Elan with a caliber of skill above the others. A practiced swordsman, he gained the advantage, pushing her into retreat. But she sidestepped a deadly thrust and stayed the attack with a riposte that surprised him.

"Elan!"

Elan looked over and saw Aure with the horses. In her moment of distraction, the pain of steel plunged through her side. She turned to her foe's pitiless face as he pulled his sword from her and swiftly dealt him hard in the chest. Holding her side, she jumped to her horse, and the three women fled from the fete.

After several leagues the women pulled up on the side of a grassy slope and looked back for their pursuers, knowing they would not let them rest.

"Jiuffe, return to the inn," directed Elan. "I will take Aure off-road." The two took flight into the thick forest, not daring to draw on their reins until they were far in the wood. Elan led them up an incline, and they finally halted their horses behind a mass of shrubs.

The Valier took a white cloth from her satchel and secured it around her waist. A shudder passed through her as she became aware that she could no longer protect her ladyship. She drew a pistol from her belt. "Aure, are you familiar with this weapon?"

"Yes."

Elan handed it to her. "Prime it, and keep it so. If we are discovered, I charge you to ride with all the skill you rode today along that river." She pointed in its direction. "Follow it east, and you shall surely find help."

Aure saw Elan clutch her side yet dared not move closer to her. The mere flick of a breeze could betray their position. The voices of their pursuers could be heard echoing around them as they scoured the broad landscape.

Three riders came into view near the riverside. Elan slipped her sword from its scabbard. Aure raised the pistol. The men stepped their horses toward them, then abruptly turned away, one of them deciding, "They probably stayed on the road to the inn." The sound of hooves drummed the forest floor, gradually diminishing beyond the brush.

After the woods returned to silence, Aure looked over to the Valier and saw her leaning over the saddlebow. "Elan?" she asked, trembling.

The Valier slowly looked up. After a few steps down the incline, Elan swayed in her saddle, causing her mount to swing wayward. Aure swiftly grabbed the bridle and directed them near the riverbank. She dismounted and ran worriedly to the Valier.

"My saddlebag. Herbs for a paste," Elan whispered with an odd pain in her voice. The sky tilted away, and she fell to the ground, exposing her blood-soaked shirt.

Aure gasped. "Oh, dearest Elan, that my folly should put you in such jeopardy!"

She emptied the saddlebag of its contents. Remembering how the village healers had once tended a servant's wound, she filled a small bowl with river water and flinted a fire to boil it. Returning to Elan, she gingerly opened the bloodied shirt. The lacerated skin was repugnant, and Aure withdrew in fright. Mindful of the duty with which she was now charged, she forced her shaking hands to clean the wound and applied the paste, guessing its proper proportions. Then she secured a nightshirt around Elan's waist to bandage the injury. After wrapping the Valier in blankets, Aure sat by her side. Stroking her hair, she lamented, "Elan, I know not what more to do."

A chill of a breeze slipped across the terrain as evening began to cloak the earth. Aure kept an uneasy watch long after the sky had dimmed into night. Beyond the light of the fire, the strange sounds of the forest rankled her attempts to remain calm. The chirp of a cricket, the splash of a fish, each rustle of leaves became a foe lurking in the darkness. Attuned to the smallest noise, Aure suddenly cocked her eyes in the direction of an eerie moan. She groped for the pistol and lifted her head. The light of a pale moon illuminated an owl sitting on a nearby branch of an oak. Aure lay back down again at Elan's side.

Having exhausted her courage, she softly cried, "Elan, do not leave me. I beg you, live so that I may show you that my heart is not cruel." Praying to the grace of heaven for her Valier's life, she finally lapsed into a fatigued sleep.

As daylight woke, Elan was drenched under sweat and fever. She drifted in and out of consciousness, not knowing which world she was in. Alarmed, Aure changed the poultice and wiped away the sweat. She lifted her head and gently brought water to her lips.

By midafternoon the Valier's fever finally lessened. Feeling calmer, Aure allowed herself a short bath in the river. She found the ointments she had bought at the fete and anointed herself with them. Then she decided to lavish Elan's body with almond paste and perfumed oils. The scent of the oils rose into Aure's emotions, and she lingered on the sight of the Valier. Elan's skin was sun-warmed yet soft to her touch; her arms, artistic in their strength; her face, contoured in a magnificent yet womanly image.

Aure's eyes dwelled on the soft sculptures of Elan's breasts. She raised her hand to her own breast, cupping it, and the sensuality of her own skin moved her. Emboldened, she touched Elan's chest. Her fingers slowly pursued the line of one breast to the other, pressing inquisitively into the pleasure. A hunger ran through Aure, and her lips traveled from Elan's stomach to her nipples as if nothing less would content her. The smooth skin tasted sweet and generous. The naked sensation pulled Aure to and fro, swaying her in erotic rhythm.

Elan moved, and Aure held herself in fear of waking her. Unable to prevent her rush to passion, she rolled off to the side and rocked on her own fingertips until the sky burst inside her. Lying in her heated breath, she murmured remorsefully, "Oh, Elan, that I be so selfish to steal what has not been offered to me!"

The strictness of her breeding caused Aure great regret for her wickedness. Ashamed, she promised not to lend herself to it again. Yet even as she spoke her vow, an inner wildness tugged at her soul. She struggled to escape from her moral bondage, using every excuse to tend closely to the Valier's recovery.

Every few hours Elan woke. She took some water and even ate a few morsels of food. When she winced in pain, Aure gave her brandy to dull it and held her until she rested easier. When she became unsettled in her sleep, Aure gathered clumps of moss for a soft pillow to give her comfort. Elan's breathing figure pleased Aure so much that she soon lost all fear about their circumstances.

As evening blanketed the land, Aure stayed awake and watched Elan, curiously aware of the contours of her face, the lay of her hair across her brow. The Valier had joined her heart, causing her to feel alive in a way she never imagined.

Aure's desire to be near Elan soon grew more powerful than any virtuous caution. Without any thought to the consequence, she slipped off her nightshirt, crept under the covers, and leaned close so that her wealth of hair mingled with the strands of the Valier's. Trembling with moistened fervor, she pressed herself against the woman. Elan's warmth ignited her, and Aure found it impossible to stay herself. She grasped Elan's breast to her lips, nourishing her abandonment.

Suddenly a hand seized her chin. Startled, Aure looked into Elan's awakened eyes. In a rabid motion Elan pulled her to her mouth. Aure's body responded instinctively, opening and pursuing with her lips, her tongue. A hand searched for entry. Finding it, Elan clung to Aure with a domination that freed her from any restraint. A tempest surged through her limbs. Her breath became hard and swift. Her body whirled into the stars, riding a relentless rush that twisted and knotted until she cried out beyond the heavens. A thousand strikes of lightning exploded her entire being, and she shook, with the last of herself spent. Falling against a layer of sweet moss, Aure closed her eyes to remain in the daze of seductive warmth. Before the moment could escape, a gentle kiss caressed her cheek, and an arm cradled her closely.

In the next days they created lather upon lather, explored each other's softness and savagery. Indeed, Elan and Aure found it impossible to exhaust their pleasures in one another. This little plot of land became a place of their own, where they would be content to live and die as a passionate force of one.

"My love, that you have blossomed in a place so far from the comforts of your home — "

"I prefer pillows of moss," Aure replied contentedly as she nursed Elan's injury. "It is almost healed." Aure kissed her lover's pink scar, then stood up. "I must exercise the horses. Will you be here when I return?" she asked flirtatiously.

"I would not leave heaven," answered Elan, gazing at the woman who had laid siege to her heart.

Aure took her horse along the riverside as she had done daily for the past ten days. When she rounded the bend, her freed spirit allowed her to ride farther than her usual jaunt. Beyond a craggy thicket she overheard voices in the distance and cautiously moved closer. In the clearing she saw a farmhouse and several riders questioning its chubby owner.

With a fallen heart she quickly made her way back. Her eyes welled up with tears when she reached their campsite, and she dug her wet cheek into Elan's shoulder. "They are searching for us, Elan. I saw them."

"Who?" Elan pulled back, ready to seize her sword.

"The marquis's guards. They are at a nearby farmhouse."

The revelation was more painful than any number of the bandits of Darau discovering them. Elan desperately searched for a reassuring thought. "They could ride very near and never discover us. We could have a day, perhaps two."

"Elan, I have finally found you. I want no other's touch."

Elan shrugged, aware that she now had to be the forceful heart. "We cannot stay in the woods forever."

"Then let us run to the Swiss cantons or to Austria," Aure implored her.

"It would bring disgrace to both of us," the Valier answered, trying to reason.

The rationalization sounded like an evasion. Aure pulled angrily away from Elan. "So you have your victory, Valier. And now you may joyfully return to your queen and gloat about your feats with the Lady Aure."

"Aure! Do not tear my heart and then call it a triumph of my own," Elan yelled back in agony. She cupped Aure's face in her hands. "You are my heart. I shall worship you every day of my life. But I cannot compromise you."

Elan took her lips and hushed Aure before she could dispute the inevitable once more. The Valier laid her down gently and mounted her, determined to drink every taste of her before they were separated.

The scouting party discovered them the next morning and escorted the two women to a well-equipped hostelry in Vils, where Madame, Jiuffe, and Simone greeted them with great relief. The following day her ladyship's coach stood ready. Several armed guards would accompany Lady Aure the rest of her journey, less than two days' ride to meet her future husband. The procession took on an air of nobility with saddles studded with silver, velvet horsecloth, and a footman waiting at the open door of the carriage.

Aure lay in Elan's arms until they heard a knock at her door. They broke from each other as Madame entered. "They are almost ready, Aure." She looked from one to the other. "I will delay them. Goodness, I am always losing my jewels! I am quite certain I will need several guards to help me find them." She plucked off an earring and whisked herself out the door, smiling at two grateful faces.

A long silence made both women painfully aware that their time together was ending. Elan gently kissed Aure and walked a few paces away to observe her. Aure was dressed in the finest of cloth and truly looked as if a life of nobility was meant for her. The sight gripped Elan's hopes, and she turned away.

A soft and knowing arm slipped around her. "My dearest, I am not a foolish maid who makes promises beyond her keep. It is a visit of introduction, not a marriage ceremony. I swear to you, you are my heart, and I shall find my way back to you." Aure sealed her pledge with a kiss of truth. And they lingered in each other's arms until an attendant announced their departure.

The Valier pulled her emotions within and accompanied the noblewoman to her carriage. She ceremoniously kissed her lover's hand. "I remain your humble servant, my lady."

Aure quickly turned and entered her carriage, fearful that someone might notice her tears. The door closed, and with the lash of a whip, the horses tracked forward.

Jiuffe and Simone ran a few paces beside the carriage, exchanging farewells with Madame. They both skipped back in good humor and retired to the inn for a drink. After several toasts to themselves, to Madame and Lady Aure, to the queen, and then to themselves again, Jiuffe and Simone stepped outside to join Elan and start their journey home.

Alight with satisfaction, Jiuffe took the lead and gaily sniffed one half of a white lace kerchief before stuffing it in her coat pocket. Simone ran her horse joyfully back and forth over the trail with the other half of the kerchief draped around her neck for display. And Elan, clinging to Aure's last words, paid the strictest toll for her desires. She traveled home with the soft, promising cambric of her lady's handkerchief wrapped around her wound.

Bangkok in the Rain
by Jess Wells

"Telegram for Muriel Fitzwater!" she heard as she came down the stairs with her brown leather rucksack and her college diploma.

"Come at once Andover House. Nanna dying."

At her grandmother's house the old woman's companion, Tricksey, gravely handed a small manila envelope and a list to Muriel.

"You must go to every one of these people on this list," her grandmother, Abigail, said, "in the order in which you receive their names." The woman stopped for breath, "Tell them…I have always loved them. Thirteen million dollars to be inherited if you take part in our little…project."

"Thirteen million? For me?" Muriel said. "But what if I'm gone…for weeks?"

Abigail laughed and tiredly closed her eyes. "I expect you shall be, my dear. I certainly expect you shall."

Muriel pursued her task, envelope to envelope. Seven countries had yielded seven lovers. She leaned her head against the starched linen headrest of the train seat and closed her eyes. The movement of the train became her back rocking against bamboo matting. Her arm dropping off the seat was the languishing gesture of the moment she gave in to being laid across a table. The train coursing around a corner was the time a lover had spun her through Mediterranean water until the sea and the sky had only her naked body between them for definition.

She became aroused each time she raised her hand to knock on another door. She walked through the women's houses with an eye to each woman in the room: Who will be my lover now? She was deliriously free, and she felt that the train speeding along was her, cutting through the drudgery that others had to endure, her flying through a life of wide-open time. People labored in the fields around her; they brought her extravagant lunches and afternoon brandies. She ate and drank with the working rich men whose lives were trapped in briefcases and calculators, the wrinkles of their faces and the hollowness of their eyes revealing that they too operated in repetitive cycles.

Muriel's life had no walls. She spent her time at the opera, museums, promenades, art studios, theaters, in the markets sipping coffee, on the rural hillside looking for the shepherdess, in the stacks introducing herself to the librarian, in the lab seducing the chemist. She lounged on sofas and beds inventing new ways to approach, caress, lunge, bite, take a woman to the place where she "unhinged herself," as Muriel liked to think of it, separating her thinking mind from her body, divorcing the logical brain from the dark and amorphous place where the woman became the surrendering animal.

Muriel's nipples were erect nearly all day and night. Her posture was impeccable. Her movements were languorous and infused with the tension of someone who is waiting, poised, confident. She was electric. She walked down unknown streets with the nerve endings in her vulva tingling, her movements driven by the gnawing center of her body. She drank coffee with slightly pursed lips that were full and moist as if she were seconds away from a kiss. Her hands fidgeted around a wineglass, thirsty for a wrist, a thigh, a breast. Muriel became predatory.

In Bangkok, Muriel drank a tall glass of thick orange tea. She felt uncertain, unskilled, unwanted. The vitality had been sucked from her, she had let it drain into the sheets of her lovers, had left it puddled in the rain in Dublin.

The noon heat crowded around her. The women in the marketplace fanned themselves slower, putting up sun umbrellas and finally bringing out small bits of fish and rice to eat when their customers refused to venture into the heat. Muriel felt the sweat collecting around her breasts, dripping down her cleavage. The sweat and humidity soaked her white shirt until it was transparent, the outline of her nipples and the trim on her bra pointed and erect, like the domed Buddhist temple across the water.

Four thin boats, bright yellow with wood canopies and flowers hanging off their dragon-face prows, bobbed beside the café.

"You need a friend," a soft voice beside her said as an arm was slid over her shoulder. "A good friend like Mai," the woman said, pushing her tiny breasts against Muriel's arm.

The woman took Muriel to a hotel that bordered the river and, pushing Muriel ahead of her as if she were a reluctant child, checked her into a room that jetted on a pier into the water. Mai checked the quality of the sheets, inspected the corners for insects. Muriel squatted over the seatless toilet and then threw a small pan of water from an open cistern down the commode. The hotel was built on stilts. Muriel saw the water and the piss fall directly into the mud below her.

Mai fussed in the room, and when she turned to see Muriel standing stark naked as if in a trance, she pulled a chair into the center of the room, in front of the door, and set Muriel on it.

"I've lost the connection," Muriel said to Mai, not sure if she understood English.

Mai unrolled a canopy of mosquito netting, hooked it to the ceiling, and made a small tent over Muriel's nakedness. She muttered in Thai and opened the door so Muriel could stare out at the winding river, the shimmering temple, and the old teak boats. Mai sat on an end table and crumbled Thai stick into a small pipe, then filled the room with the pungent smell. She ran hot water into a large pan, brought the pipe, the pan, a rough sponge, and a small stool to Muriel's tent. Mai lifted the netting and moved her stool behind the exhausted traveler, put the pipe into Muriel's mouth, and scrubbed her back with the hot water and the sponge. Mai soaked hot towels in mint water and wrapped them around Muriel's shoulders, hid her hair within a turban of white towel, and beat the tired muscles of her back with the loofah.

Mai tied up her skirt around one hip and strode Muriel's leg as she massaged her neck muscles. The soft skin of Mai's upper thighs and the tickle of her pubic hair should have brought Muriel to her senses, should have made her reach out and cup Mai's buttocks with her hands, bring the woman's leg up to her own cunt. Instead, she sat motionless, only tipping her head from one side to the other as Mai worked. The smoke circled around them, trapped inside the fine mosquito netting. Outside, the Bangkok sunset made the golden temple glow.

Mai retreated to her stool and brusquely grabbed Muriel's breasts. She pulled Muriel between her legs and squeezed her nipples, massaging her breasts as she bit into the fleshy spot between her shoulder blades and neck. Mai moved her hand over Muriel's long abdomen and got up to retrieve a small bag. She sat down on the stool again, reloaded the pipe, and in the dense smoke pulled out a dildo that she sheathed and slid into Muriel's unsuspecting cunt. Muriel's breathing deepened.

Encouraged, Mai began to tease the dildo back and forth, then changed her mind and abandoned it inside Muriel's pussy. She pulled a rope out of her bag, and, standing on her stool so that the coarse hair of her crotch grazed Muriel's turban and her smell filled Muriel's nostrils, she tied Muriel's hands together and threw the rope over the ceiling struts for the mosquito netting.

For the next several hours (or was it days? Muriel couldn't tell), she sat on her little stool with her arms above her head as her Thai friend hung beads from clips pinching her nipples, circled her, added shiny chains to the beads. As the night air wafted in the open door, she added weights to the chains, talismans in the shape of golden pomegranates and flowers. The pain in Muriel's nipples was a luscious sting that made her dream of needles shooting out from her areolae, her nipples suddenly little porcupine mounds. Every time the woman clipped a brass monkey or a copper bird onto the chain, Muriel closed her eyes and let her head fall backward. Soon the tearing sensation in her nipples had her panting, the perspiration gathering on her top lip.

Muriel rode the stool, pressing on the dildo while the chains jingled with her efforts. Boats passed the open door with their running lights on, shining skeletons of ships. Still, there was no connection between the white-hot pain in her nipples and her mind, her ability to climax. Muriel may have had breasts that were on fire, but she was mentally celibate.

Mai crossed her arms in front of her chest and stared at Muriel with determined dark brown eyes. It was clear that other measures would be required to bring Muriel back, Mai explained, to reconnect her pieces into a sexual whole.

Mai cut her down and rolled her in stiff linen sheets, laid her on the hard narrow bed to sleep.

In the morning Muriel opened her eyes to see Mai bringing in tea on a small flowered tray and beyond her the bright choppy water of the Bangkok Noi.

"We go on a journey now," Mai said.

The two women sat shoulder to shoulder in the narrow boat as its dragon prow rose above the water. They turned into the labyrinth of narrow backwater canals where the houses rose on stilts on each side of the boat, the floorboards high above their heads. The teak floors of the houses gleamed with moisture, and the humid air plastered Muriel's shirt to her breasts.

The boat pulled up to low, undulating docks, and passengers rearranged their parcels, passed back a few silver coins, and clambered onto the rough planks. Mai and Muriel were the last to disembark, setting down in front of a brown teak house with an upturned roof.

Mai escorted Muriel into a small room with no furniture where one entire wall was latticework. Muriel sat limply on the floor.

An hour later Mai came in and stripped Muriel of her clothing, then left without speaking. Muriel felt like a hollow gourd. Without moving she stared at the pinpoints of water that twinkled through the lattice.

Evening began to descend, the light grew pale, and Muriel heard snatches of music made by tight stringed instruments and drums. Mai entered again and turned Muriel toward the door, handing her a goblet of sweet drugged tea. She left the door open when she departed.

By the time the goblet was drained, there was a soft haze around the edges of Muriel's eyesight. Candlelight flickered in the hallway, and the sound of drums rose around her. People were amassing outside the door, but she sat very still, unconcerned with her nakedness.

It began to rain, and the water poured off the sides of the building. Muriel saw it coming down in sheets beyond the hallway, heard it splashing off the eaves on the other side of the latticework. The rain closed her in, rinsed the inside of her.

Two women entered the room and laid grasses around her. Two others came in and poured scented water over her shoulders.

Another pair stood her up and slipped thin shoes on her feet. A final set draped her shoulders with a bright cape. The drums pounded outside the room.

The women took her by her passive arms and led her into the hallway, where she stood in front of two dozen people, the cape straight down her back, the rest of her naked to the assembled group. Her nakedness made her feel as if the rain were pelting against her skin.

They walked her to a long table on the balcony of the house, with the rain pouring in a gray sheet beyond the ceiling and the candles dancing around her. They laid her out on a table. Muriel felt the drums pounding against her belly and the strings vibrating against her nipples. Her mind fell into a blur of drugs and rain and candles, and she was aware of being carried on a pallet around the balcony. First with leaves and palm fronds brushing her chest and belly, then with flowers, then with the hands of what seemed like scores of people touching her as she, lying immobilized on her pallet, passed them. They draped her with beads, they laid berries and nuts on her flat belly, they pushed flowers into the crevice between her torso and arms.

They set the pallet down on the table again and circled her with the candles. Two dozen hands slipped underneath her, and as she closed her eyes they lifted her up, set her down again, slipped hands under her buttocks, and lifted her. She couldn't make out faces, couldn't distinguish genders.

The music seemed to be on all sides of her, to have entered her, and now, in a fever pitch, the drums called each of the throng to climb onto the table and lie on her, to rub their cool flesh against her, some hard between the legs and some not, some soft in the chest and some not. They kissed her, they entangled her legs, they lightly grazed her skin and dismounted, they pushed themselves hard into her chest and hips. There were so many people that they blurred into a shifting, morphing mass of rhythm and tenderness. Muriel felt as if she had been robbed of her mind, and since her will had already deserted her, she was just a body that was vibrating like the stringed instruments and the drums playing around her.

Taking the dragon-prow boat back to her hotel late that night, Muriel felt as if every tiny light along the canal were the candles that had been around her and felt herself attached in some way to each of the people who had pressed little bits of their sexuality into her. To rejuvenate her. There was a thread running from her to Mai, to the group in the rain, to the dancers, to Jana in Stockholm, and back to her grandmother, who lay dying in her bed. Sex was a gift that connected them, not just each to each other but each to the previous generation and the stories they told, the fears they instilled, the secrets they shared that their daughters might grow up to know passion and pleasure. It was a strong thread, invisible, spanning time and geography. Muriel again felt like the tip of the needle that stitched them together and was refocused in her pursuit.

Caribbean Wave
by Jane Futcher

She is my mother's best friend, and her eyes are the same blue as the Caribbean waves beneath our bow, her breasts inches away as she offers me hummus and Greek olives. We are running before the morning wind, upright and fast, our main sail swung out over the water, our jib split to the starboard side. Eddy, her son, the once awesome older brother with black leather jacket and movie camera, is a sportswriter now and stands at the helm, remembering his days as a helicopter pilot in Vietnam. My father is below, studying charts; my mother sunbathes on the foredeck. Genevieve's husband, red-faced, gripping the gunwales, interrupts his son to tell him the jib is luffing.

California and Emily and the winter rains seem far away as we pass Tortola on our port side, high and green against the water, Virgin Gorda still ahead. I think about this afternoon and pray that it will happen, that Genevieve and I will be able to break from this group of six so that we may touch at last, so that I may trace my fingertips across her cheek, along her neck, down her shoulder to her clavicle.

"How are you, my princess?" she asks now, resting one hand gently on my knee. I look into her eyes, and she holds my gaze, eyes gay, laughing like a girl as she pushes a strand of white hair from her forehead. My stomach twirls. How much longer can I hunger on this edge?

I have lied. I want more than to touch Genevieve. Since we boarded this boat in Roadtown four days ago, I have wanted every part of her. In my dreams I see us on the island, where we hike at the end of today, in the hours before sunset, while my father and Genevieve's husband remain on board to read and clean the decks and coil the sheets. In my dream Genevieve and I row to shore in the dinghy with Eddy and my mother, who go a different way, to the shops for rum and limes since cocktails are their sacred prayers.

And that's just how it happens, with my mother and Eddy cajoling us to come with them as we laugh, pulling away.

Moments later Genevieve and I are winding up on a narrow trail that runs along the cliffs above the beaches, a breeze cooling us, the water below rocking our breath, in a silence that is heavy and full. I am sure she wants this as much as I do, but she will not make the first move to cross the sea that separates and draws us — our ages, the family ties, her children and husband.

I can't recall exactly when this feeling started. I am thirty-five now; she is sixty. Perhaps it began when I was a child, blindfolded, and Genevieve turned me three times at her daughter's eighth birthday before I slapped the piñata with a bat. I know that my heart pounded in San Juan four days ago in the airport, where all our planes converged, when she walked toward me, her straw hat cocked to one side, her blue cotton dress clinging to her hips, her smile so fond and sensual and eager that I forgot my battles with Emily and my fatigue from the long flight from San Francisco.

We are ascending now in the heat, I in my shorts, my bikini underneath, ready to swim after we find the beach through the hot tangle of gorse along the path. A lizard darts in front of her, and she cries out, reaching for my hand, which she holds now as she asks about my life with Emily and how I knew that I preferred women. Desire makes me choose my words too carefully; I speak in an odd, awkward way, as if I had swallowed helium, as if each word were the kiss I long to place on her lips.

I am afraid to break the spell, so I ask how she spends her days. She says she has many meetings, about the environment and overpopulation and reforming the courts. She, like my mother, like myself, has many causes. My cause has become finding the way to her.

It is hot. A green bird, perhaps a parrot, flies over us toward the ocean. "What do you read?"

"Read?" she says shyly.

"Novels? Biographies? Religion — like my mother?"

She likes Anne Tyler, she says, because her odd characters are amusing and because she writes about the city where Genevieve lives. She enjoys Doris Lessing for her strong, political women who struggle with relationships and social justice and love.

"Love?" I ask, hoping for a glimpse into her marriage with her stiff, aristocratic husband.

She blushes. The skirt of her bathing suit lifts in the breeze. Her legs are so smooth that I stumble on a stone, and she catches me. "It's hot," I manage.

"The beach is just there," she points, leading me down a sandy path that opens suddenly onto a white crescent beach, as graceful as a woman's body. At both ends of the cove, gray rocks drop into turquoise pools. Miraculously, no boats are anchored here.

"It's heavenly, my darling," she smiles.

There is an open straw *palapa* partway down the beach. I follow her to the cool white beneath the thatched roof, which has fallen in places.

"What fun!" It is her Vassar '40s voice. Behind that formal exterior I am longing to find the sensual woman whom I can feel but have not yet been able to reach. I know that her breeding will not allow her to touch me first. That is up to me.

I inhale, reaching for courage from the waves gliding into the cove. "Yes, go ahead, push on," they say. I think of that goddess chant: *Every act of love and pleasure is a ritual in my name.*

"You mean," I say finally, "that it's fun being together, alone, just the two of us?"

She looks down at the handful of sand leaking through her long, tanned fingers onto the beach. Her body, her breasts are smooth and unwrinkled. "Yes."

"You have the most amazing body," I say.

She is blushing, but she leans her shoulder against mine and looks into my eyes. "So do you."

"I don't," I say quickly.

She takes my hand. "I have been looking at your body a lot." Now I am blushing. It is strange and exciting to be so intimate with my mother's best friend, the mother of my nursery-school classmate and her older brother. I lean back, letting my right hand rest just behind her hips.

She sighs.

"Genevieve," I say, touching her waist. She moves closer. "Do you believe in God?"

She laughs.

Before I can explain, she leans back and pulls me down next to her. Our lips touch, her hands wrap around me. *Yes,* I think. *Yes.*

"Yes, I believe in God," she whispers as my knee rises between her legs and my hands fold around her waist. "I've never done this," she says.

I can't answer. Desire has wadded my mouth with cotton.

"You realize," Genevieve says as she pulls down her bathing suit, "that I have loved you for years."

The words turn me molten; my breath catches. I am gazing at her breasts, round and pale and lovely, which she is offering to me as her fingers slip under the straps of my bikini.

"Since the piñata and the three-legged race," she whispers. "A long time I've wanted you." The waves come closer as her fingers brush my clit rhythmically, lovingly. She pulls me to her breasts. "I thought I wanted you on this sail for Eddy, but I wanted you for me."

I cannot believe the heat that comes from the intensity of her love. "My milk comes down," she whispers as I take her nipple in my mouth. I have never been offered so much. "Drink my milk. Drink as long as you want." I want to swallow her, feel her breast go down through my throat, into my breath, into my stomach and my womb. I look into her eyes, her gaze so hot, surprised, and alive that my clit stands up, my womb turns over and tumbles against her, over and down and inside and beneath.

Her arms tighten around me. This woman is loving me through my reserve, has found my broken garden, gone beyond the weeds and scattered sandbox of my childhood. She is holding me, spinning back, carrying me forward. She will not let go of me, will not let me fall.

When I lie on her, she moans, pulling me closer and closer. Her womb closes around me as I touch the woman who has loved me since childhood. "I want all those years back," she whispers, "all those times when I couldn't take you in my arms and hold you like this and make love to you when you came to play with my daughter."

"You have me now," I say.

She is crying, smiling. I cry with her, my fingers swirling so fast and hard against her clit that she arches and rises and shouts, so generous, so responsive that I hold her closer than I ever held my mother.

The air is softer, cooler. We are naked and sandy and wrapped in each other's arms, listening to the sea's waves, feeling our own. We walk naked into the water, my body white and thin; hers, full and tan, her beautiful breasts and hips streaked with sand. I swim into her arms. She holds my slippery form next to her slippery form, rocking me against her, holding me as the waves dip over us. "This is heaven," she says and laughs like a girl, her white hair gold in the setting sun. "I can't tell you how much I love this."

"Tell me."

"I love this more than I love everything."

A gull squawks above us. "Will you come to California?"

"How could I not?" She gazes at the horizon, where a sail catches the sky. "Everything has changed."

I nod.

"It's much better," she says, kissing me.

I laugh. Her lips are soft. "This feels like a great, huge love."

She nods, wiping something from her eye. "Very huge."

We dress, gazing at each other, savoring each moment.

She brushes her hand through my hair so tenderly, in such a familiar way that my heart trips. Slowly, arm in arm, we climb the path to the wider trail, then look behind at the blue cove, at the shadows in the white sand beneath the *palapa* where we lay, at the edge of the water. I wrap my arm around her waist; she wraps her arm around mine.

We row back to the boat, where we have dinner and gaze at each other across the cockpit. Much later, when Genevieve's husband goes to bed in the forward cabin and my parents are asleep below, Eddy and Genevieve and I sit beneath the stars, he and I smoking a joint, she sipping vodka, and we tell him that we are lovers. He smiles and looks from his mother to me and says, "I know. I have never seen you so happy."

Salt Water
by Barbara Wilson

She's in one of those photo albums that I rarely open anymore: plain blue vinyl cover, stick-on pages going yellow at the corners. Why would I think to open it? It's full of photographs of a foreign place, of a woman I lost contact with long ago.

But if I did open it, I would find her on an island off the coast of Sweden. The wind is blowing her fine brown-gold hair as she sits on a bench at the harbor. Our bikes are parked nearby, my old straw hat dangling off my handlebars. We're waiting for the ferry to the mainland or perhaps another island where we plan to take a ride. There are several photos like that in this album, of us waiting for a ferry; I must have asked passersby to snap a shot or two of both of us. I'm smaller than she is, wearing glasses, my short blond hair ruffling in the breeze. We both look brown, cheerful, very young, though we were in our early thirties. Other photos show her in her garden, all rocks and tiles and ceramic pots, the pink roses and red and purple hollyhocks climbing up the side of her yellow wood house. There are a few of her on the rocks where we used to sunbathe, by the two pools at the edge of the island. She's never fully clothed in the garden or by the sea. She didn't like my taking pictures, I remember now. Perhaps that's why she's frowning, just slightly but impatiently.

Most of the photos are from that one week in June when I visited her more than ten years ago.

None of my friends ever knew her, and few of them would remember if I said her name now: Monika Diechmann. "One of those straight women you were always fantasizing about?" Beth might tease, amused and sure in our love that those days are long behind me. Or Evie might say vaguely, "Wasn't she *German* or something?"

But the photo album isn't where I would look if I wanted to remember her. I would probably pull out the packet of thin square blue envelopes, twelve in all, with a postcard of a whitewashed Greek village tucked on top. I might trace the lines of her script to try to recall what was important to her to tell me. I suppose I would find a lot of words about solitude and loneliness, about her longing for a full-time, absorbing creative life. Fingering the letters might give me back that sense of possibility and joy I had every time I found one in my letter box; it might bring back her precise and considered speech. I might hear her say again, "Oh, Anne, how can I make you understand?"

If I really wanted to see her again though, I would dig through the many boxes in the studio and find my sketchbooks from those two Swedish summers, when I first began life drawing. She would not be posing — she had her own work to do — but standing before an open window, the curtains white, diaphanous, blowing into the room, with the sea beyond, roaring silently on the page. I think I would not be ashamed of the drawings, even though they were often rough and crude (the foreshortening a struggle then, the angle of her thin neck and narrow shoulders always a problem; I never captured her exactly).

If I could find that box of sketches underneath everything that has piled up since, I would probably also find the watercolors that I did, single sheets placed carefully in a portfolio. I once planned to have them framed, for I thought them fresh and lovely. I wonder if I still would or if I would be indifferent, would shrug them off, the way we do so many things we loved once, as faulty and imperfect.

It all seems longer than ten years ago that I first met Monika. At the time I was finishing up a six-month stay in Norway, where a Fulbright had given me the chance to take a semester off from my position teaching art history at a small college in Minnesota. A few years before, I'd finished my dissertation on a circle of Norwegian women painters active in the second half of the nineteenth century. Now I was narrowing my research to study two of the most prominent of the circle, Harriet Backer and Kitty Kielland. In the large galleries of Oslo and Bergen and Stavanger and in smaller provincial museums and private collections, I had looked long and hard at all the paintings of theirs I could find and had read what I could about them and about the feminist movement in Norway at the turn of the century. I was preparing to write a monograph when I returned home and perhaps some less-academic articles.

I was an ambitious but not driven 32-year-old, full of great enthusiasm for my subject. I'd been teaching for about five years at my college and was hoping to get tenure soon, though most of my work had been on women's art and the school was rather conservative. I was closeted, of course, but not particularly miserable about it. I lived alone, and though nothing lasting had yet worked out for me, I was sure it would. In general, things had gone well for me. Without thinking much about it, I would probably have considered myself happy and, except for not being able to talk about my personal life with most of my colleagues or family, quite well-adjusted and socially at ease. I was still pleased about having a Ph.D. and having some connection to the world of ideas and culture. I had come from a small town in Minnesota where people did not get above themselves, at least not very far, without being punished, either by God or gossip, so I was used to being modest about my accomplishments, which did not prevent me from being secretly proud.

Oslo, then, in the early '80s, a cool bright summer evening full of delicacy and possibility. An acquaintance called Astrid, another art professor, had picked me up and was taking me to the opening of a show of contemporary Swedish women artists. Imposing as usual in a handwoven tunic and heavy wooden beads, Astrid lectured me until we got there on women's liberation and the female artist, a subject she had recently discovered.

The gallery was packed with tall Scandinavians imbibing freely. The art was the usual mix, for that time and place, of styles and subjects. A few sentimental figurative paintings of mothers and children; some nudes of men, meant to shock; a great number of murky and jarring abstracts; and plenty of wall hangings and sculpture constructions making use of Swedish craft techniques. A few pieces had an obvious, even mythological female sensibility, such as the painting of a woman giving birth to the planet Earth. Most, however, were reflections of current preoccupations with medium as opposed to subject matter. There was something huge and paint-slathered and industrial and thick and rope-twined and plastered about almost everything there.

There was only one artist, one set of paintings that drew me. Each of the six canvases was small compared to the those in the rest of the exhibit, and each had the dominating image of a rock or a rocky island in the center of a stained color field that suggested the unsettling pale blue of sky or water but that had no horizon. Around the rock at the edges of the canvases marched and spun meticulously rendered seashells and pebbles. The effect was one of lightness but not playfulness, a little vertiginous and very solitary.

I asked Astrid about the painter, whose name I could see was Monika Diechmann.

"She's not really Swedish, you know," Astrid whispered. "Some of the others seem to think she shouldn't be in the show. Her mother's Swedish, and she spends her summers in Sweden on some island off the coast near Göteborg, but she's really German, and most of the year she lives in Cologne."

I went over to the woman Astrid pointed out. She had a perfectly oval face with a broad brow on a fragile, even spindly neck. Her brown-gold hair was pulled back into a knot, and she was wearing thin gold hoops. Her eyes were large and light green, slightly protuberant with thin, bluish lids. She had on some lipstick and was wearing a cream knit pullover that showed a naked brown shoulder. If it had not been for her tan, which was quite dark, she might have looked like a Madonna from a Northern Renaissance painting.

I'd learned Norwegian to pursue my research but was still better at reading than speaking, for almost everyone I worked with in Norway spoke perfect English. I stumbled even saying something simple to her, namely that I found her work interesting, and she answered me in a clear, steady voice in English. Her accent was German.

"And what interests you?"

"The translucency. Everything around the island shimmers with light. The seashells look as if they have tiny bulbs inside them."

Afterward, when Astrid asked me what we'd talked about, I told her that Monika had said, "Thank you for not asking what it all means."

We had talked instead about technique and had quickly come to an agreement that we did not care much for anyone else's art here but hers. "And are you an artist yourself?" she asked me.

"No, an art historian. A professor." I told her about Harriet Backer and Kitty Kielland and the research I had done and was completing on the circle of women painters in Norway a hundred years ago.

I was explaining to her how thrilling it had been for me to discover the existence of this group and to see the ways in which women had helped each other in the earlier wave of the feminist movement, when Monika interrupted. "And weren't there any women who were not part of this circle?" She had a quizzical, not unfriendly look.

"Yes, there was one. At least one. Oda Krogh. She doesn't fit into my research very well. She was not a spinster who saw art as the only alternative to being a governess. She was not quite respectable. She married young and had two children, then began to study painting with Christian Krogh, the bohemian painter and novelist. She divorced her first husband and married Krogh and had two more children. She was the girl in the bad-boy gang of the 1880s."

"Why don't you write about her?"

"Because I'm interested in the larger picture, not the anomaly," I explained.

Monika's broad brow knitted as if she were trying to understand. "But the important thing is, do you like her painting?"

"I like her paintings almost more than anyone's," I admitted.

"That's very strange then that you write only about Harriet Backer and Kitty Kielland."

"I like their paintings too," I said, but Monika turned away. She surveyed the room, which had gotten even more stuffy and crowded, and she waved her hand at the walls. "I wonder," she said, "in a hundred years if this will be called a circle, if I will be mentioned as part of a circle of Swedish women painters."

"It's easier for art historians to see painters in groups," I said. "Those outside the groups sometimes don't get seen."

"I want to be seen. And yet I feel I have nothing in common with them," she said, fixing those large light eyes on me. They were the color of just-peeled green grapes and that shape too under-neath the thin eyelids. She was so delicate that it seemed she might break, but when I looked at her hands, I saw they were long-fin-gered and strong. I found myself wanting to take hold of one of them. "Not as a woman, not as a painter," Monika said almost wistfully, looking around.

"Oh, I hate that kind of opportunistic person," Astrid said afterward, dropping me off at my rented room. "Doesn't want to call herself a feminist, hardly even a woman, yet is perfectly happy to be asked to exhibit in a show called 'Swedish Women Painters.' I mean, she's not even really Swedish!"

"She lives there three months of every year," I protested. "On that island. She said I could come visit her next week. Before I leave for home."

"She asked you to come stay?" Astrid stared. "Are you sure you didn't misunderstand? You talked only a few minutes. And all the Swedes have been complaining how unfriendly she is."

Silently I held out my hand. In it was a tiny slip of paper, and it said in tiny letters: "Monika Diechmann. Take the train to Göteborg. Walk to the bus station and take the bus to the ferry dock at R. Take the ferry to A. Anyone can tell you my address."

The island of A. was the last stop of a ferry that traveled through an archipelago of small stony islands. A. seemed as we approached it to rise straight out of the sea, a pyramid of rock with pastel houses scattered up and down its slopes and red boat sheds clus-tered around the natural harbor. It was midafternoon, all sparkle and light; the scent of diesel oil, fish, and the ocean mixed togeth-er in the sunshine. I stepped over fishing nets on the dock and avoided children and dogs. As a stranger I found it all looked fes-tive and yet unwelcoming, the way a new place can seem to be. I had been traveling by train, bus, and ferry since 6 this morning.

I had written a card to Monika to tell her the day and approx-imate time I'd be arriving, but she wasn't there to greet me at the dock. I asked a fisherman working on his boat where I might find her. He jerked his head up the hill without saying anything, and I began to walk along the dock, past a small store and a line of red-painted boat sheds and then up the only street I could see, a narrow, winding path paved with large stones and occasional steps. From this path other smaller paths led off to painted wood cottages, some rather shabby, some bowered by climbing roses and clematis, with cats in the windows and weather vanes on the roofs. I asked the few people I met on the path about Monika's house, and they always pointed up and higher.

What if she hadn't been serious about the visit? What if she'd forgotten all about my coming? What if the postcard I'd sent hadn't gotten here? What if she weren't expecting me, didn't want me? What if she didn't live alone or had a lover here?

I had told my landlady in Oslo so gaily that I was going off to Sweden for a week. I had told everyone I knew. It had made me feel happy and special and as if something amazing were about to happen. I had held in my mind the picture of the dancing seashells around the mysterious rock and the picture of those light green eyes in the brown face.

There was one last house, high up on the hill, with an unhampered view of the sea. It was yellow and had been newly painted. There were small-paned windows, red shutters, a garden in back protected by a drystone wall with plants growing over it and in the crevices. I walked the last steps up the path and up the stairs of the red porch with its potted geraniums. I knocked on the door. I could smell the ocean, the salt of it, in every breath I took. There was no answer, and unsure of what else to do, I sat down on the porch and after a moment fell into a doze.

"Oh, there you are," she said, waking me up, coming around the side of the house, pulling on a shirt over her bikini bottom. "I was working in the garden."

She pressed her body quickly close to mine and kissed my cheek. She smelled of nut oil and dirt. I felt her breasts, careless, under the open shirt.

"Did you get my card?" I said.

"Oh, yes. How amazing that you actually came!" A sudden shyness seemed to come over her. "I don't have many visitors. None, in fact."

I still dream sometimes about the house that Monika lived in, and when I dream, it's always summer, always June. I still wake wishing I lived there, in that house that managed to be large and light and high on a stone hill and yet secretive and hidden too, surrounded by flowers and drystone walls wound through with cubbyholes and crannies.

Downstairs it was old-fashioned, with heavy furniture and objects left from earlier generations. There was a sunporch with a writing secretary piled with bills and letters; two pantries, one of which had been remodeled into a bathroom; and a dark, rather dingy kitchen, which had only a two-burner stove and a small refrigerator. There was a dining room, its carved table also piled with papers and boxes and laundry to be sorted, and, through etched glass doors, a large parlor with crumbling leather chairs and a horsehair settee, a tall clock with a painted, unmoving face, a piano that was out of tune, worn thick red carpets, and shelves of leather-bound books and old music scores and literary journals. There was a large tile stove, its tiles decorated in bright folk fashion, like something you might see in a painting by Carl Larsson, but sadly stained with smoke. It had been years since the house had been in frequent use. Most of the journals, brown-edged, were from the '50s, when Monika's uncle had lived here for a time, she explained. "He was running from the world," she said. "He was a book critic who wanted to write a novel and never did."

Upstairs, however, all was light and bare. In the small room Monika showed me to, there was only a single wooden bed painted French blue with a yellow-striped comforter. A painted table and a brass lamp. A straight-backed chair. No closet or dresser but an old-fashioned washbasin and pitcher set under a window that faced the sea. When Monika opened the shutters, I had a view of other islands of the archipelago and could hear the waves crashing below on the rocks.

There were two other small rooms like it upstairs, one of which Monika slept in, but they were above the garden and faced the harbor from which I'd climbed. Red and purple hollyhocks had climbed up nearly to the second floor. When I looked down I saw a white ironwork table and chairs in the midst of roses, geraniums, and stock. The largest room, once a bedroom, had been turned into a studio, which Monika called her atelier. Like my room, it fronted the sea, and its windows, tall and narrow, small-paned, in a row, took up most of one wall. The windows were slightly open, and the strong fresh ocean breeze came in and blew the long curtains of some thin ivory material, perhaps chiffon, in streamers toward us.

"I work in this room every morning," said Monika. "Sometimes all day."

The smell of oils and turpentine mixed with the warm ocean breeze; there were two mismatched old walnut tables, on which lay paints and sketches and shells and stones. A chair or two and a bookcase haphazardly filled with battered and interesting art books in several languages. Large canvases everywhere, too much to take in all at once.

Monika stood before the open window, looking out to sea, breathing deep, and her darkly tanned body — still, unself-consciously half nude — made a shape, cut out of shadow, in front of the light.

Then she turned and smiled at me. "Do you think you could be happy here?"

The island did not have beaches, sandy or otherwise. The edges ran for the most part straight down to the sea except at the natural harbor, which was protected by a breakwater. This harbor was the focal point of the small community. It had the store and post office and one café; it was where the foot ferry arrived and departed and where the small fishing boats jostled uneasily with the sailboats and cruisers of the summer people and visitors.

No one swam at the harbor. In fact, you couldn't swim off the island at all; the rocks were too steep and sharp and the currents too unreliable. Parents took their children to one end of the island, where the rocks sloped into a shallow inner pool and where someone had constructed a slide. The other place to take a dip wasn't far from Monika's house, though it was a bit of a scramble down over the hill and a over a series of vertically angled slabs of smooth dark rock. Because it was hard to get to, it was not much frequented and certainly not by many of the summer visitors or children. However, it was one of the nearest places on the island to the sea, and the area had flat dark rocks all around it, perfect for sunbathing.

As I've said, you couldn't actually swim in the sea. There were instead two pools. One was shaped like a bottle or a vase. It had a channel carved by the waves, which led to a pool filled with cold green water that was about shoulder high. Even though it wasn't terribly deep, it would have been impossible to get in or out of without the help of a ladder, which had been bolted to the side of one of the smooth rock slabs. The other pool was much shallower and lay even closer to the sea and was more subject to its movements, for the larger pool was protected by its channel from the roughest of the waves.

This was not true of the shallower pool, although at first I found it the quieter, warmer, more restful place to be. I had, the first day I went to the ocean with Monika, lowered myself down by the ladder into the vase-shaped pool and been shocked by its coldness, its tartness. I hesitated and then plunged: Immediately there was a fresh stinging at my eyes and nose, and when I surfaced I had the taste of salt adhering to the corners of my mouth.

I had never swum in salt water before.

I did not find it refreshing. I felt as if my heart had stopped from the cold plunge and from the harsh briny taste of the sea. I had nothing to compare it to, for I had swum only in lakes and ponds before, and they were freshwater, though often muddy and full of bugs.

I got out immediately, gasping. Although the air was warm, my body was covered with goose bumps and even looked slightly bluish. As my skin dried, a faint white powdery residue remained on the surface, and when I tasted it, it was salty. Of course the sea is salt — you learn that as a child — but a book fact is different from a physical one.

Monika had plunged in after me and was still there, splashing and standing up and swimming small strokes around the rim of the pool. Her brown head poked out, seal-like, and she kept her face. upturned and laughed at me. "Too cold? No, it's just right. It's *perfect.*" She had taken off all her clothes, which only meant her bikini bottom and short T-shirt, before she went in. I had only my conservative one-piece tank suit, which I now rolled off wetly into a lump, and a towel, which I wrapped tightly around me until I was warmer.

After a few minutes, however, having gotten my breath back, I thought that I would try the shallower pool. I edged down to it and put in a foot. There was only about four inches of water, and it was warm. I sat at the edge of the pool and put my feet in. I looked at the small animal life that was flourishing there; found a crab and several snails. I had not put my wet suit back on, and now the sun beat down on my back. In a minute I would have to smear on sunscreen, for I was fair and burned easily, but for just this minute the warmth was seductive. Behind me I could hear the strength and movement of the sea, slapping lightly and then harder at the rocks, a rhythm that went on unvaryingly and yet always with new variations, softer, softer, now harder, harder, harder.

"Anne," called Monika.

She was standing on a rock directly above me, still wet from her swim, the water dripping off her brown-and-gold triangle and down her legs. Her hair was streaked back from her forehead, and she was drying her ears with the towel.

"Anne," she said again, more forcefully, pointing behind me.

But I didn't turn for an instant, didn't understand. I simply sat and stared up at her, at her dripping body, brown all over, at her triangle almost above me, at her finger pointing.

Only at the last second did I turn and face the sudden large wave, which roared up the side of the rocks and hit me full in the face with a cold sweet hand. I had my mouth open somehow, perhaps in surprise, and so I swallowed some of it, and it got in my eyes and my nose. And yet this time it was not such a shock. In a strange way it was exhilarating, this smack, this drenching, this sudden flare of cold in a hot world. It was like waking up, like being kicked into being more alive.

"Oh," I said when I could speak and then "Oh" several times as I could see another large wave forming. I jumped up and scrambled to where Monika stood, laughing at me, and watched the next wave hit where I had been.

It must have been the second day that I began to draw. I had not really had a plan for this visit. I'd brought my notes on Harriet and Kitty and perhaps thought I could do some work on my monograph. But the parlor downstairs was dark during the day and musty. Out of curiosity I explored the shelves and flipped through the journals. They had yellowed paper covers, old-fashioned type, a formal feel. A few had penciled comments in the margins. I looked at the sepia and the black-and-white photographs on the walls, many of which dated from the early part of the century. The island had had fewer houses then; the harbor, sailing ships. Trunks and kegs and wooden boxes of salt cod were piled at the dockside. In those days the house had seemed to burst at the seams with family and friends, prosperous, sturdy blond Swedes on summer holiday in beautiful Edwardian dress that gave over to French-style striped shirts, baggy white cotton trousers, and espadrilles.

I read a little, stared out at the windows, tried to understand where I was and what world I had walked into. Then I took a walk around the island, which took less than an hour, it was so small. I sat in the tiny café and wrote a postcard to my parents and one to Astrid and one more to my cousin Nancy. Then I went back to the house and asked Monika to give me a sketchbook.

I was shy about using even a pencil at first. I had hardly drawn for years. Once, as a child, my hands had told me what I saw in the world, but later everything went through my eyes and was given a name and a date and a history. I learned to talk about brushstrokes without feeling a brush in my fingers, about contour and mass without touching or trying to describe that touch except through my vision. I learned for research purposes and in order to teach students who had never held a brush to focus on paintings for their subject matter more than their style. Students were always interested in biographies, and I had come to think biographically too, especially as I began to resurrect the lives of the forgotten women who'd painted the pictures I was studying.

So my earliest sketches in Monika's studio, done sitting in a corner of the room on a stool, were feeble and unsure. My first drawing of her was little better than a nursery-school stick figure. My first attempt to recall the rules of perspective made the windows behind her look like flying carpets. My first reaching back into what I had known of how to create volume and mass through the use of shadowing — not what I knew intellectually — resulted in shells that looked like alien spacecraft. I hid those first drawings and kept working, remembering back through my fingers to how I'd drawn as a child and adolescent, before I learned too much about what art should be.

Monika paid no attention to me. She was utterly absorbed and lost to everything but the canvas before her. All year she taught art in a primary school. Summer was her time to do her own painting. She set up her easel before the window that faced the sea, but she didn't paint the sea. Neither of us painted the sea. Monika painted from objects on a table covered with stiff white butcher's paper, mostly seashells, and from drawings and photos of seashells.

That first summer I was there, she was still working on a series of paintings of islands and shells. Sometimes the shell was large, and the island hid inside it; sometimes the shells lay in a broken mass of fragments at the bottom of the picture while the island loomed very large above; and sometimes the shells seemed to be whirling above the island in an aerial and threatening perspective. But usually the color harmonies were the same: thin blue background, shells (usually some sort of conch or cowrie) painted very meticulously in pinks, whites, and pale yellows with accents of brown-orange, and the island always gray and rocky and lifeless, closed in upon itself like a fist. Perhaps *lifeless* is the wrong word. The island rocks had a magical quality of stillness.

I sketched and painted Monika. At her easel, at the table, with the windows behind her, with her seashells. Sometimes I used charcoal or pastel; one day I did a watercolor series; often I simply scribbled in pencil and ink. This was how I got to know her body, for after the first halfhearted attempt to cover herself politely, she went back to wearing what she usually wore in summer to paint, which was precisely nothing.

That's how I saw her, how she allowed me to see her. Nothing hidden, nothing pretend. Narrow, slightly rounded shoulders, a faint hump beginning below the back of her neck. Not much hair, just the simple triangle and two soft patches under her arms. Long fingers and toes, with a high arch in her foot. High applelike breasts with brown nipples, a rounded belly like a little girl's, with an outie belly button. A long scar on one forearm, a compound fracture after falling from a tree when she was eight, and another scar, a little white one on her forehead from a piece of flying glass, a car accident in her teens.

Her brown hair was streaked with gold, and she usually wore it in a simple ponytail when working, sometimes with a band around her forehead to keep the wisps out of her eyes. I've described before her green eyes and oval face. Her nose was bent a little to one side, the nostrils flared easily. It was a small oddity; it made her look feral, as if she were sniffing the air. She had asthma and said that as a child it had been quite bad but that now she was mainly fine, though sometimes she could have trouble catching her breath and she was still plagued by hay fever and sinus problems. That's why the ocean air was so good for her in summer. Perhaps because of her asthma, her lips were often slightly parted, the better to breathe. Those parted lips, never dry, always moist even without lipstick, were what I had the most trouble with. I would look and look at them, never able to get the shape quite right; I would usually make them too sweet, too bow-shaped.

I often thought of Dürer when I drew her or Lucas Cranach. Those luminous, translucent eyes, that neck that looked like it might snap in the breeze, those breasts that sat so high on the rib cage. That protective modesty of expression, that oval face, those narrow shoulders all were of the German Renaissance and went oddly with her complete lack of interest in wearing clothes.

She was a good subject for me in that she never moved too quickly or abruptly but always with economy and simplicity. She was a slow and careful painter. Two or three brushstrokes and then she put the brush down, stepped back, and considered.

That same ease and focus were also how she went through her day. She habitually woke up early, around 6, and had a cup of black tea with milk. She did something in the garden for half an hour that looked like tai chi but which she told me was bioenergetics. It was a way, she said without explaining, of dealing with past losses and unlocking tension and opening channels. A quiet but forceful sound came out of her when she did these exercises, something like "H-a-a-ach!"

Afterward, with another cup of tea and a slice of bread and cheese, she went up to her studio. She was always at work by 7, sometimes even earlier. I joined her later, but as the days went on, I rose earlier too and with more excitement. I could hardly wait to get to the studio myself. On waking I would always put my head out my window and take deep lungfuls of the sea air, and the salt wind would burn a little as I took it in.

We rarely spoke while we were working, but when it came time for lunch, at noon or 1, she had me look at her work for the morning and would ask me what I thought. Occasionally I showed her my sketches. One day I remarked how familiar it seemed, visually, to draw her standing before the open window. "So many nineteenth-century paintings show a woman in front of a window. In the foreground it's terribly cozy and bourgeois: green plants, pictures on the walls, chairs and tables with tea sets. What could they want that wasn't inside that room? They have their book, their piano, their sewing. And yet the figures always look pensive and confined. Outside is the world, glowing with light, strangely distant and blurred. The window is open, yet they can't get to what is out there. Being women, they were trapped and passive."

"Don't you think it's still true?" asked Monika, not turning her eyes from her painting. "Here we are, two women inside while the beautiful world is out there."

"It can't have the same meaning now, now that we're free to choose whether to stand in front of the window or to go out."

"Are we so free?" she said.

"Well, of course," I answered and began to go into all the obvious ways in which the feminist movement of the last decade or more had given us new possibilities.

Monika listened politely — or perhaps she didn't listen at all. For after I'd finished my long exposition, she merely said, "I think we still look out the window and want what we cannot have."

In the afternoons we sunbathed by the rocks and pools or took trips to the other islands, bringing along battered bikes she'd pulled out from her small basement. Monika, who paid so much attention to the details of life, would make us sandwiches — smoked salmon and cucumbers, Jarlsberg and sharp mustard — for these outings and would take along bottles of water that she'd lightly squeezed with lemon. If we passed a café, we had an ice cream and a coffee with cream, sitting outside.

One afternoon, two days before I was to leave, we took a long bike trip. Usually Monika could go faster and longer than I. But that day, perhaps because it was very hot or perhaps because we went too far, she became very tired. She began to cough and to gasp, to have trouble breathing. I could hardly get her on the ferry and had to leave the two bikes at the harbor, leaning against a post, while I helped her walk home.

"What can I do?" I kept asking. "Shall I call a doctor?"

"No, no," she kept saying between gasps. "There's no doctor here." And then when she could speak a little easier, she explained, "It's just my asthma. I usually don't have it here. I don't understand. It was just a little too much today."

At the house she took some asthma medication and used an inhaler, then lay down. When she got up for dinner, she was fine. After I had helped her to her bed, I went back down to retrieve the bikes and bought some smoked shrimp and new potatoes at the market. I was worried about Monika, but still I had a kind of singing feeling in my veins. I had supported her up the hill, had held her brown sweaty body close to mine. I could still feel her skin on my palms.

That evening we had dinner in the garden. I did everything the way Monika would have: put a checked tablecloth on the table, set out mismatched good china, fit new candles into the tarnished silver holders. I went down to her cellar and pulled out a bottle of cool white German wine. Every year, she said, she brought a case of it from home. I boiled the potatoes and sprinkled them with dill from the garden and arranged the shrimp on butter lettuce leaves. I cut thin slices of rye bread and put out cheese and butter.

"How lovely!" she said when she came down, breathing normally, her nostrils only a little flared. She had on the cream knit shirt I remembered from the Oslo gallery, and her brown-gold hair was pulled back in a knot. "How lovely of you to make this for me! It's good, isn't it, to make things beautiful, all the details of life, to make them right?"

I was thinking, *See, I can be the way you want. I can be like you.*

The evening was warm, and in the garden we were protected from the wind. We stayed there late, lighting the candles at 11, though they were still hardly necessary, drinking one bottle and then another. Monika talked about living alone in Germany, how it was different there than here. "In Cologne I often find myself lonely, but here I rarely am. There, the phone rings, and there are letters, and I go out with friends, but I'm lonely all the same. Here, nothing ever happens. Sometimes I go days without talking to a soul, and yet I never feel odd about it."

"I can imagine that you have a lot of friends," I said. I was really very curious about her life in Cologne.

"Not many. It's so much work, keeping up with people, and then they feel bad that you don't call them. Sometimes I'd prefer to spend the evening by myself, even though I know I will not get any work done and in a way I will feel miserable knowing my friends are out having fun without me. But being alone is the only way I know to keep the channel open to my imagination. Painting — even not painting but thinking about painting — involves a great deal of solitude."

"Tell me about your flat in Cologne."

"It's not like this," she said. "This is a magic place. There, well, it's neither old nor modern. The building comes from the '50s and has a kind of square solidity to it. I have a room for my painting, not a proper atelier because of the light, but still filled with my paintings and art supplies. I have a chair there, and often in the evening I just go there and close the door to the rest of the apartment. I will sit reading something, poetry perhaps or letters between writers or artists. There is a window overlooking the garden. And I will dream of being here in summer and of the sea."

"It sounds very romantic to me," I said.

"*You* are the romantic one, not I," said Monika, smiling. "For me, being alone is partly a matter of habit and partly one of practicality. Perhaps it's also been a kind of burden that I wish to throw off — this reluctance, this loneliness."

"Then how am I romantic?" I said. "I often feel the same things."

"You're romantic because you think that feminism can somehow solve this feeling of loneliness that we all as human beings share. You dream of a kind of utopia where women could be both alone and together."

"Why is that a utopia? Women have managed it in the past. I'm sure there are many women still trying it today."

"If you believe in this utopia, then why aren't you trying to live it?"

"Well, because, you know that I...because of where I live and teach..." I stumbled. I certainly couldn't say to Monika that I thought she and I had been living it this past week.

"No, you are not *not* living it because you live in some tiny town in Minnesota. You are not living it because it is an impossible dream. You imagine that Harriet Backer and Kitty Kielland and their group had something of what you want — but you only imagine it because you don't know anything about what their real lives were like."

"No, that's not true. I do know quite a bit about their lives, and there's no reason to suppose they didn't successfully blend close companionship and a strong network of colleagues with plenty of time alone. Their work itself has a very solitary look to it. The landscapes Kitty did look as if there's no one else around for miles, and Harriet is constantly showing a woman seated by herself in a room somewhere, working, reading, playing the piano."

Monika pulled apart her bread. "It's good when you defend yourself," she said. "It's good you want to fight me a little."

"I don't want to fight you!" I said. "I want — "

"What? What do you want from me?"

To be the Harriet to your Kitty? I couldn't tell her that. "I don't want anything."

"That's good," she said. "That's for the best. Don't ask anything from me. Then you won't be disappointed." She smiled as if she were joking, but her eyes were serious.

While we had been sitting there past 11, a stiff little wind had come up. We went into the parlor, and Monika lit a coal fire. She began to tell me about the photographs on the walls.

"This is all my mother's family. A typical bourgeois Swedish family. They were in shipping in Göteborg and built this house to spend summers in. In earlier times there were lots of kids, but my grandparents had only two, my uncle Edvard and my mother. The house isn't really mine, you know. It still belongs to Edvard. He's rather old now, about seventy-five, so he doesn't come out here much. He lives in Stockholm."

"You said he lived here once?"

"Yes, for a time in the '50s. He was getting a divorce and was having some kind of breakdown, I suppose. He announced to his family that he was finally going to write his great novel. But he did no novel writing that anyone has ever seen. Instead he wrote a book here about Swedish literature. It's a very cruel book," she added. "He was reviled across the country, and that made him feel better. He made a full recovery. His daughter Sara is the member of the family I'm closest to; the rest of the family — " Monika broke off and straightened one picture and then another. Then she went on, "They treated my mother very badly after the war. Of course, everybody hated the Germans, and then my mother went and married one!"

"Was your father in the war?"

"No, his family had him in school in Sweden early, and then he went on to study at Göteborg. That's where he and my mother met. He was not a soldier, and so what if he had been? All my friends in Cologne had fathers who were soldiers, eighteen-year-old boys who were forced into the army. But my father was only German, and that was enough for my mother's family."

"And you're the only daughter. Do you feel Swedish or German?"

"If I had a choice, I'd be neither," Monika said. "I'd be something nice, like a Laplander or Cherokee Indian. But I'm afraid I have no choice. Your family, what is it?"

"Scottish and Norwegian," I said offhandedly. My family was completely uninteresting compared with hers.

"If I had a choice," said Monika, "I would live in a place that had no nationality, that was not even on the map."

"I looked on the map when I planned to come here," I said. "And I didn't find this island."

Monika looked pleased. "You see? Perhaps it's happening already."

That night she told me about something that had happened to her as a child. She had been only two years old. The war had been over for a few years, but the economy was still shaky. Her parents were in their twenties, unsure about their parenting. Monika had gotten tuberculosis. She went to the hospital and was transferred to a special TB hospital for children in another city. She was to stay there for eighteen months.

Her parents never came to visit her.

Afterward her mother would say that they had been told not to visit. Afterward her father would explain how poor they were. To take the train to this city far away, to have to find lodging and meals, to take off time from work (he was just rising in his field as a petrochemical engineer), all this was difficult if not impossible.

"It wasn't until years later that I realized my mother had come from a wealthy Swedish family. They would have certainly made it possible for her to visit me or to stay in the city where I was. But the family quarrel had not been made up then, and she didn't want to ask them for help.

"They say that I cried very much when they left me at the hospital but that after that I didn't cry at all. The nurses wrote to them and said what a good child I was. I took my medicine and obeyed all the rules. And I never cried at all.

"When I was cured and they came to collect me at the hospital, I was almost four. I didn't know who they were. I didn't want to go with them. The hospital and the nurses were all I remembered, all I knew. 'Imagine that,' my mother will say. 'Monika didn't even know her own parents.' "

Painting is lovemaking, Picasso said somewhere, and as a feminist art historian, I despised him for saying it. When I taught even my most basic Introduction to Art History courses, I tried to alert my students to the fact that the heroic male artists made use of women's bodies in particular ways, which led to a dichotomy of men as artists, women as subjects. "Ripe fruit," Renoir called his models. Other artists called them worse.

But with the charcoal or the brush in my hands, my fingers moving about the page, I understood in a way I never had before that drawing is a kind of touching, a kind of sexual touching that, while not the same as lovemaking, is certainly near to it. To make a flowing mark on the page is not so different from running a finger along the slope of a shoulder, over the roundness of a breast, down to the softness of a belly, the curve of a hip.

I don't know now, looking back, if Monika was indifferent to my constant scrutiny or whether she only pretended that she was. At the end of the day she would sometimes look at my drawings of her, but all she would say was "Good" or "You're improving."

She never drew me, of course, and I kept my clothes on when I worked. For me to remove them would have had a different meaning. A sexual meaning. It would have been a sign that I wanted her.

Her nudity was not a sign. At least not enough of one for me to be sure.

On the last evening of my visit we took a walk to the sea, down to the two pools. We had, in fact, spent a large part of the afternoon there because it was so hot, and I had gotten more sunburned than I should have. I felt a little feverish, though that might have also been due to drinking more German wine at dinner. When we clambered over the rocks, they were still warm, and we lay down to watch the sky and sea. The sun even at 10 o'clock was very far from going down. I was warm through and through, and yet the slightest breeze kept tickling the surface of my skin.

We lay there and talked about all kinds of things in the most easy, friendly way possible, and still I kept a hold on myself, still I watched what I revealed.

"Do you ever think about having children?" she asked.

"Well…no." All week I had wanted to come out to her, but I couldn't find words that I didn't think might scare her off. These days past had been so perfect, so fragile and magic, that I didn't want to break their spell. I wanted to do nothing that was not natural for both of us.

"Like your women artists of the nineteenth century," she teased. "Career and children are incompatible."

"Without a…partner, it would be difficult," I said. "In twentieth-century America."

"I find myself thinking of a child more than a partner. I suppose I would like to know what it feels like. Pregnancy. But I don't know if I would be a good mother."

"You must really like children," I said, "to work with them every day."

"I don't know if I like children so much," she said calmly. "I like the part of them I see when we make art together. But would I like to be a mother — all that noise and disruption? That's the question. I don't suppose I will ever find out."

A few moments passed. The sky was turning pink and yellow like the luminous interior of one of her shells.

"Are you..." I had to ask, "seeing anyone?"

There was a silence, then she said calmly, "A man, you mean? Oh, no. I think those days are over. They were always so serious, those German men. Swedes too. People say men don't want commitment. That's a lie. They are dying to get married and have you wash their socks."

I laughed, feeling unreasonably happy. "Why don't we have one last swim?"

We took off our clothes and jumped, one after the other, into the larger, vase-shaped pool. As always, the coldness took my breath away. "I thought it would have warmed up during the day."

"This one never warms up," she said. "Because it's deeper and because the channel goes directly into the sea. It's always filled with fresh water."

"Salt water."

"Yes, fresh salt water."

I wanted to get out immediately as I usually did but forced myself to stay. And then a strange thing happened. The water began to feel not exactly warmer but more familiar to me. My limbs were all outlined with cold as if I were a pencil drawing, but inside the lines my body was lush and swollen. My arm brushed against Monika's, then my leg, and it was as if the pencil edges broke and smeared. How warm she was! She came around back of me and pressed her body up against mine a moment. Her breasts were shells, her triangle a tickle of seaweed against the backs of my thighs.

"It's been very good for me, having you here," Monika said. "I will miss you when you're gone. Can't you stay longer?"

My younger sister was getting married in a week's time, and I was supposed to be her maid of honor. I had to; there was no way out. I felt embarrassed to say this, though, to Monika. I said instead, "I could come back."

"Oh, you'll get busy."

"No, I won't."

"When I feel easy around someone, I feel almost normal," she said, and now she held my shoulders and let her body float up to the surface behind me as if I were a pole and she a flag. "As if the loneliness is just part of life and not the whole thing."

"My ideal is Harriet Backer and Kitty Kielland," I said. "Two women, two artists, living together for most of their lives yet having separate spheres. To me, that's what love — feminism — is all about."

"Oh, you and your feminism," Monika laughed and let me go and swam away. She didn't say anything about love.

We were quiet then, happy, I think, even though I was also in pain, hot and cold at the same time, my mouth brushed with salt instead of sweetness. We paddled around the little pool by the sea in a world that was turning peach and rose and lemon yellow.

"I won't get out till you do," I said, teeth chattering.

"I'm never getting out."

So then I had to.

Maggie's Hands
by J. M. Redmann

When the train entered the tunnel, Eleanor paused in her reading. In that dark, unexpected moment when daylight was swallowed by an underground passage, Maggie's hands would have...would have gone to unexpected places. Even after all their years together, Eleanor still hadn't known where to expect Maggie's hands to travel. Her breasts, between her legs, sometimes her thigh, down her back, under her ass.

"Touch should occasionally be unexpected," Maggie would say as her hands caressed Eleanor. And with Maggie it sometimes deliciously was.

The train left the dark tunnel, the bright sunlight suddenly blinding off the snowbanks. Eleanor was on the train from Boston to New York. Another academic conference. A paper to present. *We all must have our passions,* she thought, *whether it is the nineteenth-century novel or the local football team.* Her fellow academics would look askance at her if she voiced such a thought. A cause should elicit the passion; passion shouldn't be searching for a cause to attach itself to. Maggie had talked of the courage to follow your passions, adding, "I'm not talking about sex now, you know." Maggie's passion was photography, the play of light and dark, captured images of people in the daily routines that made up a life. For Eleanor, it was the words on a page written long ago. She wanted to talk across those centuries, to reach into lives long gone.

Eleanor remembered how dislocated her life had become when Maggie entered it. That first night, when the only passion between them was sex. Eleanor's first one-night stand.

It had been an ill-fated hiking trip, organized by some women Eleanor barely knew. Three cars and one van of nature-loving lesbians transformed into two cars and one van of cold, wet, and tired women who wanted to get home. One car had been lost to an arguing pair of lovers (ex-lovers by the next weekend, she later learned). Eleanor was one of the displaced. Three women stared at the two remaining seats in the van. Maggie had solved the problem by turning to Eleanor and saying, "You're too tall to sit in my lap, so I guess I get to sit in yours." They had crammed themselves into the backseat of the van, sharing it with the piled-high hiking gear.

At first Eleanor had felt stiff and awkward; she wasn't used to women she barely knew sitting in her lap. She was unsure of where to place her hands. Would Maggie think she was trying something if she opened her legs a bit? Eleanor thought of herself as the shy, gawky bookworm, one of life's observers. She was five nine and a half and had worn glasses since she was five years old. Maggie was shorter, her hair a mass of golden brown curls, in contrast to Eleanor's straight dark hair. Maggie had been the one telling the jokes that the other women had laughed at, taking pictures, cajoling them into revealing unexpected, intimate pieces of themselves. She was a professional photographer, had already had an exhibit of her work in some downtown gallery.

If Maggie felt uncomfortable about sitting in Eleanor's lap, she didn't show it. Eleanor had once asked about it later. Maggie had replied, "Stiff? No, of course not. I couldn't wait to be sitting on top of you. You were one of the quiet ones, a challenge. By the time the rain started, I knew I wanted to bed you." Eleanor wasn't sure if she really thought that or if she was just playing out the myth of Maggie as the great adventuress.

That night Maggie's hands had traveled. Eleanor would have never dared. She was both taken aback and pleased when Maggie put a hand on her breast. Just like that. It was only a few inches — what worlds can be traveled in a few inches! Maggie's hand on Eleanor's breast changed them from two strangers shoved together to potential lovers.

The train entered another tunnel, and with her face dark and unobservable, Eleanor allowed herself the luxury of fondling the memory, letting her mind linger on that first rush when the warmth of Maggie's hand had encompassed her breast. At first that was all, her hand on the breast, as if asking, "Is this all right?" Then Maggie's fingers began slowly moving, circling closer and closer. By the time her fingers finally reached Eleanor's nipple, it was hard and erect. As Maggie said later, "Of course I didn't stop. That nipple of yours was waving a bright red flag in invitation."

No, Maggie didn't stop, but she moved slowly, almost teasing-ly. From one breast to another. Then away to Eleanor's neck or jaw, then back, her fingers hovering inside Eleanor's shirt, resting at that place where the breast begins to rise from the chest.

But the train left the tunnel, exposing Eleanor to the sunlight. Those memories created in the night — it felt unseemly to sub-ject them to this glaring daylight. Eleanor was abashed to notice that her breasts had responded to the memory, her nipples erect and straining against her bra.

She remembered the harsh sunlight in the doctor's office. Cancer. A harsh word in the harsh light. That night she and Maggie had made love in a frenzy, clinging to touch, the physical. Six years together, and that one word reminded them of how quickly things changed, how mortal they were. Touch could not be held on to. It would leave. So that night they grasped it as tight-ly as they could. Maggie's hands traveled over Eleanor's body, touching, probing, as if trying to reach some essence of her, to mold a memory that would endure.

The chemo took away Maggie's brown curls, still not a gray hair in them. It came back white, all white, rushing her into a future that Eleanor thought they would share together, but Maggie aged quickly, leaving Eleanor still in her prime.

She fought that memory: Maggie withered, her head sur-rounded by tufts of white so fine, it could hardly be called hair. She preferred the Maggie from the first six years, the real Maggie, as Eleanor thought of her. *Let the sunlight expose my breasts,* she thought as it glittered off the snow. *Let me remember Maggie and the heat that had been between us.* Defying the conductor, who almost walked close enough to catch any glimmer of her emotions, Eleanor remembered that first night.

Maggie's simple "Come to my place" after they were left off. Odd how Eleanor had never thought to say no. Resisting Maggie didn't seem possible. It was four blocks to Maggie's apartment. She had taken Eleanor's hand to lead her around a corner, then didn't release it until they were at her door and Maggie was taking out her keys.

Her memory was clear, pristine up until that point. She could remember all the details, the name of the corner store, Maggie's hand in hers, even the precise color of the leaves in the trees they passed. But once they were inside, images started cascading, one atop another. Her jacket came off. She couldn't remember Maggie taking hers off, but of course she did. They were in each other's arms. Kissing.

"I knew you weren't quite as shy as you seemed when you put your tongue in my mouth first," Maggie had said later. Eleanor had denied it. Maggie was the bold one. It didn't make sense that she, the shy, quiet one, would be the first to touch so deeply. But she wasn't sure, couldn't chase down the halls of her memory to find exactly what had happened. "I almost came right then and there," Maggie had added. Eleanor had still shaken her head in denial, but she rather liked the idea that she had a daring, sensual streak and could get lost in passion.

One clear image that surfaced was of them standing together, fiercely kissing, tongues thrusting back and forth as if vying to see who could press deeper, holding each other tightly, all hesitation long gone. She felt Maggie's arms letting go of her, her hands searching for Eleanor's breasts. This time they hadn't stopped at her shirt, at first pushing the cloth aside, then pulling her shirt off, tossing it quickly away. In the morning Maggie had apologized for the wrinkled mess when Eleanor had nothing else to wear. But in the night, in that moment of passion, it hadn't mattered.

Eleanor usually worried about things like that, took care of things. Remembered to turn off the stove and turn down the thermostat. Matched the socks into pairs. But that night all she wanted was Maggie's hands on her breasts.

"Get on the floor. I want to get on top of you." Another clear moment. Maggie's command, the coolness of the floor on her bare back. The sudden warmth and weight as Maggie let herself down onto Eleanor. The erotic shock of their bare breasts touching for the first time. Then the visions overlapped each other, fierce kissing, all the places that became wet: her breasts from Maggie's licking and sucking, the creeping wetness between her legs, from between Maggie's legs, their fingers immersed in that wetness, trailing it across thighs and stomachs. The release of orgasm over and over again. She couldn't clearly remember the first time she came; before the night was over, she came again and again. Eleanor wanted to remember that Maggie had called out her name for the first time, but it could have been the second time. Maggie had called out Eleanor's name sometime in the night. Perhaps that was what really counted: her name, the harsh, possessive way Maggie had said it.

"Five times," Maggie recounted the next morning as they sat for breakfast at an hour better suited to lunch. "I made you come five times."

"I didn't count. I don't count things like that," Eleanor had responded somewhat defensively. She couldn't be sure of the number and was a bit abashed that Maggie knew so well what they had done. "I came, you came. Are you complaining?"

"No, I came six times. No complaints, ma'am, not a one."

Sometime later, after they had moved in together, they tried to puzzle out the sexual charge between them.

"I always wanted to fuck a virgin," Maggie had said.

"I'm not a virgin. And wasn't when you met me."

"Oh, I know. Not a literal virgin. You were the reserved, quiet type. Glasses, always carrying a book. A coolness and restraint about you. I wanted to push that aside, to find the passion in you. Take you to erotic places you'd never been before. I imagined it would take weeks to seduce you."

"Instead of mere hours? You were the popular girl, the one the others wanted to be near, the kind who never paid attention to serious women with glasses who always carried a book."

Was that it, the sum of their desire? Opposites attracted? *No, it went beyond that,* Eleanor thought. Maggie had opened up something in her, gave her permission to be sexual in a way that her previous timid lovers with their shy hands never had. It had been okay to sweat and groan with Maggie, to be dripping wet and mess up the last set of clean sheets, to beg and curse and demand more. She opened a door that Eleanor had wanted to enter. Maggie liked playing her role — teacher to the younger, shier woman, a provocateur who made suggestions at the edge of shocking.

She remembered the time in the crowded elevator, Maggie behind her. Maggie had put her hand between Eleanor's legs. Eleanor remembered being astonished that she would dare. And nonplussed that there was nothing she could do to remove Maggie's hand that wouldn't bring attention to what was happening. The door had opened, and Eleanor had hurried out of the elevator, sure everyone knew. She said nothing as they walked down the hall. It was her first job teaching; they were going to her office.

Once there, with the door shut, she had turned to Maggie.

"When's your next appointment?" Maggie had cut her off.

"Next...?" She obediently glanced at her schedule. "Not until after lunch."

Maggie locked the door.

"I can't do this here," Eleanor had protested. "And that stunt in the elevator — "

"No one saw a thing. You know I don't mind shocking you, but I won't embarrass you."

Eleanor realized that it was true. Maggie played at limits but didn't violate them. There was that trust between them, the covenant that proclaimed, "I will not knowingly hurt you." It had built slowly in the three years that they had been together then. But in that moment in her office, Eleanor saw it clearly, how sturdy that protective wall of trust had become. It wasn't just sex but encompassed everything, from helping her get up in the morning for that 8:30 class to holding her late in the night when tension or vague fears wouldn't let her sleep. Eleanor marked it, that epiphany produced by Maggie's hand in a crowded elevator, like a plaque recounting the history of a place that might seem inconsequential.

Maggie circled her to close the blinds at the window.

"What if the chairman of the department knocks on my door?" Eleanor asked.

"Don't open it." Maggie now stood next to her, close enough for Eleanor to feel the heat of her skin, smell a faint waft of her perfume.

"But what if he hears something?" Eleanor only made the protest because she wanted to keep alive the tension that she might say no.

"We'll be quiet."

"Seduce me." And Maggie had, her hands traveling slowly down Eleanor's neck to her cleavage, a tease and a promise. Then her hand went back to where it had started, between Eleanor's legs, pushing and insistent, rubbing hard against the seam of her denim jeans.

Eleanor closed her eyes, shutting out the mundane world of an office painted beige, piles of the usual books. She let Maggie's hand become her only focus. First the pushing and rubbing through her jeans, then the slow unzipping of her zipper. Maggie quickly pushed aside the barrier of Eleanor's underwear.

"I love you," Eleanor murmured as Maggie's hand touched her directly. She had said it before, many times, but she still marveled at how the meaning changed, all the faces and levels of love. That it could be so alive here, in this quick sex in an office.

"And I love you," Maggie answered. Then she kissed Eleanor as her hand entered her.

Eleanor remembered clearly how Maggie's hand thrust into her. Other details blurred. They had been standing but ended up sitting on the ragtag couch that Eleanor had inherited from the previous occupant of that office. She couldn't remember moving, only Maggie's hand inside her, touching a piece of her soul. And Maggie kept that touch alive, as if she sensed that something had changed. Her hand slowed, keeping Eleanor at a plateau, prolonging the moment. Then long, deep thrusts, physical touching that echoed the emotional reach of their lovemaking. Eleanor remembered how vulnerable she allowed Maggie to make her, spread across that tattered couch, her pants shoved down around her ankles, face flushed, only a door between that and her professional life.

The train slowed as it came into New Haven. The change in motion interrupted Eleanor's memories. Maggie would never ride a train beside her again. Was there any point in remembering what had been?

After Maggie's death, Maggie's mother had invaded their apartment. To her, Eleanor was nothing more than a lover, but she was the mother. Of course, she hadn't been rude, asking very nicely if Eleanor minded if Maggie's brother could have her Leica, daring Eleanor to place a greater claim on the left-behind pieces of Maggie's life than the family that had birthed and bred her. Not married, no children, two women: It didn't count with Maggie's mother.

Eleanor had retreated to the kitchen, claiming the cups and bowls that they had shared and eaten from. A turn to take a dish from the sink had revealed Maggie's mother going through the box of their photos. Eleanor took a step to stop her: These weren't Maggie's professional work; they were the record of their life together. It incensed her that Maggie's mother (her name was Jill, but Eleanor rarely called her that, just as she usually referred to Eleanor as "Maggie's friend") felt she could look behind any door in her daughter's life. But Eleanor had turned back to the sink. Maggie would get her final revenge for all those years that she had struggled to get her mother to accept Eleanor as more than just a friend. Her mother had refused to see it. Now she would. She would see the photos Maggie had taken while they made love. She would see her daughter in heat and passion with another woman. No, not just friends. If she wanted to look in that box, let her find what was there.

Maggie had needed a picture of two women kissing. She had offered to take some pictures for a writer friend, and that was one of them.

"Why not us?" she had asked Eleanor. "It'll be artsy, backlit, no one will recognize us." She knew Eleanor would be shy about such a public display.

Safely assured of being only a blur and a shadow, Eleanor had agreed. The picture had been hard to set up, with Maggie running back and forth between the camera, Eleanor holding a pillow stand-in for a while so Maggie could play with lights and exposure. But the picture that resulted was quite good. Eleanor knew, given that she was in the photograph, that she couldn't really judge it against Maggie's other work, but it was one of her favorites. Maggie had given her an enlarged copy, framed, for her birthday. On the back it said, "To Eleanor. Love always, Maggie." The picture still hung over her bed. Love always. Eleanor thought of those words. But it hadn't been love always. Love had gone. No, that wasn't true. Love was still here; she still loved Maggie. But it had become immobile, only memory, no forward motion possible. Like that picture.

It had been interesting and mildly erotic to see that image of themselves, their lips barely touching but mouths open, waiting,

sunlight streaming through the window they stood before, turning them into silhouettes of passion. She remembered how pleased
Maggie was with herself for so clearly catching their desire. And
Eleanor had to admit that she enjoyed seeing it so distinctly captured. She remembered the look that they had exchanged and
how easy it was to go from that look to Maggie's suggestion that
she could take some more pictures only for them.

Eleanor had agreed. At first she was awkward in front of the
camera, too concerned about how she looked. But slowly desire
took over. Maggie was too used to cameras to let one, even in this
intimate a place, intimidate her. She worked Eleanor, her hands
slow and relentless, relaxing her and exciting her both. She lingered on Eleanor's breasts, keeping her touch light, kisses soft, until
Eleanor had to thrust forward for Maggie's mouth. The camera
caught that moment of passion, caught all those moments of passion: Maggie's hand as her fingers slowly separated Eleanor's slick
hairs, Maggie between her legs, the arch and stretch as Eleanor
came, a quiet moment as they lay in each other's arms, then
Eleanor as she traveled the same path down Maggie's body, the
sucking and the probing, a cry that still almost seemed to echo
from the silent picture. Those pictures they kept in a private place,
hidden in an envelope in the bottom of the box.

Eleanor remembered the anticipation as Maggie developed
the pictures, both of them standing close in the red light of the
darkroom. Slowly a record of their love and desire emerged from
the pans of chemicals. After hanging up the pictures to dry, they
had made love again, goaded into desire by the images of themselves and their desire just past.

Sometimes Maggie would leave one or two pictures out, a
signal for Eleanor. One day she had come home from teaching to
find a trail of those pictures leading to the bedroom, with Maggie
waiting naked under the sheets.

As she stood in the kitchen listening to Maggie's mother in
the living room, Eleanor had again turned to cross that distance
and take the box from her. But a startled gasp told Eleanor that it
was already too late. Maggie's mother had left shortly after that,
and she had not asked again about taking Maggie's best camera
for her brother. Whatever guilt Eleanor may have felt was

assuaged by this victory. And by realizing that she knew Maggie well enough to know how she would have reacted. Eleanor could almost hear Maggie's voice saying, "I bet now she regrets giving me that first camera when I was ten. Not to mention pawing through my stuff."

After Maggie's mother had left, Eleanor had sat and looked through the pictures, reclaiming them from those prying eyes. She remembered all the tears that the images had brought forth, sobbing and crying as she held the picture of Maggie, naked, her hands clutching Eleanor to her breast. How could Maggie be gone but that ghost of a photograph still be here?

The New Haven passengers were boarding. Eleanor shook her head, physically dislodging the memory. It had been almost a year now. Maggie was gone. She picked up her book and started to read again, hoping that her disinterest would keep anyone from taking the seat next to her.

She had spent that last year in libraries, doing research, taking her passion to the words written a few lifetimes ago, trying to find solace in books that somehow managed to live beyond their authors.

The train began to slowly pull away from the station. No one had seated themselves next to Eleanor. She was relieved to be given the private space.

It was so mundane and so profound, this train ride. It was the first time Eleanor had taken the short, boring train ride from Boston to New York without Maggie beside her or waiting for her return. Perhaps that was why the memories crowded in. They needed to fill this empty space.

Eleanor remembered Maggie in the darkroom, outlined in that faint red light. She often sat on a stool in the corner and talked or listened as Maggie developed her photos. Only later did Eleanor realize what a measure of their partnership that was. Maggie trusted her to watch the pictures come forth, and sometimes a roll of film yielded only one good shot. At first Maggie had asked for only minimal approval from Eleanor ("This is the best shot, don't you think?") but the years had slowly changed that ("Take a look at these. What do you think?") and Eleanor's judgment had become almost equal to Maggie's.

At times Eleanor desperately missed those quiet times in that dim light. But even in the moments when she still had them, thought that those evenings with Maggie could go on without end, she knew the import of them, the quiet moments that make up a love and a life.

One night they were quiet, not talking. Eleanor was watching Maggie, the sure way she developed the negatives, taking them from one tray to another. She found herself watching Maggie's face, noting the lines that were now faintly etched at her eyes, the familiar way her brow furrowed as she concentrated, the curl that would not stay with the others but insisted on falling over her forehead.

Suddenly Eleanor wanted Maggie. Her desire was usually more decorous than that, waiting for bedtime or after a romantic dinner or when Maggie summoned it with a look or a word. She got off the stool, standing next to Maggie, close enough to almost touch. Eleanor pretended to look at what Maggie was doing, but her concentration was on Maggie, who seemed oblivious to Eleanor's desire, though Eleanor thought that it must be palpable, so strong as to send off visible sparks. Her hand rested on Maggie's shoulder, but that was not where she wanted her hand to be. Could she just change this evening, insert sex into it all on her own, with no sign or signal from Maggie? Maggie could, of course, but...Maggie was Maggie.

Eleanor remembered her hesitation, that even after all these years together, she hesitated to be the one to push for sex. Usually she didn't need to. Maggie offered or suggested or hinted. What was she so afraid of? Rejection? Or was she really afraid of change, creating a new path, one that she was responsible for?

Eleanor let her arm drift from Maggie's shoulder down to her hip, her breast just brushing against Maggie's shoulder. Maggie remained intent on her pictures. Maybe she should just sit back down on the stool, Eleanor thought. Feeling the warmth of Maggie's hip under her hand didn't do much to lessen her desire. Then it came, the thought that preceded a change, like a door opening into a new room: Eleanor, five years younger than Maggie, usually let her lead. That had been the pattern in their relationship. Why, Eleanor wondered, why not change? They'd been together long enough for her to acquire some of Maggie's boldness. Why not add a few more possibilities to who and what Eleanor could be?

Instead of retreating to the stool, Eleanor moved directly behind Maggie, her breasts touching Maggie's shoulders, her hands on Maggie's hips. Maggie leaned slightly into Eleanor but only with the familiarity of touch, not with passion. Eleanor slowly but firmly tugged Maggie's hips, pulling her against Eleanor's crotch.

"These chemicals turning you on?" Maggie asked, but she didn't move away from Eleanor.

"No, you are." Eleanor let her hands travel, slowly sliding them around Maggie's hips, stopping just short of the place where her flesh rose between her legs.

"I've got to finish these."

"Am I stopping you?" One hand went to the top of Maggie's zipper. Very slowly she began unzipping it. The years they had been together had sharpened their communications to nuance and bare gesture. There were many ways Maggie could have said stop. She used none of them. Eleanor didn't stop. Her hand slipped through the open zipper.

"No, you're not stopping me. But you're proving to be…quite a distraction." Maggie pushed her hips into Eleanor, inviting her hand to go farther.

Eleanor remained slow and deliberate, her hand tracing Maggie's hair through her panties. For the moment she didn't go beyond them.

Maggie finished whatever she was doing with the negatives and after rinsing her hands started to turn to face Eleanor.

But Eleanor held her in place, wouldn't let her turn around. One pattern was broken; she wanted to break a few more. Her hand was no longer languid. It slid beneath Maggie's underwear, finding her hair, dividing it, going deeper.

A fierce possessiveness overtook Eleanor. Maggie was hers, had given her the gift of touch and desire. She could stroke Maggie's hot secret places, explore them at will. They were the only two travelers on this journey of love and desire. She shoved Maggie's pants down, got them to her knees with her hands, then used her foot to take them down to Maggie's ankles.

Who else could she do this with? Who else had ever given her this power? Only the woman in front of her, with her pubic hair and tops of her thighs already slick and wet. Eleanor ran her hands over Maggie, touching the power and desire.

"What are you going to do to me?" Maggie gasped.

"Whatever I want," was Eleanor's answer. "Bend over," she said. She twirled Maggie away from the counter of chemicals, then leaned her over the stool. Maggie obeyed the commands of Eleanor's hands.

Slick as she was, Eleanor's fingers easily entered Maggie. She thrust in, unrestrained, physical sex. Maggie rode her hand, thrusting her hips back, grunting and moaning in response.

It was quick, but at times profound things are. Maggie came with a gush of wetness that soaked Eleanor's arm to the elbow and a loud cry that subsided into harsh, gulping breaths. Eleanor draped herself over Maggie, one hand cupping a breast, the other still inside her. For the first time Maggie had given all the power and control to Eleanor. Or was it that for the first time Eleanor had taken it?

When Maggie's breathing had returned to its usual rhythm, Eleanor had simply said, "Get on your knees."

Maggie had obeyed, not even bothering to pull up her pants. Eleanor had unzipped her jeans and then let Maggie spread her legs. She knew what Eleanor wanted, where to put her tongue and lips. Eleanor sat back on the stool and watched Maggie with her tongue pressed between her legs, Maggie's curls damp with sweat. Eleanor tried to hold off, prolong the moment, but her desire, building for so long, demanded release. She came and, unusual for her, came again.

She and Maggie didn't talk much about what happened in those few minutes (only half an hour had passed, they later realized). What was there to say? Was it just Eleanor's sexual peak, her mid thirties? Perhaps that was part of it, Eleanor admitted, but she felt it was more, that it was an understanding and owning of her power, not just in sex but in how she could influence the world. It was a lesson that Maggie had taught her.

A year — one brief year — later Maggie had gone to the doctor's office. And Eleanor has used that lesson, had fought for

Maggie when the drugs and the cancer weakened her, pushed the doctors for better answers and, in the end, for relief from pain. She had cared for Maggie, carried her shit from the portable toilet in the bedroom and flushed it away, held her hand in the night when pain and nausea ruled Maggie's world. It was a brutal way to die, a slow creeping inch by inch away from life.

That was another lesson that Maggie had taught her: the despair of having a future taken from you. What might have been and now would not be. Eleanor was thirty-six, single, and riding a train by herself. Caring for Maggie had so consumed her life that when Maggie died, she felt lost and confused, barely able to stumble through the routines of her days. Maggie was also teaching her the lessons of grief and letting go. Slowly, so slowly, she was learning them.

The train again slowed, pulling into Stamford, Connecticut. Eleanor resigned herself to a passenger in the next seat; the train was too crowded for her to hope otherwise. A young college boy with a well-fed arrogance to him started to sit, then he spotted something better — something younger and blonder, Eleanor suspected. Several other people passed Eleanor by with the foolish optimism that the next car would be less crowded. She wondered which of them would come back this way to reclaim her empty seat on the rebound.

Then a woman stopped beside her and asked, "Is this taken?" At least she was polite enough to ask, unlike the rude college boy who thought the world owed him a train seat.

"No, it's not." At first glance the woman looked like another college student, but a second glance told Eleanor that she was older, mid to late twenties. She stretched to put her suitcase in the overhead rack. The sight of her breasts with the cloth of her shirt pulled tightly over them stirred something in Eleanor. *Nice,* Eleanor thought before turning her head back to her book. That's what she got from thinking about sex from Boston to New York. Now she was staring at some strange woman's breasts with what could only be called lust. Eleanor resolutely opened her book.

But the bundles' being placed in the seat next to her, the woman's jockeying and jostling to get settled, drew Eleanor's attention. The woman bent down to pick up a briefcase, revealing her cleavage. Eleanor didn't turn so quickly back to her book. The woman had attractive breasts, soft and rounded. Her skin hadn't spent too many summers in the sun, and they still promised to be soft to the touch.

Eleanor looked back down at her book, not to read but to shade her face while she thought of the feel of a warm breast against her hand, the comfort and thrill of that touch.

The woman gave Eleanor a smile and a nod as she sat, then opened up a laptop computer. She didn't seem inclined to talk, so Eleanor left her gazing at her screen. Eleanor felt faintly chagrined by her moment of lust. She read books; she didn't stare at the breasts of strange women on trains.

Eleanor tried to read again, but the glare of the sun broken by flashes of telephone poles and buildings made the pages too bright. She closed the book.

For the last year she had paid no attention to women, not sexual attention. Maggie's death was an end, and Eleanor had spent the year living in the wake of that ending place, numb to a future that didn't include Maggie. But she was here, in the future, and Maggie was not a part of it.

Eleanor didn't look at the woman but called back the image of her bending over, the inviting depth of her cleavage. She realized that it was the first time she had thought of another woman, imagined herself touching another woman. Some faint beginning beckoned. Perhaps she could find touch and even love again.

Maggie had gone quickly, too soon, too young. But age would consume Eleanor too. It was inexorable; this journey would not stop. She was thirty-six. If fate was kind, she had a few decades left. But only that, a few decades. Sometimes a year, two years, ten seemed such a short time.

The train entered the tunnel for the last time, leaving the glinting daylight, the final minutes before they arrived at Penn Station and her destination. Another memory of Maggie's hands came to her, not the rushed grope for fun and titillation in the dark but from the last time they had ridden this train together. Another visit to another doctor, one last chance. Maggie had held her hand as they had traveled under Manhattan. They had said little, just that touch of their hands.

In the dark, by herself, Eleanor let go of Maggie's hands. They were only memory now.

The woman next to her clicked off her laptop computer. She stood up to retrieve her things from the overhead rack. Eleanor allowed herself to look at the woman's breasts again, their swell against the cloth.

Yes, she would find other women to cup her hand around their breasts; one to love and hold, if she was lucky. Eleanor knew there were no guarantees. Love came as a grace, ephemeral, and it could go so quickly.

The light changed from the dim flashes of the tunnel to the flat fluorescence of the station. Eleanor gathered her things, putting the unread book back in her briefcase. Her overnight bag was up on the rack, but she was in no hurry. She thought of saying something to the woman but could think of nothing. She couldn't very well thank her for letting Eleanor fantasize about her breasts. They were only strangers on a train.

The motion of the train stopped. They had arrived. The woman got up with another smile and nod at Eleanor, and she made her slow way up the aisle.

Eleanor remained in her seat, letting the milling passengers elbow themselves and their luggage off the train. A few minutes of waiting would make it much easier to disembark. But she no longer merely watched the people with the detachment of numbness and grief; instead she saw hints of possibility. She looked at women, their hair, their eyes — were they confident or timid? Oh, yes, and their breasts. She let her glance linger on the women who looked smart and confident and who had nice breasts.

The train ride had not been long, but the most profound journeys involve more than just distance.

With the aisles now clear, Eleanor gathered up her things and got off the train.

Impulse
by Sora Counts

The last time I was between lives we got into one of those free-for-all discussions about what it would be best to go back as. What existence actually was desirable, what was improvement, freedom, what was worth going back to Earth for? The animals, yes. Everyone wanted to go animal. The grace of the antelope, the freedom of some well-wrought bird of prey. You'd like to know what wings are like, their fine bony spread and being lifted on pillows of air, becoming just an edge of such a pillow. The living physical, yes. The excellence of a forest and to be the tree in it that grows highest and holds a spirit that everyone recognizes. Some vastness of ocean so deep, it colors the sky. A wind that gets to go everywhere and touch everything.

As the timeless night wore on, we covered it all. Someone went on and on in lustrous detail about life as an illuminated manuscript — the silence, the reverence, the hands and eyes gently on you for ages. Well, if it's touch you want, said someone else, and passionate at that, it's music — be an instrument, expertly crafted so that only the most talented hands can even touch you and the touch is always exquisite. Or be the song, the music itself, one of those enduring airs without words that, long after the playing, lives on in each hearer's blood, the pleasure of its influence spreading.

We talked and talked, and gradually each voice separated itself out into a choice. I decided to return to earth as an erotic impulse.

I leaped high and fell deep into fertile turf — I am coming to life at a sex party.

I had thought I'd be born in the cunt, but no, I'm here in the eye, Tera's eye, looking at that cane across the room. Over the heads of twenty people I watch it flex, holding Tera's eye to it. I jump from eye to cane to eye, making a path between them. Exploring a little, I run down Tera's arm so that she stretches out her fingers in an anticipatory grasp. I move her legs to cross the room, enter her mouth to say, Can I borrow that? The woman who holds the cane looks at her — at us, really — and then at the almost naked body waiting patiently at the opposite wall. I enter this woman, this holder of the cane, and prompt her to say yes. And now the cane is in Tera's hand, and I am in her arm again, running down to her hand and stretching into the cane, which she taps lightly on her other hand as she walks back.

Diane, waiting at the wall, sees me, sees how I animate Tera. I rush to Diane, dive into her, somewhere in the chest in the throat in the belly I make a melting and ooze down. From some landing place in there, I send up a ripple that surfaces as a blush. She tilts her head to one side while I settle a moment in her eyes. Then I arc over to Tera, still approaching. I go directly to her eyes, which widen to give me space. I slide down along the cane and leap off the end to Diane. She is still hot when I arrive, I push off and fly back to Tera, I am riding the open air between them. I am leaping back and forth between them, pulling them, drawing them together.

Finally Tera is back. Her hand is on Diane's shoulder, and I am there, guiding that hand down the back slowly, keeping it warm, yet I send a shiver through Diane and a smile to Tera's mouth. I guide the hand under the ass, a light finger between the cunt lips so that now — she cannot help it, this has already been a long journey for me, but Diane only now is recognizing its beginning, she's been lost in a frozen moment, but now she feels herself being felt wet, feels the heat of her own body, and she cannot help it — she groans. Have I made this music?

I ease myself into the cane as Tera shows it to Diane. Holding it near each end, she glides it slowly across Diane's breasts while I move in that closed circle — arm, hand, cane, hand, arm, heart... And at each circumnavigation I rub the nipples, wake them to a confusion of irritation and longing, drawing them out to me, to Tera.

Now I'm in her mouth, Tera's mouth and throat. I have her say something rough and taunting in a low voice. Diane strains to hear, catches not much beyond the tone but searches the eyes — and finds me there. And still the cane and I coolly enamor the nipples.

I allow myself to diffuse throughout both their bodies. I am a mist. Diane closes her eyes and seems to suck me in all over. The pores of her skin open to me. I press myself into the muscles of her legs, which makes them weaken a little and at the same time makes her wet! What a surprise to me! I wallow there awhile. The heart is on automatic pilot. The lungs take little breaths as though not to provoke a disturbance. The brain is home on a warm night with no one on guard. It does not notice the cramp in the shoulder. It does not wonder what time it is. It does not know the name of the song that's playing or any other names. It is waiting.

I keep the skin awake. A door to the next room opens, and Diane's skin prickles to goose bumps. The nerves are alive too — also my doing. A loud whack occurs just a few feet away, and Diane is at attention, then instantly annoyed and ashamed of her oversensitivity. The body is waiting.

Tera is behind her now, not touching her but watching her hardly move, letting a little time pass. I fill the space between them. I fill the time with my growing.

Diane is facing the brick wall, leaning on her palms. I protect her nakedness with my heat. I halo her ass with desire. It reaches out. I elongate myself into a sliver, like liquid lightning passing through blood, Tera's blood, Tera's eyes, Tera's arm, Tera's cane. I become food. I become song. I become flight. Whatever satisfaction or impossible desire they ever felt, I become that. I become the condensation of every passion, the essence of every discovery and fear of discovery. I leave only one thing to be wished, and I make myself the path between the two halves of that wish. I am air. I am lighter than air. Tera's arm stretches out. The cane sings through me and strikes.

Suddenly I am everywhere in the room at once. I didn't know this was possible! I light on every shoulder, whisper in every ear. I am dancing from one person to another, eyes to eyes, mouth to mouth, hand to breast, whip to skin. The music is beating around us, and I move so fast, I'm standing still. I'm welcomed everywhere. I'm in their hearts and lungs. I guide their hands. I urge out their words and cries, their very breath. The more they have of me, the more and more they want. I could live here forever!

The Motel Trilogy
by Linda Smukler

Econobox

Econobox motel   your mouth on my thighs   you are doing
bicycles on the bed stretching your calves   my elbow rests on
your forehead   the white noise dry heat computer propped
on a pillow   I wake with cramped fingers   worry about
money and dog and the extreme comfort of this king-size bed
you lie next to me   share my pillow   we inhabit a box in
Buckhorn PA on the edge of a mall   black light   curtains
drawn   no one knows where we are   earlier we arrive and
you run to find a soda   I rush into the little wedge of a bathroom to strip off jeans   shoes and socks   to put on my cock
but you come back sooner than I thought   One minute I
shout and I have to let you in because the door is locked and
my pants are off   there is no choice   I open the door and
I'm standing there in a T-shirt no pants two minutes after you
left and I say I'm peeing   you know what I'm doing but you
do not say anything back   I close the door to the bathroom
and I think as a man I would definitely go up a size in pants
my jeans now too tight stuffed that huge dick   I come out
you say You had to put your pee-pee on to pee?   no secrets
or surprise here   I say yes and we drink soda   turn on the
TV   look at the view   close the curtains   turn down the
heat   sealed in our box   bed firm   and the blackness gets
bigger   a roar and a cliché to say velvet but that's what it is
no boundaries   no will   no phone   no time   just the touch
of your body as you lie on top of me and stroke my dick which
is hardly more than a picture in my mind   hardly more than
your head somewhere below my belly   I want to know what
that tip is actually doing in your mouth   how the roll of your
tongue feels along the base   I have a cock that is true and you
are treating it like a cock   I push in and out of your mouth
but I want to know the whole of me down your throat   the
inside of you as you mount me   I place my finger on your clit

as you ride   breasts a brush above my lips   stomach muscles
holding us steadfast until you come and fall on top of me   still
black in here   still white noise

Days Inn

It was astonishing to walk into room 233 at the Days Inn   the
door open for us   to turn on the lights and to close the curtains   to see you first locked into that tan recliner as I sat on
the (slightly darker) tan carpet   my back up against the coarse
blue bedspread   to smell disinfectant and to drink bitter tea
to feel the minutes of our short afternoon slip away into nervousness and the prints on the off-white walls   then how you
lay down on the bed   and I lay next to you   to kiss   no to
talk   to get comfortable with each other again   we heard
raised voices from somewhere   from the side or overhead
we couldn't figure out where   perhaps a meeting or ten TVs
screaming children or a gathering of boys to watch the football game   these were all possibilities as gradually the voices
got so loud I called the front desk to complain   the desk clerk
said the voices were coming from below   something religious
for sure   evangelists or a revival meeting   I told the clerk
that I would call her back if we needed to move   then you
asked me to turn off the hard lights and I did and lay back
down next to you and then on top of you and I finally forgave
myself for letting you wait at the train station   I remember
you turned me over and how delirious I became at your touch
and at a certain point I was overwhelmed with the desire to
enter you and all the while beneath us they called on the Lord
they called for salvation   the desk called and out of breath I
answered and said we were fine and did not want to move and
it was true   the room had become as if lighted by candles and
we lay on a sacred bier accompanied by hosannas and hallelu-
jahs   and the chalice of your scent   the icon of your face
the idols of your breasts in black lace   the staff of your finger in my ass and my cock in your cunt   our coming joined
from below by shouts and applause and the exalted blessings of
the possessed

Henry Van

There was a mud slide at Dobbs Ferry so you must come up the Harlem line instead of the Hudson   you call before you leave to say you are ill   do you really want to come?   I thought I heard a hint of something in your voice   we dodge obstacles like the quarterback now in the end zone who dances and lifts his head to heaven and so do we when I find you at the train station and we drive and discover a sweet motel in an unlikely place   clean   clear   a dark private space for which we pay money to be with each other on a sunny day   you worry and we do not touch right away   you get up and pace and turn on the TV and divert yourself from me as I do from you with talk   for hours we talk and I tell you that I do not want to get so used to leaving you after loving you   that I do not stop wanting you   I do not stop the night before nor the night after and the night after that   so I say and so it happens that it is the right thing to stop your talk with my fingers in your mouth   the right thing to stop the pacing the diversion the TV   the right thing to give you more than you think you can take   the right thing at the back of your throat at your nipple and finally at your clit   the right thing to drink orange juice in between   to fuck you again   and finally to let you take me and to hear you whisper to your little boy who you ask to sit on your lap   it's the way you push him down by his left shoulder as he tries to reach up and touch you   the way you lift your large full breasts just out of the reach of his mouth and hands   the way you make him struggle and do not give and finally he does reach you and after I think yes   let us return to this place   to the whole of you and me   meeting for 20 dollars apiece at the Henry Van along a highway near the train somewhere upstate

Riding the *Silver Meteor*
by Marcy Sheiner

I've been riding the *Silver Meteor* from New York to Miami once a year for the past decade. I get culture shock from airplanes that transport me too quickly from one climate to another; the 24-hour train ride gives me time to ease into the right attitude for the annual family reunion at my parents' home. The slow, relaxing journey enables me to shed the stress of my workday world, while the return trip gears me up to face it again.

Sometimes I think I was born into the wrong century, that I belong in a world without telephones, E-mail, and supersonic jets, a world where people still find romance in a place seemingly as mundane as a train. When I sit in the lounge car drinking a martini, speeding through the darkening landscape, I envision the poker games that were played here in the '20s and '30s, the glamorous people who gambled, fought, and loved on the railroad. There's something about a train that's inherently sexual — its strength, power, and speed; the vibrations caused by moving steel upon steel; the way the train bucks and rolls to a stop. Lying in my efficient little sleeping compartment, I fondle myself in the darkness, conjuring up the ghosts of all the railroad romances I imagine were consummated on my foldout bed.

About three years ago my cabin was situated across from a lesbian couple. I don't know if they were playing a game or if this was their ordinary demeanor, but they looked like they'd walked straight out of some '30s Parisian salon with their short sleek hairdos, satin blazers, and bejeweled pipes. They cut exotic figures, sipping brandy from snifters and gazing into one another's eyes. During the night I heard the sounds of their lovemaking — raw, ferocious growls of unbridled lust. Alone in my sleeper I masturbated to the sounds of their passion, while the motion of the train rocked me to a deliciously prolonged orgasm.

Even just moving around on a train is erotically charged. Maneuvering through the corridors requires cooperation among the passengers. Usually someone will duck into an empty room to avoid a collision, but when that's not possible, one of them has to flatten up against the wall while the other sidles past. I've often brushed against hard nipples or allowed my breasts to graze someone's chest or spine, then later used the memory of the encounter in my fantasies.

Every year I try to talk my lover, Donna, into joining me. But we both know it would be a disaster — she's too much of a type-A personality to endure the confinement. Most likely she'd end up pacing the corridors like a caged animal. But we do have a semi-open relationship, which means we occasionally dabble in extra-marital affairs, and she's given me her blessing to seek out an erotic railroad adventure. The right someone just never materialized.

Until my last trip.

Maybe it was my own vibes: I'd decided to go all out, to dress the way the railroad makes me feel. With padded shoulders and trashy jewelry back in vogue, I had no trouble looking like a gun moll in a calf-length black dress with rhinestone buckle, fishnet stockings, spiked heels, and a floppy feathered hat. When I boarded I settled my luggage into my room as quickly as possible and headed for the club car, surreptitiously peeking into compartments along the way. Enviously I eyed an empty first-class car with its sofa-size seat and double foldout bed, imagining the scenarios that must have been played out there.

In the club car I drank a leisurely cup of coffee, then headed to the dining car for breakfast, then back again to the club car for more coffee. This frantic back-and-forth activity was carefully choreographed to provide me both optimum exposure and an opportunity to assess my traveling companions.

A family with six kids trouped past my table — yawn. A pair of newlyweds sat across the aisle. An old woman tottered in on a cane, assisted by a young porter. A tall, elegant woman in a purple jumpsuit slithered through the door, and my heart fluttered: Sizing her up, I decided she was bisexual and eminently seducible. Just as I was contemplating how best to proceed, she appeared: my ultimate railroad fantasy.

She might have stepped out of a time machine, so much did she resemble a '30s Chicago gangster. She was tall and thin, wearing a double-breasted three-piece tweed suit and silk tie, a natty fedora pulled over one eye, her patent leather shoes spit-shine clean. She consulted an old-fashioned pocket watch as she stood in the entrance to the club car, a serious expression on her face. Her skin was chocolate brown, and her features delicate: long nose, thin lips, sleek jawline. Her eyes roved the room, briefly pausing when she saw me. Casually she slid into the booth facing mine.

My initial reaction was to flee, so terrified was I to let this marvelous apparition see the naked lust that had crept into my eyes. But then I pulled myself together to present the composed, worldly woman who lives inside every seemingly fragile femme. Looking directly at her, I lifted my cup in salutation. An almost imperceptible smile played at the corners of her mouth as she nodded and raised a hand to tip her hat. This silent exchange, lasting perhaps ten seconds, conveyed a wealth of information. There was little doubt in my mind that at long last my fantasy would be fulfilled.

After several minutes of pointedly ignoring her, I slowly stood up, offering her a full view of my bod, and strode past her on my spiked heels, feeling her eyes observing every move I made. Back in my compartment I bided my time, imagining making love to the tall, dark stranger. When I felt the moment was right, I headed for the dining room, three cars ahead.

In the second car I saw her approaching. The blood sang in my veins, and my nerves tingled with anticipation. In the few seconds it took for us to meet — during which our eyes remained steadily fixed on one another — I tried to figure out the best course of action. Should I flatten myself against the wall? Wait for her to do so? Sidle past frontward or backward? There are some things our mothers simply failed to teach us.

As I should have expected, she took control of the situation. Flattening herself against the wall, she gallantly waved her arm for me to pass. I made a hasty decision to offer the feel of my ass rather than my breasts and turned my back to her. Despite her wool suit and my rayon dress, I distinctly felt something hard nudging the crack of my ass: My God, she was packing! Right here on the *Silver Meteor*! The woman had balls. It was all I could do not to totter on my heels as I kept on walking, feeling her eyes boring into my spine.

I sat in the dining car unable to eat my lunch, my panties getting wetter and wetter. Suddenly it occurred to me that I had no clue as to which compartment or even which car she was staying in. For all I knew she would disembark at the next stop. Near panic, I left the dining car and made my way through the sleepers, through first-class and the club car, even up and down the coaches. Not a sign, although she could have been behind any closed door. Defeated, I returned to my cubicle, where I spent the next few hours brooding that I might never see her again.

It was late afternoon when one of the porters appeared at my compartment bearing a glass of sherry on a tray along with a tiny envelope. Opening it, I found a note saying simply, "Dinner at 8." It was unsigned.

"Who," I asked the porter — though I knew very well who — "sent this?"

"The gentleman in the next car, madam. In Compartment B." I laughed at the porter, at his assumption that my beautiful butch apparition was a man. Baffled, he smiled politely.

Hastily I scribbled "Yes" on the note and gave it back to the porter with a hefty tip. Alone, I stared at the drink. I'd always thought sherry was for ladies with delicate sensibilities and had never even tasted the stuff. I downed it in one gulp, then sputtered as an intense heat spread across my chest, making my nipples tingle.

I spent the next few hours watching the landscape speed by through the twilight hours. I had no idea where we were — Virginia? Georgia? For all I cared we could have veered off into Tennessee. I felt suspended in time and space, in another world altogether. The little drama between me and my '30s gangster was a play I'd long wanted to star in, and in this atmosphere it was easy to pretend that it was real, that I was indeed a gun moll and she a mobster. I fantasized becoming her steady girl, her "wife," spoiled with furs and jewels, living a dangerously thrilling life on the lam.

In this persona I changed into a red low-cut dress and gaudy rhinestone earrings and sashayed into the dining car, feeling people's stares — for the most part approving, though some were amused. She was waiting at a table that, unlike the others, had been adorned with real roses and a lace tablecloth. A bottle of French wine accompanied the standard railroad fare of greasy chicken and instant mashed potatoes.

As we sipped our wine and poked at our food, I followed her lead and hardly spoke. We didn't even exchange names but just gazed at one another, occasionally allowing our knees to touch beneath the table. Once or twice one of us remarked on the quality of the food or the service, but for the most part we simply allowed ourselves to experience the electricity crackling between us.

At the end of the meal, she paid the check, then rose and motioned for me to follow. She led me to her compartment — which, much to my delight, turned out to be the first-class cabin I'd earlier admired. The bed had been unfolded, the covers pulled back to reveal black satin sheets. Before I could laugh or make any comment, she had her mouth on mine, her hands roaming hungrily up and down my torso. She blew in my ear, kneading my breasts with such intensity, I felt faint. She reached behind and unzipped my dress, then stared at me appreciatively. Gently she pushed me onto the bed and proceeded to take off her clothes.

When I saw her naked body, I was momentarily taken aback — she was so skinny that every rib stood out. The dildo, harnessed around her bony hips, was enormous against her wiry form. She dropped to her knees and knelt before me, put her mouth on my crotch, and blew hot breath through my silk panties. She removed my underwear and kissed my belly, lightly circling my navel, then moved down and rained passionate kisses all over my mons. She bit and nipped at my inner thighs before turning her attention to my stiff, enlarged clit. With the tip of her long tongue, she licked around the outer edges, avoiding the sensitive head, until I clutched her hair and urged her to take my clitoris into her mouth. All the while the train was speeding through the night, its motions and vibrations intensifying our movements.

She worked her tongue deep inside me, moving it in and out with what seemed like superhuman force. I'd never felt anything like it. She continued tongue-fucking me while she pressed a finger to my clit until I came, thrashing and moaning and pressing her head against me. Laughing with pride, she climbed on top of me and thrust her dildo inside, pounding away until she too grunted in orgasm.

She was so light, I hardly felt her weight on me as we drifted into sleep. Eventually she rolled off, and we curled around each other. I wouldn't say it was a restful night, since every few hours one of us would wake up and paw at the other until we were fucking again.

Daylight found me on my knees, exploring her pussy with my tongue. As I was savoring the musky smell and taste, the train began to slow down until it was crawling along, stopping and starting, barely moving an inch a minute. From the corner of my eye, I saw that we had entered a freight yard where a crew of men were working. I moved to close the shade, but she grabbed my wrist. "Wait," she said, reaching for the dildo and harness. Quickly she put it on, then pulled on my hair, pushing my face between her legs.

"Suck it." I hesitated, glancing toward the window. Workmen were leaning on their shovels, watching the train go by, hoping no doubt for a scene such as ours. Supporting herself on her elbows, my gangster looked out the window, then at me.

"Come on, sweetheart," she coaxed. "You'll never see these guys again. Show them what you can do with a cock. Show them how good you suck girl cock."

A thrill danced up and down my spine. She was right: Why not use these guys in this already theatrical scenario? I pulled my long hair to one side to give my audience a full view and lapped hungrily at her long, sleek girl cock. I played the scene for all it was worth, excited by the workmen's imagined reactions. Would they realize that we were two women? Would this excite them? Outrage them? Briefly I noted that most of the men were white. We were not only two women but also two women, black and white, having sex in the Deep South. With renewed excitement and a feeling of delicious rebellion, I bobbed my head up and down on her cock.

"That's right, sweetheart, show the boys what you can do. Show 'em how good you suck girl cock. Yeah. Show 'em how much you love it."

Her words excited me even more. I fingered her clit furiously as I sucked, feeling her mounting excitement. Rubbing myself against her shin, I came just as she did, picturing dozens of hard cocks shooting come into their pants out in the freight yard. Then the train picked up speed again.

An hour outside of Miami, I gave my gangster lover a long juicy kiss and returned to my compartment, where I washed up and put on plain cotton slacks and a blouse. The porter carried my luggage to the end of the car, accepting my tip with a knowing twinkle in his eye.

My parents happily embraced their little girl, and I kissed the cheeks of a bevy of siblings and cousins — the whole damn family had come to meet me. As they urged me toward the car, I managed to peer through the circle to catch a glimpse of her. Briefly she turned and tipped her hat before striding off into eternity.

Everybody's Going to Seattle
by Kate Allen

The blond woman crouching on the edge of the mat had a knife. She was certainly not the only one in the hall with a knife — there was a ton of hardware being toted on costumes. If the party had been busted, half of the women there could have been arrested immediately for having concealed weapons. The other half would have been arrested for being too near-naked. This woman was both.

The invitation had said, AMAZON FEAST — TRIBAL DRESS ENCOURAGED, but the tribal part had been translated pretty loosely. There *was* a huge contingency in furs and beads and necklaces made of plastic bears' teeth — the cultural-appropriation girls wouldn't have known where to begin being offended — but there were also women from outer space and cowgirls who had forgotten to wear anything under their chaps and gladiators and women in evening wear as well as the gals who had just worn their dress leather.

The woman with the knife had gone the beads-and-leather route — she had on a wooden necklace and a kind of skirt made of slashed black-and-purple suede and, as far as anyone could tell, nothing else. It was hot in the hall, and there was a fine sheen of sweat across her shoulders and breasts, which were femme-pretty with pink nipples. She stood with her dagger in one hand by the mats where the women were wrestling, screaming "Fuck her! Fuck her!" whenever anyone went down. Just as she was not the only one with a knife, she was not the only one thinking this. She was just, as yet, the only one screaming it out loud.

Another woman, also blond, though her hair was cut short and spiked up, came and stood behind her, rubbing the bodice of her black gown against the other's bare back. There was music — some kind of New Age Nubian slave stuff — and in a moment they were dancing. Those who knew the woman with the knife knew she played only with butches — and rough-trade butches at that — but she had been doing a lot of femme-on-femme energy that night, dancing and flirting with other women in dresses and high heels for the appreciation of the butches around her.

The dancing became so hot, a little circle of the wrestling fans broke off to form a ring around them. Then the woman in the gown was swirled off by a crowd of serving wenches carrying platters of whole chickens over their heads. The woman with the dagger went back to her place at the very edge of the mat.

"Fuck her!" she screamed when one of the women went down, and then, because it was someone she knew, she added, "Just lie down and let her fuck you, Josie! She's going to kill you otherwise!" This elicited a laugh from the crowd, and there was another laugh a minute later when the ref, who had been getting more and more nervous about the enthusiastic way in which the woman was wielding her dagger — as if she might at any moment decide to leap out onto the floor and gut one of the downed wrestlers — attempted to take it from her. The blond broke into a big smile and without warning slammed the blade into the base of her neck as if she were Juliet, and the plastic blade retracted as prop daggers had been doing for stage Juliets for years.

Only butches had been wrestling thus far, but now a small woman draped mostly in jewelry and scarves stepped up to the edge of the mat. She kicked off her high heels and turned to face the woman who was following her. The second woman was little-boy butch and had at least forty pounds on the first. Everyone was silent for a moment, wondering how this was going to work out. Then, when the ref brought her hand down, the femme leaped at least three feet into the air, throwing herself at the other woman, who caught her at chest height. She was big enough that she didn't go down under the femme's weight, but she could not pin her nor even get her off her shoulders. The women in the crowd began to laugh and stamp their feet, cheering for the pluckiness with which the femme clung — even upside down, for the butch woman had managed to turn her — and the way that she was attempting to topple the butch using her hanging weight alone.

"Fuck her!" screamed the blond, even though the other woman was not technically down, and for the first time the other women around her joined in the chant. Everyone wanted to see the pretty femme get her cunt pumped while she was hanging upside down with her legs around the waist of the boy butch.

But the femme was not giving up that easy. She managed to swing herself upright, and it was this movement that sent the butch boy careening off the mat and into the startled crowd. The blond with the dagger was caught squarely in the chest, and she dominoed into someone behind her, who caught her head and kept it from crashing into the floor.

"Fuck her!" yelled someone in the crowd, because even though the blond had gone with a crash, you could tell that she hadn't been hurt, and it was too funny to have the tables turned. Especially since her ragged leather skirt had been pushed up, and, as everyone suspected, she was wearing nothing underneath. Her cunt, like her tits, was as pink and femmie as if it had been made to order to match her outfit. Her pubic hair had been trimmed short, and she had a ring through her labia. She was wet.

She looked up at the crowd around her, and a look that equally commingled fear and excitement crossed her face. She made a move as if to push herself up with her hands, in one of which she still held the dagger. After that one call the crowd had gotten almost silent, so it was easy to hear the next sound — the snap of someone's pulling a latex glove tight over her hand.

"Don't."

Until that moment the blond had not noticed the woman who had saved her head from striking the ground. At the sound of her voice, the blond froze and then looked up slowly, an unreadable expression on her face, an expression that could have been passion or horror or excitement or fear. Anyone in the crowd who had talked to the blond for more than five minutes that weekend knew the woman who had spoken was her ex. The blond had told perfect strangers she hadn't known the ex was coming, she was having trouble with it, that after all this time she still hated seeing her with other women. Her friends knew beyond this that though the two had not spoken for almost a year, the blond still loved this woman with a doomed passion and that, despite the dancing and flirting, no one had touched her — not to play with, not to make love to — since they had broken up the previous autumn.

A woman in a gladiator costume, a friend of the blond who had driven up to the conference with her, made a move as if to help her to her feet, but she was stopped by the woman who had snapped the glove over her hand.

The ex was a beautiful butch with dark hair that was long in back and spiked on top. Her translation of tribal was a long black duster and a black cowboy hat, and she looked sexier fully clothed than many of the women who were wearing next to nothing. She looked down at the blond and then up at the crowd, and her look said there was not going to be a gang rape, consensual or no, that she would have to be killed first for that to happen.

There was a discernible shift in the crowd — everyone moved back half a step. Then the dark-haired woman leaned down and put her hands on the waistband of the blond's skirt. She lifted slowly, until her ass was almost a foot off the floor, and then she bent closer to her face and said softly, "I'll wrestle you, baby." She swung her back and forth between her legs and then let go so that the blond was thrown backward onto the mat, landing on her back with a little "Woof!"

There was no heckling as the blond scrambled to her bare feet. The dark-haired butch began to disrobe as if the match had been agreed on, as if the two previous women didn't have the right to two more rounds. She was wearing a heavy harness under her coat. The blond was topless, obviously to show off her tits. The butch was topless because she had a beautiful back. She was the kind of woman you would like to watch chop wood, bare to the waist, and then afterward dig your nails into as she fucked you standing against the house.

A woman wearing only a collar helped the butch remove her black cowboy boots. The blond had backed up to the edge of the mat, crouched down as if she were going to fight yet looking anxiously over her shoulder as if she wanted to make sure the option to run was still open. The ring was packed solid with women who wanted to see her thrown down, and it was obvious she was pinpointing her friends in the crowd, women she could count on to back her up if she decided to safeword out.

Once again the woman in the gladiator's costume made a move toward the blond, bending down to put a hand on her shoulder. "Don't do this," she said in a voice that was audible to the crowd. "You got away from her once. Stay away!"

The blond squeezed her hand but made no move to back out of the ring.

And then it began. They had wrestled before — that was obvious from the stances they took. They had played together and played hard. That was obvious from the way that they came together without any regard for the pain when their bodies met.

The butch was bigger and heavier. And she was the top. The blond had submitted her body and soul to her, and she had replayed those submissions over and over in her fantasies during the year they had been apart. It gave the butch a tremendous psychological advantage.

But the blond was strong too. And though there was part of her that wanted to lie down for this woman, she was pissed. You could see that in her eyes as she went for the butch's legs — could see the anger of betrayal and abandonment. They both went down, and the femme scrambled away from the other, knowing she would never be able to flip her once the butch got on top.

The dark-haired woman looked at her almost lazily, as if she had not fallen but had somehow ended up full length on the mat as part of a plan. At the last possible moment, she reached out one large hand and wrapped it around the blond's ankle. And that was the end.

The blond might have been able to fight back if she'd kept her head. And she might have kept her head if the crowd hadn't taken up her chant, if every woman surrounding the mat hadn't started to yell, "Fuck her! Fuck her!" That was what finally threw her off, made her lose every little bit of strategy and disintegrate into tossing herself futilely from side to side and cursing as the dark butch proceeded to reel her in, hand over hand.

The blond flipped herself onto her front and began to push herself up with her arms. The butch reached up beneath her skirt with the gloved hand and shoved three fingers into her cunt. The blond cried out as if she had been struck, and she struggled to pull away, but by now the butch had her by the hip, and she slowly pulled her down on her hand. The blond kicked back, hitting her shoulder, and with a roar of anger the butch pulled out of her and used both hands to slam her onto her back. She snapped her left arm down between her breasts, her elbow on her sternum, her hand around her throat. Everyone there who had ever watched them play had seen her use this hold before.

"Safeword out, Tina!" The blond's friend had stepped out onto the mat, which of course should have meant the match was no good and would have to be restarted. Except, of course, everyone, including the ref, had forgotten how it had started or the fact that there were once rules.

The blond turned her head toward her friend. But friends are always so much wiser than we are, and their eyes could not really meet because the blond's had shrunken to a pinpoint, and it was obvious that she not only was not going to use her safeword but that she probably had forgotten what it was.

The dark-haired woman cracked her sharply across the face. She had never liked the blond's attention wandering when she was topping. The blond cried out in pain, a cry that was barely audible over the chanting, which had renewed itself to a feverish pitch. The butch moved her hand directly from the blond's face to her cunt. With one brutal shove her fist was in. "Fuck her! Fuck her!" the crowd was shouting. But the woman with the dark hair was not listening. She was looking into the eyes of the blond as she reached deep inside her, as if she were reaching up to grasp her heart in her hand.

And the blond was not listening either. She was gazing back into the eyes of the other woman, and with one hand she was stabbing the dagger over and over into her back.

Contributors

Kate Allen grew up in Idaho and currently lives with four cats in Denver. She is the author of five novels, including the popular Alison Kaine mystery series, which features a Denver cop involved in the local leather community. She likes to make quilts and two-step, and her fantasy is to someday have to work only one job (as opposed to three) to support her writing. She is currently working on a crossover novel involving queers, cats, and vampires.

Elaine Apthorp teaches literature and American studies, mostly to budding computer scientists and engineers, at San Jose State University, where she is an associate professor. She has a Ph.D. from the University of California, Berkeley, which is difficult to explain, since she spent most of her time there playing softball and writing stories about lesbians with angst when she was supposed to be studying scholarly tomes about King Lear's heart condition and postmodern poststructural postness. "Stealing Home" is part of the novel in her desk drawer.

Lucy Jane Bledsoe is the author of *Sweat: Stories and a Novella* (Seal Press, 1995), which was a finalist for the Lambda Literary Award for lesbian fiction, and of a novel, *Working Parts* (Seal Press, 1997). She is the editor of *Heatwave: Women in Love and Lust* (Alyson, 1995). She is also the author of two novels for young people, *The Big Bike Race* (Holiday House, 1995) and *Tracks in the Snow* (Holiday House, 1997).

M. Christian has been to many countries on many continents and just about every state in the union but calls San Francisco his spiritual home (though it's not nearly queer or hip enough). His stories can be seen in such anthologies as *Best Gay Erotica, Best American Erotica, Power Tools,* and *Happy Ever After.*

Sora Counts is a craftswoman who makes S/M toys for her business, Sorodz. She lives in Oakland, California.

Myrna Elana has contributed to Joan Nestle's *The Persistent Desire* and *Dark Voices 5: The Pan Book of Horror* as well as the *San Francisco Chronicle, Trivia, The Chicago Review,* and *Outrageous Women.* "Hourglass City" is dedicated to loved ones with HIV and cancer.

Martha Equinox has worked as a waitress, ice-cream–truck driver, auto mechanic, psychic healer, astrologer, law-office manager, and accountant. Her published work has appeared in *Coming to Power* (Alyson, 1987) and *The Rock,* and she has written and performed autobiographical work on death and loss, aging, and lesbian sex roles.

Jane Futcher is the author of three novels: *Dream Lover, Crush,* and *Promise Not to Tell.* Her short fiction has appeared in a number of anthologies, including *Heatwave, Afterglow,* and *Lesbian Adventure Stories.* She lives with her lover, Erin Carney, a home-birth midwife, in Novato, California.

Veronica Holtz lived and studied in Europe for several years. She now lives in the Philadelphia area. Still, she believes the most erotic meal is French bread, cheese, and wine.

Michelle Latiga is from the Northeast: New England, where she was raised, and New York City, where she grew up. She moved to Texas seven years ago for a job that sends her traveling around the world. She lives in Dallas with her partner of six years and their two cats and extended family. Latiga has worked as a professional musician and playwright. If you ask her, she'll tell you she's six feet tall. She's not. And when asked about her best accomplishment, she smiles, "I've been in gay bars on six continents!" Next? To ride across Alaska on a Harley!

Bonnie J. Morris earned her Ph.D. in women's history from Binghamton University in 1989. Now a professor of women's studies at George Washington University, she spends her winters writing and her summers working at women's music festivals throughout the United States. She also tours with her one-woman play, *Revenge of the Women's Studies Professor.* Her work has appeared in over twenty anthologies; her first two books, both addressing the recent history of American Jewish women, will be published in 1997.

Shelly Rafferty is a writer, parent, teacher, and poet whose recent work will appear in *Close Calls: New Lesbian Fiction* (St. Martin's Press). She is a regular contributor to *The Lesbian Review of Books* and currently writes about medical research in upstate New York.

J. M. Redmann lives, works, and frolics in that swamp known as New Orleans. She is the author of three novels, *Death by the Riverside, Deaths of Jocasta,* and *The Intersection of Law and Desire,* winner of the 1995 Lambda Literary Award for lesbian mystery.

Marcy Sheiner is a writer and editor who doesn't get to ride the rails nearly as often as she'd like. Her most recent book is *Herotica 4* (Penguin), with *Herotica 5* soon to follow, and she's working on a collection of essays.

Linda Smukler is the author of two books of poetry: *Normal Sex* (Firebrand Books, 1994) and *Home in Three Days. Don't Wash,* a multimedia project with accompanying CD-ROM (Hard Press, 1996). She has been nominated for a Lambda Literary Award and has received fellowships in poetry from the New York Foundation for the Arts and the Astraea Foundation. She also won the Katherine Anne Porter Prize in Short Fiction from *Nimrod* magazine. Her work has appeared in numerous journals and anthologies, and she is coeditor with Susan Fox Rogers of *Portraits of Love* (St. Martin's Press, 1997).

Judith Stelboum is an associate professor at the College of Staten Island, City University of New York, where she teaches English, women's studies, and lesbian studies. Recent writing has appeared in *Common Lives, Lesbian Lives, Sinister Wisdom, The Lesbian Review of Books, Sister and Brother, Not the Only One, Dyke Life, Tangled Sheets, Heatwave,* and *Resist: Essays Against a*

Homophobic Culture. Her biographical/critical essays on Olga Broumas and Marilyn Hacker will appear in *Guide to Twentieth-Century Literature in English* (Oxford University Press).

Robin Sweeney is an editor and writer who lives in Oakland, California, with her sweeties, one child, and a great number of housemates and/or cats. She is the coeditor, with Pat Califia, of *The Second Coming* (Alyson, 1996). Her work has appeared in bunches of anthologies, which isn't bad at all considering she's disabled by chronic fatigue immune dysfunction syndrome.

Jess Wells's eight volumes of work include a novel, *AfterShocks* (Third Side Press, 1992); short stories, *Two Willow Chairs;* an anthology, *Lesbians Raising Sons* (Alyson, 1997); and an erotic novella, *The Common Price of Passion.* Her work has appeared in nearly two dozen literary anthologies within the lesbian, gay, and women's movement, including *Women on Women, The Femme Mystique, Lavender Mansions, Lesbian Culture,* and *When I Am an Old Woman.* Her work is included in university curricula and textbooks, and she is a two-time winner of the Lebhar-Friedman Award for Excellence in Journalism.

Gabriella West lives in San Francisco. This is her first anthologized piece. She is currently trying her hand at a lesbian romance novel.

Barbara Wilson is most recently the author of the novel *If You Had a Family* and of the memoir *Blue Windows: A Christian Science Childhood.* She has published several mysteries featuring translator sleuth Cassandra Reilly and is herself a Norwegian translator. She lives in Seattle, where she writes and runs Women in Translation, a nonprofit publishing company. "Salt Water" is excerpted from a novella of the same title.